THE
YOUNG GENERATION

Books in
The Fairfields Chronicles Series
by Sarah Shears

THE VILLAGE
FAMILY FORTUNES
THE YOUNG GENERATION
RETURN TO RUSSETS

Published by Bantam Books

THE
YOUNG GENERATION

Sarah Shears

BANTAM BOOKS
NEW YORK · TORONTO · LONDON · SYDNEY · AUCKLAND

THE YOUNG GENERATION
A BANTAM BOOK 0 553 40263 3

Originally published in Great Britain by
Judy Piatkus (Publishers) Ltd

PRINTING HISTORY
Judy Piatkus (Publishers) Ltd edition published 1986
Bantam Books edition published 1992

Bantam Books are published by Transworld Publishers Ltd,
61–63 Uxbridge Road, Ealing, London W5 5SA, in Australia
by Transworld Publishers (Australia) Pty Ltd, 15–23 Helles
Avenue, Moorebank, NSW 2170, and in New Zealand by
Transworld Publishers (NZ) Ltd, 3 William Pickering Drive,
Albany, Auckland.

Printed and bound in Great Britain by
BPCC Hazells Ltd
Member of BPCC Ltd

PART I

Chapter One

It was not often that young Julian Franklin noticed the beauties of nature as he raced through the park. His head was down over the handlebars of his bicycle, and he had a train to catch.

At the age of seventeen, he was even more impatient than he had been at the age of seven, and now he was impatient to be finished with the last term at Grammar School, and into an adult world. Neither an academic nor a sports enthusiast, his one absorbing interest in life had not changed in the past decade, and the collection of model aircraft in his bedroom at Russets was still his most treasured possession in this Year of Our Lord – 1936.

His handsome dark head seemed either to be hanging over the handlebars or bent backwards at an awkward angle as he stared at the sky.

'One of these days you will walk straight into the lake,' Aunt Lucy threatened mildly, because this boy she had fostered was as dear to her heart as her own four sons. In a sense he did belong to the family, but it was a closely guarded secret. As a small boy he had often enquired about the father who had disappeared before he was born, and the young mother who had died in childbirth.

3

That he was a Franklin, and a grandson of Sir Neville Franklin, had been a proud boast in those early years. But a whole era had passed with a grim finality on that Autumn day in 1925 when the last of the old Franklins had been thrown from his horse. The Big House had been empty but for caretakers for some years; and it was only recently that it had been purchased by a rich American industrialist with a shrewd eye for investment in Britain.

Any hope that Aunt Lucy used to keep alive regarding another useful pair of hands on the farm had long since been abandoned. Julian was not interested, and had to be bribed to help. His long, lean body was tough as whipcord, and he kept himself fit in the school gymnasium and vaulted all the farm gates for one specific purpose – his eventual enrolment into the Royal Air Force.

He could not explain why he had lifted his head from the handlebars on that particular Autumn day and saw, for the first time with dazzling clarity, the glory of Autumn in the spreading beeches. And framed in the picture was a girl on a black horse – a beautiful girl in a green riding habit that fitted her slender figure like a glove.

'You're trespassing,' she said, with cool deliberation.

He laughed when she had expected an apology, and his mocking laughter floated back as he raced away across the Park.

Her dark eyes flashed with annoyance. She hated to be laughed at. Diane Maloney, at seventeen, was every bit as impatient as Julian Franklin to finish with school, and even more indifferent to the glory of Autumn in Marston Park. She was still at the Academy for Young Ladies in Paris, where she was expected to perfect her French and acquire a sense of dress and deportment that

4

befitted the daughter of Harry B. Maloney. An English governess could hardly be expected to satisfy his exacting standards in this respect, though she had certainly proved a good investment – and Harry had to admit that this self-willed daughter had not been an easy pupil. Anyone but 'Sammy' would have quit years ago, but Sammy belonged to the bulldog breed, and hung on. Her real name was Amelia Jane Sampson. 'Call me Sammy,' she had said, when he had engaged her in that posh Park Lane Hotel some thirteen years ago. She was still with them, but there was no schoolroom at Marston Park now, and Diane had outgrown a governess. To manage without Sammy was unthinkable. She was the go-between, the general factotum, the stabilising influence in a family in which the Irish-French temperaments often exploded.

It had taken the whole of six months to restore the mansion to its former grandeur. An army of workmen and charwomen were brought in daily from the village, and Sammy had been there to supervise. Her first job had been to furnish the flat – which the Franklins had occupied during and after the War. She had thoroughly enjoyed her new role. Her employer's wife, Kitty Maloney, stayed in London to keep house for Harry in their luxury flat at Maida Vale. Harry liked home cooking, and Kitty was an excellent cook, for she had spent her early years in the kitchen of a famous restaurant in Manhattan. The French chef, monarch of his kingdom, was a tyrant to be feared and obeyed, for his violent temper and scathing tongue. A staff of foreign servants had been engaged in London for Marston Park, with an English butler called Bates, and an unmarried cook called *Mrs* Davy. She told Sammy it was customary. Only the butler and the cook had actually seen Marston Park before their engagement was verified.

Harry and Kitty had been near neighbours as adolescents, in a predominantly Irish working-class district. Harry was an ambitious youngster, never missing an opportunity to make an honest – or a *dis*honest – dime! He had no scruples and no conscience. Kitty adored him, but nobody had been more surprised than Kitty when her slavish devotion had been rewarded. They were married at seventeen, and shared a tiny apartment that was Kitty's pride and joy. She was strong and sturdy, and a conscientious worker. The hours were long and it was sweated labour in the basement kitchen of that swell restaurant in Manhattan, but she never neglected Harry. He was often away 'on business', but she did not enquire into the nature of the business. She had discovered in the early days of their marriage that he couldn't bear to be questioned. 'Master of his fate, and Captain of his soul', that was Harry B. Maloney.

Kitty had been secretly appalled at the size and grandeur of Marston Park, but she was not the least bit jealous of Sammy who had taken over the responsibility, for she knew her limitations, and her natural inclination was to obey orders, not to give them. She was fond of Sammy, and Sammy was fond of her, and that was all that mattered. No woman could have been more proud of her clever husband and beautiful daughter than Kitty Maloney, yet they hardly noticed her. She was too insignificant, and their combined personalities too strong. It was a mystery nobody could explain how such an odd looking couple had produced such a beautiful daughter. Harry was a small man, with a pallid face, sparse black hair and shrewd dark eyes. Kitty was short and fat, with mild grey eyes, and untidy brown hair. She was a comfortable soul, and quite unsuited to the sophisticated world to which her husband and daughter belonged. They said her husband was a wizard, with an uncanny instinct for a good investment, but she did not pretend to understand how a boy from such a humble background could make a fortune in less than twenty years – and Harry had no intention of enlightening her. He never discussed his business affairs with his wife and daughter, and kept his public image apart. Business associates were lavishly entertained in the best hotels and restaurants, and a suite of offices had been opened in Oxford Street some twelve months before the purchase of Marston Park. Harry travelled back and forth to the States with the easy assurance of a seasoned traveller, but Kitty stayed at home. They were keeping on the apartment at Maida Vale for Diane's convenience. She had her own small car, and would bring her young friends down for weekends, but London was the Mecca, and for all the grandeur of Marston Park, Diane could not see herself being buried in the country.

She had never known a time when they were poor, and never met any of her Irish relatives. Kitty had three miscarriages before Diane was born, and Harry finally came to the conclusion that it was due to the heavy lifting of copper pans in the kitchen. Without hesitation, he picked up the telephone and informed the chef his wife would not be reporting for duty from henceforth. So Kitty stayed at home, and lifted nothing heavier than her own pots and pans, and gave birth to a beautiful baby girl. Those early years in their modest apartment, before Harry began to move around into bigger and more luxurious apartments, were the happiest that Kitty would ever know in the whole of her married life. The baby, Diane, seemed to act as a spur to Harry's ambitions, and his determination that only the best was good enough for his adored daughter. Kitty was amazed to hear a child of three conversing in French, but Harry, who was bilingual (he had a widowed French grandmother living with the Irish family in New York) said it was quite natural. The only French words that Kitty was familiar with were connected with the menu in the Manhattan restaurant, so it soon became a game, to tease Mama by speaking French with Papa.

When Sammy joined the family, she found it was already too late to correct the child's deep-rooted conviction that her Papa was clever and her Mama stupid. But Sammy insisted on the King's English being spoken at the meal table, and her championship of the child's mother found an immediate response in Kitty's affections. Sammy endured all the temperamental scenes with her young charge with her own particular brand of humour and patience. It was not the child's fault that she was so precocious. She blamed the doting parents. Sammy had never married, and never mentioned a family, so it was assumed she had no near relatives. Harry was concerned only with her qualifications and her personality when he engaged her as governess to his self-willed little daughter. She was a woman in her late thirties by the time they moved from New York to London, and Diane was already in France. Like her father, and Sammy, Diane was a seasoned traveller, and had often accompanied Harry on his business trips to London. They always stayed at Brown's Hotel, and met Harry for dinner in a small French restaurant in Soho. A proud and indulgent Papa, he gave Diane and Sammy money to spend, and they shopped at Harrods and in Bond Street.

Sammy dressed neatly in tailored clothes, and she always wore a hat and gloves. Her tall figure had a distinction that was completely lacking in her employers. It was an intelligent face, with wide grey eyes and a friendly smile. A single glass of wine and her eyes were sparkling. Diane had been accustomed to a small

8

glass of wine with the evening meal even before Sammy joined the family. It seemed to do her no harm, and it amused Harry. It was just one of the habits of which Sammy disapproved but had to accept. She was a sensible woman, and knew her authority was not absolute. Her employer had a quick temper, and you did not take liberties with Harry B. Maloney. Their relationship was friendly and congenial, and there was never any question of intimacy. Harry was a faithful husband, probably because it had not yet occurred to him to take a mistress. All his energy and enthusiasm was poured into the one absorbing obsession – to make money. And his heart belonged to his daughter, Diane. He always spoke of her as 'my' daughter not 'our' daughter, and Kitty was merely the instrument who had produced this masterpiece. There was no time for friendships or recreation. He was a self-made man, and completely indifferent to class.

When young Julian Franklin raced away on his bicycle, that mellow Autumn day, Diane Maloney trotted her horse towards the farm called Russets. At one time the farms had been part of Marston Park estate, but the late owner – Sir Neville Franklin – had bequeathed them in his Will to the tenant farmers. Sammy had discovered quite a lot about the history of the place by talking to the charwomen who were brought from the village for cleaning when the workmen had finished.

It was a fascinating history of an era that had vanished completely; of a class of society called 'Gentry', and a servants' hierarchy. Sir Neville, it appeared, had an ailing wife and four rather plain daughters, and no son to inherit the estate, while Farmer Blunt, at Russets, was blessed with a buxom wife and three good-looking boys.

Farmer Blunt had fallen off a hay-wagon and broken his neck, and Sir Neville had witnessed the accident and comforted the poor woman. Lucy Blunt had everything that was lacking in his lady wife. She was pretty, plump, and warm-hearted, but her greatest asset was her strong, healthy body. He saw her as the perfect mother for his son and heir, and when a year had passed after her husband's death, he bedded Lucy. The village women still remembered the scandal, for it was no secret that Lucy Blunt was carrying Sir Neville's child as proudly as though it had been conceived in holy wedlock. The village women had been eager and willing to talk over their cups of tea to Sammy about the late owner of Marston Park – about the handsome boy called Charles who was allowed to stay with his mother at Russets until he was seven, then taken to the 'Big House' for his formal introduction into upper-class society, and the traditional education that befitted the son and heir. From that time he was permitted only to visit his mother for a day or two in the school holidays. Sammy agreed with the village women that it was an unkind ultimatum for both the boy and his mother.

'Then Miss Cynthia, the second daughter, wouldn't 'ave nothing to do with that silly lark of being presented at Court, and 'aving what the Gentry called a season, and went orf to a London 'ospital to be a nurse, and that didn't 'arf upset the Squire!' a blunt charwoman explained with a chuckle.

'But that wasn't the end of it, Miss.' Another woman took up the story. 'Miss Cynthia married into a working-class family, a nephew of Lucy Blunt. Mind jew, this young man in question was doing quite well for 'iself as a solicitor's clerk, but 'is brother was still serving be'ind the grocery counter, and another brother was a farm labourer. Their Mum didn't agree with it, Miss, and no more did we. Class is class, and she reckoned it were asking for trouble. As it 'appened, it turned out all right, that marriage, for she stuck to 'im, and you 'ad to admire 'er, for 'e came back from the War with only one leg.' All the women sighed sympathetically over the teacups, and Sammy begged to hear more of the fascinating saga.

Marston Park had been converted into a convalescent home for officers during the War, and two of Sir Neville's daughters were working as VAD nurses. Lucy Blunt lost her eldest son in the War, and another son came home badly wounded. Then the youngest Franklin girl got herself in the family way, and died in childbirth, and nobody knew who was the father. Lucy Blunt fostered the child, who went to the village school, then on to the Grammar School. That young Charles Franklin, with a public school education, had grown up to be a bit of a rake – chip off the old block, you might say, for Sir Neville was no saint. There were ugly rumours about young Charles, but he had cleared off to America, and hadn't been seen since the day of Sir Neville's funeral. As for Lucy Blunt, she had had her share of trouble, what with getting mixed up with the Gentry, and her son Tom being in love with his brother's wife, and that same brother getting killed in the old Dutch barn that young Julian set alight one Christmas Eve. You would think the poor woman would be grey-haired and careworn, but she was still a pretty woman, plump as a spring chicken, the Mistress of Russets.

Sammy kept in touch by telephone with the London flat during the six months she was supervising the restoration of Marston Park; Harry was interested in its history, and impatient to take possession. When at last it was ready, he drove Diane and Kitty from London, together

11

with a consultant from a famous London store to advise on furniture, carpets and curtains. His advice was invariably over-ruled by Diane, however, and his patience and courtesy almost exhausted by the end of the day. Three extra bathrooms had been installed – Harry had an obsession about bathrooms, remembering his childhood and the tub in the kitchen.

Diane knew exactly what she wanted for her own bedroom and sitting-room, for she had already been conducted round the showrooms in the various departments of the London store, and made her own personal selection. The rooms she had chosen had been occupied by Beatrice and Cynthia Franklin. Harry and Kitty would occupy the room known as Her Ladyship's boudoir, and Sammy would be comfortably installed in the old schoolroom. She would not be spending much time there, for Kitty would need her company, and Harry would be annoyed if they made no use of the beautiful drawing-room, with its period furniture, velvet curtains and Chinese carpet. Sammy's throat would tighten with tears to see the dumpy little figure in a brocade chair, busy with her interminable knitting. Why couldn't Harry see for himself that it was wrong for Kitty? It was right for Diane, this luxurious setting; and everything revolved around Diane. It was like a new toy to a girl whose young life was crowded with excitement and variety – an expensive toy, provided by an indulgent parent with the mistaken opinion that money could buy a place in English upper-class society for his lovely daughter. He envisaged her stepping into the shoes of the disinherited Franklins. The tradesmen, the workmen and the charwomen who remembered the family with pride and affection despised the 'New Rich', and served them only because of their urgent need to earn a living. 'Beggars can't be choosers,' they said.

The Gentry had known instinctively how to treat their servants and train their children. Tradition was not something you purchased, but something you inherited. They remembered the plain little girls from Marston Park, riding to the village in the governess cart. They remembered their impeccable manners and shy smiles. They all had a wide-eyed innocence, and it was a pleasure to serve them when they had pennies to spend in the shops. The 'New Rich' might impress their London associates, but not the villagers. A rich American industrialist, who appeared to have more money than sense, would have no interest in village affairs.

Harry B. Maloney would attend the Catholic Church on Sunday morning, with his wife and daughter, whenever he happened to be in residence, and contribute generously to the various charities. They would drive up in the Jaguar. The chauffeur's immaculate uniform matched the car. Miss Sampson, who was Church of England, would be dropped off at the church gates, and collected again after the service. They would make no friends in the village. 'They don't rightly belong,' was the general opinion among the working class. And it was true.

The 'good old days' when the Franklins drove up in their carriage, and the parson was waiting at the door to greet his distinguished patron, were gone for ever. They remembered the handsome figure of Sir Neville on a huge black stallion, following the funeral cortège of his tenant farmer, Tom Blunt. And if his roving eye had already detected a pleasing substitute for his ailing wife in the farmer's pretty widow, wasn't he entitled to bed her, after a decent period of mourning? Those were the days when the ruling class could claim to rule with dignity. There was no dignity in the rich industrialist, with his pallid face and shrewd black eyes, or his dumpy little

13

wife, so obviously subservient to husband and daughter. As for the foreign servants who knew no loyalty to their employer, they would soon be bored in the country mansion, slipping back to London that first Winter. Sammy would be on the phone to the Agency in Tunbridge Wells to send replacements, and the most unlikely girls would report for duty – girls who giggled behind Bates's pompous back, and upset Mrs Davy – girls who had to be reminded to change their caps and aprons, and wipe the lipstick from their sulky mouths – girls who flirted with the married men on the staff, and entertained their boy-friends in their bedrooms. Only Kitty was aware of the burden that Sammy carried on her willing shoulders, and the problems that almost defeated this remarkable woman whose loyal friendship and affection had spared a neglected wife complete obscurity. Neither Harry nor Diane were concerned with such mundane domestic matters, only with their own comfort.

When Diane's London friends arrived to spend the weekend at Marston Park, the house echoed to their shrill, excited voices, jazz records, and the strumming of Spanish guitars. It was a new era of unrestrained emotions, and sexual indulgence. Money could oil the wheels of this new era at Marston Park, but the young generation were too busy and too impatient to notice the changing seasonal pattern of the formal gardens. They were concerned only with the tennis courts and the heated swimming pool, framed in tropical vegetation, in the basement. Park keepers and gardeners were part of the landscape – a useful commodity scattered over the wide acres. Only Sammy knew their names and enquired after their families. They cycled from the village every weekday, and provided their own bread and cheese and flasks of tea. They had no status, and could be replaced as easily as the maids.

It was Sammy who noticed that the boy raking the gravel drive had outgrown his clothes. His thin legs and arms were blue, and the small, peaked face under the man's cap was bent against the tearing March wind. She hurried out and brought him to the kitchen for a bowl of hot soup. He was only a child of fourteen, and had left the village school at Christmas. This was his first job, and he was lucky to get it, he told Sammy, because several other boys had been after it. His name was Jimmy, and his mother took in washing. He gave her all his wages, and she gave him back a shilling for his pocket. It was customary, he said.

'Me Dad always 'anded over 'is wage packet to me Mum and she gave 'im back a shilling for beer and baccy,' he explained, gravely, as he supped the hot soup.

'What was your father's job?' asked Sammy.

'Ganger, Miss.'

'Ganger?'

'On the railway, Miss.'

'I see.' But she didn't see.

Even his wife hadn't realised until it was too late that it was no job for a man with a weak chest. But they were living in railway property, and there was no alternative.

'What age were you, Jimmy, when your father died?'

'I were eleven years old, Miss, and I were the eldest of seven.'

'*Seven*?'

'Yes, Miss. You see, there's two lots of twins.'

Sammy was appalled, but the cook showed no surprise. The railway cottages were swarming with children. She had no patience with parents who couldn't control the birth rate, but then she had never been bedded with a man who spent a tanner of his weekly shilling every Saturday night, and claimed the right to a dutiful wife after he had dropped his trousers on the cracked linoleum.

15

When Jimmy had finished the soup, he picked up his cap and smiled his thanks.

'I'll be getting back to work now, Miss,' he said. The smile had a shining radiance that lit his small, peaked face with surprising beauty. Sammy was touched, and she let him go with a strange reluctance.

'He's so *thin*, Mrs Davy,' she sighed, as she watched him running back to the interminable raking of the gravel drive.

'What can you expect, Miss, with all those mouths to feed.'

'What would he bring for his dinner?'

'Bread and jam most likely.'

'But there's no nourishment in bread and jam!'

'His mother will have a plate of stew waiting in the oven, I shouldn't wonder. There won't be much meat in it. Just a few scrag ends from the butcher.'

'Could we give him his dinner, Mrs Davy, or just a bowl of soup?'

Cook shook her head. 'It wouldn't do to favour the boy, Miss, and he wouldn't expect it. You wouldn't be pleasing his mother, neither, if that's what you had in mind. They don't take kindly to charity, the working-class mothers. I should know, Miss. I come from a working-class family.' She paused; 'As for being married, I like my bed to myself, Miss, and that's the honest truth!'

'In that respect, Mrs Davy, I share your sentiments!' Sammy chuckled, amiably.

With the coming of Spring, Kitty left the house and took long walks alone. She had grown accustomed to spending many hours and days alone in the London flat, when they moved from New York, but she was more lonely at

Marston Park, and she missed the cooking. On the cook's free day, she enjoyed herself in the kitchen, but was careful to put everything back in its rightful place, for Mrs Davy. Martha, the young kitchen maid, was a village girl, and she also enjoyed this one day in the week when the mistress took over the kitchen. Mrs Maloney didn't give her orders. She spoke quietly, as though to her own daughter, but she was an excellent cook, and knew how to make some very tasty dishes with French names because she had worked in the kitchen of a famous restaurant in New York, in her younger days. Mrs Maloney was no snob, not like that stuck-up Miss Diane! She was nice and homely, and when they shared a pot of tea, she would talk about the early days in New York, when they lived in a small apartment. She had to hang the washing on the fire escape, and drag the pram up two flights of stairs because she was not allowed to leave it in the hallway. She smiled at the memory, as though it had been a happy time, and Martha felt like a kindred spirit when the mistress talked of those early days. Didn't her own mother drag the pram up the stairs, with the baby tucked under her arm? Her father was a groom on another big estate a few miles away, and they lived in the rooms over the stables.

'Me Mum says it was an 'appy release to 'ave three miscarriages for there wasn't enough room for any more children,' she told the mistress.

A happy release to lose three babies? Kitty was remembering the girl's remarks the following afternoon, on her lonely walk across the park. That poor woman.

Away in the distance she could hear the rattle of the tractor and the shrill voices of the children at Russets. She knew the history of the old farmhouse from Sammy, and she invariably found herself walking in that direction. She was too shy to introduce herself, and watched all their activities from the shelter of a giant oak tree in the Park. She envied Lucy Blunt her busy days and her four grandchildren. It must be such a satisfying way of life, she was thinking as she watched the servant crossing the yard with a heavy basket of washing that had blown dry in the orchard, and a boy of about nine or ten, driving the cows into the milking shed. It was a way of life with a pattern and a continuity. The changing seasons would be their barometer. The markets could be precarious, but not as precarious as Harry's sporadic investments. She was not as stupid as Harry and Diane liked to pretend, and she was no fool.

Their own world, built on speculation and gambling, had no firm foundation. It could collapse like a pack of cards, and Harry would be bankrupt.

When the puppy wriggled through the boundary fence and a little girl climbed over it and gave chase, laughing and shouting excitedly, Kitty knew her hiding place would soon be discovered, for the puppy ran straight for the tree followed by the child – a pretty little girl, with tight curls, a chubby face, and bright blue eyes.

'Hallo,' she said, for she was friendly, and was always delighted to be the first to discover anything new. It could be the first lamb or the first primrose, both of equal importance to a six-year-old. Snatching up the puppy, she kissed it fondly, and giggled when it licked her face.

'You're Mrs Maloney from the Big House, aren't you?' she decided.

'That's right.'

'I'm Mary Blunt, but everyone calls me Midge 'cause I'm so little. Did they call you Midge when you were a little girl?'

'No, I was always called Kitty.'

'Were you coming to visit Granny? She likes having visitors.'

'Well, I hadn't reckoned on calling.'

'You're welcome. Everybody's welcome at Russets.'

'Thank you, dear. Another day, perhaps.'

'I wouldn't like to live in the Big House. It's not as nice as Russets. This is the best place in the whole world.'

Kitty smiled and asked, 'How come you are not at school?'

'There's whooping cough in the village, and Granny is keeping us at home.' So it was Lucy Blunt who still had the last word at Russets. 'That's my twin brother sitting on the fence. His name's John. He's backward. Granny says I'm much too forward, but I'd rather be forward than backward.' Her blue eyes shone with lively intelligence. Her pinafore was torn, and her knees were grazed.

'When I'm grown up, I shall live here always, and so will Dick. He's ten, and he's very clever. He can milk a cow and nearly drive the tractor. My sister Maggie is going to be a missionary, like Auntie Harriet, only she's not our real Auntie. When Maggie was eight last birthday, she decided to be a missionary because her Sunday School prize was all about the heathen children in Darkest Africa. Maggie reads her Bible and says her prayers to Jesus.'

'And you don't?'

'Granny says I don't have to if I don't feel like it, and I don't ever feel like it. Granny says you can be a good Christian and never set foot in a church or chapel. You can say thank you to God just as well outdoors as on your knees in your bedroom. Daddy and Mummy don't want Maggie to be a missionary, and they think she will outgrow it like Dick has outgrown flying his kite. But she won't, 'cause Maggie always knows 'xactly what she wants to do, and she wants to be a missionary when she's grown up.'

'It's a swell thing to know what you want, Mary.'

'Julian wants to fly an aeroplane. When he's eighteen he will join the Royal Air Force.'

'I guess I know all about that young man.'

'Who told you?'

'A little bird told me.'

Midge giggled. 'You are funny, and you talk funny.'

'That's because I'm American.'

'Americans are rich, aren't they?'

'Some rich and some poor. I guess it's the same over here.'

'Granny says only a rich American could afford to buy Marston Park.'

'I reckon your Granny knows what she's talking about.'

'She knows everything, my Granny. She knows where babies come from. I asked Daddy and he said to me ask your Granny.'

Kitty smiled whimsically at the bright-eyed child. It must be rather wonderful to have such a reputation, but Lucy Blunt was a legend in her own lifetime, if you could believe all the tales those village women told Sammy. A woman who had tamed Sir Neville Franklin was very remarkable. They said he had spent more time at Russets than at Marston Park, and never looked at another woman after his son went away. They said she never shed a tear when they told her he was dead, but just went on with her work as though nothing had happened. But she knew her place. The mistress of Russets could have been mistress of Marston Park, they said, but it wouldn't do, and she would never leave Russets.

'Midge! Midge!' Lucy Blunt was calling over the fence, and the little boy was hugging her round the neck.

'That's my Granny,' said the child proudly. 'Now you have to stay. Come on!' And she dragged the reluctant Kitty by the hand.

Her shyness made every new encounter an ordeal, but she was not shy with children, and this friendly little girl had paved the way for an introduction.

'Is she being a nuisance, Mrs Maloney?' Lucy asked, as they shook hands.

'She's real cute, Mrs Blunt. I reckon you're a very lucky woman to have such a big family.'

'Come and meet them. I'll open the gate.' She smiled a welcome, and there was such warmth and natural friendliness in her manner, it would have been churlish to refuse. 'This is John, my youngest grandson. Say hallo to Mrs Maloney,' she prompted.

He mumbled obediently, and stared at the visitor with a blank face. A thin little boy, with straight flaxen hair and pale blue eyes, he bore no resemblance to his lively twin.

A younger woman was crossing the yard from the dairy, carrying a slab of yellow butter on a blue dish. The likeness between the two women and the child they called Midge was quite extraordinary.

'My daughter-in-law, Carrie,' said Lucy, taking the butter.

'We've been wondering when you would call, Mrs Maloney.' Carrie's hand was hard, like her mother-in-law's, and her grip as firm as a man's. They were hard-working women, and there was no time for feminine vanity.

'I found her first, didn't I, Granny?' Midge interrupted, excitedly. And they laughed at her.

'Time for milking, Mrs Maloney. Come and meet my husband Tom, and my eldest son, christened Richard but always called Dick,' Carrie invited. 'I don't know why we bother to give our children proper names for we seldom use them!' she added. 'Maggie wouldn't answer to her proper name of Margaret, and as for Mary, I can't remember who christened her Midge.'

21

'It was Dick,' Lucy reminded her as they walked towards the milking shed. Tom was already seated on a stool, and the boy stood beside him. For Kitty Maloney this was another new experience, to watch a cow being milked and to smell the cattle, standing so patiently in their stalls. Tom lifted his head from the cow's flanks to grin at the visitor, but his hands were moving expertly on the swollen udders, and jets of milk splashed into the pail.

'I'll be with you in a minute, Tom.' Carrie spoke quietly, and beckoned to the boy who came to stand beside her. She bade him shake hands with Mrs Maloney. He had inherited the curly hair and vivid blue eyes and the natural friendliness.

'Where's Maggie?' Lucy demanded. 'I thought she was helping you in the dairy, Carrie?'

'She was, but she was so clumsy I sent her away. I get on better without her.'

'You should let her help. She will never learn if you discourage her.'

Carrie shook her head. 'We shall never make a farmer's daughter of Maggie, Mrs Maloney. She's just not interested.'

'Maybe she'll take to it later, when she's grown a bit.'

'Not Maggie. You can always tell, right from the start. Dick had a feeling for it even before he could walk, and Midge has taken to it like a duck to water.'

'I suppose we can't complain if two out of the four of the young generation will carry on the family tradition,' Lucy concluded, sensibly, and had the last word on the matter. 'Won't you join us for tea, Mrs Maloney?' she invited. 'I usually have tea with the children about this time, and Tom and Carrie have theirs after they have finished milking. Julian will be home from Grammar School by that time – the only one of the family you haven't met.'

When Kitty hesitated, Midge took her hand and urged,

'Come on. There's new bread and butter and strawberry jam, and gingerbread and lardie cake, and Granny makes everything all her own self, don't you Granny?'

'Get along with you, child!' Lucy gave her favourite grandchild a playful push, but she still led the shy little boy by the hand, and he had nothing to say. The servant had the tea laid ready on a starched white cloth. She had changed her apron and tidied her hair.

'This is our Katie,' said Lucy, and she greeted the visitor with a polite 'Good afternoon, Ma'am.'

The years had left no visible mark on Katie. An illegitimate child, conceived in the barn, of a passing tinker, she had been taken into the orphanage where she had spent her childhood. She was a big, strong woman with the mind of a child, and she still had to be supervised. But Lucy was a kind mistress, and Katie knew she was luckier than most of the orphan girls sent into service at the age of thirteen, while the boys were apprenticed to tradesmen, carpenters and wheelwrights for seven long years.

'You can brew the tea now, Katie,' her mistress reminded her. 'Put the puppy in the basket, Midge.'

The servant and the child both obeyed promptly, and the older girl came downstairs as soon as she was called, Kitty noticed. Maggie had been reading in the bedroom she shared with Midge. She was a serious little girl, with long flaxen hair and an elfin face. She shook hands with the visitor and sat down at the table.

'Have you all washed your hands?' Lucy looked from one to the other enquiringly, but only Maggie had clean hands. Dick, John and Midge were ordered to wash.

'Course she's clean. She doesn't do any work,' Dick complained.

Midge giggled happily as she dragged her twin to the scullery sink.

23

Chapter Two

Walking back across the park, Kitty turned to wave to the woman and children on the farm gate – a woman with the bloom of youth renewed in the joy of her grand-children and their need of her. Lucy Blunt would never grow old, for the children would keep her young, and be-cause she had been married at sixteen, she would live to enjoy her great-grandchildren.

'Come again, Mrs Maloney. Always welcome,' she called after Kitty, and Midge echoed, 'Come again, Mrs Maloney!'

Lucy held on to the two younger children who had climbed the high gate. John stood halfway, Midge at the top. So they would grow through childhood into adult life, the girl leading, the boy following, the girl fearless, the boy seeing danger everywhere.

Kitty walked slowly, savouring the warm friendliness of the past hour at Russets. Her nearest neighbours, yet it seemed another world. By comparison, their own world at Marston Park seemed shallow and artificial, yet she had no authority to change it. Harry held the reins, and their future would depend entirely on his management of their affairs. He had always been a gambler. The only time he played safe was when he had married Kitty O'Brien.

A whimsical smile touched her lips but did not reach her eyes. Why had he married her, and, so far as she knew, remained faithful to his marriage vows when he hardly noticed her existence? She felt no bitterness, only a deep-rooted sadness and disappointment as she looked back across the years.

When Dick had run off to the milking shed and Maggie had been reminded to help Katie with the washing up, and Midge had settled down with drawing book and crayons, Lucy sat at the kitchen table to help John with his homework. It was not compulsory to do lessons in the evening for children attending the village school unless they were studying for examinations. But Lucy had decided her youngest grandson must be encouraged or he would just accept the general opinion that he was backward, and not bother to learn. Every child has some potential, and it is not always obvious to his family.

When Julian was nine, he had begun to study for the Grammar School scholarship, and Lucy had supervised his evening studies because she had taken the place of both parents in his young life, and knew the importance of education. After all, as she had constantly reminded him, the next hurdle he had to face for his entry into the Royal Air Force would be difficult, and not confined to the manoeuvres of aircraft. Yet he found all kinds of study irksome, and was easily bored by subjects that had no relation to his ambitious plans. Sometimes Lucy could see his father in the boy's disarming smile – the father whose identity was known only to herself, to Sir Neville Franklin, and to the girl who had died in giving him birth. Yet he had inherited his mother's features, and some of her mannerisms. In just the same manner, the young Penelope Franklin would toss her head and laugh at her critics in those few short years of independence she had enjoyed after she had finished with the governess and the schoolroom. The War had changed all their lives, and the two Franklin girls had enjoyed their war work as VAD nurses in the hospital at Marston Park.

Penelope had been the most popular with the young officers, and had a reputation as a flirt, while her sister Sylvia had been faithful to a Canadian captain. She had married him at the end of the War, and made her home in his country. All the attention and the spoiling had gone to Penny's head, they said, and she seemed to enjoy shocking her sisters and contemporaries. Be that as it may, Penny had received the biggest shock when she discovered she was pregnant, and the whole village had been saddened by her death. It was a long time ago, but Lucy was constantly reminded of the girl as Julian grew in her likeness.

Midge was not concentrating on the crayoning. She was listening for the tinkle of the cycle bell. She adored Julian, and could not settle to anything until he was safely home.

'Julian!' she shrieked, and dropped the crayon. She was out of the door and racing across the yard before her twin had lifted his eyes from the simple sum on the slate. She swung the gate wide. It took all her strength, but Julian let her do it.

'Hallo, young Midge,' he grinned. The light from the cycle lamp lit her curly head. Her bright eyes danced with excitement. He had never known a child to be so constantly happy. Her happiness was infectious. He laughed, and scooped her on to the saddle. Twice round the yard, then indoors. He had taught her to steer while he held on to the saddle. She thought she had full control of the bike as they circled the yard. Her small pink tongue licked her lips, and her cheeks were flushed. The lamp illuminated the pathway. They ran into a sprinkling of hay near the Dutch barn that Dick had dropped on his way to the stable, and a wet patch where the mare had stood harnessed to the trap.

'The little bugger always does her piss in that exact spot. Been doing it for years,' Julian grumbled.

Midge giggled. She loved that word 'bugger', but Granny wouldn't allow it. And piss was vulgar. Julian was seventeen and a law unto himself. His escapades as a young boy, retold by Granny, had enhanced her hero worship. Her brother Dick would never have dreamed of running away from Russets to spend a whole day with a family of gypsies, from whom he caught scarlet fever, and a night with the hop-pickers on a farm near Cranbrook. As for jumping in the river when he couldn't swim and nearly getting drowned, that was downright stupid, according to Dick, who swam like a fish in the same river. She had listened to the horrifying story of that Christmas Eve when Julian had crept downstairs with a candle at midnight to see whether the cattle were kneeling in homage to Jesus. They weren't, of course, and the practical Midge, who discovered the myth of Father Christmas during her first week at school, was surprised at Julian being so fanciful. But he dropped the candle and set the hay alight, and the barn was nearly destroyed. Poor Uncle Albert was killed. It was a long time ago, but Granny remembered every detail of that sad Christmas, when a little boy set fire to the barn, and the Fire Brigade were called out, and nobody wanted to pull crackers or sing carols. Now Julian was grown up. He could jump higher and run faster than anybody else in Midge's small world. He was teaching her to ride the pony that his grandfather had given him. Round and round the field on a leading rein. Next Summer he would teach her to swim, for he had conquered his fear of the river by learning to swim in the baths at the Grammar School. It was a matter of compulsion, he told her. To refuse would have branded him a coward for the rest of his school days.

Fear was natural, but it must be conquered, he insisted.

'I'm not afraid.' It was true.

'I dare you,' he would say – and she dared.

But Julian was a Franklin, not a Blunt, and it gave him distinction. He looked like a Franklin and behaved like a Franklin. Tom called it arrogance, but Lucy said it was natural. She would not listen to complaints about his behaviour, though she often had to speak to him privately when he upset Tom or Carrie, or boxed Dick's ears for being cheeky. That was the pot calling the kettle black, she would remind him, since only Julian had the cheek to ride across the Park when the new owners of the estate were in residence, and only Julian would dare to laugh at the haughty Diane Maloney.

'She told me I was trespassing, Aunt Lucy. Didn't she know I was a Franklin? Stuck up little bitch!'

But Lucy ignored the incident, and invited Diane's mother to tea at Russets. The young ones could settle their own differences, or carry on the feud. It was no concern of the older generation, she considered.

The distance between London and Marston Park seemed to shrink with the new family in residence. Harry and Diane, in their respective cars, thought nothing of the journey, and lapped up the miles with the same easy complacency as they travelled from London to the States. Travel was not a pleasure but a necessity, a means of getting from one place to another, and Harry

28

always carried a briefcase full of important documents to be perused, so that he saw nothing beyond the windows of his comfortable limousine, driven by a competent chauffeur. Even Sammy was surprised at their casual acceptance of their new way of life.

Since they had finally settled into Marston Park she seldom went to London, but when she did go, she phoned for a taxi to take her to the station because she couldn't depend on either of the cars being available. She would give Kitty a treat, this year, she had decided. They would do their Christmas shopping in Oxford Street, and have lunch at one of the Lyons Corner Houses and tea at another. Kitty didn't care for Harrods or Slaters. She liked to be in the company of the English working class when she did her shopping, and she particularly favoured Woolworths. Tea at Lyons, with hot buttered tea cakes and a plate of fancy cakes from which to choose, pleased her enormously. She was like a child in her enjoyment of such simple pleasures, and grateful to Sammy for arranging it.

Any kind of outing relieved the monotony of her days. Never in her life had she felt so idle, so useless. Yet she had not taken advantage of Lucy Blunt's kind invitation. She was afraid to trespass on a new relationship not yet consolidated, and she had not mentioned the visit to Harry or Diane, who would probably assume that Mrs Blunt was being friendly out of curiosity. The New Rich had provoked much speculation from all classes of society in the village. Kitty was waiting for a definite invitation from Russets, and when it came – in the shape of a note, delivered by hand – she was delighted.

Tom and Carrie would soon be celebrating their eleventh wedding anniversary, and she was included in the family celebration. All anniversaries had a special significance at Russets, for Lucy loved parties. Dick had been surprised to discover his birthday followed so quickly after his parents' wedding anniversary, but he was a farmer's son, and the facts of life were no mystery.

'If I was conceived before you married Dad, that makes me a bastard, doesn't it, Mum?' he told her. Only a Blunt could be so devastatingly blunt, she thought, as she was reminded of her disloyalty to Bertie, Tom's brother, and her first husband. She could still blush like a young girl, and she often found the questions of her growing children embarrassing. It was so stupid, for she had lived at Russets since she was seventeen, and had married Bertie when he came home from the prisoner-of-war camp in Turkey. The horror of those early years, of her first marriage, had left an indelible mark on her personality. Even in the security of Tom's arms in the marriage bed, once shared with Bertie, she could still shudder at the memory of Bertie's terrible deformity.

'I tried to escape. This was their punishment,' he had told her on their wedding night. Their sexual relationship had been a travesty, an abnormal and endless experiment in new ways of compensating for his bitter frustration.

Tom was a gentle lover, and a dear, considerate husband. Only once had he taken her forcibly in all those long years of purgatory with his brother, and she had been shamed and shocked by the passion she had aroused in him. That was a long time ago, when Michaelmas Day was a holiday, and everyone flocked to the Michaelmas Fair. A long time ago, but fresh in the memory, for Carrie. A woman always remembered the exact hour when she lost her virginity. A long time ago, and now her firstborn son was reminding her that she had been bedded with his father before marriage. Tears pricked her eyes.

'Don't cry, Mum. It doesn't matter to me.' He seemed

surprised at her distress. 'Even the best families have skeletons in the cupboard. What about the Franklins? Charles was a bastard. So is Julian.' He gave her a hug. 'Cheer up, Mum. What's for supper?'

'A letter for you, dear, from Marston Park.'

Aunt Lucy had been dying to open it since it was delivered soon after Julian left the house to cycle to the station. Propped on the kitchen mantelpiece, it had tantalised her all day, but it would be taking liberties to open a letter addressed personally to a seventeen-year-old, and past experience of four growing sons had prepared her for yet another on the verge of manhood.

Tom and Carrie had already started on their tea when Julian came in with Midge. She would sit beside him and wait for tit-bits from his plate, as she had been doing since her high chair days. All the family gathered in the kitchen at this hour of the day. It was a leisurely meal for Tom and Carrie, after they had finished milking, and also for Julian, before he started on his homework. Maggie was reading her Bible in the rocking chair, with a kitten in her lap, completely absorbed in the story of Ruth. She was quite unaware of the speculation that centred around the letter.

'It's scented, dear,' Aunt Lucy hinted, but Julian simply took it up, sniffed at the mauve envelope, pushed it under Midge's nose, and laid it down.

'It smells like that scent Dick bought in the market for Mummy's birthday,' she said.

Dick glowered. 'You've been pinching it!'

'Only a small little drop on my hankie.'

'You leave it alone. It's not *yours*. Why can't you keep your meddling hands off other people's property?'

'I don't know.'

'She takes my marbles. It's not fair,' John grumbled.

'You can have them back. I don't want your silly old marbles.'

'That's enough!' Lucy reminded them sternly, as she poured more tea for Tom.

'Aren't you going to open your letter, Julian?' asked Carrie. He was teasing them deliberately.

'Who would be writing to you from *that* family?' Tom had a very poor opinion of the new owner of Marston Park, shared by Lucy and Carrie. Even the dairy produce was delivered from Harrods. Lucy intended to speak to Mrs Maloney about placing the order with Russets, but it was not a subject to be mentioned at their first meeting.

Julian glanced about the table, a disarming smile on his handsome face. He loved to keep them guessing. He held out his cup for more tea.

'You've had two,' Aunt Lucy reminded him, but she refilled his cup for the third time and begged, 'Open it, please.'

'I need a knife. A clean knife, Midge, that's jammy.'

Katie was paring apples at the small table under the window, but she missed nothing that was happening at the family table. She belonged, and she knew she belonged. Now she wiped the knife on her apron and handed it to Julian.

'Thanks, Katie.' He slit the envelope carefully, and took out a single sheet of matching notepaper. 'Phew, it pongs!' He flapped it across the table, and they all laughed. He loved an audience, and he knew how to switch on the charm. He was a Franklin.

Scented notepaper was a novelty at Russets. Only Aunt Lucy wrote letters, and she kept a threepenny packet of stationery on the mantelpiece.

Now the silence was impressive, and their expectant

faces turned towards him. Only Maggie took no part in it, and went on rocking to and fro, absorbed in her Bible. They watched Julian's humorous mouth twitching with amusement. They seemed to be holding their breath while he scanned the page. Then a blush crept over his face. Julian was embarrassed by the contents, and Julian was never embarrassed.

'Is it private, dear?' Aunt Lucy prompted.

'It's from Diane Maloney. I'm invited to a party on Saturday. *In*formal dress. Ha! Ha! That's a joke. I don't possess anything else, do I?'

'Are you going?' they chorused.

He shrugged. 'Why not? It would be interesting. I've never met a rich American industrialist.'

'What shall you wear, dear?' Aunt Lucy was slicing the lardie cake.

'Flannels and blazer.'

She nodded.

He was wondering what sort of a party it would be that started at 9 o'clock, but Diane Maloney and her London friends would be sure to think up something original. He couldn't imagine them playing charades or hide-and-seek, the favourite games at the homes of his school friends once they had finished with hunt-the-thimble and musical chairs. He was good at charades, but hide-and-seek was a bit of a gamble. You might find yourself pulled into a dark corner by a hot, clutching hand, obliged to kiss somebody's kid sister. Alternatively, it could be exciting if you played your cards well, and the prettiest girl at the party had you taped. His reputation was at stake if he missed the chance of a stolen kiss – the reputation of a Franklin. He knew all about his grandfather's mistresses and the scandalous affair with Aunt Lucy. He knew his cousin Charles was bedding the village girls while he was still at his public school. 'A chip off the old block,' they called him. But he left Marston Park in rather a hurry, some years ago. They said he got a girl in the family way, and grandfather had thrashed him. They said he was living with a wealthy widow, old enough to be his mother, in California. They said he had a fatal fascination for women – whatever that might mean. At seventeen, Julian's sexual curiosity had still to be satisfied. Flirting was fun, but he was not such a devil as he would have them believe.

When the table had been cleared, and the two younger children sent upstairs to get ready for bed, he settled down to his homework at the kitchen table, but found his thoughts wandering from the French translation to the girl, Diane. Why had she invited him to a party when they hadn't been formally introduced? It was so *un*-English. But then, Diane Maloney was American – Irish-American obviously, with a name like Maloney. That patronising manner she had displayed at their first meeting could be deceptive. It was easy to be patronising on the back of a thoroughbred. He remembered his grandfather on the handsome black stallion. One thing was certain; he would soon remind her he was a Franklin, if she started to give herself airs! The New Rich had no breeding and no background. He had both, and he was proud of his heritage. Aunt Lucy had not failed in her duty. She had encouraged this pride.

Growing up at Russets, riding the wide acres of parkland on his pony, he had often stopped to admire the Big House, and wondered what it would be like to live there. It was sad to see it so empty and neglected. In his grandfather's day it had been so alive, so pregnant with his strong personality. But this was home – the warm kitchen, the clatter of dishes, the hot smell of ironing, children running about overhead, Katie busy with cans of hot water, Tom smoking his pipe in the rocking chair,

Carrie playing those interminable Indian love lyrics on the parlour piano, and Aunt Lucy, bless her, the beloved matriarch on whom they all depended. He sighed, and bent over the essay.

Julian propped his bike against the ivy-clad wall, climbed the steps to the terrace, and stood there, staring at the house that had once belonged to his forebears. He felt a tremor of angry resentment, an objection to the new owner flaunting his wealth at Marston Park. It was a kind of desecration.

On this warm Autumn evening, the French windows were open on to the terrace. Lights blazed from every window, and a jazzy recording of the latest song hit was drowned by the shrill clamour of voices, and the screeching laughter. They couldn't be drunk, surely? It was only a little after 9 o'clock. If it was just high spirits, it was pretty awful, and he felt like an intruder. It had seemed strange to start out for a party when the rest of the family were getting ready for bed, but it was a new experience, and he supposed it was one of those parties that went on till the early hours of the morning.

As he stood hesitating on the terrace, a young girl, in a short yellow frock and short hair, ran screaming from a window, chased by a boy in pale blue trousers that fitted his backside as tightly as a glove. A matching silk shirt was open to the navel. In his school blazer and flannel trousers he was already feeling ridiculously over-dressed and was turning away when the girl stopped him.

'Hi! Don't run away.' She had clutched at his hand, laughing and breathless, and when the boy caught up with her, she squealed excitedly, 'Darling, look what I've found.'

The boy laughed mockingly. 'Straight from school by

the look of it,' and draped his arm possessively round the girl's waist.

'Don't take any notice of Gerry. He's just kidding,' she told Julian, still clutching his hand. 'Are you gate-crashing, or has Di invited you?'

'I'm invited.'

'You see, a genu-*ine* guest. Come on in and get acquainted. Say, what's your name?'

'Julian – Julian Franklin.' The name meant nothing to this young American or her boy-friend. They had grown up in a society far removed from the English aristocracy. They had no shyness, no inhibitions, only a brash confidence in their own importance. The world was their oyster, and to be young was swell, if you didn't stop to think. The mind was an empty vessel waiting to be filled. You lived on your nerves and your emotions.

The girl in the yellow frock was pert and pretty, the boy as lean as a greyhound, with a cropped head and a weak mouth. Products of a new generation, they were enjoying, as Diane Maloney was enjoying, the benefits for which an older generation had worked and slaved and denied themselves. At seventeen and eighteen, they had sampled the dangers and delights of sex, and the stimulating vapours of alcohol. To be different was to be rejected by the herd.

But Julian, on the threshold of this new world, was not yet aware of its danger or its fascination. That would come later.

'Hi! Di! Come on over!' The girl in the yellow frock shrieked above the clamour, gave him a reassuring pat, and drifted away with her partner.

Diane Maloney was dancing with a tall blond Adonis. They were entwined together in a close embrace. The girl's dark head had the shining gleam of a raven's wing against the blond. Every curve of her slender body was

36

accentuated in the sheath-like frock. It was so revealing, she could have been naked. Her long legs were bare, and her feet were bare. The boy's feet were bare. They were equally matched, beautiful in the flowing rhythm of their young bodies.

And Julian stood watching and waiting, conspicuous in his school blazer and flannels, hot with embarrassment. The noise was deafening, the lights dazzling, and the swaying couples had a sameness as though they had been made in the same mould and poured into the scanty, revealing clothes. Then she was skimming across the floor, smiling a welcome, hands outstretched. She was like a flame in her scarlet frock.

'Hallo, Julian. So you came? I guess you thought I had a cheek after being so darn uncivil the other day. Am I forgiven?'

He nodded.

She took his hands. A tremor ran through his whole body – not an angry tremor, nor yet a resentful feeling of her claim to his rightful heritage. He smiled nervously as she removed his blazer and draped it over a gilt chair.

'Take off your tie and your shoes,' she said, and when he obeyed, she looked him over with approval, raised his hand, and called out, authoritatively, 'Hi! Look who's here! Say hallo to Julian, our next door neighbour.'

Twenty or more couples called 'Hi, Julian!' and then went on dancing cheek to cheek. Somebody had put on another record.

'Can you rumba, Julian?' asked Diane.

'No.'

'I'll teach you. Come on.'

He was an apt pupil, and she was pleased with him. The blond Adonis was watching. He was drinking something he had poured from a jug on the sideboard. This was the original dining-room that Julian remembered from early childhood. It was oak-panelled, with a parquet floor – a spacious room, in which all the couples could move freely. Refreshments had been arranged on a long table, covered in a starched white cloth. The wailing saxophone drowned their voices. It was bedlam, yet strangely exhilarating. But where were the grownups? How could they stand such a racket? Julian wanted to know, as she led him away.

'Daddy is in London, and Mummy at the flat, looking after him. That's the whole point of the party,' Diane explained. 'Come and meet Sammy. She's in the study, glued to the wireless, listening for the latest bulletin on Eddy and Wally.'

Julian looked blank.

'Your Edward and our Wallace. We've all been betting she'll be sitting on that throne before Christmas.'

'You're wasting your money. Never in a million years!'

'You sound as if she is not good enough?'

'She's not. Firstly, she has divorced two husbands. Secondly, she's a commoner. Thirdly, the Archbishop of Canterbury would never sanction such a union.'

'How come the Archbishop can play the dictator?'

'Because the King is the supreme Head of the Church and the State.'

'It's crazy. The whole set-up is crazy. He's in love with her. Isn't that a good enough reason?'

'No, there's a thing called duty.'

'Then how the hell will they sort it out?'

'The King will abdicate.'

They found Sammy in the study. She switched off the wireless and stood up to greet Julian with a smile and a firm handshake.

'Good evening, Mrs Sampson.' He returned the smile.

'Call me Sammy. I feel I know you, Julian. I've heard so much about you, and indeed, all the Franklins. It's a fascinating story.' She glanced at his open shirt and stockinged feet. 'I see Diane has been disrobing you already. Don't let her bully you, Julian. She's had her own way since she took her first steps.'

'Sammy, that's not fair!' the girl protested.

'It's true, dear.'

'Has there been any new development in the royal romance?'

'Not since the last news, but it seems to be a foregone conclusion.'

'That the King will abdicate?'

'Yes.'

'Of course, you two would stick together. It's not democratic. It makes me real mad to think of that stuffy old Archbishop having the last word.'

'Somebody must have the authority to decide such an important issue,' Julian argued. 'It's a great pity, though, for Edward was so popular with the people when he was Prince of Wales. This affair with Mrs Simpson has been a shock. One expects a king to do his duty. Mrs Simpson must be a very strong character to have weakened all his good intentions.'

'Of course she's a strong character. That's why she would make a good queen,' Diane insisted.

Sammy shook her head. 'We don't want a King who could be overruled by his Queen. That would be a disaster for this country. Don't you agree, Julian?'

'I certainly do.'

'Shucks! What's the use of talking. You're prejudiced. Come on, Julian. Let's get back.'

'Go easy on the cocktails, Diane,' Sammy warned.

The girl laughed mockingly as she dragged Julian away.

'Sammy's a honey, but she's so old-fashioned, she would have me drinking lemonade if she had her way.'

'I suppose it's difficult for a governess to realise the time has come for her pupil to start thinking independently.'

'Sure thing. It's almost twelve months since she gave up teaching me, but I reckon I'll always be her special baby.'

'Do you like going to school in Paris?'

'How come you know all about Paris?'

'Everyone knows. Servants talk. The new family at Marston Park has provided a fresh topic in the village.'

'They don't like us, do they?'

He shrugged. 'What do you care?'

'I don't understand. Nobody could be more generous than Daddy. He contributes to all the local charities. What more do they want? You tell me, for I sure would like to know.'

'Country people are slow to accept fresh faces. You'd be surprised how long it takes. Even a man or woman in the next village can be regarded as a foreigner in our village,' he explained. But he knew the Maloneys would never be accepted. To be labelled the New Rich was detrimental to a friendly relationship in any class of society but their own. The girl beside him was as alien to himself and his young contemporaries at the Grammar School as the boy from Peking eating his noodles and rice with chopsticks in a Chinese restaurant.

The blond Adonis was draped over a gilt chair, glowering at the dancing couples. So Diane had slipped up in her arithmetic, Julian was thinking, and he, Julian, was odd man out at the party. It was going to be quite a lark if this fellow tried to monopolise their young hostess, but he was ready to do battle for her favours, as ready as his forebears in shining armour. The honour of

40

the Franklins was at stake! It had not occurred to him until tonight that he was a romantic at heart, but then he had never been associated with such a beautiful girl. It came as no surprise, however, when he found himself back among the dancers, that a hand clutched his shoulder, and an arrogant voice demanded, 'Move over, boy!'

'Not yet, darling,' cooed Diane. 'Wait for the tango. That's your speciality.'

'OK,' he agreed, and drifted away.

'Keep it under your hat, Julian. We are secretly engaged. That's why Carl is acting so possessive.'

'Engaged? But you are still at school.'

'Sure, and Carl's still at college.'

'He's not English or American?'

'No, German. An only son. Pots of money. Ever heard of Richters?'

'No.'

'You will. Grandfather Richter made a fortune during the War, and his son stepped into his shoes when the old man died last year. Carl reckons they could make a second fortune in the next War, and he could be a millionaire before he is thirty.'

'What's the family business?'

'Armaments.'

Julian whistled. 'Where did you meet him?'

'I was dining with Daddy in our favourite French restaurant in Soho when Carl came in with his friends. They dared him to introduce himself – and he dared!'

'Cheeky blighter!'

'That's typical of Carl. Don't breathe a word. Daddy would be real mad at me if he knew we were engaged. He reckons we shall be at war with Germany again before the end of the decade. Daddy used not to talk business with me till recently. Maybe he thinks I'm old

41

enough now to understand what it's all about. Or maybe he's lonely. We are not a close family, Julian,' she sighed. 'Gee, isn't that record terrible? Let's switch off. Are you hungry?'

'No, thanks.'

'Neither am I. We'll eat later, shall we?'

Carl was waving a glass.

'He wants me to sample his new cocktail. Come on, else he will get mad at me.'

When she switched off the record, the dancing couples still went on jigging and jerking like marionettes on invisible strings. Carl flung an arm round Diane's neck and she looked at him with adoring eyes as they sipped from each other's glass. Julian sipped his own cocktail and moved away gradually.

Out on the terrace he gazed towards Russets in tormented uncertainty. Should he stay or go? It was so contradictory. Only a short time ago he was ready to do battle for Diane's favours. Now he was wishing he was back in the kitchen at Russets, drinking hot cocoa. This was his first cocktail. He found it very over-rated and tipped it away. Blast! Why couldn't he make up his mind?

When the strains of a tango drifted out to the terrace, he moved back to stand in the French window. Now Carl and Diane were alone on the floor while the other couples had moved away to gather round the refreshment table, chattering and giggling. Their dancing had a professional quality that Julian would never acquire. Swaying in graceful union, their slender sensuous bodies belonged together. Even as they danced they were making love. It was so revealing Julian could feel the excitement in his own racing pulses. But they were not aware of him, only of each other. This was the prelude to sex. That would come later, when they

42

tired of dancing and went below, to the basement. The swimming pool was the high spot of Diane's parties, and only Julian was ignorant of the pleasures in store.

Feeling peeved and neglected, he sat on the balustrade, reminding himself that Carl had every right to claim Diane. They were engaged. He could not tell how long he sat there, but when, at last, the gramophone stopped playing, Diane came to look for him, profuse in apology. She was flushed and starry-eyed, and when she took his hands and pulled him off the balustrade, he was once again enslaved by her beauty and vitality.

'Cheri, it was naughty of me, but I so love to dance, I forget my guest. Come now, we all go down to the pool. You can swim, of course?'

'Of course.'

Carl had gone on ahead, and now she shooed the rest of her guests down the stone steps that had once led to the wine cellars. Now it was like a tropical hot-house at Kew Gardens. The transformation was so exotic, Julian gasped and exclaimed boyishly, 'Gosh! It's fantastic!'

'I thought it would surprise you.' Diane was searching the green, translucent water for the blond head. In a matter of seconds, the white wicker chairs were draped in colourful garments, and boys and girls were jumping in the pool, hand-in-hand, stark naked! Diane stepped out of her frock. It was her only garment. She slipped into the pool and gazed up at him, teasing and provocative.

'I dare you, Julian Franklin!'

He dropped his clothes on the same chair that held her frock, dived into the pool and came up in the centre, his dark head streaming. The water was warm, but he was shivering. Then she was there, dragging him down, like a mermaid with her victim. Her warm wet body and her long legs were entangled in his own. He could not escape. He had no desire to escape. Boys' nakedness he had known in the communal bath after a rugger scrum, but a girl's body was still a mystery for all his pretence to intimacy with the opposite sex. First his young cousin, Wendy, and then of recent years, young Midge, he had rubbed down with a towel after a swim in the river. Their firm little bodies were beautiful, and innocent of sex. But now his little cousin was thirteen, and when she stayed at Russets in the Summer vacation, she was shy of him, and undressed and dressed behind a bush. They had been like brother and sister until this Summer, when he was surprised to discover she had suddenly developed little pointed breasts. That explained the shyness, of course.

But he wasn't thinking of Wendy tonight. The four years that divided them had widened, and he was a man, with a man's racing pulses and throbbing loins. It was a kind of torture, and the clinging wet body could both repel and attract. To lose his identity was a shock, but he was losing it now, in this tortuous sensuality, as they clung together.

Then she was wrenched away, and he was fighting and struggling with Carl. Caught unawares, and exhausted emotionally, he was no match for a jealous lover, fighting for possession of his love. Seized with the old terror of drowning that he had not known for several years, he was gasping and choking. He thought he was dying. His lungs were bursting. But he didn't want to die. In desperation, he kicked out savagely, heard a yelp of pain, and was free. A few frantic strokes and he was climbing out of the pool. Snatching up his clothes, he ran for the steps. They let him go.

At the curve in the stairway, he stopped to pull on his shirt and trousers. He hardly glanced at the cluttered room, and was out of the French windows and across the

44

terrace in long, loping strides. Then he remembered his blazer, shoes and tie, and rushed back to gather them up. Once on his bicycle, he went like mad across the Park, and into the sanctuary of Russets.

The grandfather clock was striking eleven as he crept into the warm kitchen. Only two hours, and the pattern of his life had changed, though he was not yet aware of the implication. It had been a traumatic experience. In those two short hours, he had known every kind of emotion, and all his latent senses had been awakened to sex.

He was still shivering, and he pulled up a chair to the stove, opened the door, and felt the warmth of the banked-up fire. A mug of cocoa was standing on the hob. Dear Aunt Lucy! Had she wondered if he might have had enough of Diane Maloney's party before her other guests? Her intuition where her family was concerned was remarkable. She seemed to know and understand all their needs, and not only their bodily needs. She fed them like fighting cocks, encouraged and scolded them. She could be stern, but never shocked or surprised. The burden of responsibility was heavy on her shoulders, but she bore it cheerfully.

Tom had never been a strong character, and Carrie had never fully recovered from the mental and physical suffering of her first marriage. So they were glad to lean on Lucy, and to let her decide everything. Their children went naturally to their grandmother, not to their parents, to settle even the smallest matter. It could be argued that Tom and Carrie were too dependent on Lucy, too ready to allow her to carry the burden of the farm and the family, but it was inevitable that a strong personality should dominate a weaker. Her husband, Bert, long since dead from that fall from the hay-wagon, had been an easy-going character, quite happy to let his

45

young wife hold the reins. So it was naturally assumed, by the young generation, that Granny was the person who had the last word on everything.

The cocoa was hot, not lukewarm. So Aunt Lucy had not retired to bed with the rest of the family, but had made the cocoa quite recently. Perhaps she was still awake, and had heard him come in? He was tempted to go and see. A warm hug would be comforting. He remembered how often he had crept into her bed as a child, crying with earache or toothache. She had a cure for all their ailments, and called the doctor only for serious accidents, or childish infections such as measles and chicken pox. He remembered the time when he caught scarlet fever from a gypsy boy, and had to be segregated from other children for six weeks. He remembered his grandfather riding over from the Big House with presents. He remembered, with vivid recollection, the day he was killed, and that he had wondered what it was like to be dead. Grandfather was the most alive person in his small world. He was like a king in his kingdom of Marston Park. They said it was a splendid funeral, and that the groom led the handsome black stallion behind the cortège – the horse that had taken fright and thrown his master. They said the whole village was there to pay its respects; the shops had closed, the bell tolled all day, and the children from the village school had walked in procession to church, the boys wearing black armlets, the girls with their hair tied with black ribbon. It was a long time ago, and a whole decade had passed.

With his feet on the fender, sipping the hot cocoa, he was suddenly choked with tears. It could have been reaction, but he was a boy again, young and vulnerable, crying quietly for his lost innocence.

Chapter Three

It was the one topic of conversation in all classes of society, from the humblest croft to the grandest castle – *The King had abdicated*! His speech had moved many of his subjects to tears, for he spoke of 'the woman I love' in the tenderest way. It was the end of an era, one of the shortest in history, when a monarch had to choose between his kingdom and a woman. The romantics insisted it was a wonderful gesture, worthy of a king. But for many of his disappointed subjects it was an act of deplorable folly and self-indulgence. Between the two, he was stripped of every virtue, banished from his country and his people, and condemned to a lifetime of wandering abroad in search of happiness. Families were divided on the issue, the women more sympathetic than the men. Children fought each other without knowing the crucial importance of such an unprecedented abdication; and Diane Maloney lost her bet.

The patients in the Hospital for Women in the Marylebone Road stopped talking about their operations. This new topic of conversation in the wards lasted for several days, and Sister Simmons – the mother of young Wendy – was constantly consulted. She was considered the supreme authority on all matters, and took precedence over Matron.

Sister Simmons was strict with her nurses, but kind to her patients. They said she was the daughter of the late Sir Neville Franklin, but her private life was kept strictly private, and only her closest friends and colleagues were aware that she had married into the working class in defiance of both classes of society, at the outbreak of War. They said her husband had lost a leg in the War, and she had stayed on at the hospital after she had qualified to supplement her husband's small income as a poor man's solicitor.

But that was not the only reason she was still there, eighteen years later. Sister Simmons was a dedicated nurse, and the hospital her second home. She drove up every morning from their little terrace house facing the Common in Tunbridge Wells, and hardly used the flat provided for her convenience. Her mother-in-law – the twin sister of Lucy Blunt at Russets – enjoyed a free hand as cook-housekeeper, and the lasting gratitude and affection of her son's wife. They had never moved from the little terrace house because it suited them all admirably. Freddie had his office conveniently near to the town, and Ruby an easy walk to the shops. Wendy was a weekly boarder at the Seminary for Young Ladies, an exclusive establishment under the patronage of three maiden ladies, all sisters, of gentle birth. It was not snobbery that decided Cynthia Simmons on this particular school when Wendy was five, but its reputation. Apart from a little tennis for the seniors and rounders for the juniors, sport was not included in the curriculum. Music, painting, needlework and deportment were subjects of vital concern and importance to the three Miss Wallaces.

It had proved a good choice, for Wendy's musical

talent had been encouraged, and she had passed her examinations with distinction. It had also discouraged her natural tendency to be a tomboy. When she complained of being smothered in silly old restrictions, her father smiled indulgently.

'Your mother knows best, my pet.'

'That's what you always say, Daddy.'

'Well, it's true.'

'As far back as I can remember, Mummy has been the one to decide everything. Don't you mind? Shouldn't a man be the master in his own home?'

Freddie Simmons shook his head. 'A marriage should be a partnership, dear, with the man and the woman having equal rights. Your mother has her profession, I have mine. We understand each other perfectly, and you are wrong to assume that your mother has the last word on everything. We consult each other on important issues.'

'You love Mummy very much, don't you, Daddy?'

'Yes, I do.'

'More than you love me?'

'It's a different kind of love, dear, neither more nor less. One day you will understand.'

'I love you best, so why can't you love me best?'

He pulled her on to his good leg and she perched there, hugging him round the neck. He was shy of endearments, but he adored his daughter, and could not bear to see her punished. Cynthia was inclined to discipline the child as she disciplined her nurses. They were not very close, and Wendy had a strong will of her own.

The years were slipping away too quickly for Freddie Simmons, and his small daughter had grown into a leggy schoolgirl. Her long fair hair was another bone of contention between mother and daughter, for Cynthia would not allow it to be cut.

49

Perched on his knee, that evening in November 1936, they had been discussing the Abdication, and, like so many of her sex, Wendy was in favour of the King's decision. The girls at school thought it terribly romantic and could talk of little else.

'Mrs Simpson is not pretty, is she, Daddy? I suppose she must have sex appeal?'

Freddie was taken aback. 'What do you know of sex appeal, my pet?' he asked anxiously.

'I know it's something I haven't got, that my special friend Belinda Jackson has got, because the boys whistle after her, and I've seen the music master touching her breast. Do you think my breasts are nice, Daddy? Julian didn't even notice them, the last time I stayed at Russets.' She sighed.

'I think perhaps Julian has a one-track mind, dear, and now he is in his last year at Grammar School, the Royal Air Force is no longer a dream, but will soon be a reality.'

'Yes, and he sees me as a sister. Growing up together, well, almost, is a great drawback. I mean, can I ever make Julian notice me if I haven't got sex appeal?'

'Every male is not attracted that way, pet. Personality is a very important factor, and intelligence. A plain girl or woman can also be attractive to the opposite sex. A pretty face will not always be pretty.'

'Was Mummy pretty when she was young?'

'Your mother is not old, dear,' he rebuked her, gently. 'No, she was not pretty, but she had beautiful eyes. She still has beautiful eyes. Have you never noticed?'

'You mean *expressive*. When she is pleased, her eyes are soft, like brown velvet, and when she is angry, they are black!'

'So, you have noticed?'

'Of course. I'm not a baby and I just wonder what attracted you to Mummy in the beginning, apart from her eyes, I mean? Was it love at first sight?'

He shook his head. 'That's a question you should ask your mother.'

'Why?'

'Because she will probably tell you that it was love at first sight for her, but it took a long time to convince me that she had actually made up her mind to marry me, when I lay unconscious.'

'How? When? Why have you never told me?'

'I don't know. It happened very suddenly. I was racing across the Park on my bicycle to keep an appointment with Lady Franklin, when Cynthia Franklin almost ran me down. I think a hoof must have caught my head when her horse shied. I don't remember anything else till I opened my eyes, several days later, on Aunt Lucy's sofa, in the parlour at Russets, and saw Cynthia sitting there. I had concussion.'

'Poor Daddy.'

'Poor Mummy! She couldn't realise what she had let herself in for. The class barrier was almost impregnable before the war, and it was sheer madness even to arrange a meeting in London.'

'Go on, Daddy. It's exciting, and very romantic.'

'Mummy was working very hard at the hospital. She was in her first year as a probationer, and we arranged to meet at a tea-shop when she was off-duty in the afternoon, which was not very often. I had rooms in Soho, and an office there, but was earning hardly enough to pay my landlady. We both seemed always to be hungry when we met in that tea-shop, and consumed a plate of currant buns. I remember the waitress was a motherly soul with a cheerful smile. Your mother wore white gloves to pour the tea, and I thought it was because she

51

was a lady, but when she took them off, I was shocked to see her hands were red and roughened by hard work and hot soda water. She told me a probationer was just a glorified charwoman.'

'Then what happened?'

'War was declared, and I joined the Army – and your mother proposed!'

'*Mummy* proposed?'

'She had to, my pet. I would never have got round to it.'

'Oh, Daddy, you are so sweet. I love you best of all. Then I love Grandma next best, then Mummy, then Julian, though I sometimes think Julian may be second best one day.'

'Or even best?'

She shook her head. 'I'm not like Mummy. I won't ever propose. I would sooner be an old maid.'

'That would suit me fine, pet. Then I wouldn't lose you,' he teased her. 'I can hear the car. Run upstairs and tidy your hair. You look as though you've been tangled in a bush.'

'I have, on the Common. I was chasing Jock.' She slid off his knee and ran upstairs. Hanging over the banisters, she watched her parents' warm greeting. 'Anyone would think they had been parted for weeks,' she told herself. 'It's not fair! I hate Mummy!'

Life was so difficult, so puzzling. When she was a little girl, in the kindergarten, she had supposed that all families were close, and all parents lived happily ever after once they were married. But it soon became clear that it was not so. In her own family, at a very early age, she had felt hurt and neglected because of that very special love between her parents. She often felt left out when she longed to be included. When she was a little girl, she would hang around Daddy's neck and refuse to let go when Mummy came back from the hospital. Then there was a scene, with Mummy struggling to release Daddy, smacking her hands, and ordering her to let go. Tears and tantrums. Poor Daddy! And Grandma always taking her part.

'You are not to spoil her, Mother. I won't have a disobedient child!'

'But she's only a baby, love.'

'She's not a baby, and she's not stupid. She knows exactly what she is doing, causing such a rumpus. It upsets Freddie. I won't have him upset. You know it brings on a migraine, he is so sensitive. Please don't fuss the child, Mother. Send her upstairs. When she has calmed herself, she can come down and apologise.'

More tears, as she was pushed off the warm, comfortable lap. Grandma couldn't bear her little love to be scolded. That was a long time ago. She would never behave that way now, but it still hurt, and she still felt neglected, crouching there on the landing, holding her breath for fear of being discovered. To see Daddy holding out his arms, and Mummy enfolded in those arms, with her head on his shoulder. It was so contradictory. Mummy wasn't like that. She was strong and capable and rather bossy. She just didn't *need* a shoulder. Once she had actually heard Daddy say, 'My darling girl, you are worn out.' Now that really was a surprise, for Daddy was shy of endearments. Grandma had explained that it was because of the way he was brought up, in a working-class home and by working-class parents who called their children by their Christian names, or sometimes luv, but never dear or darling. It was only one of the many differences in her parents, Wendy had discovered, even before she started school. They had different voices, different manners, different tastes in food. Mummy was proud and dignified. Daddy was a

53

gentle person. Daddy was so sweet.

It was Saturday again, the happiest day of the week, if Mummy was on duty at the hospital. She had alternate Saturdays and Sundays free. Today they had walked along The Pantiles, she and Daddy, arm-in-arm, and had strawberry ices at the tea-shop. Leaves were falling, and there was a lovely smell of Autumn. Every season had its own particular smell, and every season was beautiful. She had been taught to notice such things.

One of her earliest memories was here, at The Pantiles, with Daddy pushing the pram, while she toddled along, picking up the Autumn leaves, one by one, and placing them carefully on the pram cover. They would sit down to rest his poor leg. It was called James, and people would stop to enquire after James. That was also a long time ago, but The Pantiles was still their favourite walk on Saturday or Sunday afternoons, while Grandma had her forty winks. She was so lucky to have a father who hadn't to go away on business all the week, like so many fathers. He kept office hours, but was often available in the late evening for the convenience of a client. All his clients were working class, and could not afford to pay the high fees that other solicitors charged. He also did work for a trade union.

Some of the girls at school had divorced parents, or parents who were not living together, and the children had to spend part of each holiday with either the mother or the father, but not as a family. They had no choice in the matter, and were not consulted. When her best friend, Linda, confessed to her own parents' frequent quarrels, and her fear of divorce, it made Wendy anxious.

'Don't worry, my pet. It won't ever happen in our family.' Daddy was very positive.

Some girls had two lots of grandparents, but she had

only Grandma, Daddy's mother.

'Am I upper class or working class, Grandma?' she had asked one day, when they were talking about families.

'Neither one nor the other, love.'

'Why?'

'Because one parent is upper class and one is working class.'

'I would like to be upper class, but then I wouldn't have you or Daddy, and I love you both very much. I've just remembered. Julian is neither one thing or the other, so I don't mind.'

'Julian is not sure where he belongs, love. He knows he is a Franklin on his mother's side, but his father is still a mystery. He could be upper class or working class, and he may never know his father. In all the seventeen years, there has been no word from him.'

'Perhaps he will confess his sin on his death bed? And it was a sin, wasn't it, to leave a little baby without parents when the mother died in childbirth?'

'It was wicked, love. It gives a child a chip on the shoulder.'

'He never mentions it now, but he once told me it might spoil everything. Supposing he discovered his father was a dustman, or a butcher, or an ex-convict! It would be so humiliating.'

'But his mother was a Franklin, and not likely to allow just any Tom, Dick or Harry to take liberties.'

'To tell you the truth, Grandma, I don't actually know what it means – taking liberties. A girl of thirteen should know about babies, shouldn't she?'

'Yes, love.'

'Couldn't you tell me, *please*?'

Ruby shook her head. 'It's not my place, love. It's a mother's place.'

'I could never ask Mummy such a personal question, and if I ask Daddy, he will be sure to say, "Ask your Mother, pet".' She sighed. 'It's pretty hopeless, trying to discover the facts of life. I bet you sixpence Maggie knows how babies are made, and she's only ten. I could ask Julian, but we are not on speaking terms at the moment.'

'What's he done to upset you?'

'He hasn't even noticed my breasts!'

Ruby stifled a strong desire to laugh, but it was no laughing matter to her young grand-daughter. She wished Cynthia would enlighten the child. Too much curiosity could be dangerous. She remembered her own initiation had been as natural as breathing. In a working-class family, birth and death held no mystery. She and Lucy, her twin sister, had enjoyed themselves in the hayfield. They both had known exactly what they were doing, at the age of fifteen, with Bert and Tom. Both married at sixteen, and babies on the way.

'Why am I fair, when Mummy and Daddy are dark?'

Questions! Questions! But who better than a grand-mother to answer questions about the family? Her memory is good, she has the time and the patience, and can satisfy the most avid curiosity. To be told she was like her Grandmother Franklin was very satisfying to Wendy. It seemed to prove her theory that she rightly belonged to the upper class.

'Tell me about my other Grandmother,' she coaxed, as they shared a bench on the Common one afternoon in the long Summer holiday.

'I only saw Lady Franklin once, when I happened to be doing a bit of extra charring at The Three Nuns one Sunday morning. The family from Marston Park drove up in their carriage to attend the morning service at the church. It was before the youngest child was born. Your

56

mother was in the carriage with her two sisters, Beatrice and Sylvia. Also the governess and the ladies maid. Sir Neville was on horseback. When the youngest child was born, they said your Grandmother Franklin was so disheartened, she refused to have any more children, and became a semi-invalid.'

'Why was she disheartened?'

'Because it was another girl, and Sir Neville wanted a son and heir.'

'But he *did* have a son later, didn't he? His name was Charles, and he lives in America. Julian told me about him one day, when we walked across the Park to look at the empty house.'

'Yes, he had a son.'

'But you said Grandmother Franklin refused to have any more children. Did she change her mind?'

'No.'

'Well, then, who was the mother of Charles?'

'My own sister, Lucy, at Russets.'

'*Aunt Lucy*? Why has Julian never mentioned it? Was it another skeleton in the family cupboard?'

'Yes, love.'

'It's fabulous! Tell me more. I'm dying to know what happened. How did Aunt Lucy come to be the mother of Charles Franklin?'

Ruby sighed. She got so involved these days with her favourite grandchild. How to explain to the child that her own sister had been bedded with the Squire for one particular purpose – to conceive a son and heir. It was a bit of a gamble, but Lucy had three healthy boys, and it seemed likely that she could produce another. If not, they would try again.

'They say your Grandfather Franklin made no secret of the fact that he admired our Lucy. She was pretty, and plump as a Spring chicken, as the saying goes. And she was strong and healthy, never had a day's illness far back as I can remember. Mind you, my love, we were all flabbergasted. It was such a scandal. But Lucy had no shame. She carried that child so proud you would think they was man and wife.'

'So Aunt Lucy was Grandfather Franklin's mistress?'

'Well, not exactly.'

'What then?'

'I can't say no more, love. I've said too much already. Your mother would be cross with me if she knew what we had been talking about.'

'Then we won't tell her. What was he like, Charles I mean?'

'The handsomest little boy I ever did see. They said he was a chip off the old block. But there was always trouble in the family after he was born. Lucy's own boys were jealous. They called Charles the cuckoo in the nest. You couldn't blame them, for she doted on that child. They were half-brothers, you see, but Charles got all the attention and all the spoiling. Sir Neville was proud as Punch. He promised my sister the child should stay at Russets till he was seven, then he would live at Marston Park because he had to be educated properly as a gentleman's son. Perhaps she thought he would change his mind when he saw his son growing so strong and healthy at Russets, or perhaps those early years went so quickly she wasn't prepared when the time came. It broke her heart when he was taken away, and only allowed to visit her for a day or two during the school holidays. It was a mistake, I reckon, to take a child from a working-class family, where he felt he belonged, to grow up with the Gentry. Must have been very unsettling to a little boy of seven, especially when he was sent away to boarding school. It was the start of the mix-up between the classes, and the young generation, to this

58

day, don't seem to know where they rightly belong. If your Grandfather Franklin had lived, I reckon he would have claimed Julian as he has claimed Charles. They say it's an ill wind blows nobody any good. When Miss Cynthia married my Freddie, I were proper flummoxed, but she were cool as a cucumber. "May I call you Mother?" she said, the first time we met.'

She smiled at the memory.

'I love that word flummoxed, Grandma, but it's ages since you used it.'

'It's working class, my love, and you will never know what I suffered when I first came to live here; speaking working class and dropping my aitches came natural, but I had to talk proper. It was my duty. From Richmond Row to Tunbridge Wells was a big step, Wendy love.'

'I should like to see where Daddy was born.'

Ruby shook her head. 'They say it's being pulled down, and a good riddance.'

Christmas 1936 at Russets was no different from any other of recent years. With four children, Julian still agreeable to join in the fun and games, and Katie forever a child at heart, Lucy was in her element. Puddings, cakes and mincemeat were made in November with John and Midge stoning raisins and eating the sugar in the candied peel. Tom and Julian had brought in the holly from the wood and dug up the Christmas tree that was replanted in the garden every year.

Julian had supervised the decorations. The tree sparkled with tinsel and glittering coloured balls when the candles were lit. All the decorations were packed away carefully year after year. Nobody ever thought to buy new. The fairy doll for the top of the tree was looking rather tatty, and she had lost her wand.

'I could make the Star of Bethlehem,' Maggie suggested, but nobody wanted her star.

Carrie had taken all the children to Tunbridge Wells as a rare treat to do their Christmas shopping in Woolworths. They travelled by train, another rare treat, and met the Matron of The Firs Preparatory School with her two young grandsons. The outing was arranged for the first Saturday in December, so that Wendy could join them. She felt very grown up and superior, though she was not much taller than Dick, and her long fair hair was tied with an Alice band.

When all the children had spent the money they had saved in their money boxes, they walked to The Pantiles to have lunch in the tea-shop. Matron had telephoned to ask if fish and chips could be provided for the whole family, and since the pupils and their parents were good customers, it was agreed. Trifle would follow.

Eight-year-old Mark and six-year-old Matthew were pale and listless, and had to be coaxed to eat. This would be the boys' first Christmas in England, and they had been invited to Russets on Christmas Day with their grandmother. They had not recovered from the parting from their parents in September. It had seemed such a big, exciting adventure to travel all the way from the Congo with their parents who were missionaries, but they had completely forgotten about boarding school at the end of the three months' leave. Even with Grandma as Matron of the school it was a strange, frightening place. They sadly missed the native children at the Mission, and were stifled in the school uniforms.

Maggie took them under her wing, however, and regarded them as privileged children because their parents were missionaries. When the little family had visited Russets in the Summer, she had listened enthralled to the tales of the Mission in Darkest Africa.

She had begged to be allowed to keep a snapshot of the little scholars with their beaming black faces, gathered on the forecourt of the school house. Dick had made a frame for it, and it hung on the wall over the bed she shared with Midge. There were texts on the walls and a picture of Jesus as The Light of the World.

Midge had a collection of china animals on the dressing table that she had collected from the Michaelmas Fairs. She never looked at the texts, or the picture of Jesus, because she was not religious like Maggie.

'You can pretend I am your sister if you like,' Maggie told the boys while they waited for the trifle to be served. They were seated one on either side in the tea-shop.

'When I'm grown up I am going to be a missionary, and I shall ask to be sent to the Mission in the Congo. We shall all be one happy family.'

'I don't want a sister! I want Mummy and Daddy!' wailed Matthew.

'Now look what you've done,' Mark scolded. 'Now he won't eat his trifle.'

'I'll eat it,' Midge volunteered obligingly. She was flushed with excitement, and her fur-trimmed bonnet made a halo for her curls. Compared to the family from Russets, the two little boys from the Congo were pathetically frail, but it was too soon to expect any improvement, their grandmother was thinking.

This was the penalty that parents and children must suffer when their work took them overseas. It was five years before Harriet, her daughter, and Philip were due for their next leave; they would hardly recognise their own children. It had all started when she had fallen in love with the young Scottish missionary and married him. Such years of heartache, with her own boy left in England at the age of six, though she had been allowed

61

to keep the two girls and to educate them herself. When her beloved Malcolm died of a fever, she brought them home, and her son was a stranger. Now a new generation would grow up the same way, and it saddened her to see Matthew crying.

'Come to me, my darling,' she coaxed, and gathered him on her lap.

It was no use to expect Julian to play all those childish games again on Boxing Day. Enough is enough. He was off to the meet at The Three Nuns, Lucy reminded her grandchildren as they sat down to a late breakfast. Midge looked puzzled.

'What meeting?'

'MEET – silly, not meeting.' Dick spelled it out irritably.

All the farm children were irritable, and it didn't surprise Lucy. Too much excitement and too much to eat on Christmas Day. She had been up in the night with John who had a bilious attack, and she had taken him into her bed. Mark and Matthew had stayed overnight with their grandmother. They had eaten sparingly, and thought the Russet children were greedy to eat so much. They were not at all impressed by Maggie's production of the Nativity Play in the barn, or the doll in the manger.

'We had a real little baby at the Mission, a black baby,' said Matthew, importantly. 'And the Virgin Mary was black. Her name was Tuppenny, and she was my best friend,' he added.

Maggie was not too pleased at being upstaged by Tuppenny.

'But the Virgin Mary was *white*. In all the pictures she is white,' she insisted.

'That's what Daddy said, but Mummy wouldn't listen.

They nearly had a quarrel,' Mark explained gravely. 'They were all black children at the Mission, you see, and no white children, only Matthew and me. Mummy said we could be angels, only we didn't want to be angels.'

'Boys can't be angels. Only girls are angels,' Midge interrupted, but they ignored her.

'It takes me back to my own time at the Mission,' the boys' grandmother was saying, and her eyes were sad with memories. 'Your grandfather always insisted we had a black baby in the manger. He said there was no evidence to prove that Jesus was white. He had some very strong views on the matter, and I'm afraid I disagreed. But I was a parson's daughter, and we were very class conscious in those days. The colour of your skin was terribly important. I must confess I always had the feeling at the Mission that we were superior to the natives. It was very wrong, of course, and I was ashamed of such feelings. I am still ashamed.'

Mark and Matthew looked at her in surprise. Grownups never admitted to being ashamed, and seldom said they were sorry.

'Let's not have a Na'vity play next Christmas. Let's have a circus,' Midge suggested, brightly.

'Ha! Ha! Very clever!' Dick jeered.

'We've got all the animals here, 'cept the lions and the elephants. We could teach Jock to jump through a hoop, and I could practise standing on Betsy's back. It's a nice big back. Maggie is ever so clever at cartwheels and walking on her hands. John can be a clown, and you could be the ringmaster.'

'Don't want to be a clown,' muttered John.

'Some circus!' Dick yawned. 'One thing I know for sure. I'm not playing Joseph in your silly old Nativity Play any more, Maggie Blunt! I felt a proper ninny this

63

year. It's because I'm ten, and too old for that kid stuff.'

Lucy chuckled as she buttered more slices of toast. Black or white, children were much the same all over the world, she reckoned – and the idea of a black Virgin Mary *was* rather appealing!

Julian led his horse from the stable that it shared with the old mare, Betsy. It had been a gift from Aunt Cynthia when she received her share of the inheritance from the Marston Park estate.

'I do think it's too bad to have to wait till you are twenty-one for your legacy,' she explained.

It was a generous gesture, but it was typical of Aunt Cynthia. He was a little in awe of her as Sister Simmons – a rather formidable person in her starched uniform, but even her own daughter, Wendy, was not at ease with her mother in that uniform. He supposed Wendy would be going to London again, to see the Boxing Day matinee of *Peter Pan*. Once upon a time they had been taken together, but that was a long time ago. Captain Hook was the best part for a boy. All that flying stuff was silly. He supposed Wendy would be going to the theatre with a school friend. He had always regarded Wendy with a brotherly affection. She was a good sport, and not at all fussy about her clothes. When he remembered she had given him quite an expensive fountain pen for Christmas and he hadn't bought her anything, he felt a little guilty. But it quickly passed.

Riding away across the Park it was Diane Maloney he saw in his mind's eye. He had tried in vain to rid himself of that tantalising memory in the swimming pool. His dreams were haunted by a mermaid with Diane's laughing face, pulling him under the green water.

It was mild for late December. The worst of the

weather in the Weald could be expected in the New Year. He was still young enough to enjoy sledging with Dick and Midge as keen as mustard. Uncle Tom had to make a new sledge every year, they were so rough. To turn a somersault in the ditch, or crash through a hedge, was all part of the fun, and Midge was game for anything. He really loved that child. Of course he would be expected to help in digging the sheep out of the snowdrifts. Most of the lambs would be born within a shelter of hurdles, but sometimes they found a ewe and her newborn lamb frozen stiff in a snowdrift, if a blizzard had sprung up suddenly overnight. There was something very pathetic about such a discovery, and his throat would tighten with tears.

He had none of young Dick's natural aptitude for farming the land or looking after the farm animals, but then he was not a Blunt, with a long history of farming forebears. He was a Franklin, and he loved horses. The Franklin men had all loved horses, and some of the women too, according to Aunt Cynthia, who had shocked propriety by riding astride. His own mother, the youngest of the four sisters, had preferred to drive in the governess cart. Aunt Cynthia had all the family photographs in an album, but he felt no emotion when he studied a photograph of his mother. He could see there was a likeness. In the uniform of a VAD nurse, taken during the War when Marston Park was a Convalescent Home for Officers, the young Penelope Franklin was very attractive. All four sisters had been rather plain little girls, but their looks had improved as they grew older, according to Aunt Lucy. However, they all had one redeeming feature – wide, intelligent eyes.

Skirting the small area of parkland reputed to be haunted was an automatic gesture for Julian, and he was taking no chances. It was here that something had frightened Grandfather's horse and he was thrown to his death. But there were earlier incidents in the same area. The rumours had been started by Hetty, the ex-housekeeper, and the groom, and country people tend to be superstitious. It was here that Aunt Cynthia's horse had shied and nearly killed Uncle Freddie on his bicycle. That was before they were married. And it was here, according to rumour, that Charles Franklin had fought his father and left him lying unconscious while he rode over to Russets to tell his mother he was going away and not coming back. It was all rather strange and eerie, for the only explanation – if such it could be described – was a hollow tree. Why hadn't it been chopped down? Julian asked himself, as he rode past.

It was only in the past few years that he had attended this traditional Boxing Day gathering in the village – since he had outgrown the *Peter Pan* matinees with Wendy. It was such a heart-warming scene on the fore-court of The Three Nuns; but he didn't really care to hunt the fox. The first year he had witnessed the kill, and it had turned his stomach. Henceforth, he had dropped out at the last fence, turned his horse, and ambled home on a detour. The publican and his barmaid were busy handing up stirrup cups to the riders, and Squire Ellesby, Master of Hounds, was a splendid figure on his chestnut stallion. It was a scene from Dickens, for nothing had changed. Scarlet coats, black hats and white breeches. The hounds were fretting to be away. A number of children were mounted on their ponies alongside their parents. This was one of the few events in the country calendar in which only the upper class were actively engaged, though a number of followers trailed behind on a medley assortment of nags, but usually lost sight of the field after a few miles.

Julian reined in his horse at the churchyard wall,

waiting for the Master to give the signal to move off. A small crowd had gathered in the High Street, and children were strung along the churchyard wall like swallows on the telegraph wires. The second day of the Christmas holiday was more energetic than Christmas Day, and families would walk for miles to see the hounds and huntsmen gathering at The Three Nuns. Tomorrow the holiday would be over, and everyone back to work.

Suddenly he saw her, on the outskirts of the milling crowd, like himself, an interested spectator. His heart thudded. He could feel his cheeks burning with embarrassment. That well-groomed figure on the thoroughbred horse could not be compared to the naked mermaid in the pool, but beneath that immaculate costume, she was the same person. Not one of those snooty girls, giggling over their stirrup cups, could hold a candle to Diane Maloney, but she was ignored. She had all the things that money could buy, but money could not buy her entry into this élite society, and she was fully aware of the barrier that divided her and her kind. Now she had spotted him, and lifted a hand in salute. It was like a royal summons. She would not come to him. He must go to her. This was one way she could get her revenge and snap her fingers at the snobs. She had only to beckon, and one or other of her admirers would be there. Today it was Julian Franklin.

So she waited, proudly erect as a young goddess, and their meeting did not pass unnoticed. Tongues wagged and lifted eyebrows told their own tale. That nice boy from Russets had already been ensnared by that young madam from Marston Park.

Diane smiled and offered her gloved hand. 'Hi, stranger!' was all she said, but there was a wealth of meaning in that brief greeting.

'Hallo, Diane. How are you?'

67

'OK.'

'Me, too,' he said. He knew for certain now that she was also remembering their last meeting.

'Where's Carl?' he enquired, conversationally.

'Germany.'

'Germany?'

'Sure. Home for Christmas.'

'Yes, yes, of course he would be. And your other friends, are they here?'

'No. *Home for Christmas!*' she jeered. 'Yesterday I was so darn bored I could have taken a high jump in the lake. We did all the right things. Went to church in the morning, stuffed ourselves with turkey, plum pudding and mincepies. Daddy played Santa Claus, and handed round the presents from the Christmas Tree. All the servants had presents. Sammy played the piano and we sang carols to please Mother. After tea we played silly games, roasted chestnuts, and ate a lot of candies. Christ! Could anything be more boring than Christmas Day?'

Julian laughed. 'Serves you right!' he told her, meaningly.

Her eyes flashed dangerously. He enjoyed making her angry. She couldn't have it all her own way.

They were moving off now, and the High Street echoed to the clatter of hooves. The hounds swarmed about the Master. A pale sun filtered through the clouds, and Diane forgot her annoyance in the picturesque scene that was so typically English. Julian would discover that her moods were quickly over. She lived for the moment. There was no past and no future for Diane. Only today, to be lived dangerously. She was smiling again, a provocative smile that would have warned him had he known her better.

They trotted their horses behind the main body of

riders, turned off at the village green, and cantered down the lane. Soon they were spreading out across a field, and the hounds had their noses down, sniffing the damp earth. They flew over the first hedge, side by side – a girl and a boy, with nothing to choose between them because they both had been riding and jumping since childhood. It was, for Julian, an exhilarating experience to have such a companion on Boxing Day. He knew young Dick was only waiting to be invited, but the mare couldn't jump, and they would have to stop and open gates. The thrill of the chase would be lost. With this glowing girl beside him he lost all sense of time, and Russets was a whole world away. Their mounts seemed to be sharing their excitement – up and over! – up and over!

Then, without any warning, Diane had decided she had had enough of following the hunt, left her companion to scale the approaching hedge, and galloped away across the field. When he caught up with her at last, and grabbed the reins, she was laughing breathlessly.

'What's so funny?' he demanded.

'You! I nearly died laughing to see you flying over that hedge, and me going some place else! Poor Julian. Are you mad at me?'

'I could shake you!'

'Carl doesn't wait to warn me. He's very masterful.'

'Cave man stuff, eh?' She nodded. 'There's a streak of cruelty in every German,' he told her.

'How come you know so much about the Germans?' He made no answer. 'You've been reading too many books.'

'I don't want to talk about Carl.'

'But he is my fiancé.'

'Then why didn't he take you to his home for Christmas?'

'I told you. It's a secret engagement.'

'If you marry a German, you must live in Germany.'

'Sure. Would you mind?'

'Yes.'

'You're jealous?'

'Yes.'

'Kiss me,' she said.

When he leaned over to kiss her, he found her lips were parted, and her mouth was wet and warm. Her tongue flicked over his own tongue with a tantalising sensuality. It was unlike anything he had ever known. To kiss a girl was no new experience, but this was a kind of torture. When his own tongue responded, she dropped the reins and took his face between her hands. He was enslaved, hypnotised into a state of unbearable yearning. She knew he was a novice, and that he had no defence against her. She knew she had already awakened latent sexual senses in his young, virginal body that night in the pool, and she had only been waiting for an opportunity to get him alone.

When she let him go he was trembling, and she knew he would not be satisfied now until he had lain with her. Had she known the shepherd's hut was so conveniently near? he would ask himself, later. But now when they walked their horses in that direction, hand in hand, he went with her and asked no questions.

The hut was ready for the shepherd's use at lambing time. It was freshly white-washed, with a camp bed in one corner, and the floor spread with clean straw. They did not speak as they stripped off their jackets and laid them on the straw. Diane stepped out of her clothes with the practised ease of familiarity, but Julian was fumbling and shy.

Stretched on the jackets, the girl waited, smiling and seductive. In the dim light of the small window he could

70

see the lovely curves of her breasts and thighs, her flat stomach, and long slender legs. When he had dropped his clothes on the straw, she held out her arms enticingly, and he slid to his knees and knelt there, staring and shivering, till she reached up and dragged him down. Her body was burning, and her clutching hands frantic.

'Take me! Take me!' she was moaning, and arching her back. Her sex was too demanding to wait for his caresses. Sex was her master, and dictator, and her lovely body an altar.

Now that she had challenged his manliness, he would be compared to Carl, and in one respect he had every reason to be proud. Measured against his school-fellows in the communal bath, after a hectic game of rugger, his penis was a much coveted organ! He knew already, at his initiation, that no gentle lover would ever satisfy Diane. In this second encounter with her nakedness he was discovering not only his own potential as a lover, but the meaning of sex-appeal. It was not mere prettiness. It was elemental.

'Darling. That was fabulous,' she whispered.

It was all that he wanted, to please her. With her head on his shoulder, he sighed with satisfaction, closed his eyes, and slept.

Chapter Four

Wendy was working hard to win a scholarship to the London College of Music, and Julian had joined the Royal Air Force.

'He looks very handsome in his uniform,' Cynthia told her daughter.

They had met by chance at Victoria Station – Julian on a short leave from the RAF Station in Cumberland and on his way to Russets – Cynthia rushing for a train to Tunbridge Wells. Her car was in dock.

'Does he like being in the Royl Air Force?' Wendy asked.

'Adores it!' Her mother had always used words extravagantly, Wendy was thinking. Her mother was a snob, though Grandma strongly denied it.

Wendy had reached the age of critical assessment of adults. Only two people were beyond the scope of her youthful criticism – her father and her grandmother, who had been endowed with every virtue and none of the vices. The gulf between mother and daughter had widened, and the adolescent girl was not entirely to blame. A mother who refuses to recognise her daughter is no longer a little girl, and persistently ignores every stage of her development is asking for trouble. The weekends were disturbed by tears and tantrums that could have been avoided, and the school holidays had a way of turning sour with boredom. Wendy was spending more and more time at Russets in the long school holidays, but she was not allowed to travel alone. This was another bone of contention, since so many of her school friends travelled long distances by train.

'Your grandmother enjoys a few days' break, and her sister is glad to see her. You can travel together, and she will come over to collect you when you are ready to come home,' Freddie had pointed out diplomatically.

She had outgrown so many things in the past twelve months, but had not outgrown her clothes. Her neat little figure and long flaxen hair still reminded her mother of Alice in Wonderland, so she may have been forgiven for neglecting to admire those little pointed breasts!

In the Summer of 1937 Wendy spent three hours every day practising on the parlour piano. Aunt Lucy had agreed to one hour each morning, afternoon and evening. The piano had been tuned, though it hadn't the special quality of tone of her own piano. Not one of Carrie's four children had any musical talent, but Maggie could manage a verse of 'Onward Christian Soldiers' and 'Now the Day is Over' with one finger.

Dick declared Wendy's piano playing gave him a belly-ache, and Midge's little dog howled dismally. Only John was impressed. He would sit outside the open window, propped against the wall, hugging his knees, a dreamy expression on his peaked face. It was the first time that Wendy had stayed at Russets without Julian, but she was constantly reminded of him by the photograph on the kitchen mantelpiece. He had joined the rest of the collection in a fretwork frame – Tom's hobby on Winter evenings.

When Julian's door stood open one evening, she went in and wandered around, inspecting the model aircraft he had been assembling since he was a little boy. The walls were plastered with photographs of aircraft, from the earliest to fly the Channel to the most modern, designed both for speed and comfort. Soon he would be flying real planes, and his boyhood dreams of being airborne would come true. In two years, if he passed his examinations, he could be a pilot. She could not visualise the technicalities of such examinations any more than Julian could visualise her musical exams. They were worlds apart, yet once they had been so close. Did it matter? She was not sure, but then she was not sure of anything these days. She cried easily, and often felt depressed and miserable.

'She was such a happy child,' her mother sighed impatiently, forgetting her own difficult adolescence.

In Julian's room she found a reminder of those happy days when they were close as brother and sister – a packet of cards, dog-eared and dirty. As she turned them over she could see the two children kneeling on the hearth-rug in the kitchen, and hear their shrill voices shouting, 'SNAP! SNAP!' She brushed away a tear, and put the cards back on the shelf, wishing she could put back the clock.

She was given little jobs to do, but they were clean little jobs like feeding the hens, collecting the eggs, laying the table, and drying the dishes. She wore a white pinafore, and couldn't bear to soil her hands. It was only fair to the other children, Aunt Lucy had explained, patiently.

'You are not a guest at Russets, dear. You are one of the family.'

But she didn't really belong at Russets any more. Was it because Julian was no longer there? Completely

74

absorbed in her world of music, it was annoying to be reminded to lay the table for dinner, or take a tea-cloth and dry the dishes. Couldn't they see she was Different? The Russet children had no claim to distinction. They were working class, and they smelled earthy. She could claim to have Franklin blood in her veins, like Julian. But mother had renounced her claim to the upper class when she married into the working class – or so she would have you believe.

'Once a lady, always a lady,' Grandma insisted, and she was usually right.

There was something called 'breeding' that distinguished the species, both human and animal, it had been explained. She had recognised the breeding in her mother's aristocratic features, and her compelling personality. Uncle Tom had talked for years of his dream to breed a pedigree herd of Jerseys, but with a family of four children to support, it would always remain a dream. Sometimes Wendy thought she could see a trace of that indefinable 'breeding' in her own features, and the proud tilt of her head. If only she could grow tall, with a beautiful bust like Sonja Lefeaux. If only she had sex-appeal. . . .

To have a special talent was a gift of God. To use it was pleasing to God. To waste it was a sin. This sensible philosophy had been ingrained in Wendy since her first music lesson with her teacher at the age of seven. Cynthia had chosen wisely. Herr Muller was a dedicated teacher, and a strict disciplinarian. He lived in lodgings, taught the pianoforte and the violin six days a week, and was organist and choirmaster at St Saviour's on Sundays. He was a fiery little man, with a mop of untidy hair and piercing blue eyes. You did not love Herr Muller, you simply obeyed him, Wendy had soon discovered, when she had her knuckles rapped for allowing her thoughts to wander from the interminable scales and exercises. It was humiliating to start at the beginning again when she had been playing nice little pieces from mother's repertoire since she was six. Herr Muller was not impressed. He pushed the scores away in the stool, spread out the first elementary lesson, and barked, 'You vil start 'ere. Dat is understood, yes?'

'Yes, Herr Muller,' Wendy agreed, meekly.

He never praised. He bullied. But he got results. Wendy was an apt pupil. Whenever she went away to Russets, she was given specified work, and instructed to practise for three hours, six days a week. It was not a chore or a duty, for she had long since decided on a musical career. First the scholarship, and three years at the London College of Music. Then the Youth Orchestra. She knew exactly what she wanted to do. She had always known – as Julian had always known about flying.

In his new world of men, Julian Franklin found himself a nonentity. His status had the same insignificance as a new boy at public school still living with the proud memory of being head boy at his prep school. He was indeed a very small fish in a big pond. To sink or swim would depend on his own determination and the ability to survive. He had these qualities, but he had still to be reconciled to the crowded communal living at the camp, the complete lack of privacy and individual preferences. Since he had never been subjected to the rigours of boarding school, it was not easy to adjust. Furthermore, he had grown up in a close-knit family, under the protecting wings of Aunt Lucy.

In many ways he was a very young eighteen-year-old, and very conscious of his youth as he fought for a place in the jungle of humanity, more varied and surprising than anything he had ever conceived. His seriousness and dedication to duty did not lend itself to popularity. He was neither a dare-devil nor a lady-killer, and moderate in his consumption of beer and cigarettes. Only a small minority seemed to be whole-hearted in their application to their chosen career, but he could have been mistaken. None could foresee a time when their courage and dedication would be largely instrumental in saving their country from enemy invasion. Their superior officers and instructors had long since been aware of the dangers, however, and were kept informed of every new development in Nazi Germany. The powerful administrators in their Whitehall offices were deceptively quiet, but it was a brooding quietness. All over the country new recruits were pouring in to Army and RAF camps, and the Senior Service was boosting its own propaganda for those who favoured a life on the ocean wave. A rash of recruiting posters had suddenly appeared on every available placard, and disused dwellings. Even the village constable had been obliged to remove the posters for missing persons and lost property and to substitute the colourful recruiting ones. Young men were invited to leave their rural occupations for the exciting world of the uniformed services. They were promised good pay, free board and lodging, smart uniforms, and an opportunity to travel the world at the expense of the State. As always, the older generation was wary, and inclined to scoff. Many remembered a time when Kitchener had stared down at them with his magnetic eyes and pointing finger. The single word 'YOU' was intended to halt every faltering step, and it had an irresistible appeal. Mothers, wives, and sweethearts had wept and pleaded in vain. 'Kitchener's Army' grew to alarming proportions – and few came back from the holocaust of the Western Front.

Ruby remembered that her youngest son, Jack, with a wife and four children dependent on his earnings, had seen the Kitchener poster pinned to the notice board at the village hall. He had gone straight back to the Grocery, untied his apron, and volunteered to serve his King and Country. Jack was one of a number of volunteers from Fairfields who had marched away so proudly with the village band, and whose names were inscribed on the plaque in the church porch. Freddie was the next to go, and he lost a leg. Lucy's Harry was not spared to come home to Russets, and Albert came back a physical wreck. Now Lucy was anxious for Julian. She didn't trust that ridiculous little man called Hitler.

'Just a strutting little bantam cock, Aunt Lucy!' Julian had insisted, with manly derision. In his neat uniform he was a stranger, and the 'crew cut' gave his face a lean, hungry look. She wanted to cradle him in her arms, as she had cradled him so often as a small boy in need of comfort, for she knew, instinctively, that he was finding the camp life strange and difficult. He was a grown man now, and she could not reach him. In a few short months they had deprived him of his boyhood, and stripped away all the natural impulses of adolescence. He was clothed in a kind of protective armour. Was he protecting himself from any one person, or from the awful possibility of being grounded? she wondered. Nothing less than a pilot's certificate could satisfy her Julian.

It was not a sudden resolution inspired by all those recruiting posters, but a boyhood ambition, nurtured through the years. Something was troubling him, and her heart ached to see him so closed up, and so reluctant to talk about his training. Only Midge could coax a smile from her hero. Midge adored him, and had no hesitation in showing her adoration. He was showered with hugs and kisses, and she sat on his knee while they rocked back and forth in the old rocking chair, her curly head on his shoulder. But they all were disappointed that he said so little about his new life in the RAF camp.

'What exactly do you *do*?' Dick persisted.

'You wouldn't understand even if I tried to explain. It's too technical. Aeroplanes are not like tractors, you know. It's a hell of a life. We are constantly being bullied by some bloody-minded instructor. There's a lot of drill on the parade ground, and PT thrown in for good measure. Physical fitness and mental alertness are what they are aiming at – one hundred per cent, not ninety-nine and three-quarters!' He laughed at his own joke.

'But do you *like* being in the RAF?' Dick persisted.

'You bet I do!'

'Tell us about the WAAFs,' Carrie interrupted. 'Are they disciplined as strictly as the men?'

He nodded. 'Their quarters are out of bounds, and they call their officers "Ma'am". They say it's even worse than boarding school, but they do have fun with the boys when they are off-duty. The local people are jolly decent, too. We have the loan of the village hall for dances every Saturday night, and there are three pubs.'

'Do the girls drink beer?'

'They certainly do.'

'And smoke?'

'Yes. It's a case of when you're in Rome, you do as the Romans. You'd be darn lonely if you didn't.'

'Have you got a WAAF sweetheart?' Midge asked innocently.

'No.'

'Why not?'

'Because I've got a sweetheart at Russets.'

Midge squealed with delight, and flung her arms about his neck. 'You won't marry that horrid Diane Maloney before I'm grown up, will you?'

'Whatever gave you that idea?'

'Mrs Maloney asked Granny for your address.'

He still could blush, Lucy noticed.

'Did you get a letter from Diane?'

'Yes.'

'Did you write her a letter?'

'Yes.'

'That's quite enough, Midge. No more questions,' Lucy scolded, and Julian gave her a grateful look. He had read the letter and destroyed it, but he could remember every word. Her large, sprawling writing had covered the single sheet of scented notepaper. He was disturbed by the summons to Marston Park, but even more disturbed by the threat to visit him at Russets if he failed to keep the rendezvous in the Summerhouse beyond the rose garden. They had not met since Boxing Day. Sexual intercourse and its emotional aftermath was best forgotten, he had decided. He knew that a number of the trainees in his group indulged in sex on Saturday nights, but his initiation in the shepherd's hut had left him strangely reluctant to repeat the performance – and it *was* a performance! Why couldn't Diane be satisfied with Carl? To compete for her favours had lost its attraction since he joined the RAF.

He was utterly and completely dedicated – wasn't he? Then what was he doing on his bicycle, at midnight, pedalling across the Park, when he should have been enjoying a good sleep on the last night of his leave? An invisible cord seemed to be drawing him towards Diane. He was shivering again, and all his newfound manliness had been left behind in the neatly pressed uniform laid out on the bed.

'You little devil! You've been teasing me!'

The husky voice came out of the shadows as he pushed open the door. He closed it carefully, and stumbled towards the voice like a blind man groping for human contact. It smelled musty, and there were scufflings on the roof. The small window was draped in leaves from an overhanging branch. When the moon slipped out from behind a cloud, it lit the dusty interior momentarily, then left it again in shadow.

Diane was perched on a bamboo table, swinging her legs. She was wearing a loose bath-robe. It was white, and her slippers were white. The dusty Summerhouse was an incongruous setting for such a beautiful creature, but she had not found the shepherd's hut distasteful. She seemed not to notice her surroundings. Perhaps she was absorbed in her own image, and her own demanding sexuality.

'Why have you kept me waiting till the last night of your leave?' she asked, as she wrapped her arms about his neck.

'You know why,' he muttered, sulkily.

'I don't. Tell me.'

'I have to concentrate on my work. It's terribly important. I can't afford to get emotionally involved. Some of the chaps take sex every Saturday night as easily as they take a pint of beer. I'm different, Diane.'

'You are so sweet, darling. I could almost believe you,' she said. Her eyes were gleaming like cats' eyes in the dim outline of her face, and her soft lips brushed his cheek.

'Let me go. You have Carl,' he pleaded, in a desperate attempt to break the spell she was weaving over his reluctant senses. He stood there, tense and stiff, in the circle of her clinging arms, till her mouth captured his own mouth, and her tongue flicked over his own tongue. Then his body sagged, and she knew she had conquered his resistance. His hands cupped her breasts under the bathrobe. The nipples were hard. Her body was warm and scented. He could feel her heart throbbing, and her stomach quivered under the gentle touch of his exploring hands. She let him alone, controlling the urge to fling off the bathrobe. She had to convince him, now, tonight, that sex was not a hindrance, but a necessity to his growing maturity. His clean young body was ripe for sex, and she gloried in her own power to stimulate his senses. His initial reluctance had been no surprise. She had learned through her mother's frequent visits to Russets that young Julian Franklin was a serious and dedicated recruit to the RAF. His letters had been read aloud, and his Aunt Lucy was very proud of the boy she had fostered.

Diane had not been blind to the combination of strength and weakness, from the beginning of their association, and it was the weakness in his armour that was so vulnerable – the weakness that would provide for her own sweet indulgence. She would play on his reluctant senses with the skilful manipulation of a courtesan. She remembered how easily she had seduced the bearded art master during her last term at the Academy in Paris. She was only a child in years, but a woman in her understanding of her own lovely body. Sammy had called her a cuckoo in the nest, for Sammy had recognised the sex-appeal even in the schoolroom.

Once again she held him captive by her tormenting tongue. She had taught him in the shepherd's hut on Boxing Day that it was a deadly weapon, but tonight he was more conscious of his own swift response. Then, with a shuddering sigh, she dropped the bathrobe on the dusty floor, slid off the table, and they fell together, entangled.

Carl Richter returned to London in the Autumn of 1937, already a dedicated member of the Nazi Party, and totally absorbed in its doctrines. The playboy who had gone home to Germany for the Summer vacation had returned a serious student of Nazism.

Diane was bored. He could talk of nothing else but the Fatherland, its glorious past and even more glorious future, and the splendid spectacle of 20,000 uniformed members packed into a vast stadium. Those ardent blue eyes that once had seen nothing but perfection in her dark beauty, were more discriminating. He would not dare to introduce her into the select company of his new friends, and his secret engagement had become an embarrassment. Yet his father had insisted he could be very useful in establishing a permanent link with the American industrialist, Harry B. Maloney – and Carl was still a dutiful son.

Now the engagement was no longer a secret. Marriage was a serious step to take, and Carl was not yet ready for it, but he was persuaded into the wisdom of such an alliance. They were both only children. *Their* children would inherit a vast industrial empire. It was a fascinating prospect to an ambitious young man.

So he courted Diane with a single-minded determination, was charmingly attentive to Sammy and Kitty, and extremely courteous to Harry. The noisy house parties were discontinued, for Carl was a very possessive lover, and refused to share her favours.

They were a handsome couple, almost inseparable once their engagement was officially announced. Carl was the perfect foil to Diane's demanding sexuality. He had no scruples and no tenderness. His love-making had a brutal intensity, and they shared a pagan enjoyment of their beautiful bodies. For Diane it was a period of almost total disregard of all her former acquaintances, and Julian was forgotten.

But for Carl it was only one facet of the new world. He would serve two masters, and know the best of both in the forthcoming two years.

They were married in the Catholic church at Fairfields, and Carl duly promised to have the children of the marriage brought up in the Catholic faith. It was another big occasion in the village, and attracted a crowd of children on the churchyard wall, and a bevy of aproned Mums on the tombstones. Everyone agreed that Diane Maloney was the loveliest bride the village had seen for more than a decade. They said her wedding dress made in Paris had cost a fortune, and the young couple would spend their honeymoon in Paris. They said she was marrying a German, the only son of a rich industrialist, but then nobody expected her to marry a local chap. The New Rich label had stuck, and she had no place in the upper class. They said her poor Mum wasn't half upset because she never expected her daughter to get married so young, and because she might have to live in Germany. But her opinion was not asked – they said.

The foreign servants at Marston Park kept the village grapevine buzzing with gossip. This was no fairy tale romance, according to the Austrian parlourmaid, but an arranged marriage between two ambitious parents. She was probably right. But the bridegroom's parents had not attended the wedding, so there was something odd about the marriage.

But when the confetti had been swept up, and the church bells stopped pealing, an aged crone, propping up the bar at The Three Nuns, would have the last word.

'They been apeing the Gentry ever since they took over at the Park, but the silly buggers ain't got no breeding!'

Andrew Robinson, the ex-village schoolmaster, was enjoying his retirement, but his wife, Martha, was still missing the lively environment of the School House.

Every Thursday afternoon, Winter and Summer, in all kinds of weather, she walked to the village to do her shopping. It was never any other day but Thursday because she was regular and methodical in her habits, as befitted a good housewife.

When she had finished her shopping, she made her way to the School, walked along the narrow path leading to the playgrounds, and stood at the fence, watching the children at play. She was still at heart Teacher who had ruled so kindly over the Infants' classroom for so many years. Now she wished she could put back the clock.

It was a common failing in retirement, she had discovered, when she stopped for a gossip in the High Street. Very seldom did she find an elderly couple mutually content and happy with so much time on their hands. Those hard-working years and the struggle to bring up a family on such meagre wages, now seemed, in retrospect, the happiest years of a woman's life.

With only one child of her own to rear, Martha had satisfied her strong maternal instincts in the Infants' classroom. She had put on a lot of weight in recent years, but there was still a likeness to Mrs Noah in her dumpy little figure. In the faces of the children in the school playground she often saw a likeness to one of her old pupils – a grandson of Millie Sillitoe, with the same red hair and freckles – a grand-daughter of the irrepressible Tommy Larkin, with the same snub nose and mischievous blue eyes. Family likeness was a fascinating study to an ex-school teacher. She had an album full of photographs, a cherished memento of the village school where the local photographer was invited to take photographs once every year for posterity. The whole class would be lined up on benches, the girls in pinafores, the boys in a motley assortment of jerseys and jackets, standing stiffly to attention behind the girls. It was a very solemn occasion

No smiles were demanded or expected.

Yet for Andrew, those years behind the headmaster's desk had left no mark and no nostalgia. The chapter was closed, and he had no wish to be reminded. His straggling grey beard matched his grey head. He seldom listened to Martha's chatter. His mind was occupied, in this year of Our Lord, 1938, with the Munich Agreement in which Neville Chamberlain, the British Prime Minister, had conferred with Daladier of France, Mussolini of Italy, and that ridiculous little man, they called the Führer, who seemed to have some kind of magnetic quality, only apparent to the Germans. International affairs had long since taken priority over local affairs, whilst Martha's interests were wholly parochial. He listened to the wireless, was an avid reader of the *Daily Telegraph* and *The Spectator*, conservative in politics and in every aspect of his character.

His high principles had always been a little difficult to live up to, and his dogmatic attitude to those who fell from grace was not shared by his soft-hearted spouse. Her grandsons, Mark and Matthew, who spent part of the school holidays at Fairfields, provided a constant source of interest and enjoyment, but Andrew was jealous of the time she spent with the two little boys, as he once had been jealous of Philip. No amount of reasoning or coaxing would change his stubborn attitude. He could neither forget nor forgive Martha for her neglect – it had seemed like neglect – when her whole heart and mind had been devoted to her son's welfare. How could he feel the same affection for Philip, who was not his son, but born out of wedlock? He was *fond* of his stepson, and interested in his development, but quite incapable of understanding why a promising career in the Law should have been sacrificed for some remote Mission in the Congo.

Now he had to bear with the noisy demands of Philip's children, and watch Martha's smothering maternal love all over again. The only refuge for his disgruntled ego was to be found in his book-lined study, and the boys were kept out of his way.

They had been encouraged at their boarding school to be independent and self-reliant, so they were put on the train at Tunbridge Wells, and were met by Martha at Fairfields. Both boys had their mother's features and personality, but Martha had discovered small mannerisms that reminded her of Philip.

When they tumbled out of the train, dropped their cases and ran into her outstretched arms, she was a whole woman again, and the empty years when they were growing up at the Mission were forgotten. They snatched off their caps, hugged her exuberantly, and clamoured for the front seat in the station taxi. Gran was ready to spoil them. With Grandma, who was also the School Matron, they were obliged to behave, otherwise she could be accused of favouritism. It made the relationship rather strained.

'What's for dinner, Gran?' would be Matthew's first question, and the answer never varied.

'Sausages and baked beans.'

'Goodie! What's for pudding?'

'Treacle tart or chocolate blancmange, or both?'

'*Both*!' he shouted.

The porter chuckled as he picked up the small battered cases that had travelled all the way from the Congo.

'Gran, are we going to Russets on Sunday?' was Mark's first question. He loved the farm, and had already decided to be a farmer. Matthew had changed his mind half a dozen times, and was currently considering a bus conductor. Neither had any intention of following in the footsteps of their dedicated parents. They were completely weaned away from the Mission, and had almost forgotten their black friends.

The Firs was a happy place, where every day followed its own particular pattern. They knew what to expect, and they liked it that way. Just as they knew what to expect from Gran. Grandfather was a grumpy old stick, and they kept out of his way. Providing they behaved impeccably at the meal table and did not interrupt his boring monologues – How did Gran put up with it? – they managed to convey the respect that was due to him. 'Once a schoolmaster, always a schoolmaster,' Gran would remind them, when they finally made their escape.

They always ran on ahead, for they were too big to hold her hands. She followed behind with her tripping steps, carrying a bag of toffees and their school caps. They chewed happily all the way, and dutifully handed back the toffee papers. She loved them dearly.

They squeezed into Philip's bed, and 'borrowed' his books and his bicycle. Nothing of Philip's was sacred any more. In the happy atmosphere of The Firs, both boys had developed into normal, healthy children, their fears and tears forgotten. Music was encouraged. Mark had chosen the piano, Matthew the violin. The younger boy's performance was so excruciating even Martha had to admit he would never make a Kreisler!

It was Mark who mentioned quite casually one afternoon, as he swung from a bough of the old plum tree in the garden, 'Gran, did you know there is going to be a War?'

She looked up from her knitting to ask, 'Who told you there is going to be a War?'

'Headmaster. It's no secret. Everybody knows. Headmaster thinks we may have to evacuate the school to the Cotswolds.'

88

'Why the Cotswolds?'

'Because it's what they call a safe zone. Tunbridge Wells is too near the Kent coast if there should be an invasion. It's exciting, isn't it, Gran?'

A cold hand clutched her heart. Andrew had seen the red light two years ago, but he was such an old pessimist she had turned a deaf ear.

'Then you wouldn't be allowed to visit me in the holidays?' she said. Her mouth trembled. Tears pricked her eyes.

'I don't know.' He slid off the bough and came to sit beside her. 'You could evacuate to the Cotswolds, then we could still visit you in the holidays.'

'Your grandfather would never leave here.'

'Don't cry, Gran.' He gave her a hug.

'I'm not crying.' She smiled through her tears at the grave young face. Now she could see a likeness to Philip, in the concern for her.

'Headmaster says it would all be over in six months, and the British always win the last battle.'

She nodded agreement. Headmaster was an authority on *everything*!

When the boys were tucked up in bed, and Andrew listening to a favourite programme on the wireless, she picked up the telephone in the tiny hall and dialled the exchange. She wished in the Winter months that she could chat to her friends in the comfort of the sitting-room, but it would disturb Andrew. The phone was a link with Russets and with Ruby. She often spent a pleasant half-hour chatting to one or the other. Lucy and Ruby had both lost sons in the last War, and had a second son severely disabled. Was it selfish of her to be thankful now that Philip was thousands of miles away, and her grandsons too young to get involved? she asked herself, as she waited for someone to pick up the phone at Russets. It was Carrie who answered breathlessly impatient.

'Hullo, who is it?'

'It's me, dear. Teacher.' The childish name had stuck, and the long friendship was precious to both. She recognised anxiety in the voice of the younger woman, and asked sympathetically, 'What's wrong, Carrie?'

'It's John. He's had a fit.'

'A fit?'

'Yes. Aunt Lucy thinks it may be epileptic. She phoned the doctor for advice, but he's out.'

'Has anyone else in the family suffered from fits?'

'Not as far as we know.'

'It could be another kind of fit, not epileptic. John is a very nervous little boy, isn't he?'

'That's what Aunt Lucy says.'

'Well, she should know, dear, for she must have coped with just about everything in the nature of illness and accident with her big family.'

'She's wonderful, and she never panics. I find myself depending on her more and more, and I shouldn't, for I'm their mother. But she's so strong and capable. Last week it was Midge. She fell off the milk float and gashed her leg. Tom had to take her up to the surgery to get it stitched.'

'Poor Midge.'

'There's always something happening here. Never a dull moment! Mark and Matthew all right?'

'Fine, thank you.'

'Were you phoning for anything in particular, or just to have a chat?'

'Just to have a chat. Carrie, does Tom think there will be another War?'

'My dear, Tom's mind wanders no farther than Russets. This is his whole world, bless him!'

'Mark was telling me today that their Headmaster is pretty certain that another war is inevitable. He is even planning to evacuate the school to the West Country. As a participant in the last War, he would probably recognise the danger signals. He lost an arm about the same time that Freddie lost his leg.'

'I didn't know.'

'It gave me quite a shock to hear Mark saying it was so exciting, but I suppose it would seem to be so at his age. When you look back, Carrie, it seems no time at all since the last terrible war. Only twenty years. They must be mad!'

'Yes, I wonder why men have to fight wars.' Carrie was remembering that day in 1918 when she stood on the platform at Fairfields station, staring at her future husband. She had hardly recognised Bertie in that pathetic scarecrow. Four years in a Turkish prisoner-of-war camp was just about the worst place to find himself after their ship was torpedoed. 'I know it's selfish, but I can't help being thankful that Tom is past the age to volunteer, and Dick is too young,' she said.

'Well, you needn't feel guilty, Carrie. I have just been congratulating myself that Philip is away on the other side of the world, and Mark and Matthew are too young to get involved. But there's Julian.'

'Yes, there's Julian – and he's got his wings.'

'I know. Lucy told me. She was so proud.'

'She's here. She wants a word with you.' Carrie handed the phone over.

'Well, Martha, that was a bit of a shock, but it was quickly over, and he seems to be none the worse. It was my first encounter with a fit, but there is always a first time with children. Did you have any trouble when you were teaching?'

'I only ever had one child who suffered with fits – Lena

Larkin – but that was hereditary, and it *was* epileptic. She just had to lie on the floor till it passed. I always slipped something into her mouth to prevent her biting her tongue.'

'Yes, I did that with John. I remembered reading it in *Doctor Sanders' Medical Journal* all those years ago, never dreaming it would come in useful one day . . . Martha, is there going to be another War?'

'Andrew has seen the red light for some time. He says we must be blind to ignore the fact that Germany has never accepted defeat as the final humiliation. With all those thousands of men in uniform again, and a new generation indoctrinated with the same creed, all those demonstrations of loyalty to the Fatherland, it's all too obvious they are preparing to fight another war. He is usually right, Lucy.' She sighed, and Lucy echoed the sigh.

'Yet with so much at stake, my dear, I can only think of Julian. We women are still enslaved by our own limited horizons. Nothing has really changed fundamentally, since 1914, when I was on tenterhooks for Harry and Albert. It's natural, I suppose, for a wife and mother to want to hang on to her own. I remember how I clung to Tom, insisting he could better serve his King and Country on the home front. I don't think he ever quite forgave me, and Albert taunted him for staying at home. Even with the land-girls we were working like niggers, and it won't be any easier next time. I'm twenty years older, but I'm tough. We shall manage. We shall *have* to manage. The children will help.'

'I shall envy you, Lucy.'

'They might want you back in the Infants. Would you go?'

'Like a shot!'

'You were not really ready for retirement, being so

much younger than Andrew?'

'No, but we had to get out of the School House. There was no alternative, and this cottage was vacant, so Andrew bought it.'

'Couldn't you have carried on teaching and cycled to school?'

'Andrew wouldn't hear of it.'

'There is such a thing as self-assertion!'

'Not with Andrew!'

'You shouldn't allow yourself to become a doormat, Martha.'

'Alas, I haven't your resilience.'

They had only one thing in common. Charles and Philip were both born out of wedlock, but their circumstances were poles apart. Lucy was sorry for Martha. To see her adored only son once in every five years was a bitter pill. But children must be allowed to live their own lives, and Philip had to break the strangling umbilical cord.

The house overlooking the canal at Little Venice in the Maida Vale district of London – a wedding present from Harry B. Maloney to his beautiful daughter – was a convenient base for Carl Richter and his friends, and Diane was the perfect hostess. It was a cosmopolitan household, with the Austrian parlourmaid 'borrowed' from Marston Park, a Belgian chef, and two Dutch housemaids – all bi-lingual.

Diane had been obliged to learn German, but she enjoyed the tuition at the School of Languages in Oxford Street, and it kept her out of mischief while Carl was away. He was often away, presumably on important business for his father's expanding corporation, but he did not confide in her, and she had not yet been invited to meet his family. There was always an excuse that it was not a convenient time, and Carl had the last word on the matter.

Marriage had changed Carl from a doting lover to a domineering husband, and his views on the precise role of a marriage partner were old-fashioned and dictatorial. Under the charming façade was a hard core of pride and ambition. Their relationship was based entirely on physical attraction, and when their emotions exploded, they would abuse each other in a shouting match in three languages. Diane would slap Carl's face, and he would instantly retaliate with a blow that would send her staggering across the room, with streaming eyes. Then he would stand over her in a threatening attitude till she begged for mercy on her knees. This was his moment of triumph, his sweet revenge. There was no love between them, only this compulsive physical attraction that could not be satisfied except in tortuous sexual indulgence. It could not last, this marriage, and the son who would have inherited the accumulated wealth of the Richter-Maloney Enterprises was born dead. Carl felt he had been cheated. It was unreasonable and unkind to blame Diane, but without love there can be no trust.

The Nazi Party provided a mistress. She was young. She was a virgin. And her strong, healthy body would produce a perfect creature to inhabit the Third Reich.

Chapter Five

This would be his last visit home. All leave would soon be cancelled. It was a long journey home from the RAF station on the West Coast of Scotland where he had been posted when he finished his training. He missed the friends he had made at the Camp. But this was the real thing, and there was no looking back. It was a man's world with only a few girls, and they all were young and not yet fully conscious of the important role they would play in the near future.

The train was crowded with service men and women, but Julian was the only one in the uniform of the RAF in that particular compartment. He had slept for the first part of the journey, and when he opened his eyes, he sat quietly in his corner seat, listening to the Army and Navy fighting a battle of wits. In a haze of tobacco smoke, their faces were blurred and their language ripe with profanity. They were sweating in their ill-fitting uniforms, and had flung their jackets on to the luggage racks, with their hats and kit bags, opened their shirts, and rolled up their sleeves. With their cropped heads and weathered faces, all the men had a similarity. Only Julian was different in his tailor-made gaberdine uniform, and pale complexion.

The sliding doors were open, and the corridor was crowded with squatting figures and baggage. To reach the lavatory was an obstacle race, helped along with kicks and curses. There was no privacy anywhere in this long, hot Summer of 1939 – only at Russets, in his boyhood bedroom that Aunt Lucy always kept in readiness for his homecoming, with clean linen and wax polish. But so much time would be taken up with travelling, there would be only five days left to enjoy it.

They had to queue for refreshments at Crewe, and two hefty seamen stood guard at the door, ready to fight any intruders. Their pals came back laden with mugs of tea, sandwiches and pies, and they all ate ravenously, nobody bothering to enquire into the contents of the snacks. They grinned at Julian back in his corner with a mug of tea and a packet of biscuits. He was not hungry. They felt very protective towards him. He was so young, but he had his wings, and in their noisy company his quietness had a certain distinction. Now they were talking of women they would bed, with a rough vulgarity that sickened Julian. Yet why should he object to their coarseness when he still was shamed by his own disturbing sensuality.

He had lost touch with Diane since her marriage, and he would keep away from Marston Park. His initiation into the rites of sexual intercourse had left him strangely reluctant to associate with the girls at the RAF camp. Several of his travelling companions would be spending their leave in London, and staying at the Army and Navy Club. They would pick up their women in the bars of Piccadilly and Soho. They knew the risk of such casual associations, for they had been warned in the early days of their training, but it was a risk they were prepared to take. The harsh discipline of their world of men would be forgotten on the soft breast of a woman.

Julian closed his eyes, and remembered Diane in the shepherd's hut, and again in the Summer house. He did not want to remember. He would like to forget it had actually happened, but it was quite impossible to forget. He wondered about her marital relationship with Carl, and whether it had satisfied the passionate demands of her beautiful body. Even when she had been engaged to Carl, she had seduced him with such easy and natural abandon; it was obvious that she had had other lovers. It was a dangerous game to play, however, with a possessive husband, and a man so soon to be recognised as an enemy. They said she had a child and it was born dead. They said Carl was seldom at home, and that he used the house at Little Venice as a hotel, for the convenience of his friends. Servants talk, and the Austrian parlourmaid still kept in touch with the servants at Marston Park.

How would it end? War with Germany was inevitable. It was not his business, Julian reminded himself, not very convincingly. Diane had no scruples about getting what she wanted, and she had wanted Carl Richter since their eyes met across that crowded French restaurant in Soho – and Carl wanted her. If one could believe all the rumours, there was no love between them. Perhaps she had never been taught the meaning of love? With such odd parents, could she be blamed for such an egoistic view of life?

His own family background at Russets was so different, with its solid foundation and continuity. He was lucky, and never more aware of it than now, when it was threatened. He had no illusions about the danger they faced, and the squadron of Spitfires lined up on the airfield seemed a frail and vulnerable weapon to use against such a powerful enemy. Yet already he was familiar with his own particular Spitfire. He felt quite an affection for her, and had named her Lucy. If only he could have shared the terrible fear that he might discover he was a coward when the testing time came. But their true selves were cloaked in deceptive disguises and light-hearted bravado.

Aunt Lucy always deplored the fact that he arrived at Fairfields without a welcome, but it was impossible even to guess which train he would catch from Victoria. So he hired the station cab, and sat back, savouring the beauty and quietness of the surrounding countryside.

It was hay-making time at Russets, and when he had paid the driver, he leaned on the gate, breathing the sweet scents of hay and the roses climbing over the old grey walls of the farmhouse. Away in the distance he could see several figures busy with rakes and pitchforks, and Uncle Tom on the wagon. The sun was setting in a ball of fire, and long shadows were creeping across the hay-cocks. The three women wore old-fashioned sun-bonnets and long print dresses; Aunt Lucy, Carrie and Katie. A small, girlish figure in a pinafore was up on the half-filled wagon with Uncle Tom. She would soon be ordered to come down, for Aunt Lucy had never forgotten that bright Summer day so long ago when her husband, Bert, had fallen from the top of a loaded hay wagon and broken his neck. The boy, Dick, was holding the reins of the big Shire horse. That would be Duke. Midge was chasing a dog round the hay-cocks, and two other children – that would be John and Maggie – were sitting in a nest of hay, drinking lemonade from a bottle.

It was a familiar scene, photographed on his memory since early childhood, when he was carried to the hay-field and the harvest-field on the broad back of Duke or Prince. His throat was suddenly tight with tears, for he could be seeing it for the last time. Now that it was threatened, he wished he had taken a bigger share in the work. Compared to the life he had chosen, the land had a timeless quality – Spring, Summer, Autumn, Winter. It would still be here long after – long after . . .?

He shivered, rubbed the back of a grubby hand across his wet eyes, and yelled 'HALLO THERE!' It reminded him now of the playground at the village school – a tableau in which the figures suddenly froze at the summons of a teacher's shrill whistle. The figures in the hay-field had frozen at the sound of his voice, but only for a split second, then all were waving and shouting, and Midge was running with the dog, calling excitedly, 'Julian! Julian!'

He draped his neatly folded greatcoat over the gate, dropped his bag in the yard, and waited. She climbed up on the other side and they hugged each other over the top of the gate. She hadn't grown much in the past three years. As her father would say, 'Midge was plump as a Spring chicken.' The same could be said of Aunt Lucy and Carrie. It was an endearing plumpness, and like her mother and grandmother, Midge smelled of earth and sweat. Her curly head was full of hay-seeds, her kisses were wet and her breath smelled of liquorice. He was laughing now, all his sadness forgotten in the warmth of her welcome.

'How long are you staying? When do you have to go back?' she demanded, breathlessly.

'A fine question I must say, and I have only just set foot in the place!' he teased.

Her mouth drooped. 'I didn't mean it that way.'

'I know you didn't. I've got five whole days.'

'Goodie!'

Over in the hayfield they were waving their rakes and pitchforks.

'We'd better go,' he said, and swung his long legs over the gate. Midge took his hand and he ran with her, the dog barking at their heels.

99

Under the sun-bonnets, three smiling, sweating faces were waiting to be kissed. Katie was never left out of anything. John and Maggie tumbled out of their nest to offer him the bottle of lemonade.

'Thanks,' he said. It was warm and sticky from their mouths, but he remembered how he had liked to drink straight from the bottle at their age, ignoring the big earthenware crocks of cold lemonade and the mugs in the shade of the hedge. Then he saluted Uncle Tom, and the girl on the hay wagon, and realised he was looking up at Wendy.

'Hallo,' he said, and she answered 'Hallo'.

'I didn't recognise you. What have you done to your hair?' he asked, with brotherly directness.

'Had it cut. Don't you like it?'

'No.'

She shrugged and smoothed her pinafore with clean, slender hands. She was fussy about her hands and her clothes these days, and had long since outgrown her tomboy ways. But she was used to his bluntness.

'I bet you sixpence your mother was mad,' he told her.

'She was.'

'It was naughty of her. It was such pretty hair,' Aunt Lucy insisted.

'It wasn't at all pretty. It was dead straight. Only curly hair is pretty.'

'I like it short. It suits you,' said Carrie, soothingly.

'Come *on*!' Dick was getting impatient and hungry for his supper, so Tom asked quietly, 'Shall we finish the loading?'

'Jump!' Julian commanded.

But Wendy scrambled down from the wagon, ignoring his outstretched hands. She could not bear it if he touched her, and she felt quite sure she would faint if he kissed her. She was not his little sister, and he was not her big brother. She was nearly seventeen, and a grown up young woman, and he was even more handsome in real life than in the photograph she had begged from Aunt Lucy. It was hidden in the secret drawer where she kept her diary. Under her pinafore her heart was beating like a little hammer, and she wanted to cry. It was all so terribly wrong to be in love with her cousin. His up-turned face and his dark searching eyes had been too much for her young resolution. She dodged round the wagon and fled to the shelter of the beech wood. Julian would have followed her, but Aunt Lucy advised, sensibly, 'Let her alone, dear. It's adolescence, and quite a bit of temperament from the Franklin side of the family. Wendy lives in another world most of the time – a world of music.'

'Of course. I had forgotten.' He grinned at the children – no temperament here! – and sat down in the nest of hay, relaxed and happy, with Midge and Maggie cuddled in his arms, and young John squatting on his heels, gazing at him with wide-eyed worship.

'You're very quiet, Maggie.' He wondered if she'd had an overdose of sun, or too much lemonade, but it could have been that Midge always seemed to steal the limelight. They were all completely different, Carrie's children, and it was interesting to see their differences developing as they grew older. Maggie's solemn little face was framed in a curtain of hair.

'I was thinking,' she said, quietly. 'What about Diane Maloney?'

'Wht's she done?'

'She's married a German.'

'I know.'

'He's going to be an enemy alien soon, then he will be interned, won't he?'

'He won't wait to be interned, Maggie. Carl Richter is

101

much too clever to be caught on this side of the Channel when War is declared.'

'Is he a Nazi?'

'I should imagine so.'

'Why does Hitler hate all the Jews? Jesus was a Jew.'

'Was he? To be honest, I'm a bit out of my depth.' He grinned boyishly, pecked her cheek and asked, 'Shall we change the subject?'

Maggie sighed. It was awfully difficult to be a good Christian in a family who shied away from any mention of Jesus, but she was still determined to be a missionary in Darkest Africa. Sunday was the happiest day of the week, when she started out after breakfast to walk the two miles to Sunday School, carrying her Bible and Prayer Book. Both had been won for regular attendance, and would remain with her for the rest of her days. The Prayer Book also contained over three hundred hymns, and she knew every word of all the familiar ones. After Sunday School, all the children filed into church, and she loved every minute. The senior girls stayed behind when the juniors were led out before the sermon. There were no senior boys.

'It's bad enough having to attend day school, but I'm buggered if I'm going to walk all that way on Sunday morning. Anyway, it's not compulsory,' her brother Dick had reminded her – and she had reminded *him* not to swear.

The Vicar, who liked to be called Rector, preached rather dull sermons. They said he was a lonely man since his frivolous little wife had eloped with a travelling salesman. They said the salesman had deserted her when he discovered she was pregnant. They said she had begged her husband to be taken back, but he had refused. So his sermons had a bitter flavour, denouncing the lust of the flesh.

'Poor man, he's to be pitied,' they said.

Many of his working-class parishioners had been weaned away from the church to the cheerful atmosphere and hearty singing of Chapel. The children of these parents now attended the Chapel Sunday School, but Maggie's loyalty to the church was unswerving. She loved all the important festivals of the church calendar – Easter, Harvest Festival and Christmas. And when the Rector's droning voice sent many of his upper-class parishioners to sleep, and her companions began to fidget – and suck sweets – Maggie settled down to listen, her mind emptied of every secular thought. Of course she loved Julian. Everyone loved Julian. But his views on the Creation, the Virgin birth and the Resurrection were quite blasphemous. She was frightened by such heresy, since she believed so profoundly in the teachings of Jesus of Nazareth on which the Christian Faith had been based. Maggie was still too young, however, to defend her beliefs against the opposing views of adults, and she lapsed into sulky silence.

In the nest of hay, cradled on Julian's arm, she watched the three women feeding the hay to her father on the wagon, and wondered why she had no real sense of belonging to Russets and this farming family. She was a cuckoo in the nest. If only she had been born Auntie Harriet's daughter, she would be growing up at the Mission in the Congo. Her heart ached for the love and understanding of this wonderful woman. Surely they were kindred spirits? Yet her own two sons, Mark and Matthew, were not going back. They had none of their parents' dedication. Both boys spent part of their holidays at Russets. Granny loved boys. 'God moves in a mysterious way', according to Auntie Harriet. If you had faith, all would be made clear one day.

'You children could be laying the table for supper,'

said Granny, decidedly, pushing a damp curl under her sun-bonnet. She was hot and tired, and feeling a little irritable, and probably a little envious of the children's light-hearted approach to hay-making.

'Ah, supper! Good show!' Julian was suddenly reminded he was hungry, and they all trooped away to the house.

Wendy was disappointed that Julian did not follow her to the wood, but of course he would prefer the company of Midge – that precocious little pest who was everyone's favourite, and getting to be quite objectionable. Wendy couldn't bear to be overlooked for a child of nine. She had passed all her examinations with honours which gave her a rather exalted opinion of her own importance. Nobody at Russets really appreciated her cleverness. Only Daddy understood how hard she had worked, and how desperately she wanted to make a career for herself in the world of music. Mother now had other plans for her daughter of course, and she was so tired of being reminded, 'Your mother knows best'. It was not true! And it was so humiliating to be treated as a child, and all her dearest wishes discouraged. Mother had arranged for a twelve-month course of tuition at the local Secretarial College, since it would eventually lead to a nice cosy little job as somebody's secretary. She was due to start at the beginning of the Autumn term, and had been allowed to 'enjoy' several weeks at Russets after their usual family holiday at the seaside – too boring for words to describe.

'A carefree period before settling down to work,' Mother called it. How stupid could parents be! How easily deceived into thinking their offspring had accepted the fate they decreed! Even her darling Daddy had been persuaded into thinking that Security was the ultimate achievement, and that her outstanding talent could be regarded as a means of occupying leisure hours – a hobby, in fact. She was furiously angry that her brilliant success as a pianist should be described as a mere HOBBY!

Well, she was not going to comply with Mother's wishes, at least, not for more than a few weeks. She hadn't any definite plans, only this fierce determination to escape from a future in which she would be confined to an office five and a half days a week for fifty weeks of the year. The mere thought of such an existence had set her mind working on ways and means of escape. So much would depend on this war that all the grown-ups were discussing with such morbid relish. Daddy said we were better prepared to fight another war with Germany than in 1914. Mother declared emphatically that if it had to be war, the sooner the better, then they could get it over before Christmas. Gran shook her grey head sadly. She had lost her son, Jack, in the last war, and Daddy, her eldest son, had come back from France with only one leg. If you hadn't actually lived through a war, on what Mother called the Home Front, it was difficult to imagine all the changes in their way of life. Mother had been swept into the strange world of a busy London hospital, while Daddy had locked the door on his small office and walked away to volunteer at the nearest recruiting centre. They were married suddenly, like thousands of other young couples caught up in the desperate urgency to be together in a few brief hours of happiness. It was Gran who filled in all kinds of facts for the child's questioning mind, not her parents, who shied away from the subject of the last war.

But she belonged to the young generation – Julian's generation – and the prospect of another war was an exciting challenge. She was still a virgin, innocent of sex, because all her senses and emotions had been directed into the channels of a musical education. There was a kind of sensuality in the union of her sensitive fingers to the keyboard, but it was not sexual. Several students at the college had found her attractive, and would have explored what Gran called 'her private parts'. Since she had no brothers, and only a vague idea of the shape and nature of the male genitals, she was much too frightened to allow such liberties. It was romantic to be in love with Julian, and there was no risk of losing her virginity. It could be lost quite easily, according to one of her more knowledgeable friends, and you could find yourself pregnant after only one involvement. It was a solemn and dreadful possibility, and sexual intercourse was a mystery.

In the shade of the beech wood she walked slowly and pensively, her slender hands twisting the hem of the white starched pinafore. She looked much younger than her actual years, but her thoughts had the brave independence of the young generation.

Some time later, the rattling of the wagon wheels on the cobbles suggested they had finished loading the hay. When they all had washed at the pump, they would sit down to a supper of home-cured ham, home-baked bread, their own dairy butter and cheese, jam from their own gooseberries, cake, and raspberries and cream. She had helped Maggie to pick the raspberries, and complained about the stain on her hands and pinafore. The big teapot on the hob would be emptied and refilled several times, for tea was still the most refreshing beverage. This meal was actually high tea and supper combined because of the hay-making. Meals at Russets revolved around the work on the farm, and were timed accordingly.

It would be fun, Wendy was thinking, to walk into the kitchen late with a nonchalant air, and see all their faces turned in her direction. Her self-importance would be restored by such an entrance. So she took off the pinafore, folded it neatly, and smoothed the creases from the pretty flowered muslin – one of several frocks Gran had made for the seaside holiday – and left the wood behind. The kitchen door stood wide open from dawn till dusk on these warm Summer days, and the family was gathered round the table. The range shone with black lead, and Katie's energetic elbow grease. A marmalade cat was stretched in a pool of sunlight on the floor. Bright red geraniums crowded the window sills. It was a picture she would carry in her mind's eye through the dangerous and difficult years ahead, yet she had no premonition of such a future.

'So there you are, dear.' Aunt Lucy smiled a welcome and poured another cup of tea. Her face was glowing from the quick wash under the pump.

Carrie looked up anxiously. She was remembering her own youth, when she had often fled to the beechwood to cry in private. But there was no trace of tears on Wendy's flushed cheeks, or in her sparkling eyes. Tom was grinning, the children stared, then went on eating. Katie was slicing more bread at the end of the table, but she did not look up. She had told the Mistress that Wendy was a little madam and should be kept in her place, but the Mistress had reminded her it was not *her* place to interfere.

Wendy's darting glance travelled round the table and came to rest on Julian. He was looking at her with a strange expression, a kind of tenderness that was new in their relationship. Then he stood up, pulled out a chair, and she sat down beside him and began to sip the sweet, hot tea with a lovely sense of belonging. Julian had changed out of his uniform into his farm clothes – a check shirt, open at the neck, corduroy trousers and canvas shoes. Katie had been instructed to carry up a can of hot water.

He was very conscious of his young cousin sitting so close, and the clean, sweet smell of her clothes and hair. Wendy would never smell of earth and sweat. She was too fastidious. He supposed she must be aware that the new hair style was most becoming, and she had blossomed into a very pretty girl. When he could get her alone, he would ask her what she intended to do. He felt protective towards her, and would like to think of her here, at Russets, when war was declared. But the setting did not suit her, and if she stayed, she would have to work hard, like a land-girl. It was ludicrous to imagine such a dainty creature in breeches and boots, mucking out the stables and feeding the pigs.

Even here, at Russets, the threat of war was the main topic of conversation. Aunt Lucy, Tom and Carrie hung on his opinion as though he had access to secret documents because he happened to be wearing the uniform of the Royal Air Force.

'We take orders. We go where we are sent. We are not expected to ask many questions – and if I knew, I wouldn't tell you!' he added, with a disarming grin.

'The postman is our main source of information, apart from the wireless, but then our country postmen have always delivered news as well as mail.' Aunt Lucy was off on another topic, a safe topic, thank goodness. This was his last leave, and he wanted to forget the war.

'I well remember when the old Queen died. It was Percy Philips who told us why the bells were tolling,' Aunt Lucy was saying.

'That was Queen Victoria, wasn't it, Granny?' Midge interrupted.

'That's right, love.'

'I like history. It's my favourite subject.'

'Is it, love?'

Wendy sighed. Midge – always Midge!

They lingered over the meal. It had been a long, hot day in the hay-field, and there would be another long day tomorrow, for the barometer was set fair. There were few grumbles when the weather was kind.

Midge was prolonging her bedtime, but it was getting late, and John was falling asleep at the table. It was never any trouble to get Maggie to bed, for she always had a book to read till Granny switched off the light. As for Dick, he had grown away from the rest of the family, and had almost forgotten how to play. Lucy had recently put him in complete charge of the poultry, and he was proud of his new responsibility. He managed the incubators and handled the broody hens to the manner born. To feed and water the hens was his first job after breakfast, before he started for school, and his first thought as he raced home. He was bored with school and was a poor scholar.

It reminded Lucy of the days when her own three boys had shown little interest in learning the three Rs – reading, writing and 'rithmatic – at the village school. But children were allowed to leave school at the age of thirteen in those days, if they could satisfy the school inspector that they had a useful job of work waiting for them. Dick was already fretting that, under the new regulations, he must stay at school till he was fourteen. In the meantime, there would be plenty of work to keep him busy in the six weeks of the Summer holiday, when the village children were picking hops on the other farms. He would whitewash the chicken-houses, repair the fences, and enjoy the pleasure of seeing his own chickens and eggs being sold on the market stall. He was still a little squeamish about wringing their necks, but it had to be done when the hens stopped laying.

As Lucy had explained to her grandson, 'It's the only way we can make a living by selling our produce. Your father is always reluctant to take his lambs and bull calves to market, but it's all part of the cycle of farming, Dick. You can't afford to be sentimental.'

He listened to Granny. She knew what she was talking about. There had been good years and lean years at Russets, for farming was a precarious livelihood. Dick would help with the harvest before he went back to school, and this Autumn there would be a good crop of cereals as well as the best crop of hay they had seen for several years. To fill the big Dutch barn that had been partly destroyed by fire before he was born, and rebuilt by his father and the neighbouring farmers, this was achievement and satisfaction. Russets was his whole world, and he wanted no other.

'Thank God for Dick. He's a true Blunt,' Lucy reminded Julian.

'A poor look out for Russets if you had to depend on me, eh, Aunt Lucy?' Julian retorted. 'It's the Franklin blood in me that sees the land as a demanding taskmaster. That doesn't mean I don't admire those who spend their lives struggling with it,' he hastened to add. 'But you need to be born to it.'

'I wasn't born to it, love, neither was Carrie, but we both married farmers, and when you marry a farmer, you marry his work and his world, or should do.'

'The young generation of women may not agree to that kind of devotion. They are more enlightened, and some see themselves as equals. This war could prove they are right. There are thousands of young women already in uniform, doing a man's job, and the Home Front will be manned almost entirely by women and old men. I foresee a revolutionary change in the status of women, Aunt Lucy.'

110

'You know, Julian, my generation of women may have *seemed* to be subservient to our menfolk, but actually we managed to rule the roost! Your Aunt Ruby was a tower of strength in her family, and she definitely wore the trousers, as the saying goes. I could name quite a few, and not all working class. Old Parson's wife was another example of petticoat rule, as it was called. With Old Parson so gentle and easygoing, her strong character was necessary, and many of her husband's poor parishioners had reason to be grateful for her autocratic ways. No, my dear boy, you are wrong to suppose we women were all condemned to a life of servitude and obedience.'

Julian kissed her affectionately. When she called him 'my dear boy' he had a feeling that he was greatly loved by Aunt Lucy – the youngest of her family of boys, and not even a Blunt. But then, she had loved his Grandfather Franklin. What a woman!

PART II

PART II

Chapter Six

Maggie, John and Midge went back to school the following day, but Dick had persuaded Lucy that he was indispensable in the hay-field. She was easily won over, for Dick was such a splendid little worker.

Soon all the children would be on holiday, but it would not be all play. Each child would be expected to help. There were no idle hands on a farm.

Julian slept late, and found his breakfast in the oven. Aunt Lucy came back to the house at mid-morning to brew another pot of tea, and bake a batch of scones for elevenses. Julian watched her nimble fingers from his end of the kitchen table. He had been reading the daily newspaper that a boy had delivered on his bicycle before school. The half-crown he earned was welcomed by a mother of a large family, and a labouring husband earning only thirty shillings a week.

The news was bad. Across the Channel, the Nazi war machine had gone into action, and nothing would stop it. This peaceful backwater was no place for him now.

Aunt Lucy was smiling at him across the table. The bodice of her print dress was tight across her ample bosom, and her bare, plump arms were dusted with flour. With hay-seeds in her hair, her flushed cheeks and wide blue eyes, she was a picture of healthy, lusty womanhood. But she had had no lover since she lost her lord, and she shared her bed only with a sick child.

'Leave out your dirty washing, dear. Katie will put it in with the rest tomorrow morning. We shall be finished with that field today,' she said.

'Thank you.'

She knew by his absent-minded answer that his thoughts were far away. 'Is anything happening over there?' She pointed to the paper.

'Plenty. It's Poland they're after, and I have a very strong feeling we are going to let them down – the Poles, I mean. If we moved now it might be prevented, but we shan't move till it's too late. Of what use is a pact or pledge if it's not honoured? Nothing more than a bloody scrap of paper!' His dark eyes were blazing with such false pretences, and she did not chide him for swearing.

She was brushing the scones with a small pastry brush dipped in milk, and Poland was so remote. She was not even sure she could find it on the map. But Julian was already involved and impatient to get into action. Her heart ached for his youth and the dangers he must face. She could not spare him, and he would not wish to be spared. The young generation were as ready and eager to serve as their fathers in 1914.

'It's not fair. Their long history has been nothing but invasion. Their position is so vulnerable. They can be attacked on so many fronts. But they are a brave people, and they will fight to the last man.' He was still talking about the Poles, and she wished he could forget the war and enjoy his leave.

'Wendy has been looking out for you, dear,' she reminded him kindly.

'Has she? I don't honestly know what to make of her. She blows hot and cold.'

116

'She's very fond of you.'

'I'm fond of her.'

The telephone was ringing and Aunt Lucy's hands were floury.

'I'll answer it.' Julian dashed away and picked up the receiver.

'Hello, Russets here.'

'Hello, may I speak to Julian, please?'

He did not recognise the voice and asked cautiously, 'Who's speaking?'

'Diane – Diane Maloney.'

'It's Julian here.' His voice was hoarse. He was nervous and tongue-tied. 'Who – who told you I was on leave?' he stammered.

'You're Aunt Lucy told Mother, Mother told Sammy and Sammy told me.'

'I see.'

'How come you missed out on letting me know? I thought we were friends?'

'We are. I'm sorry, Diane.'

'It was fun last time, wasn't it, darling?'

'Yes.' He was blushing at the memory. 'Where are you speaking from?' he asked.

'From the London house. Julian, I *must* see you, *please!*'

'I only have four days leave.'

'PLEASE!'

'Could you come down to Marston Park, tomorrow or the following day?'

'I can't leave the house, and I can't explain on the telephone. The servants are not all loyal.'

'Where's Carl?'

'Where do you think? Back in his beloved Fatherland. . . . When do you go back?'

'Thursday.'

117

'What time?'

'I shall be leaving here after breakfast. It's a long journey. It takes all day.'

'Break your journey, darling. Take a taxi from Victoria.'

'I – I can't promise, Diane.'

'You *must*. I've *got* to see you, *please*!' She was crying.

'All right. Don't cry.'

'You'll come?'

'Yes.'

'Promise?'

'Promise.'

When he put down the receiver it seemed that an eternity had passed but it was only a few minutes.

'That was Diane Maloney phoning from London. I have promised to break my journey to see her on Thursday. She was crying. I couldn't refuse, could I?' he asked.

'I suppose not.' Lucy had no time for Diane Maloney, but she had grown quite fond of her nice little old-fashioned mother.

He carried the tray to the hay-field, and they greeted him exuberantly and crowded round. Aunt Lucy filled the mugs with hot, sweet tea, and Wendy handed round the buttered scones.

'I think I'll just pop along to say hello to Aunt Martha and Uncle Andrew. It won't take long on my bike,' he told them with assumed casualness.

'Very well, dear.' Aunt Lucy was not the only one to be disappointed that he was going visiting on his first day at home, but Wendy was too proud to protest. He drank a mug of tea but refused a scone. It was too soon after his favourite breakfast of sausages and bacon. And he hadn't recovered from the telephone conversation with Diane. She was too hard-boiled – or was she? Something

118

had upset her pretty badly, and it couldn't only be Carl, for he was always coming and going to Germany.

Wendy was looking pensive and very young in another clean pinafore. What would she say if he told her he and Diane Maloney were lovers? He would never tell her, of course. One did not deliberately shock one's little cousin.

They watched him ride away and settled down to work. Wendy was choked with tears as she raked up the loose hay into a hay-cock. Why couldn't he have stayed to help? It was mean of him. She hated the hay-field. She was hot, and her head ached, and she asked to be excused.

'Lie down on the sofa, dear. The parlour is always cool,' Aunt Lucy advised kindly.

'Has she really got a headache, or is it just an excuse?' Tom grumbled.

'I thought she was looking pale. She's not very strong, is she?' Carrie was more sympathetic. She wondered, not for the first time, if Wendy were in love with her cousin.

'Wendy is highly strung.' Lucy had the last word on the matter. A child could be excused from all practical jobs once it was labelled 'highly strung', and Wendy was not adverse to cashing it on this particular theory. The Blunt children could not claim such distinction, though Midge was showing signs of an artistic talent that might eventually isolate her from the rest of the family. Her clever animal sketches had been much admired, and several had been pinned on the wall of her classroom at the village school in the past year. She seemed not to need encouragement.

To have a child who could amuse herself on a wet day in the holidays and never asked 'What can I do now?' was in itself a blessing, as Lucy would say. Midge had

119

rejected dolls from infancy. Puppies and kittens had been her playmates. She had no fear of any animal, and had once been rescued at the age of three from under the huge hairy hooves of Duke, the Shire horse.

But Wendy's musical talent had been recognised and encouraged. Cynthia had paid for a good teacher to coach the child for examinations. Now, on this hot day in mid-Summer, with an aching heart, she knew where to find a measure of comfort. The keyboard of the parlour piano was yellow with age, but the tone was good. Lucy had it tuned regularly by the blind piano tuner from the village. She had rinsed her gritty hands under the pump and dried them on the roller towel hanging on the kitchen door. In washing all trace of the hay-field away, she was ready and eager to be wrapped about in the privacy of her own little world. Chopin was her joy and inspiration. She felt an affinity with Chopin that was almost spiritual in its depth and reverence.

A faint breeze stirred the muslin curtains. Away in the hay-field, the faint strains of the Nocturne in F sharp major reached the man on the wagon. He paused for a moment and balanced himself with the prongs of the pitchfork. There was something vaguely haunting and disturbing in that distant music – a warning, a premonition – of what?

Cycling along the country lanes to Aunt Martha's cottage, Julian's thoughts were so far removed, he was completely oblivious to the lush beauty of early Summer. A lark was ascending in full song from a field of ripening corn, but he did not hear it. The hedges were draped in pink and white roses and sweet-scented honeysuckle, but the scent escaped him as he raced past. Dazzling rays of sunlight gleamed on bright yellow buttercups and red poppies, but Julian was not dazzled because his head was down over the handle-bars, and he barely avoided a farm cart at the bend in the lane.

'Can't you watch where y're going, yer buggerin' young sod!' yelled an irate farm worker.

'Sorry!' Julian flung over his shoulder.

Only when a solitary plane droned overhead was his attention claimed, and he gazed up into a clear blue sky and remembered the squadron of Spitfires lined up on the airfield.

It had been a mistake to take this leave. If he hadn't come away, he would not have got involved with Diane, or felt so guilty at neglecting Wendy. Girls were all right, but when they intruded on a man's job – and one so important – they were a nuisance. His whole self, mind and body, should be so utterly dedicated at this crucial stage, there would be no room for distractions – and this leave was already threatening more distractions than he had anticipated.

Aunt Lucy, bless her heart, thought she understood the problems of adjusting to a few days' leave, but she didn't. Nobody in Civvy Street could be expected to comprehend the stress and strain of living at full pressure on a remote air station. He supposed the same would apply to the Army and Navy, but he had no acquaintance in either, and only a fleeting interest in their manoeuvres. All over the country, men were in training and our own war machine was almost ready to go into action. But it did not roar and rant like the Nazi engine. It moved so quietly and effortlessly, it was almost overlooked in the noisy propaganda from across the Channel.

He found Aunt Martha picking strawberries, and he leaned on the back gate watching the dumpy little figure with affection. She hadn't changed in all the years, and she still resembled Mrs Noah whichever way you looked at her! Her world was small now since Uncle Andrew had retired. She missed the lively environment of the School House, and the close proximity of the village. A country cottage in a secluded spot might be a retired schoolmaster's idea of bliss, but not for his wife.

When she looked up from her picking, and saw him standing there, she smiled to welcome him, and hurried down the garden path. He leapt over the gate and gave her a hug.

'What a lovely surprise! I was feeling a bit lonesome,' she said, offering the bowl.

He took a strawberry. It was ripe and juicy, and he smacked his lips.

'Have another?'

He took another, and another, and another, rolling his eyes at her, and she laughed at his boyish greediness.

'Where's Uncle Andrew?' he asked.

'In the study. Buried in his books, as usual. I don't see much of him. I know I shouldn't be complaining, Julian dear. I should be counting my blessings with a husband too old to get involved in this war, and a son thousands of miles away. I keep hoping the young Infants teacher will want to join in one of the women's services when War is declared, and I shall be invited to take her place, just for the duration of the war. It won't be long now, will it?'

'Not long.'

'Is this your last leave?'

'Yes.'

'It was kind of you to spare the time to call on me. You will stay to lunch?'

'Thanks, I should like to. They're hay-making at Russets, and I'm not much help as you know.'

'I know, dear. You never cared for it, only the horses; neither did Philip.'

'How are they? The Congo is a hell of a long way to go to preach the Gospel.'

122

'It was Harriet. Philip would never have dreamed of it. But they were in love, Julian. They seem to be ideally happy. I couldn't bear it if Philip had made a mistake.'

'Are the boys still at that prep school in Tunbridge Wells? The one I escaped from by the merest fluke? Do you remember?'

'Indeed I do. All the hue and cry when you were missing, and your poor Aunt Lucy nearly frantic with worry. Mark and Matthew seem happy enough, but of course they do have their grandmother on the spot as school matron. The school is being evacuated to the Cotswolds. I am going to miss the boys. They always spend part of their holidays here. Will it be a long war, dear? Andrew seems to think so, but he's inclined to be pessimistic. There's talk of it being over before Christmas.'

'That's being over optimistic.'

'I expect you are right, dear. I do hope Andrew will allow me to go back to the Infants. I hear the Teacher will join up. The uniform is a great attraction. I have not seen you in your uniform, dear, but Lucy tells me you look very handsome. I think she was wondering if you might bring a girl home on this last leave, though you hadn't mentioned any particular girl in your letters. There must be quite a few pretty girls to choose from?'

'Blondes and brunettes and a ravishing red-head! I rather fancy the red-head!' he lied gaily. It was so easy to pretend to be a Don Juan for nothing could be proved. It so happened that girls in uniform held little attraction.

Aunt Martha was enjoying his company. He was so amusing and affectionate. If she had been blessed with a second son, she would have wished for a son like Julian.

'Is Wendy helping with the hay-making?' she prompted.

Could it be his pretty young cousin had stolen his

123

heart? There would be trouble in the family if their relationship were to change. Cynthia would be the first to object since she had all the evidence of the danger at her finger tips, so to speak. As for Lucy, she would remember all the old wives' tales of abnormal children born to married cousins.

'Wendy had a rake in her hand when I left, but she was not looking very enthusiastic,' Julian was saying.

'She is not at all happy about that Secretarial College,' Martha reminded him.

'What Secretarial College? I've not had a chance to talk to her yet.'

'Her mother has enrolled her from next term, for a twelve-month course.'

'She will hate it. Besides, what was the point of all that slogging away on the piano if she is being pushed into an office?'

'Her mother thinks it would be too precarious to depend on her music, and she should have another skill. She could be right. She is usually right.'

'Poor kid. It must be quite a problem having my Aunt Cynthia for a mother.'

'She is rather strict with Wendy, but her father spoils her, so I suppose one balances the other.'

'I wouldn't know. I was a spoilt little brat.'

'You were a dear little boy. It was easy to spoil you. I always found the boys so much more responsive than the girls when I was teaching. And I adored Philip,' she added with a sigh, and Julian hugged her shoulders and pecked her cheek.

'Shall we finish picking the strawberries? The bowl looks a little depleted.'

'Would you like to? And you can pick some mint for the mint sauce. It's roast lamb for dinner. I picked and shelled the peas after breakfast.'

'You can leave me to make the mint sauce. I quite like cooking, though I don't get a lot of practice. Aunt Lucy is not too keen on handing over her job, and I'm rather slow. She made a batch of scones for elevenses this morning while I was finishing my breakfast.'

It was pleasantly peaceful in the garden. Neat rows of vegetables were proof of Martha's industry. She would not expect any help from Andrew. He usually watched her efforts from the comfort of a deck chair in the shade of the plum tree, since he did not care for too much sun on his balding pate.

When dinner was served in the small dining-room, he was called from his study, and greeted his ex-pupil with a limp hand shake. Julian listened politely to his very decided views on the impending war and the mentality of Hitler. He ate the excellent meal but made no comment. Then he excused himself, with the ponderous air of an elderly academic.

'He enjoys his dinner. Now he will have a nice little nap,' said Martha, as though she were speaking of a child. 'How do you think he looks, dear? I've been rather worried since he had that heart attack earlier in the year, but the doctor assured me it was only a slight attack.'

'I shouldn't worry, Aunt. He looks very fit.'

'Do you think so? It's good to have a second opinion. He tells me not to fuss.' She smiled whimsically as she cleared the table. Julian insisted on washing the dishes.

He left her standing at the gate – a lonely little figure, and rather pathetic. It was mid-afternoon, and he felt a little guilty for being absent from Russets for so long, but Aunt Martha had been so glad of his company, and he had discovered he could talk to her quite easily about this acute problem of adjusting to his home environment. Unlike Philip, who enjoyed a three-month

125

furlough from the Congo every five years, his own leave was a matter of days. He had told her he was seeing Diane Maloney on the return journey, and she naturally assumed that Diane was the missing girl-friend, though he had not mentioned her in his letters to Lucy.

So it was Diane, not Wendy? That was even a bigger hazard, for the girl had a shocking reputation. Servants talk.

As she watched him ride away, her heart was sad, and when he turned to wave at the bend in the lane, hot tears pricked her eyes. This war would be fought in the air, according to Andrew. Trench warfare was a thing of the past. New weapons of destruction had been invented with a deadly accuracy, and others would follow. Scientists, not soldiers, would decide the outcome of *this* war. It was a sobering thought on this bright Summer day. She had seen so many of that lost generation of youth caught up in that last terrible war, and the naughty little boys who had played pranks in her classroom, and fought each other in the lavatories, had marched away to fight for their King and Country – and never came back. Now a new generation must obey the call to serve, and Julian was already involved. A woman cannot visualise the magnitude of war, only so far as it concerns her own small world. At the moment it was Julian, but soon the village would be deprived once again, of its lovely youth, for the girls were already clamouring for uniforms and stepping out boldly into an unpredictable future.

The peace all about her was deceptive, and she felt impatient with her own security, and the pleasant pattern of her days. Julian had disturbed her complacency, and left her with an urge to get involved. Andrew would refuse to sanction her return to the classroom. She had always waited on him hand and foot, and she supposed he had never made a cup of tea, or boiled an egg in his whole life. Neither had Philip for that matter, but marriage to Harriet had changed all that. When they came on leave with two small children, she had been so surprised to see her son taking the boys to the lavatory and cutting up their meat.

There was work to be done in the garden, and Andrew would be expecting a cup of tea. This was her life. She squared her shoulders, and went back to the kitchen to put on the kettle.

A mile or so down the winding country lane, Wendy was perched on a field gate, and Julian braked clumsily and demanded, 'What are you doing here?'

'Waiting for you. You've been ages with Aunt Martha. I thought you were never coming.'

'Serves you right! Why aren't you helping them with the hay?'

'Why aren't you helping?' she retorted.

He grinned. It was like old times, this back-chat. He propped his bike against the hedge, climbed on the gate, and swung one leg over the top. She had changed her frock, he noticed. The blue print matched her eyes. Her short hair looked soft and silky. She was pretty, but it was not a chocolate-box prettiness. The firm little chin and the stubborn mouth gave character to a face still childishly rounded.

'Aunt Lucy was disappointed when you didn't come back to dinner. We had hot sausage rolls, and that horrid bread pudding.' She shuddered at the memory of the candied peel.

He laughed, and pulled her roughly towards him, to sit between his legs. They had often sat this way on top of a gate in the days when he saw himself as her big brother, and Wendy as his little sister. Her hair tickled his chin. It had a clean, fresh smell.

'You've been washing your hair,' he said.

'I had to. It was full of dust and hay-seeds.'

He could feel her small, pointed breasts under his hands; and her bare legs were twitching. 'Sit still!' His voice was gruff with repressed emotion and a sense of danger. A tear dropped on his hand.

'What's the matter?' he asked.

'Nothing.'

'Is it because I've neglected you?'

She shook her head.

'What then?'

'I love you,' she whispered. 'I didn't mean to tell you. It's wrong. I know it's wrong.'

'Why is it wrong?'

'Because we are cousins.'

'What difference does it make?'

'If you marry your cousin, your children will be born deformed, or mentally retarded.'

He swung her round, his dark eyes blazing. 'Who's been telling you such rubbish?'

'It's true! I've read about it, and a friend of mine knew a girl who married her cousin and had a mongol child.'

'Now listen to me, chick.' The pet name fell readily from his lips, and the old protectiveness stifled any danger of intimacy. 'There is absolutely no foundation for such an assumption. It's utter balderdash! – an old wives' tale. I never heard such nonsense, and for you to believe it. Where's your intelligence?'

She smiled tremulously, her blue eyes adoring. 'Then you don't mind me being in love with you?'

'I'm very honoured, Miss Simmons!'

'Now you're teasing me,' she pouted.

He kissed the tip of her nose.

'Kiss me properly,' she said, and closed her eyes. Her mouth was soft and warm, and he brushed it gently with his lips. Supposing he kissed her as he kissed Diane

128

Maloney – would she respond *as a woman*? He thought not. She was too young, and she acted like a child.

'I've got your photograph. I begged it from Aunt Lucy. I've kept it hidden in my secret drawer, but now I can put it in a frame – or does it have to be a secret still?'

'Let's keep it a secret, shall we? Just between the two of us.'

'All right.' She was so undemanding. She hadn't asked, 'Do you love me? . . . Will you marry me?'

Leaning against him, she sighed blissfully, and seemed to be perfectly satisfied with such a one-sided pact. But her nearness was disturbing, and his whole body ached with a new, surprising desire to make love to her.

'I've got another secret I should like to share with you,' she said.

'Go on. I'm listening,' he prompted.

And she told him of her plans. He listened, but did not fully grasp the significance of her intentions. His hands cupped her breasts, and his loins trembled. It seemed she was going to this Secretarial College in September, but had no intention of staying there. She was determined on a musical career, but rather vague about her plans to accomplish it.

'Something will turn up,' she insisted, with the blind faith of Mr Micawber.

'Be careful,' he warned, automatically.

'Careful of what?'

'Your mother won't like it you know, if you disobey her.'

'Mother will have to put up with it, for I shall *never*, *never* go into an office. I should die of boredom. Why shouldn't I please myself? She forgets she was a rebel at my age, yet she expects me to conform. It's not fair! Anyway, Daddy will take my part. So will Gran. You

129

know, Julian, I'm not just being stubborn. Music means more to me than anything else in the whole world. It's in my blood. It's meat and drink to me. I should die if I was deprived of my music.'

'I believe you,' he said, stifling a yawn, and feeling a little piqued to be relegated to second place. He stretched his cramped legs.

'We must go,' he said, and they slid off the gate. It was not the first time she had perched on the handle bars, but she was no little weight to heave up the sloping lane.

'Am I too heavy? I could walk?' she volunteered.

'Shut up and sit still!' he growled – still feeling a little piqued.

They were having their high tea at Russets when the telephone rang, and Carrie went to answer it, leaving the door open.

'Teacher? Yes. It's Carrie speaking.'

A pause, then a wail of protest.

'Oh, NO!'

Another pause, and then her choked voice saying soothingly, 'I'll come along at once, my dear. Yes, of course,' and the receiver clicked. They all looked up as she came back into the kitchen, and her stricken face told its own sad tale.

'That was Aunt Martha. Uncle Andrew has died very suddenly. She took in his cup of tea soon after you left, Julian, and found him slumped in his chair, unconscious. She phoned the doctor and he was there in half an hour, but Uncle Andrew was dead. The doctor said he wouldn't have suffered for more than a few seconds.'

'Poor Martha,' Lucy sighed, sympathetically.

Tom was already on his way to check whether the tyres on Carrie's bicycle needed pumping, and the children sat and stared at their mother's rare tears. Uncle Andrew was not their real uncle, and they had all been a little in awe of him when he came to tea on Sunday afternoons with Aunt Martha. It was difficult to feel at ease with a retired schoolmaster who had caned your Dad. Death was no stranger in the animal kingdom, so they were not afraid of it.

'Uncle Andrew was ever so old, wasn't he, Mum?' Midge was the first to speak.

'Not all that old. He could have lived for another ten years with a sound heart,' Carrie reminded her.

'It's a pity it had to happen just now. Aunt Martha is going to be pretty lonely in that isolated cottage when war is declared, and Philip thousands of miles away,' Julian reflected quietly.

'Shall you stay with Martha for a day or two?' Lucy wanted to know.

'Yes, I shall stay till after the funeral, if you can manage without me?'

'Of course, dear. We shall manage.'

'I'll help,' Julian volunteered.

'Me, too,' Wendy echoed.

'Then I'll pack a small bag.' Carrie climbed the stairs slowly. Her beloved Teacher would be a widow again. For the second time she would be shocked by the appalling suddenness of death. But there had been no false tears for Dick Martin, the father of Philip, only a sense of relief and freedom.

As she pedalled down the lanes so recently visited by Julian and Wendy, and passed the field gate that would linger in their memory for many a long year, she noticed a small bright object lying in the grass and slid off her bike to pick it up. It was the button off Wendy's frock. So they had met here today in secret. It was not the first time she had wondered about their relationship. Had she imagined those sly glances and unspoken questions in their eyes? Once upon a time her dear, devoted Tom

131

had courted her with such glances, and risked his brother's wrath. To be in love with his brother's wife had been Tom's misfortune, and he carried the burden for so long it seemed they were doomed to a lifetime of stolen kisses and secret intercourse. Then Bertie had been killed by a falling beam that Christmas Eve when the Dutch barn was set on fire, and she was already pregnant with Tom's child. Now Julian and Wendy, on the eve of another war, were sharing those sly glances and secret rendezvous. It could mean nothing but trouble if they were in love. Russets had known so much sorrow and heartache in the passing years, and each new generation had to battle through stormy seas to reach a safe harbour.

Aunt Lucy had known only brief periods of happiness after Bert's death – with the boy Charles, and the latter years with her selfish lover. Babies had been born out of wedlock in her family, grown sons had been killed and some terribly maimed in the last cruel war; the harvest had been poor one Autumn, and the following year all their new-born calves had died of some rare fever. But Russets stood square and solid, and under its hospitable roof men, women and children lived out their lives and were hardened, not defeated, by circumstances beyond their control.

Could that small button be proof of another clandestine love affair? Carrie wondered. Were they feeling as guilty and as desperate as she and Tom had felt? Julian was as dear to her as her own children, but Wendy was still an unknown. The unwritten law that it was dangerous for cousins to marry was as firmly established as the laws of the Medes and Persians in the minds of the working class – and Carrie was working class.

She found Martha leaning on the gate. She seemed very calm and composed. It was Carrie who wept and had to be comforted when she hugged the dumpy little figure, and Carrie who had to be given a cup of hot sweet tea before she could speak of the man lying on the sofa in the study.

'It was a merciful death, my dear. He could have suffered a long and painful illness in hospital, and that he would have found most distressing, for he was such a private person. And he has been spared all the difficulties and restrictions of another war. No, it was all for the best,' Martha insisted as they sat together over their tea in the kitchen. The doors and windows were flung wide open, but the blinds were drawn in the study.

'Andrew never cared for the sun. I always had to draw the curtains,' Martha explained, as though he were still capable of complaining. His presence would be felt for a long time. It was a domineering, humourless presence, and Martha had been a slave to his eccentricity of recent years.

'What shall you do?' Carrie wanted to know.

'I shall go back to the Infants classroom. The young pupil teacher has already given in her notice. I heard a couple of days ago that she would be leaving at the end of the month, but I hadn't mentioned it to Andrew. He wouldn't have liked it and I did not want to upset him. It's only a couple of miles, and I have my bicycle.' She sighed. 'I have to work anyway, Carrie. Andrew's pension is not paid to his widow, and I shall be back where I belong. Those years in the Infants were the happiest.'

'But it's almost time for the long Summer holiday. You can't stay here alone.'

'Why not? There is plenty of work to be done in the garden. I shall pick the fruit and make jam. It will take me about a week to spring-clean the study. Nothing has been moved in years. I could do no more than run the

133

sweeper over the carpet, and polish and dust the furniture, when Andrew was out of the way. I shall try my hand at decorating. It's all so shabby. Oh, there is plenty to keep me busy this Summer.'

'I shall come and help you with the decorating. They can manage without me for a week or so. It's not often I get away. I shall enjoy it.'

'And I shall enjoy having you, dear. It was good to see Julian this morning, but I felt a little sad after he had left, thinking about the dangers he must face as soon as war is declared. Do you think he is in love with Wendy?'

'He's fond of her, but that's natural. Wendy has always spent part of her holidays at Russets. They have practically grown up together, like brother and sister. But they are no longer children, and when they start to meet in secret, it's something more than fondness.'

'Are they meeting in secret?'

Carrie explained about the button. 'Wendy's mother would be the first to object, and it would upset Aunt Lucy. They are first cousins, you see. It's dangerous.'

'I don't altogether hold with that particular theory, my dear, and I certainly wouldn't have had any objection to Philip marrying a first cousin, but he had no cousins so the question didn't arise. The young generation do not bother about their parents' sanction in this day and age. They just get married. So many young couples will rush into marriage as soon as war is declared, as they did in the last war. I do think Cynthia has been too strict with Wendy. I hope she won't do anything foolish.'

'I think it's more likely that Julian might act foolishly. He is seeing Diane Maloney in London on the return journey.'

'But she's married.'

'That doesn't prevent her from taking a lover, and Julian is very attracted to her. She is beautiful, and on

134

the few occasions we have met, quite charming, but I don't like her, and I should hate to see Julian made a scapegoat with a jealous husband.'

'He's a German, isn't he, and we shall soon be at war with Germany? Perhaps she thinks they will soon be separated, anyway, so what matter what people say? Poor Wendy, she wouldn't stand a chance if she had to compete with Diane Maloney.'

'I'm not sure. Wendy may surprise us. She has a lot of character and a will of her own. Cynthia doesn't get it all her own way. Have you heard about the Secretarial College?'

'Yes, your mother told me on the telephone. It's a shame. The child is a brilliant pianist, and it's such a terrible waste to put her in an office. I know I sound like a school-marm, but I can't bear to see a talent wasted.'

In the silence that followed, a blackbird spilled his evening song over the peaceful garden – and the ex-schoolmaster lay at rest amongst his books.

Midge had begged for the wagonette to take Julian to the station. She visualised all the family gathered on the platform, waving her hero away to the war. But Julian was adamant. *Nobody* would go to the station.

He left Russets after an early breakfast in the station cab, and the whole family were gathered at the gate. Aunt Lucy, Carrie, Wendy, Maggie and Midge smothered him in hugs and kisses, while Tom and the boys gripped his hand. It was an emotional moment. Everything had been said and could only be repeated.

'Goodbye!' 'Take care!' 'God bless!' 'Don't forget to write!'

Midge had a final hug, then she climbed over the gate and raced after the cab, the dog barking at her heels. It was another picture to carry in his mind's eye, and he was choked with tears as they faded from sight. Aunt Lucy had provided a fat package of sandwiches for the journey – home-baked bread spread with dairy butter, and thick slices of home-cured ham. He was sorry to leave them. Yet, at the same time, he was glad to be going back. It had been an upsetting leave, with Uncle Andrew's sudden death, and his confused feelings over Wendy. There had been no further opportunity to be alone with her, so he had to take away the memory of his pretty little cousin perched on the gate, leaning against his chest, his hands cupping her breasts, and his body trembling with the desire to make love to her.

Looking back, he could not understand his own un-responsive attitude when she confessed her love for him. Had she been disappointed? Wendy was too proud to beg for favours. 'Kiss me properly,' that was all. There were so many unanswered questions troubling him now. Was she still a virgin? Was she afraid of sex? Why hadn't he persuaded her to make the best of the Secretarial College for a year, and then argue her case against an office job? To share her secret was a responsibility he would rather not have.

The familiar fields and woods of their lovely Weald slipped away. Why had he promised to see Diane? Would he run into Carl Richter, or would he be back in Germany?

Victoria Station was thronged with uniforms. Every-one seemed to be on the move. Trolleys were piled high with kitbags, and girls as well as men were pulling and pushing the trolleys in great good humour. There were no porters to be seen. Martial music blared from loud-speakers, and the atmosphere was charged with excited anticipation. He had to share a taxi with a well-dressed, elderly couple, complaining bitterly about the long delays everywhere. They had booked their passage, they told Julian, and would soon be on their way to America. He wished them luck, but did not envy them. The youth were not looking for a means of escape.

The parlourmaid took his greatcoat and bag and laid them carefully on the chest in the hall. Then she led the way upstairs, tapped on a door, pushed it open and stood aside. The curtains were drawn, and a shaded lamp on the bedside table shed a faint glow over the girl on the bed. Her face was bruised and one eye blackened. A wry smile twisted her lips. She reached out her arms, and her naked shoulders were scarred and ugly. Then, before his horrified eyes, she stripped off the sheet and revealed her bruised and battered body.

'Was it Carl?' he whispered.

She nodded.

'But why?'

'I don't know,' she lied.

Carl had returned home from Germany to find his wife in bed with his best friend, and when he had thrashed her lover and thrown him out, he tied her to the bed-posts by her wrists and ankles, and raped her with such violence she had begged for mercy. The maid had found her, barely conscious, some hours later, still tied to the bedposts, but she had no pity for her mistress.

'She's been asking for it. Now she's got it,' she told the other servants.

'The man's a maniac,' Julian muttered, as her arms slid round his neck.

'Kiss me, darling,' she said.

And when he had kissed her, they made love. Her battered body still craved for sex, but he left her weeping with disappointment and frustration. It had been a mistake to invite him. She had sensed his revulsion. He was gone, and she knew she would not see him again.

Chapter Seven

All over the country, wireless sets had been switched on. It was another unforgettable moment in the history of the British people, but few would remember the exact words of the ageing Prime Minister. It was enough to be told in his solemn, measured tones, that we were at war with Germany. The short silence that followed was profoundly moving, till a lone aircraft, flying low over the Weald, shattered the silence of that peaceful Sunday morning. Mothers clutched their children, and fathers hurried out to gaze upwards, half expecting to see the bright sky darkened by the invading Luftwaffe.

Lucy had called the children indoors to hear the momentous broadcast. They were old enough now to share whatever Fate had in store. Only John was frightened, but he was a nervous child, and Lucy took him on her lap when the others ran out into the yard.

'Is it OURS or THEIRS?' Midge was dancing with excitement.

'What would a solitary plane of the German Air Force be doing over here and the war only just declared?' Tom wondered.

'*Reconnaissance*,' said Dick, decidedly. He was

138

already prepared with maps and charts and a surprising amount of useful information he had gleaned from the daily press, and the 6-o'clock-news bulletins on the wireless. It had been somewhat disappointing, however, to find Julian so reluctant to talk about the RAF on his last leave. The exact position of Julian's station was so vague, Dick could only hazard a guess. And as for the number of aircraft and personnel on that particular station, it was still shrouded in mystery.

This absorbing new interest had spread like a prairie fire among the boys of his generation; for them the war would be fought in the air, and their hero-worship confined to the pilots and the gunners of the RAF. Since Julian had refused to allow his model aircraft to be used, and Lucy kept a strict eye on all Julian's personal possessions, Dick had to make do with paper models.

Midge and Maggie would see Julian in every daring exploit, for Julian *was* the RAF. Katie was worried about her half-day. Would it be cancelled now war was declared?

'Put the kettle on, Katie, and brew a pot of tea,' her mistress reminded her with an exasperated sigh. After all these years, the silly woman still had to be reminded that a cup of tea was the first essential to any emergency.

'Hitler won't drop any bombs on Russets, will he Granny?' John asked, anxiously.

'Never you fear, my love, he couldn't possibly find us, not in this valley.'

'Can I eat my Saturday chocolate now?'

Lucy nodded, and smiled affectionately at her youngest grandson as he hurried away. John was backward and rather babyish, but he had a certain way of getting what he wanted, and was clever enough to escape anything in the nature of work, with Midge and Maggie so ready to deputise. The morrow would see all the

139

children back at school, and the pattern of their days would still be governed by the seasons, not Hitler's war. The few concessions they would be obliged to make would be similar to those granted in the 1914 war, when they ploughed up the field behind the cow-sheds and planted potatoes. Eggs would be graded for the market, but there would still be cracked and broken ones for cakes and to eat for breakfast. Certain obligations would be demanded as regards the sale of cattle, sheep and pigs, but on the whole, they would not go short of food or fodder.

When the teapot had been emptied, Lucy left Katie to baste the Sunday joint and prepare the vegetables, while she telephoned her sister Ruby, and her old friend Martha, to chat about poor Mr Chamberlain. Martha was more concerned with getting her things ready for the morrow when she would be back in the Infants classroom, and Ruby was agitated about the attitude of her beloved grand-daughter to the Secretarial College.

'She starts tomorrow, and she don't want to go. She's made up her mind she's not going to like it, and you know how stubborn she can be.' Her voice dropped to a whisper. 'It's her mother what wants it, Luce. Me and Freddie reckons it's a mistake.'

'You mustn't interfere, Rube, not between husband and wife.'

'I don't never interfere, Luce, but it upsets me.' Her twin quickly changed the subject.

'Come over for the day on Tuesday. I've got some nice bottled plums you can take back, and more pickled onions and chutney for Freddie.'

'Thanks, Luce. I'll bring the empty jars. They might get scarce now the war's started.'

'They won't be the only things that'll get scarce, love, but you and me have been through it all before,' Lucy

140

chuckled. 'That reminds me. Best make sure of enough dried fruit for the mincemeat and the Christmas puddings. Remember the last war, when the grocer kept it under the counter? By another Christmas it could be scarce again because it has to be fetched from foreign parts.'

'*Another Christmas*? But they reckon it will all be over by this one?'

'That's wishful thinking, Rube. Ask Freddie. He'll know. He was in the last one.'

'I feel proper flummoxed, Luce, and that's a fact.'

'Me too, love, but we shall manage. It's the young ones I feel sorry for, all being conscripted from the age of eighteen. And all classes – the Duke and the dustman. Nothing like a war to level things down to brass tacks.'

Ruby sighed gustily. Her twin often spoke in riddles. What had brass tacks to do with it?

They waited anxiously for Julian's letter, but when it came, it was cheerful and confident. He spoke of 'sorties' and 'dog-fights' and 'targets', but no specific targets were mentioned, and it took Dick to explain what these mystifying terms meant. It was surprising to read such lucid descriptions of cloud formations, and the leading Spitfire shining like silver in the sun's rays, for Julian was not normally given to such fanciful observations. Lucy read the letter aloud to Tom, Carrie and Katie as they sat over breakfast, after milking, then read it again to the children when they came home from school. Midge could hardly wait to eat her tea before starting on a letter to Julian that would be enclosed in Granny's.

Lucy had been writing regularly every Sunday afternoon for the past two years, and would continue to do so.

141

'Letters mean a lot to the chaps when they are so far from home,' he told her. But there was no regularity in his own letters, and she did not expect it. Carrie and Maggie would write occasionally, but Tom, Dick and John would just send their love. There was no mention of Wendy in this first letter since war was declared, but when Lucy read it over the 'phone to Ruby that same evening, she was told that Wendy had also received an envelope from Julian.

'She don't show it to nobody, Luce. It's private, she says. Bless her heart! But it came just right to cheer her up. She was so down in the dumps at that Secretarial College. She told me all the girls have got boy friends in uniform, and they pass their photographs around when the teacher is out of the room. We never had no photographs of your Bert and my Tom, did we, Luce? But then, we was never separated, and we was married at sixteen with our first babies on the way!'

'I wouldn't change places with the young generation today, not for all the tea in China,' Lucy declared.

'Nor me,' her twin agreed. 'You and me wasn't ignorant of the facts of life. It come natural in the working class, with such big families, all crowded in together. It's my belief that Wendy don't know a half of what you and me knowed at thirteen. She pretends to know because she's too proud to ask. It wasn't my business to enlighten her, Luce, when she started the curse, and I reckon her mother has never got round to it, for they've never been close. With no brothers and sisters, and not going away to boarding school, there wouldn't be much opportunity to learn the facts of life, and she's young for her age. Anyway, she was up in her room for an hour or more after tea, and I reckon she was writing to Julian.'

'I hope she won't break her heart over him if he

doesn't reciprocate. He seems to be rather smitten with the Maloney girl, and he was seeing her in London on the return journey. We had her mother here to tea yesterday, and she hadn't seen Diane more than once since her car accident back in the Summer. I always feel so sorry for that poor little woman. It's such an empty life. Her husband and daughter have no time for her. Harry is away in the States, and he's seldom at home these days. She says he is boasting he will be a millionaire if it's a long war, but it won't make any difference to her. She still talks about the early days of their marriage, when they were poor, as her happiest. I asked her whether Diane would have to join the forces, but she said not, because they are still American citizens. That nice woman they call Sammy is English, of course, and she has already invited the local branch of the Women's Voluntary Service to make their headquarters at Marston Park. It's the first time they have shown any real interest in village affairs, but they are not entirely to blame. They were labelled the New Rich when they first arrived at Marston Park, and the label stuck.'

'Too much money can be an awful bind, Luce, though I've never had to worry on that score. Counting me pennies has been no hardship. I must hang up now, love. Freddie is expecting a call from Cynthia. She's on night duty this week at the hospital. They all have to take a turn now, with so many of the young nurses going overseas. If it wasn't for Freddie, I think Cynthia would volunteer. She's such a dedicated nurse.'

'Hang up then, Rube. So long.'

'So long, Luce.'

Carrie was waiting to phone Martha. They chatted for half an hour or so, once a week, but made no mention of the war. Martha had taken on a new lease of life since

Andrew died. She found the new generation of Infants hardly changed. They still had sand-trays and slates, still chanted 'twice-one-are-two, twice-two-are-four', still dried their wet boots round the coke stove, and still planted mustard and cress on damp flannel spread on cracked saucers round the window sills. She was Teacher again. The boys fought for the privilege of pushing her bicycle up and down the school path, and the girls brought her flowers, and sometimes a cabbage. Back in the Infants' classroom the war would hardly touch Martha, and who could blame her for switching off the 6-o'clock-news bulletins? She was 'Digging for Victory', obeying the posters plastered all over the place. Potatoes had been planted where she once had a lawn, and rows of Brussels sprouts had taken over the herbaceous border. These would be sold to the greengrocer, and the money sent to her grandsons at Christmas. Her small world was organised. There was no waste, and no extravagance. She valued her independence, and she did not fret when Philip's letters were long overdue. She knew he was not involved in the war, and her grandsons were at school in a safe area. For the first time in her life, Martha could please herself.

Harry B. Maloney's attendance at the Catholic church in the village was erratic, even when he was in residence, but Kitty never missed a Sunday. The familiar pattern of the mass was as comforting and comfortable as the marriage bed when her lordly spouse was absent.

Father O'Leary, who had succeeded Father Dominic, was a jovial priest who thoroughly enjoyed all the christenings, weddings and funeral celebrations to which he was invited as an honoured guest. His parishioners, almost all working class, would spend money they could ill afford on lavish tea parties, and often get into debt. The children loved him. All their childish fears and anxieties, confided to 'Father', had a nice way of disappearing all together. And he was still young enough to tuck up his cassock and kick a ball, or run a race, on Sports Day. Compared to the pompous, strait-laced Parson across the way, Father O'Leary was a delightful and popular servant of the Lord.

Soon after war was declared and before Harry left for the States, Father O'Leary took the opportunity to ask a favour – a big favour – but a rich industrialist could afford to be generous.

'It has just occurred to me, Mr Maloney, that you might wish to contribute to the war effort in some useful capacity?' he began, smiling disarmingly at his victim.

Harry had no such thought in his head. But Father O'Leary could be very persuasive, and Harry was remembering the prayers he had offered for Diane's lucky escape from death back in the Summer. To be under an obligation to anyone was a pain in the neck.

'I understand from Father Dominic,' the priest continued, 'that Marston Park was converted into a Convalescent Home for Officers in the last war, and that Sir Neville Franklin graciously handed over the whole house, apart from a few rooms he used as a flat, for the duration of the war. He retained only one maid-servant. Now, I am not suggesting for one moment such a complete upheaval, and what I have to suggest could be terminated with a month's notice at any time that you found the arrangement inconvenient.' He paused to smile again, with bland reassurance, and Harry wondered with some misgiving what was in store. It would seem churlish to refuse, whatever was involved, for Sir Neville Franklin had been held up as a model landlord and the most generous of benefactors every since Harry

145

took over the estate. But the Franklins were Gentry, and Harry was clever enough to realise he could never emulate such an established hierarchy.

'What had you in mind, Father?' he asked, cautiously.

'I have been asked to find accommodation for a convent school to be evacuated from the Victoria district of London. There are some sixty pupils and ten staff, including five teaching nuns, kitchen and cleaning staff, and a gardener-handyman. They would be entirely self-supporting and organised. The children would be well-behaved and obedient. I would personally be responsible for their good conduct. It would be a most generous contribution to the war effort, Mr Maloney, and, if I may say so, deserving of the highest praise.'

Harry showed no surprise at this extraordinary plan to take possession of Marston Park. Sixty children and nuns all over the place! He had forgotten Kitty until she touched his sleeve, and he turned to look at her. She was nodding agreement, and it was not often he saw her looking so flushed and eager.

'How about Sammy? What is she going to say about such an invasion?' he asked.

'Sammy will love it, and so shall I.'

'I can see all our servants giving notice.'

'Let them. Anyway, the younger ones will be conscripted. We can do the same as Sir Neville Franklin in the last war, and move into a few rooms with a side entrance, and manage with one elderly servant.'

Harry shrugged. What did it matter? He still had the London flat, and Diane had her own house at Little Venice.

'Very well. Go ahead. Let my wife know when to expect them,' he told Father O'Leary.

'God will bless you, my son,' said the priest, fervently, as they shook hands – and Kitty was squeezing his arm.

146

They wasted no time. In less than a month, all the servants, apart from Wilhelmina, the sturdy little widow from Rotterdam, had left Marston Park, and two nuns had arrived with the cook and the gardener-handyman, not only to supervise such a major operation, but to roll up their sleeves and work hard. The study was retained as the headquarters of the local WVS as promised, and Sammy, Kitty and Wilhelmina moved into the flat.

Now it was Kitty who had taken on a new lease of life. Here was work in place of idleness, and children would soon be swarming all over the house. Marston Park had been a white elephant for so long, with so many empty rooms that echoed to the ghosts of the Franklins. She and Sammy helped to move furniture and make up the rows of small beds in the main bedrooms. Vans and lorries had been disgorging beds, chairs, tables, desks, linen and blankets, kitchen equipment, hockey sticks and musical instruments, in the courtyard. So much equipment was necessary to house such a large family. It was going to be a long war, according to Father O'Leary, and the nuns had the utmost faith in his predictions, and the warmest regard for his cleverness in settling such a big problem so happily for all concerned. The children would benefit from the pure country air, and their anxious mothers be assured of their care and safety. A dozen or so small boys would be included in the evacuation, and older sisters would be instructed to help with dressing and washing and baths. The days would be organised with the same disciplined routine to which the children were accustomed, and nothing would be neglected. There would be a time to work and a time to play, a time for prayers and a time for meals, a time to attend Mass in Father O'Leary's church and a time to spend their pocket money in the village shops.

Sister Agnes and Sister Josephine were so overjoyed

147

to be bringing the children to Marston Park that they made light of every obstacle. When Mother Superior had decided to evacuate the school, it had been assumed that the children would be billeted in the village, and they were fully prepared to share the village school with the local children. Perhaps an agreement could be reached with the Schoolmaster for their own children to attend school in the afternoons, and the local children in the mornings. Now all their problems had been solved, and all their doubts removed. Sister Agnes and Sister Josephine went about their duties convinced of Divine intervention on their behalf. Kitty was frequently consulted, and suddenly found herself indispensable. Her small, narrow world had expanded, and she bustled about importantly. One afternoon, she took the Sisters to Russets, and introduced them to Lucy who escorted them over the house and the farm, then settled down in the kitchen with cups of tea to discuss the buying and selling of milk, eggs, butter and cheese, old fowls for boiling, and roasting fowls for Christmas. Sister Agnes, no longer young and rather fat, was offered the rocking-chair, but preferred to sit upright on a kitchen chair. Both nuns sat with straight backs and folded hands. There was a quietness and tranquillity in their demeanour that Lucy admired. She had expected to be embarrassed by their piety, instead of which she was joining in the laughter when Sister Agnes told a funny story.

It so happened that Maggie was home from school with a chesty cold, and smelling strongly of camphorated oil. In the short space of half an hour, she had lost her heart to the gentle Sister Josephine, and made up her mind to be a NUN – not a MISSIONARY! It was not a sudden whim that would pass, but a firm resolve by a determined little girl naturally inclined to religious tendencies. Maggie had so far received little encouragement and a great deal of scepticism from her long suffering family. Now she haunted Marston Park every Saturday as soon as she had finished the jobs that Lucy insisted on.

When the children arrived, she joined in their walks to the village, made friends with a girl her own age – a devout little Catholic called Patsy Brown – and was actually allowed to sit in a back pew in the Catholic church while Father O'Leary heard the children's confessions. It was a strange and beautiful new world, so far removed from that spartan Mission in the Congo. The smell of incense, the kneeling nuns, the Madonna and Child, the lighted candles on which every child had spent a penny, the pictures and statues of the saints, and above all, the holy atmosphere. Her first and lasting impression would always remain with her, for young Maggie Blunt, a farmer's daughter, was destined to enter a religious order at the age of seventeen, and nobody would dissuade her.

Lucy remembered the storm of protest when Parson's grandson, young Richard, the brother of Harriet, had been converted to the Catholic Faith, and was thereafter one of the teaching Brothers in a Jesuit College in Brussels. So Lucy made no protest, and allowed the child the privilege of deciding her own future.

The puddings were made, the Christmas cake rich in fruit, and a large jar of mincemeat stood ready on the pantry shelf for this first Christmas of the war. John and Midge had seeded the raisins and eaten the sugar in the candied peel. Lucy was reminded of all the other Christmases, when her own three boys had 'helped' to prepare the mixture. Then came Charles, and, much later, her little 'Benjamin' – the best-loved of all her boys. Now it was her grandchildren.

The years were slipping away, but she still had her health and strength, and she was still the mistress of Russets. Carrie was not a demanding daughter-in-law, and had no wish to hold the reins. Martha had been invited for Christmas, and would bring useful presents for everyone – hand-knitted jerseys for the children, cardigans for Lucy, Carrie and Katie, and socks for Tom. She had more time for knitting now in the long evenings, and no Andrew to complain about her clicking knitting needles. She would miss her grandsons, but she was a sensible woman, and realised there must be a measure of sadness for most women in this first Christmas of the war. Last year there had been a tree to decorate for Mark and Matthew, stockings to fill, and dinner to cook. They had manfully filled the log baskets in the woodshed, then they lay on the floor, playing with the clockwork train and all its accessories their parents had ordered from Hamleys in Regent Street. They had eaten their sugar mice before breakfast, and were most reluctant to leave the train to accompany the grown-ups to church, but Andrew insisted.

So many memories for Martha on Christmas morning of that pure young voice leading the choir in the processional hymn:

> Once in Royal David's city,
> Stood a lowly cattle shed,
> Where a mother laid her Baby,
> With a manger for His bed.

She had wept with pride and joy as her son passed by in his freshly starched surplice, but he had been staring straight ahead, and had not seen her tears. It was a long time ago, and other boy soloists had taken his place at Christmas, Easter and Harvest Thanksgiving, but to a fond mother, there is nothing to compare with the voice of her own son. This year she would be staying at Russets for three days. This year she would pray for Julian, and all those gallant young men for whom the festival of Christmas would be swallowed up in the call to duty. Lucy shared his letters, and read them over the phone. She too was surprised at his poetic descriptions of their flights and their aircraft. No fear, no horror, no disaster crept into his letters. This was a new Julian they hardly recognised, and for young Dick, who had expected to hear all the gruesome details of the bombing raids and the drama of the 'dog-fights', it was disappointing.

Wendy had dutifully completed one term at the Secretarial College, and after a week's holiday at Christmas, was due to return the first week of January. Both parents had been deceived into thinking she had accepted it sensibly, but Ruby was not taken in. Like so many grandparents, she seemed to have a better understanding of the young generation, and was much more inclined to sympathise than criticise youthful aspirations.

Wendy had no intention of enduring a second term in that hateful place. It was not true, that oft-repeated reminder of Daddy, 'Your Mother knows best, pet'. She saw the war as a golden opportunity to escape, and she haunted the reading room at the Public Library to examine all the lists of 'Situations Vacant' in the leading London dailies. She was not exactly sure what she was looking for, but she knew it must be connected with the world of music, and it must provide enough money to live independently. That word – independence –

beckoned like a beacon, and all her young enthusiasm could see a future bright with success and rich in experience. Only Julian shared her secret, and he had promised faithfully not to disclose it to a living soul. In return for his loyalty, she had encouraged him to talk about his own feelings and fears in his letters. She admired his courage tremendously. He was wearing the little silver medallion of St Christopher she had sent for his birthday, and she kept all his letters in the locked drawer in her room. He had told her he could not keep her letters because nothing was private with the chaps. Only his thoughts were private.

Dear Julian! That was rather sweet – only his thoughts were private. And she was part of that privacy. She knew now that he loved her dearly, and that love had grown out of the early relationship of big brother and little sister. Since war was declared he had signed her letters, 'Yours ever, Julian'. He wrote so frankly now of the fears and feelings he could not confide to the family at Russets. Once he wrote – 'I do not want to die, but if I must, then let it be swift and not a long drawn out agony, for then I should be a coward.' Another time he wrote:

My best friend was shot down a week ago when we were almost within sight of the coast. No trace has been found of him or his Spitfire. He was a Pole with an unpronounceable name and we called him Pete. We trained together, and won our wings the same day. In peace time he was a Count, and he was the only son. There were four sisters. Nothing had been heard of them since 1938. He was homesick for Poland, but so brave and cheerful. It seems such a waste, sweetheart. All that courage and endurance only to be snuffed out like a candle. Poor old Pete.

Another time he wrote: 'If I get out of this alive, my very dear Wendy, I shall never go farther afield than Russets!'

It was there, at last, and it seemed to stand out in bold type, directed especially to Wendy Simmons! IT read: 'An accompanist wanted for small concert party to tour the British Isles and entertain the Forces and factory workers. Small salary, but all expenses paid. Apply immediately Box 3520 of this paper.'

Her heart was singing as she copied it down in her notebook and hurried home to write and post the letter. Gran was very busy in the kitchen as usual, and showed no surprise to receive a hug and a kiss from her impulsive young grand-daughter. Wendy had always been an affectionate child. Temperamental, yes, but all clever children were difficult to live with. Ruby watched her favourite grandchild running down the road to post her letter, some time later. That would be for Julian. Wendy wrote regularly, but Julian's letters were erratic, and that was to be expected.

Climbing the steep path, her mind in a whirl of hopeful expectancy and doubtful pessimism, Wendy walked briskly across the deserted Common on that grey December day, hugging her secret. If only Julian were here. She would not mention it yet in case she was disappointed. Would there be a number of applicants? Would she be rejected because she was too young? How soon could she expect a reply? 'Please God, let them take me,' she whispered. As a child she had prayed: 'Please God, don't let Daddy love Mummy best.' 'Please God, let me pass my exam.' 'Please God, give me breasts like the other girls.'

Suddenly she stopped dead – a dreadful thought. Supposing Mother got hold of the letter. She would know it was not Julian's handwriting. Another urgent

153

prayer was called for – 'Please God, don't let Mother get hold of the letter.' She was shivering now in the cold wind, for she hadn't stopped to put on her coat and the woolly cap with the long tassle that Gran had knitted, with matching gloves, for Christmas. She turned and ran back, near to tears, with this new anxiety. The whole lovely plan would be ruined. She would never get away! She could see herself tapping a horrid typewriter in some dreary office till her hair was turning grey – unless Julian rescued her.

When Cynthia announced the following morning that she would be on night duty again, and sleeping in the hospital annexe, Wendy could hardly contain the impulse to shout 'Thank you, God!' She had often wondered in the past if God listened, but here was proof that he did. Who was it said 'Put your trust in the Lord, and keep your powder dry'? That meant you had to make a big effort yourself before you could expect help from God.

When Ruby saw her waiting for the postman, she thought, 'Poor child. I hope she won't be disappointed again.'

As soon as the letters dropped on the mat, Wendy snatched them up. A solicitor had letters every day, and the tradesmen had sent their monthly bills. Her heart missed a beat – it was here – a letter addressed to Miss Wendy Simmons in a bold, masculine hand!

'So you got your letter from Julian, love?' Ruby had no need to ask. The child's face was radiant. She waved the letter and dashed upstairs. With trembling fingers she tore it open, and read:

Dear Miss Simmons.

Thank you for your application and the charming snapshot you enclosed. With all your qualifications I am sure we should get along splendidly. We are a small company, just myself and my wife, Nancy, and our comedian, Lennie O'Brien. We three have been in show business since the last war. So we are real old troupers. However, this war has closed the theatres, and we did not fancy a long period of resting. Apart from an accompanist, we also need someone to play small parts in our comedy sketches, and I expect you would enjoy taking part. There would be ample opportunity to include a couple of classical piano pieces in our repertoire, and these you could choose. We anticipate lively and appreciative audiences, but I must warn you it will not be an easy life. Travelling will be difficult with so many wartime restrictions. Lodgings can be uncomfortable. It all depends on the landlady. As for 'theatres' – draughty village halls, smoky barrack rooms, and Dutch barns. If you have not been put off by all these obstacles, we shall be delighted to welcome you into our midst. Perhaps a month's trial period would be a good idea, then you would feel free to change your mind? I suggest you join us for lunch at the Regent Palace Hotel, Piccadilly, on 3rd January, then we can get to know each other before we leave for Salisbury the following day. I will book accommodation at the hotel for one night. Please bring only the minimum of luggage, but include at least three pretty frocks, *not* evening gowns. Looking forward to meeting you,

Yours very sincerely,
Nigel Bannister.

P.S. Look for us in the foyer. I shall be wearing a red carnation. N.B.

The 3rd January was the very day the new term started at the Secretarial College. What fantastic luck! But how to

155

get out of the house with a suitcase? She was proud of the way her mind was coping, and not being bowled over at such a stupendous decision. Never in her short life had she been allowed to decide anything, and now she was embarking on a brave new chapter that would stagger Mother with its sheer audacity.

It was quite simple. She would pack the case and push it into the wardrobe. Gran was unlikely to look there, but she would look under the bed. Cynthia had instructed her daughter during her schooldays to keep her room clean and tidy, but if Ruby hadn't taken a hand from time to time, her daughter-in-law would have been horrified at the clutter. No, it shouldn't be too difficult. Wait until Gran went out shopping, and with Daddy in his office and Mother at the hospital, she could slip out with her case, take a bus to the station, and leave it in the left luggage to be collected on the 3rd January. Of one thing she was absolutely certain. She would not change her mind at the end of the month's trial period. She would make herself so indispensable, they would beg her to stay.

'Show business' was something completely alien and mysterious. She hadn't been to a theatre since the *Peter Pan* days. It was the cinema she enjoyed. This was a weekly treat with Gran, and they shared a box of liquorice all-sorts.

Curled under the rumpled eiderdown, she read the letter through a second time and found it every bit as exciting as the first time. No words could describe the relief of being rescued from a lifetime of typing and shorthand. NIGEL BANNISTER. She was ready to adore him even before they met! He would be gallant, charming, and altogether delightful. Only a very nice person could write such a nice letter. Three pretty frocks were no problem; she had a whole range of pretty frocks that Gran had made, and they had been washed, starched and ironed ready for another Summer. She supposed their landladies would do their washing. Gran had spoiled her in so many ways, and she had never washed anything but her own stockings. She could sew on a button, but that was the limit of her handiwork with needle and thread. It was Gran she would miss most, and Gran who would be most upset. To be deceitful or dishonest was almost a crime, and the first, and most important commandment was 'Honour thy father and thy mother'. Gran had very high working-class principles. Mother's high principles were upper class. It was ridiculous to suppose she had changed when she married Daddy. He liked her that way. So did Gran. As Gran would say, 'Your Mother has only to open her mouth and you know she's a lady.'

Wendy sighed. She had a very strong feeling that 'show business' would be regarded as the ultimate depth of degradation for a strictly brought up young lady!

Everything went according to plan. She was shivering with nervous excitement as she passed through the swing doors of the imposing London hotel, into the crowded foyer, and stood there, completely bewildered by the bustling activity in an atmosphere of dazzling lights and luxurious warmth. There were people everywhere, and many in uniform, for this particular hotel in the heart of Piccadilly was a favourite rendezvous. A lovely woman in a sari glided past, holding a small black-eyed boy by the hand. They seemed quite at home in the hotel, and they crossed the foyer, stepped into a lift, and disappeared.

'It must be Wendy?'

A tall, distinguished grey-haired man was smiling down at her. She nodded, tremulously.

'And I'm Nigel Bannister. Welcome, my dear.'

'How do you do, Mr Bannister.'

He took her hand in a warm clasp. 'You must call me Nigel. There are no surnames in show business,' he told her – and picked up her case. They walked together to a nearby corner, where a smartly dressed woman sat waiting with a rather untidy little man.

'My wife, Nancy,' said Nigel Bannister. 'You see, darling, I was not mistaken.'

'How could you be mistaken, darling, when you had the photograph?' cooed Nancy, with an artificial smile. She was a handsome woman of uncertain age, rather overdressed, wearing a lot of cheap jewellery and a pungent scent. Her thick, auburn hair was piled in curls, and her hat sat precariously on top of the curls. She had green eyes – cat's eyes!

The untidy little man had jumped up to grip Wendy's hand.

'Lennie O'Brien at your service, Miss. Pleased to meet yer.'

There was nothing artificial about Lennie. Was he a Cockney? Wendy wondered. They seemed an odd sort of trio to be travelling together. The Bannisters, so obviously sophisticated and this shabby little man with his cheeky grin. In a sudden flash of enlightenment she realised why she had been chosen to complete the foursome. They wanted someone young and pretty and rather naïve. They would emphasise her youth. Nancy Bannister was staring at her with barely concealed dislike, for her husband was still holding her hand. Nancy didn't trust him. It wouldn't be the first time he had made her feel she was past her prime. She *was* past her prime, but she had no intention of losing her grip on this handsome, philandering husband of hers, who could turn on the charm as easily as turning on a tap.

'Come with me to Reception, my dear, and I will book

158

you in. You will have to sign,' he was saying, smoothly, as to an ignorant child. Perhaps she *was* ignorant of the procedure in a big London hotel. And with that look of starry-eyed wonder, she could be as innocent as a new-born babe. Such childish clothes – the knitted cap with the long tassle, matching gloves and a fawn coat, double-breasted.

When they were out of earshot, Lennie chuckled, ''ere we go again, Nance!'

'Don't be vulgar!' she snapped irritably. She did wish he wouldn't call her Nance, but she had to put up with it for the sake of his usefulness. Lennie was everybody's dogsbody. He did all the running about to find lodgings, and when she and Nigel were broke, he paid for the lodgings. A good comic was a great asset for this tour.

'There's a war on, ducks. Make em laugh!' he told her. He was right, of course. Second-rate tenors and sopranos were two-a-penny, but not good comedians. She had no illusions. Show business had always been a precarious living for second-rate artists, and they were lucky to meet Lennie in that agents' office in September. Now they had the girl, an added attraction where men were concerned, and the majority of their audiences would be comprised of men. If only she could trust Nigel. If only she were not so jealous. If only she were twenty years younger!

'Got the key, guv?' Lennie was on his feet again, ready to carry the case and escort Wendy to her room. She followed him to the lift, and he pressed the button and grinned. 'Not ter worry, kid. You'll be OK.'

'I'm not worrying.'

'In you go.' He gave her a push and she stepped inside. 'Third floor. The rest of us is all on the same floor, so you won't feel lonesome.'

She almost had to run to keep up with him down the

long carpeted corridor. She had never known anyone move so quickly. Then he was opening a door and standing back. She went inside and gasped.

'But this is luxury.'

'Not bad. They say all them 'undreds of bedrooms is exactly alike. So it don't matter which one you get.'

'It's so *warm* and comfortable.'

He frowned. 'Nah don't get the wrong idea, kid. This is only for one night. Lodgings on tour won't be nothing like this.'

'Look, there's a telephone.'

'You can order anything you like, only don't forget it goes on the bill.'

'Could I ask for an early cup of tea? Gran always brought me a cup of tea at 7 o'clock.'

'You live with yer Gran?'

'Yes.'

'She didn't mind jew coming away?'

'No.'

'You're blushing. That ain't strictly true, is it?' She shook her head. 'You mean? – oh, my gawd! Your Gran don't know?'

'She does now. I have left a note.'

'Blimey! You got a nerve!'

'You won't tell the others? They would send me home. *Please*, Lennie.'

'Okey-doke. Don't cry. Where jew say you come from?'

'Tunbridge Wells.'

'I used ter live in Kent when I was a nipper. I ain't a London born Cockney.'

'What part of Kent?'

'Village called Fairfields.'

'But that's where Daddy lived.'

'So you've got a Daddy?'

'Yes.'

'And a Mummy?'

'Yes.'

He gripped her shoulders hard. 'Nah look 'ere, Wendy. Don't try no tricks, not with Lennie. If you an' me is going to be pals in show business we got ter trust one another, see?' She nodded, near to tears again. 'Nah, start at the beginning and spill the beans.'

She told him the full story, and he looked thoughtful. 'Is yer Dad's name Freddie?' he asked.

'Yes.'

'Well I be jiggered! We was neighbours in Richmond Row. An' yer Dad married into the upper class, one of them daughters of Sir Neville Franklin at Marston Park?'

'That's right.'

'You got class, ducks. It stands out like a sore thumb.'

'Oh, Lennie, you *are* funny,' she giggled happily.

'That's what they pay me for.' He was sitting on the radiator. He also seemed quite at home in this smart hotel, she thought, but perhaps he was one of those people who quickly adapted to any situation.

'Jus' warming me bum!' he told her, and she giggled again. It was going to be all right.

'Yer Dad was always different from the rest of us kids in Richmond Row. Always got 'is 'ead stuck in a book. No football. No larking abaht with girls. Not like me. They said I was an 'oly terror.'

She could see he was proud of such a reputation, and he still looked like a cheeky urchin when he grinned.

'We was so bloody poor, our lot, we 'ad ter share two bloody bloaters between the four of us! Me brother Mike 'ad a ferret, an' went poaching for rabbits, but 'e got picked up one Christmas Eve so we never 'ad no Christmas dinner. They locked 'im up 'cause 'e 'ad no

161

money ter pay the fine. When 'e come out, 'e ran away an' joined the Army. Mike was fifteen but 'e passed for seventeen. They never asked many questions, not in them days. When I was fourteen, I left school, then I cleared art. There wasn't no future, not for any of us kids, only if we cleared art. I came ter London, lived rough, an' picked up a few coppers from the barrer boys in the market. They liked a nipper what could fetch a cup of char, an' sweep up all the muck. Then I got a chance ter serve the customers. That was ol' Jock, a cheap-jack, what liked 'is drop o' booze. So 'e give me a tanner for minding the barrer, see? Then 'e got ter leaving me 'alf the day, an' the silly old sod were proper fuddled when 'e come back. That's when I made a bit for meself on the quiet. I could charge the customers what I liked when I was in charge of the barrer. Blimey! I made a packet out of them American dames. They'd fall for anything, they was so dim. "Look, Honey, genu*ine* antiques!"' He chuckled. 'Genuine my ass. There wasn't nothing on that barrer worth more than a couple of bob!'

'But that was cheating, Lennie.'

He shook his head. 'Nah, yer got ter be crafty to make a living in the market.'

'Then what happened?'

'Ol' Jock dropped dead one dye with an 'eart attack, an' there wasn't no relations, so I took over the barrer. By the time I was seventeen, I 'ad three barrers, an' three little Cockney kids working for me. That's enterprise, ducks. That's enterprise.'

'But why did you leave the market if you were doing so well? How did you get into show business?'

'That's another story. Come on, get cracking, or we shall 'ave the boss up 'ere. Leave yer 'at and coat on the bed, an' the case. You can get unpacked later.'

'Just a minute. I must tidy my hair.'

'It don't need no tidying. It's okey-doke.'

'I wish I had hair like Mrs Bannister.'

Lennie nearly choked with laughter. 'T'ain't real, my ducks. It's a wig!'

Nigel Bannister was pacing up and down. He was not a patient man, as Wendy would soon discover.

'You've taken your time. Now we shall probably have to queue for a table for lunch, and if there is one thing I object to it's queueing,' he asserted.

Lennie had straightened his face. 'Sorry, guv.'

'It's my fault. I was looking at everything. It's absolutely super! I have never stayed in an hotel. When we go on holiday to the seaside we always stay in the same lodgings because it suits Daddy,' Wendy explained.

Nigel was amused at such candidness. It was quite a novelty in this day and age to find a girl so obviously unspoiled. But if he had heard the conversation in the bedroom, he would not have taken her on tour. It was not the first time Nancy had accused him of baby snatching. Lennie had already concluded that a girl with Wendy's background and upper-class accent would be very carefully brought up. But it took guts to leave a decent home. Not like Richmond Row, where you were glad to get away.

Nancy was looking peeved about something, and he guessed it was another pretty girl that had upset the apple cart. She was a bad-tempered bitch. Couldn't she see the kid was an asset? The boys wouldn't take kindly to a show without a pretty girl. It was going to be a bit of a lark, keeping the peace and playing nursemaid to young Wendy, he was thinking, as he followed them to the restaurant, the boss leading the way. Give the boss his due, not only audiences were smitten by his personality, he really could charm a bird off a bough.

The head waiter remembered a vacant table, and they

were comfortably seated within a few minutes, with a young subordinate hovering with enormous menus.

'That was clever of you, darling,' cooed Nancy. She enjoyed her food, and was determined to make the most of an unexpected luxury. There would be plenty of time later for fish and chips in dreary lodgings.

'It's easy, darling, when you know how,' her husband bowed, and patted her hand affectionately. He loved to play mine host. Nothing like good food and a bottle of wine to ease the strain of a new relationship, and put Nancy in a good humour. That was important, and he was not such a fool as to ignore its importance. She was jealous. It was natural, but he could always make it up to her in bed.

'Well, my dear, have you decided?' he asked Wendy.

She shook her head. She was appalled at the size of the menu and the price of each individual item.

'What are *you* having?'

'Fillet steak.'

'Me, too,' echoed Nancy and Lennie.

'Me, too!' giggled Wendy, glad to be relieved of the responsibility of choosing.

When Nigel had given precise instructions about cooking the steaks, he found the wine waiter hovering, and knew exactly what to order. Nancy was almost purring with satisfaction now. This was her kind of world. She could easily forget the war, and the hardships of show business, given enough money to stay here indefinitely. Perhaps Lennie was paying? – or Nigel had 'borrowed' another hundred pounds from some unsuspecting acquaintance he met in the bar? 'Why worry your pretty head, darling?' he would ask when she questioned the source of the bulging wallet. She had often wondered why Nigel had married her.

'The green eyes, darling. I never could resist green eyes.'

'Do you still love me, darling?' was a question that women never tired of asking.

'My darling, I adore you.'

She had to believe him. But tonight, because of the girl, she would have to be reassured again. With more good food and wine this evening, Nigel's ardent love-making should restore all her confidence.

So she watched with pleasure the girl's obvious dismay at the size of the steak and the lavish garnishing of fried onions and mushrooms, and grilled tomatoes; sauté potatoes and French beans were spooned on her dish before she could open her mouth to protest.

'Serve her right if she's got a delicate digestion,' Nancy thought spitefully. Nigel would soon lose interest in a pretty protégé who spewed up her dinner.

Similar thoughts were bothering Lennie, but he wanted to save the kid embarrassment, so chose a practical approach. When he had almost cleared his own dish, he leaned over and helped himself from Wendy's. She smiled her thanks.

'It's a swap, ducks. You can 'ave me portion of ice cream,' he told her with a sly wink.

Nigel, Nancy and Wendy spent the afternoon in the crowded lounge, where an orchestra played selections from Gilbert and Sullivan, Ivor Novello, and the ever-popular Strauss waltzes. Lennie went off to Soho to visit his old haunts, but came back in time for tea, his peaked face redened with the biting wind, and his thin shoulders hunched in a fisherman's jersey. With a check cap that he seemed reluctant to remove, a red silk scarf in place of a tie, baggy flannel trousers and scuffed suede shoes, he was an embarrassment to his companions, but quite unaware of the fact. 'Embarrassment' was not a word that had ever appeared in Lennie's vocabulary. 'Impossible' was another. Take the question of ready cash:

165

Lennie could always find something to buy and re-sell at a profit. A mug was born every minute! There never was a time when his pockets were empty. One of his earliest transactions – he loved that word, 'transaction' – had been a bit of a lark. All the little girls at the village school were not lucky enough to have half-pennies to spend on sweets, but those who did had to hand them over, or else! 'Jew want me 'and up yer drawers?' he would ask, innocent like, and they paid up. All but Maggie Styles, and she was hot stuff at the age of ten! Carrie Simmons, Freddie's kid sister, was the best bet, however, because she had three brothers who kept her supplied with half-pennies, and she carried them in the pocket of her pinafore. But that was a long time ago. Girls were safe enough with Lennie O'Brien these days, for he hadn't fancied anyone, not since Lena, and that was way back in the First World War. Lena was a prostitute, but she wasn't a tart. And it wasn't her fault because her Mum had put her wise to it when she was just a kid. Lena would break a halfpenny in half to share with a pal. He should know, for when trade was bad on the barrer, she never charged him a penny for his lodgings. Then she got took ill during the War, just when her own trade was brisk in Piccadilly, and the kind little doctor in Soho told him on the quiet it was cancer, and she hadn't long to live. Blimey! He felt terrible! The doctor wanted to send her to hospital, but she begged to be allowed to stay at home – home was a couple of shabby rooms in a drab basement. Then it was his turn to repay all the kindness he had received. He looked after her good and proper, like she was the Queen of Sheba, and she lived for nine months. In those nine months, Lennie knew the meaning of unselfish devotion, for the first time in his life.

Lena would have been so proud of his success in show

business. He could always make her laugh. Today he had stood on the pavement in Soho, looking down on that same basement, choked with bitter-sweet memories. With these memories still uppermost in his mind, he drank two cups of tea, and ate a couple of chocolate éclairs, then he began to fidget and he wished he could spend the evening in his favourite pub in Soho. The kid was looking pale, and she had refused the cakes.

'Like ter look around, ducks?' he invited.

'Yes, *please*. If Mr and Mrs Bannister will excuse me?' She had lovely manners, he thought, but she couldn't get her tongue around to calling them Nigel and Nancy, not yet.

'Off you go!' The boss was OK, and Nancy purring like a cat that had stolen the cream.

'You all right, kid?' he asked, when they were back in the foyer.

'I do feel rather sick. I am not used to such rich food. Do you think I could be excused from dinner? Would they be annoyed? If I could just lie down quietly, I think it would pass.'

'It's not only the food, ducks. It's all the excitement. Don't jew worry. Lennie will fix it.' He squeezed her hand.

Going up in the lift she held her stomach and smiled tremulously. But when he left her at the door, she was near to tears.

'Nah, don't forget to order that early cup o' tea for yer won't 'ave yer Gran to wait on yer tomorrer,' he reminded her.

'Oh, *Lennie*,' she whispered.

He kissed the tip of her nose and closed the door.

'Poor little blighter. She's bit orf more than she can chew,' he told himself, as he ran downstairs. He spent the next hour or so in the bar, then went back to the lounge to collect the others for dinner.

When the door had closed on Lennie, Wendy sat on the edge of the bed, holding her stomach, weak tears flooding her eyes. She knew already it had been a mistake, but it was too late now to have regrets. If only Gran were here to fill a hot water bottle. If only she hadn't been persuaded to drink a little wine. The taste was so bitter, she must have pulled a face because Lennie had finished it. He was kind, and she felt at ease with him, but not with the others.

When she had unpacked her case, she undressed and got into bed. It was a little after 6 o'clock, and she thought of Gran and Daddy listening to the news on the wireless. In the luxury of a London hotel, it was difficult to imagine a war was being fought and men were dying. Then she remembered Julian, and said a little prayer for his safety. She had his photograph in the pocket of the case, together with her Post Office Savings Account. It contained the sum of fifty-three pounds and gave her a pleasant sense of prosperity. She wondered how much she would be paid for her services as an accompanist, but she was too shy to ask, and would have to wait and see.

She fell asleep almost immediately, and slept for twelve hours. Lennie had pushed a note under the door. It read:

Dear Wendy,
    Ask the maid to bring your breakfast at 7.30. Meet us downstairs at 8.
    Chin up. Lennie.

Then she remembered the early morning tea. Tentatively she lifted the receiver. A brisk voice answered immediately. 'Room Service. Good morning.'

'Good morning. May I have a cup of tea now, please, and breakfast at 7.30?'

'Certainly, Madam.'

The receiver clicked. It was done! Everything was so simple. She rinsed her face, combed her hair and climbed back into bed. A grey-haired chambermaid carried in a tray and laid it across her knees, not just a cup of tea, but a tea-pot, milk and sugar, and two biscuits.

'Thank you very much.'

The woman smiled at the girl's obvious delight in what, for her, had become a mere routine service for more years than she cared to remember.

'What would you like for your breakfast, Miss?' she asked.

'Can I choose?'

The recital was automatic – fruit juice, prunes, grapefruit, cereal, eggs, boiled, poached or scrambled. Kippers, kedgeree, bacon and egg and grilled tomato, toast, rolls and butter, marmalade and honey. Tea or coffee.

'But that's fabulous!'

The woman shrugged. 'It's usual. Is this your first visit to this hotel?'

'It's my first visit to *any* hotel, and it's absolutely super!'

'How long are you staying?'

'Only one night. We have to leave after breakfast.'

'Nobody stays long. It's in and out all the time, especially now there's a war on.'

'It must be a very exciting place to work in.'

'It's a job.'

'I'm starting on my first job today.'

'You don't look old enough to be working. I thought you would probably be at boarding school and having a special treat before you went back. We get a lot of boarding school children staying overnight.'

'Oh no, I have finished with school. I have been engaged as an accompanist with a small touring company. We are going to entertain the Forces and the factory workers, and it's going to be great fun.'

'I hope so,' she answered, dubiously. This bright-eyed girl reminded her of her own youngest daughter, already in the uniform of the ATS. The young ones all had the same idea, that it was going to be fun, but they didn't remember the First World War. Fun? My God!

'Well, now, have you decided what you would like for breakfast?' she asked, kindly.

'Yes, I have – fruit juice, cereal, scrambled egg, roll and butter and honey.'

'Tea or coffee?'

'Coffee, please.'

By the time she returned with a loaded tray, Wendy had discovered a bathroom, taken a bath, dressed and packed. She was hungry now, and ate every morsel, leaving sixpence on the tray. The chambermaid, busy with a rush of orders for 8 o'clock breakfast, watched the neat little figure tripping gaily down the corridor, swinging her case. In her knitted cap and buttoned coat she looked very childish. What were her parents thinking of? They surely couldn't be aware of the dangers. But it was not her business, and the girl was soon forgotten.

Nigel and Nancy Bannister were standing with their luggage in the foyer. There was no sign of Lennie. She greeted them with a cheery 'Good morning'. They hardly answered, and did not enquire if she was feeling better. She had still to learn that early morning is not the time for cheerfulness when tempers were short.

'Where's Lennie?' she asked.

'Outside, getting a taxi,' Nigel barked irritably.

She stood there, watching impatient guests waiting to pay their accounts, and the swing doors constantly rotating. Then Lennie pushed his way in, still dressed in the odd assortment of clothes that would soon become familiar on and off the stage.

'OK, Guv,' he grinned at Wendy, picked up two of the heaviest suitcases, and hurried back through the swing doors. Nigel and Nancy each took a case, and Wendy followed them out. The taxi driver had already manoeuvred a tin trunk into position, and quickly stacked the cases while they climbed in. They travelled to Paddington through crowded streets on this grey, January day that would mark the end of Wendy's innocent youth.

The scene at Paddington was chaotic. There were no porters. Everyone carried or pushed their own luggage. The Forces had commandeered all the trolleys that were piled high with kit-bags. There were queues everywhere – for incoming taxis, for tickets, for kiosks, for buffets, and for a place on the crowded platforms. All the trains were late. Lennie scuttled off, came back with a porter's truck, and piled on their luggage. They followed in single file, almost running to keep up with the comic little figure in the big check cap. It was Lennie who elbowed his way on to the train, scattered cases and newspapers over the seats of the nearest compartment, and grinned, unabashed, at the agitated women hot on his heels.

'Sorry, ducks, engaged. Sit down, for Gawd's sake!' he growled at his admiring companions, and disappeared.

'What's he doing now?' Wendy asked, anxiously.

'Putting the trunk into the luggage van.' Nigel was stacking the cases on the racks while Nancy sank thankfully into a corner seat. She had not spoken a single word since they left the hotel, but now she wrapped herself in her fur coat and complained, sulkily, 'They haven't turned on the heating, darling.'

'They probably won't turn it on. There's a war on, darling,' Nigel reminded her.

'As if I didn't know,' she retorted.

'Okey-doke.' Lennie was back, and Wendy breathed a sigh of relief. She had already discovered the little comedian was absolutely indispensable.

Some time later, the doors were slammed and the train moved off jerkily. Conflicting emotions battled in Wendy's racing heart – excitement, anticipation – and fear of the unknown future that lay ahead.

The lofty spire of Salisbury Cathedral, blanketed in mist, reached for the sky. In the smoke-filled compartment, three much-travelled adults yawned and stretched, and a girl for whom everything was new and fresh as the morning dew, recovered her spirits. As the train pulled into the station the doors burst open, and the passengers spilled out. They would be spending a couple of weeks in Salisbury, giving shows to the various Army units in training on Salisbury Plain. Rehearsals would take up most of the first week. Nigel had been responsible for the arrangements with the various authorities, and their lodgings had been booked well in advance. Thereafter, they would just have to make do with the accommodation Lennie could find. One step at a time was as far as they could see, and in this respect the three seasoned troopers shared a common bond. *The show must go on*. This was their creed, and it served to stabilise their individual preferences and prejudices.

The young novice in their midst had a lot to learn, and there would be no sympathy, not even from Lennie, if she failed to pull her weight. If he must play the nurse-maid, he would not spoil his charge. Neither her back-

172

ground nor her innocent youth would protect her in this demanding new world of show business. It was a great test of character, and Wendy would succeed or fail. Nigel Bannister would soon know if he had chosen wisely. An accompanist played a very important part. 'Any fool can play the piano, but only a versatile performer can cope intelligently with a varied repertoire,' he had told Nancy when they first discussed the tour. Nancy was still dubious. Being Nigel, he had fallen for a pretty face and had still to prove that her qualifications were genuine. If the show was a flop, Nancy would blame Wendy and Nigel would send her home. It was a risk they had to take, he insisted. Wendy had a pleasing personality, a charming smile, and a cultured voice. For the rest, it was just a matter of practice. They would rehearse every item over and over again until it was perfect – and Nigel was a perfectionist.

Mrs Green, their first landlady, had an air of refinement, and a quiet manner. Her late husband had been a verger at the Cathedral for nearly 40 years, and their lives had been steeped in tradition in an atmosphere of sanctity and ceremony. Lodgers were a species of the human race she had only recently encountered since her address had been added to the list of accommodation in a city bursting at the seams with an influx of civil servants, clerks and typists. Her tall terrace house lent itself to lodgers, however, and she welcomed her first guests from the world of show business with a shy smile, and showed them into a sitting-room crowded with heavy furniture, smelling strongly of Mansion polish. A small fire barely warmed the room on this raw January day, and there was no sign of any refreshment.

'I think you will find the accommodation adequate,' Mrs Green murmured, and Nigel thanked her politely and asked to see the bedrooms. They followed her up the narrow stairs. Nigel, Nancy and Wendy each carried a case, and Lennie carried two. The tin trunk had been dumped in the hall. The double room on the first floor that Nancy claimed for herself and Nigel had an adjoining bathroom, and the single room was suitable for Wendy. Lennie being the obvious choice for the other single room on the second floor, the others did not need to climb any more stairs.

Nigel and Nancy dropped their cases on the bed, and wondered if the food would be as sparse as the fuel. Fresh from the warmth and luxury of a London hotel, the unheated bedroom was a chilly reminder that private citizens had already been obliged to economise.

'What time shall you be requiring your evening meal?' their landlady was asking in the doorway, after she had shown Wendy and Lennie to their rooms.

'Any time that would suit you, Mrs Green, for this first week will be taken up with rehearsals. After that, it's just a matter of fitting in with the arrangements, and the convenience of the various parties. Shall you mind providing us with a late supper after the show?'

'I hope it won't be *too* late?'

'If it is we will eat in the canteen.'

'Very well. What about lunch?'

'A pot of coffee and a plate of sandwiches would be fine.'

'I don't normally serve coffee. Most people prefer tea anyway.'

'Then we will have tea,' Nigel agreed, with a little bow, and unaccustomed patience.

But coffee was a necessity, not a luxury. They would need to provide their own. Lennie would hatch up something. Lennie would fix it.

Nancy was still wrapped in her fur coat, looking rather peevish.

'Cheer up, darling. It could be worse,' her spouse reminded her.

'I need a drink, darling. We both need a drink. Did we bring the whisky?'

'Have you ever known me to forget it, darling? What do we do for glasses?'

'Look in the bathroom, darling.'

'You look, darling, while I find the bottle.'

It was carefully wrapped in a pair of crêpe-de-Chine camiknickers. They exchanged a meaningful smile as he folded them carefully. Nancy in her fur coat lost all her sex appeal. She had not moved, so he wandered out to look for glasses. The first day in new lodgings was always an ordeal. The whisky helped.

'What about the others, darling?' she asked. As if she cared!

Nigel shrugged. They both knew Lennie would be on his way to the nearest pub – and Wendy would be drinking tea.

In the little room across the landing, Wendy could hear the clink of glasses, and Nigel talking soothingly to Nancy. Lennie clattered down the stairs and the front door slammed. She shivered. There was really nothing to complain about. It was a very clean house, and Mrs Green was a most respectable woman, but there was no *warmth* in her, or her house. She hadn't really known what to expect. Their seaside lodgings before the war had been a friendly, familiar place since early childhood. She was kissed and hugged on arrival. The hall was gritty with sand, and cluttered with boats, buckets and spades and shrimping nets. Wet towels draped the bedroom window sills. It was sad to think of barbed wire entanglements on the deserted beaches, and patrols on constant guard for enemy invasion. It all seemed a long time ago, in another world, those seaside holidays before the war.

In the chill of this strange house, her travelling

companions had left her alone. She was lost and lonely, and not yet ready for this new world in which she found herself. But she had her pride, and she would not beg to be noticed. She knew already that Nancy would be jealous if Nigel made a fuss of her. She had yet to learn that show business had many facets, and she would see all of them, eventually, on stage and off.

The face in the mirror was pale, the eyes bright with unshed tears. But this was no time for tears. She snatched off the woolly hat and rumpled her short hair. She would get unpacked. Then it would be time for their sandwich lunch and a cup of tea. It was just today that everything was so strange. Tomorrow would be better, she told herself, not very convincingly. Behind the draped muslin curtains, that lofty spire reminded her that Julian was up in the sky, far removed from her strange earthbound world. She would write to him tonight, after rehearsal. When she had set his photograph on the dressing table and scattered her few belongings about the room, it was not so bleak and bare as it had first appeared. Gran would say she had to put up with it, and she knew exactly what Mother would say. But Daddy would understand, and he wouldn't blame her. They had always been close. His dark eyes would be sad today, and there would be nobody to fetch his papers and tobacco from the little shop at The Pantiles – nobody to play his favourite Chopin. He would play his records after supper, for Gran went early to bed, and Mummy would be on night duty at the hospital. She could picture him in his favourite armchair, smoking his pipe. At 9 o'clock he would switch on the wireless and listen to the news. Her darling Daddy!

She was back at the window, peering between the draped curtains, her throat tight with tears when Nigel walked into the room.

176

'What are you doing? You are not crying, are you?' he asked, anxiously.

'No,' she whispered, and turned her head to look at him. She liked what she saw.

He took her chin in his hand and smiled down at her. 'Not sorry you came?'

'No.'

'Good girl. I knew I could depend on you.' He brushed her trembling mouth with his lips, and the smell of whisky was strong on his breath.

Lennie came back later, after they had finished the tea and sandwiches.

'He won't need any of this. It's beer and bread and cheese for Lennie. We don't bother about him. He goes his own way and pleases himself. But he's a good trouper, isn't he, darling?'

Nigel was warming his hands on the cup of hot tea. They were still wearing their overcoats. Nancy nodded, absent-mindedly. Her green eyes flicked over the girl kneeling on the hearthrug, holding out her hands to the small fire. They were slender hands, with unpolished finger nails. Her own varnished nails matched her lipstick. She had made up her face afresh in the bedroom. She always felt naked without her make-up. She was a handsome woman, and had nothing to fear from that pretty child. They were still separated by her cold hostility, and she left it to Nigel to make polite conversation.

When the bell rang, he hurried to open the door to Lennie. Landladies were sparing with their keys, and touchy about being disturbed in their cosy basements to answer the door. Mrs Green had handed him the key when she brought in the tea tray.

'Ready, Guv?' Lennie blew in on a gust of cold clammy air. A taxi was waiting at the curb. Trust Lennie to get them organised.

'Blimey!' he exclaimed, when they left the city behind and were lost in a fleet of Army trucks and jeeps and columns of marching men. Rows of Nissen huts stretched across the landscape as far as the eye could see. Nigel was surprised to discover they had been allocated a recreation hall for their rehearsals, and orders had been given that they were to be left undisturbed for two hours, twice a day.

To walk across a stage for the first time and run her hands along an unfamiliar keyboard was an unforgettable experience to the young novice. For the others, however, it was no novelty. One stage was much like another, and the chilly dressing rooms in the wings might have been found in any small provincial theatre in the country.

'Play something – anything!' Nigel commanded.

Wendy draped her coat over the back of the chair and sat down. Her fingers slipped easily into the opening bars of a Chopin Polonaise. They stared, surprised by the professional technique and quality. Then Nigel spread his hands in a gesture of satisfaction. 'I told you so,' he seemed to be saying.

Lennie tried out a few experimental steps of a new routine. Nancy's thin lips were pursed with irritation. She had no use for anything not directly involved with their own personal repertoire, and Chopin was too highbrow to be recognised. Lennie and Nigel had not recognised Chopin, for that matter, but they knew for certain now the girl would be an asset not a liability. Nigel bowed graciously.

'Thank you, my dear. That was charming. Now, let's get to work!'

Nancy was arranging scores on top of the piano – solos and duets they had been singing for the past two decades. Audiences loved them and never tired of the old favourites from 'Hiawatha', 'The Student Prince' and 'The Merry Widow' they had persuaded themselves. Nigel's 'Road to Mandalay' and Nancy's 'One Fine Day' from *Madam Butterfly* were beginning to sound what Lennie called 'shop-soiled', and the accompanist had to work hard on the pedal to help along those strained high notes. 'One Fine Day' had always been beyond the range of a second-rate soprano, but Nancy stubbornly refused to accept it. Whenever it was included in the programme, Nigel would be sweating in the wings with a tot of whisky. Poor darling! This tour might well be her swan-song. It was a ghastly thought – retirement. He would not allow himself to dwell on such a gloomy prospect. The war had saved them from the compulsory 'rest' so dreaded by their profession, and wartime audiences would not be too critical. They were saying now it would be a long war. He and Nancy would not mind how long it lasted, or how many times they had to unpack that battered tin trunk in fresh lodgings. It was their life.

'This is our signature tune, Wendy. We make our entrance from the wings, arm-in-arm, in evening dress,' Nancy was explaining, importantly.

> Tea for two, and two for tea,
> A girl for you, a boy for me,
> Oh can't you see how happy we should be-ee.

She sang blithely, with a girlish little step to the centre of the stage. Lennie winced, and went on practising his own routine in a corner. Of one thing he was certain. His own act would need no props to support it. A few chords, and a couple of hand-springs and he would be there, grinning like a Cheshire Cat, in his sloppy old clothes, greeting the audience like old friends.

''ullo! 'ullo!'

'Hullo!' they would shout back.

He knew how to handle them. He thought he must have been born with the gift of the gab. It was natural as breathing. He composed his own comic songs, and had no voice for singing. What did it matter if it made them laugh? He was sorry for the kid, who was obviously a classical pianist. She would have to learn a repertoire of songs that was not familiar to her generation. There were no scores on the piano in show business. Nancy would bully her, and Wendy was no match for that green-eyed bitch.

They had tea in the NAAFI canteen – the only civilians among all the uniformed men and women. It was an ugly colour for the girls, and only the most ravishing blonde could look attractive in khaki serge.

Wendy followed Lennie to the counter to collect mugs of tea and currant buns. It was the start of a routine that would be repeated in every canteen throughout the tour. Nigel and Nancy would sit down at a vacant table, light their cigarettes, and expect to be waited on. It was shop-talk in the tea-break, and Wendy listened absorbed but made no comment, while her three companions argued heatedly and disagreed on almost every point – their modulated voices drowned in the clatter and chatter of the lively canteen. Only at the end of the week, at the dress rehearsal for the first show, would their differences be resolved in a united front. But Wendy was not yet aware of the pattern, and it worried her.

'Not ter worry, ducks. It will be OK on the night,' Lennie told her, decidedly, when they seemed to be no nearer the harmony she had expected. Lennie was the most relaxed on stage – or appeared to be. But all three had very definite opinions about her own personal contribution. She soon discovered an accompanist was

180

nothing more than a prop on which to hang all their temperamental shindies. In this role of go-between, her own artistic temperament was submerged, and she found herself compliant to their wishes, and sensitive to their moods. It was a new discovery, that team-spirit was not confined to the school playing-fields, but was cleverly disguised to deceive audiences into thinking the performers always lived in perfect harmony. This was show business, this merging of talent and temperament, this fierce dedication and discipline.

For the young novice it was an exhausting experience. Her companions demanded too much of her, and only Lennie, with his good-humoured kindliness, recognised the first signs of homesickness when she enquired about the postal arrangements. She had her letters written, to Julian, and to Tunbridge Wells, but dare not mention the address of their lodgings. To find Mother waiting on the doorstep to take her home would be frightfully embarrassing. She would never live it down, never again know the bitter-sweetness of independence.

'Letters? What letters?' Nigel seemed surprised at Wendy's anxiety. They were not expecting letters. Neither was Lennie.

'It's like being on board ship. The mail is collected at every port, and if you miss out at one port, you find letters waiting at the next,' he told her.

Wendy looked puzzled. 'But how will they know *where* to write?'

'It's simple. I will give you a list of dates we shall be appearing at the various Army camps and Air Force stations in the West Country, and you can send it to your parents. Tell them to address their letters to the Nigel Bannister Touring Company, c/o Administration, that should find you,' he told her, importantly. 'After Salisbury, we proceed west to Oxfordshire and

Gloucestershire, and from there to Bristol. We finish this first part of the tour at Plymouth. But you mustn't be too disappointed if letters don't reach you for several weeks. You may collect a whole bunch at Bristol.'

'Several *weeks*!' she wailed. 'I couldn't bear to wait that long.'

'There's a war on!' Nancy snapped impatiently.

'And this is show business, my dear,' Nigel reminded her, with a disarming smile.

'Butterflies in the old tum?' Lennie whispered, hoarsely, draping an arm about her shoulders. She was trembling like a leaf in the wind, her eyes wide with shock as she peered out from the wings.

'Lennie, there must be *hundreds*!' she gasped. 'They are packed in like sardines.'

'Full 'ouse, ducks. Jus' what the doctor ordered.'

'But I am absolutely petrified.'

'Jus' nerves, kid. It's natural. I'm nearly wetting me pants.'

'*You*, Lennie?'

He grinned. 'It's the waitin'. Not ter worry. You're okey-doke, an' they're goin' ter love yer. Give 'em all you've got, ducks, for they're goin' to need it, them lads art there. They've got a bloody war on their 'ands. You an' me is the lucky ones, an' don't yer forget it. If I can make 'em laugh, Wendy, you can make 'em cry with that ole joanner. You play jus' luvly, ducks, jus' luvly.'

'Thank you, Lennie dear.' She kissed his cheek.

Nigel was beckoning from the other side of the stage impatiently. Lennie poked her in the back and hissed, 'SMILE, ducks, SMILE.'

She stepped out, smiling shyly. They met in the centre of the stage. She curtsied and Nigel bowed. Then he took her hand and they turned to the audience – a sea of faces in a haze of smoke, suddenly alerted, ready to be entertained.

'Ladies and gentlemen, may I present our young accompanist. Her name is Wendy.'

They had rehearsed it, over and over again, until it was no longer spontaneous but nothing had prepared her for the impact of the audience – the cheers and clapping, the cat-calls and whistles.

'Hi, Wendy!'

Her smile was no longer forced, and all those rehearsals seemed to have no bearing on this unforgettable moment. They liked her, and she liked them. It was mutual. The front row had been reserved for officers, and they smiled back at her while the ranks yelled their approval. They saw a girl in a print frock, a very pretty girl, with shining hair and wide blue eyes. She was everyone's kid sister, and those on the back row knew this was her début because the comic had told them so over a pint of beer in the NAAFI canteen.

When Nigel raised a hand for silence and slipped away, she sat down at the piano with a sense of wonderment that Nancy must have known in the early days when everything was fresh and new. Over in the wings she could see Lennie with his thumbs up, and his face split in a wide grin. Flushed and excited, her heart pounding, she struck the opening chords:

> Tea for two, and two for tea,
> A boy for you, a girl for me,
> Oh can't you see how happy we should be-ee.

They were a handsome couple, and they knew how to charm an audience. All their loving gestures in that first duet had a convincing reality. They hung on every endearment, touched lips and cheeks with a tenderness that gave their stage performance the romantic glamour of the screen. Every one of those girls in khaki serge

183

would gladly have changed places with Nancy, but not all the men found his partner fascinating. They had seen it all before in peace time in very different circumstances. But the girl at the piano was a novelty, and they watched her covertly.

The show had been carefully timed to last an hour – Nigel and Nancy to open the show with their love duet and their individual numbers – *not* 'One Fine Day', to Nigel's immense relief. Then Lennie would steal the limelight with his fooling and his naughty stories that would have the audience hooting with laughter. In his baggy trousers, he would remind some of the older men of Charlie Chaplin, for his mobile face could change from comedy to pathos in a matter of seconds. Then Wendy would play her Chopin, and the sketch would follow. Nigel had given her only a small part because Nancy had complained that her voice didn't carry to the back rows. The show would finish with community singing, led by Nigel and Nancy. Wendy had practised all the Vera Lynn favourites. 'The Forces Sweetheart' they called her, and her voice had a heart-rending quality that no other person in show business could imitate. When she sang – 'There'll be bluebirds over the white cliffs of Dover, Tomorrow, just you wait and see' – every man and girl in the NAAFI canteens from Land's End to John o'Groats, believed her. Then a quick line up on stage for the final bow, with Nigel holding Wendy's hand as well as Nancy's, and Lennie waving his check cap.

Over a glass of sherry in the officers' mess, they found themselves separated, and a very young sub-lieutenant was raising his glass to Wendy.

'That was a rare treat. I have not heard that Nocturne played so delightfully since I was a child. We were practically brought up on Chopin, my sister and I. My mother was an ex-pupil of a Polish professor at the

London School of Music,' he told her, with boyish frankness.

'And *my* mother introduced me to Chopin, and gave me my first lessons.'

'You seem very young for this sort of life. Don't your parents mind?'

'No,' she lied. 'It's just for the duration of the war.'

'Are you enjoying it?'

'Very much.' She sipped the sherry distastefully, trying not to shudder. It was one of the things she had to get used to, Nigel had insisted. It was always sherry they would be offered before and after the show. It was customary.

She would like to have stayed talking to the young sub-lieutenant about music, and about their homes and childhood, but Nigel was keeping a strict eye on her, and intervened after about ten minutes or so. He had no intention of allowing one particular person to monopolise the child. Romance, or the romantic illusion, must be confined to the stage. So he laid a proprietary hand across her shoulders and smiled at the boy, young enough to be his son, but old enough to serve his country.

'Sorry to interrupt, old chap, but the Major has asked for an introduction. My little Wendy seems to have made quite a hit.'

'I was just telling her, Sir, how much I had enjoyed it. A pity there was no time for more.'

'We shall be giving two more shows in Salisbury this week. Why not come along if you are off duty?'

'Thank you, Sir. I will.' He shook hands with them, and watched them walk away. The girl had hardly touched the sherry, and had obviously not acquired the habit. The woman was flirting with Carstairs and Bentley, and the comic still telling naughty stories. He sighed, wistfully. The girl was different. She didn't belong to show business. It was as obvious as her dislike of the sherry. He could so easily have fallen in love with her. It would take his mind off the war. To discover one could be lonely in such a crowded place was a new experience, and he was not yet sure he had done the right thing in applying for a commission. It pleased his mother to show him off to her friends in officer's uniform, but at nineteen he was younger than most of the men who called him 'Sir'. It seemed absurd, but there were hundreds more like him. Nobody noticed when he slipped away. Even in uniform he was a very ordinary young man. Away from the smoky atmosphere of the mess, outside in the cold frosty night, he could breathe more freely. Country born and bred, of middle-class parents, and destined for the Civil Service, the war had changed all that. Straight from public school to Sandhurst, and thence to Salisbury Plain. The haunting Nocturne followed him into the darkness. He would not see her again. What was the use when he was due for embarkation leave and overseas posting? Their worlds were too far apart.

He almost stumbled on a couple, huddled in the hedge, wrapped in their great-coats. He was so close to them he could sense their panic. Their faces were pressed close together, their mouths clinging, and their clutching arms desperately seeking the comfort and companionship so soon to be denied. It could be a matter of weeks or three months at the most.

He walked on, his own loneliness and longing intensified. But it was not for him, this furtive fumbling in the dark – or for the girl called Wendy, who played Chopin.

186

Chapter Eight

'I be proper flummoxed, son, and that's a fact.' Ruby had read the letter three times, and could make no sense of it.

Freddie looked at his mother across the kitchen table, and saw that she had aged in the few days since Wendy went away.

'Cynthia is furious, Mum,' was all he said, and she nodded her grey head. Cynthia, and her counterpart, Sister Simmons, demanded instant obedience. The wife and mother frequently became overlooked in the strong personality of the hospital Sister. The stress and strain of so much night duty in this first Winter of the war often clashed with the temperament of a teenage daughter. Everyone was blaming the war for all the disruption in family life, but Ruby, and her son Freddie, had foreseen a time when Wendy would rebel against her mother's domination. Now that time had come, and they were helpless in their ignorance of her exact whereabouts. Freddie would have been on his way to fetch her back had he known where to start looking.

'Who are these people, Mum? – this Nigel Bannister Touring Company – I've never heard of them. If it was ENSA, we could get in touch with them, for they would be properly organised, with a London office. These people must be travelling independently to entertain the Forces. She doesn't give any details. But how on earth did she contact them in the first place? That's what puzzles me. Have you seen any letters addressed to Wendy, apart from Julian's?'

'No, I haven't. She's always looking out for the postman these days, but I naturally thought it was Julian's letter she was expecting. It's not like her, love, to be so deceitful. Wendy has always been as honest as the day.'

'Because Cynthia insisted on honesty, since she was old enough to understand right from wrong. If she told a lie, she was punished, wasn't she?'

'Yes.'

'Now Wendy is no longer a child, and this is not dishonesty, Mum. It's the young generation asserting the right to please itself.'

'Then you don't blame her?'

'I'm sorry she had to do it this way, but perhaps there was no alternative. It has been a battle of wills for some time between Wendy and her mother, as we both know, and she stuck out as long as possible against that Secretarial College, then finally gave in – at least, that's what we thought. But she must have known what she intended to do. This was not something decided in a few weeks.' His mouth twisted in a wry smile. 'Between you and me, Mum, I can't but admire her enterprise!'

Ruby handed back the letter. 'She says it's great fun, and she feels she is contributing to the war effort, and we are not to worry.'

'Cynthia will say she could have contributed more usefully to the war effort as a VAD in the local hospital if she was bored with the typing and shorthand.'

'But Wendy isn't cut out for nursing.'

'Or for office work. She knows what she wants, and

she's just gone after it, and that takes courage. We can only hope she won't be disappointed. We shan't know, because we shan't be told – and she won't come running back.' He sighed.

Ruby filled his cup with strong black coffee. There would come a time when coffee would only be obtainable on the Black Market, and Freddie would be drinking tea like all the rest, but not yet. Freddie liked his coffee, and it was Ruby's pleasure to spoil her little family. She loved them dearly – this crippled son, her favourite grandchild, and the daughter-in-law from the upper class who ruled their lives, *but called her Mother*. For a working-class mother from Richmond Row to find herself the mother-in-law of one of Sir Neville Franklin's daughters had been the biggest shock of her life, and she had had quite a few.

'May I call you Mother?' the girl had asked, so humbly. My, but she were proper flummoxed!

A car had drawn up at the kerb, and they looked at each other, but did not speak their thoughts when the car door slammed. The front door also slammed, and the little house seemed to rock on its foundations. Cynthia was in a foul temper, and Freddie shrank from yet another scene that left them both exhausted.

When she swept into the kitchen he was on his feet to greet her, but her mouth was pursed, and she gave him her cheek and snatched up the letter in a single movement. All her movements were brisk and decisive, and he often sensed her impatience with his clumsiness. She was frowning now as she scanned the single page and tossed it back on the table.

'Little fool!' That cultured voice could be scathing, and sarcastic, as many an unfledged probationer had discovered to her cost.

'Well, have you done anything about it? Or have you

just been sitting there, the two of you?' She flung the question at mother and son, and then could have bitten out her tongue when she saw their distress. There was a likeness now between them, for Freddie's hair was greying, and they both had a gentleness and patience that never condemned her own impatience and made excuses for her bad temper.

'There is not much to go on, in this first letter,' Freddie pointed out, reasonably.

'You could try phoning ENSA. They might know of this company. No, leave it! Let her stand on her own two feet if that is what she wants. She will soon find out her mistake if she hasn't done so already. I hope you realise, Freddie, this escapade is the direct result of all your spoiling?' she snapped irritably.

He could not answer her, his throat was too tight. Ruby was filling the kettle to make a pot of tea. Her infallible remedy for every distressing situation or emergency, had long since been adopted by the British public. Ruby never interfered between husband and wife.

'No tea for me, thank you Mother. I need something stronger, and I know where to find it.' She left them standing there and marched into the sitting-room. They would never know how this poky little house crowded in on her at such times, when her nerves were ragged. She wanted SPACE – the space she had known as a child at Marston Park, and the space of a big London hospital. For Ruby and Freddie, who had never known the luxury of spacious living, claustrophobia was a condition as foreign to them as ragged nerves. When the black mood had passed, Cynthia would be shamed by their patience, but now she felt only irritation as she flung her hat and coat on the nearest chair, collapsed on the sofa, and closed her eyes. Freddie had followed her in and was

190

pouring the sherry. She kept her eyes closed till he stood over her.

'She will be all right,' he told her, quietly, and her eyes flew open.

'With a *touring company*? It sounds like a circus. Thanks.' She took the sherry with a hand that trembled, and raised the glass to her lips. But her teeth were chattering, so he took it back and put it down on the table. He knew from past experience that it was sleep she needed now when her nerves were at breaking point. He banked up the cushions, took off her shoes, swung her legs gently on to the sofa, and covered her with a rug.

'You've still got me, my dearest girl, for what it's worth,' he reminded her. His rare endearments always disarmed her. Over the years he had managed to conceal his working-class shyness of endearments, but it was still there, deep-rooted as the miracle of his marriage. He had not expected that Cynthia would wish to spend the rest of her life married to a poor man's solicitor. He had no wealthy clients, and no ambition. Every year that passed was a kind of bonus, but it was not his nature to put it into words.

'His dearest girl.' Her tired body slumped. Her eyes were moist.

'My darling, I don't deserve you,' she said, contritely – and turned her head away.

Julian's weekly letters from Wendy usually covered six pages, so he only glanced at the letter with the Salisbury postmark, and put it away to read later in the day, after he had slept. It was difficult, almost impossible now, to visualise that other world in his mind's eye, as he had last seen it at Russets, back in the Summer of 1939. All of himself – body, soul and spirit – belonged to the RAF.

There was nothing left over. Only by this selfless dedication could he continue to serve his country till his own turn came to be shot down. He had no illusions about survival.

The hay-field in the bright June sunlight, the women in their print frocks and sun-bonnets, Tom on the wagon and the patient Shire horse in the shafts, appeared as a mirage from time to time, framed in the grey Winter sky over the grey sea. Then it was gone. The only reality was the squadron of Spitfires all about him, and the sudden frightening plunge of enemy aircraft. It seemed he had never actually known that other life – never been a boy on a bicycle belting across the Park to catch the train from the little country station – never known the taste of home-baked bread and blackcurrant jam – never had his own pony, or driven the farm cart on market days – never climbed the trees in the beech wood or helped himself to apples in the orchard. It all had a dreamlike quality, that other world, so remote from the reality of war in their own particular sphere. The Army and Navy were equally remote. He had no time to consider these other tremendous forces on land and sea, bent on destruction as they themselves were destroying – and being destroyed. Because tomorrow was so uncertain, they lived for today, and snatched a little happiness in the brief interludes of relaxation. They thought he was a queer because he preferred the company of his own sex, but there was nothing abnormal about his relationships.

Since that last and final emotional episode with Diane Maloney he had avoided the girls on the station and spent his off-duty cycling alone, or with an agreeable companion, among the hills and glens of a landscape as varied and beautiful as his own Weald of Kent. He had realised, when it was too late, that Diane's obsession with sex was abnormal, and he had been a fool to break his journey in London on his last leave. That perfect body, bruised and battered by the violence of a jealous husband, was intended to provoke compassion, but it had provoked only revulsion. He had since heard, through the grapevine at Marston Park – servants' talk – that Diane was enjoying herself with Canadian officers in the house at Little Venice since, being an American citizen, she was under no obligation to join up. To reject all sexual intercourse as an obscenity was ridiculous, he told himself repeatedly, but he could not discard his sense of distaste and neither could he reveal the source of his obvious reluctance to meet the WAAFs socially. Of course they were nice girls. He admired their efficiency and their organised discipline, but he shrank from the personal involvement that the majority of his contemporaries enjoyed.

As for Wendy, she had been relegated to her original role of little sister, with her six pages of childish scribble to her 'Darling Julian' signed with 'Lots of love and kisses'. The row of kisses brought a smile to his tired eyes. He remembered that one chaste kiss on top of the gate in the lane, and a wet, warm mouth – the mouth of a child.

When the batwoman awakened him with a mug of tea, he remembered the letter with the Salisbury postmark, and groped for it in the drawer of the bedside locker. Sipping the hot sweet tea, he read:

Darling Julian,

There is so much to tell you I hardly know where to start, but I will try to start at the beginning. You remember I told you in my last letter that I had answered an advertisement for an accompanist in a small touring company, and that I was grabbing all the letters off the mat before Daddy or Gran could discover a letter addressed to me in person? Of course I had to pretend I was looking for *your* letter, darling, and it was true, in a way, because I am always expecting a letter from you, which is stupid of me when I know you are much too busy chasing those devils in that awful Luftwaffe. You didn't *promise* to write regularly, and I do understand. Now I must get back to the start of the Big Adventure or you will remind me, for the umpteenth time, that I always wander away from the subject! When THE LETTER finally arrived, I told Gran it was from you, so she wasn't surprised when I dashed upstairs to read it in private. Your letters are much too precious, darling, to hand around the family. I keep them locked away in my secret drawer. Gran gets all the latest news of you anyway. Aunt Lucy always telephones when she has heard from you.

It was a jolly nice letter, Julian, and I was surprised and thrilled to be offered the job without an interview. You see, I had taken the precaution to enclose a snapshot of myself, and all my qualifications as a pianist. This Mr Nigel Bannister obviously thought I was the most suitable applicant, though he didn't say how many people had applied. He said they were a small private company, not like ENSA, and there would be just the four of us travelling all over the British Isles, to entertain the Forces and factory workers. Can you imagine your little cousin in show business? He suggested that I should meet the rest of the company – his wife, Nancy, and a comedian called Lennie, for lunch on the 3rd January at the Regent Palace Hotel, in Piccadilly. We should be staying overnight there, and leave for Salisbury the following morning. He said to bring only light luggage, and no evening dresses. I never had an evening dress anyway!

He said to bring several pretty frocks, like the one I was wearing in the photograph. The accompanist, he thought, should be unsophisticated rather than glamorous, and when I met his wife, I realised *she* had all the glamour, and would certainly resent any competition!

I had to tell a few little white lies, darling, to the family, and I know you disapprove of this, having such high principles, but I couldn't bear to miss such a fabulous opportunity. I *did* mind deceiving Gran and Daddy, but Mother deserved it, after pushing me into that horrid Secretarial College. Actually, it was quite simple. All I had to do was to pack my case, wait for Gran to go out shopping, take a bus to the station and leave the case at the left luggage. Then, on the Big Day, I left home at the usual time so they thought I was going to the College, but I caught a train to Victoria. Wasn't it clever of me?

I am not sure that you will agree about the cleverness, and you will probably think it was a mean trick to play on them. To be quite honest, I *did* have qualms on that train, and so many butterflies were fluttering in my tummy when I saw them waiting for me in the foyer of the hotel – Nigel Bannister, wearing a carnation in his buttonhole – I nearly fainted! You see, darling, I have never stayed in even the smallest hotel, and this was *vast*, with hundreds of rooms and crowds of people, many in uniform, and a lot of foreigners. But Nigel Bannister was charming, and we liked each other immediately. Nancy Bannister was not at all friendly. I think she would have preferred a man accompanist. I should say they are both past middle age, but a handsome couple in a sophisticated way. Show business is their way of life. As for Lennie, the comedian, I wish you could have seen him. Such a funny little man in baggy trousers, a fisherman's jersey, a red scarf, and a check cap several sizes too large for his peaked little face. He talks like a Cockney, but he was born and bred – guess where? – *Richmond Row, Fairfields* – and Gran was a near neighbour! When he took me up to my room – the Bannisters treat him like a servant but he is not the least bit intimidated – I told him the truth about running away, and he promised not to tell the others. I feel I could tell Lennie anything and he would understand. Mother would be shocked to see me associate with such a person. Yet he is absolutely natural, and so kind. The Bannisters are a little artificial, and have two faces – a public and a private face.

When we went into the restaurant for lunch, it appeared to be crowded, but Nigel used his charm on the head waiter who found us a table. The menu was fabulous, but Nigel hardly glanced at it and ordered steaks for everyone. When they arrived they were huge, and garnished with fried onions, mushrooms, tomatoes and green beans. I felt quite sick. It was all too much I suppose, on top of the excitement. I must have been looking rather pale because Lennie scooped some of it on to his own plate. That is the sort of thing he does. He is so kind. I didn't enjoy sitting in the crowded lounge with the Bannisters in the afternoon. It was so hot and stuffy, and I was still feeling sick. Lennie went off to visit friends in Soho and came back in time to eat my two chocolate éclairs! The thought of another lavish meal in the evening quite revolted me, so I asked to be excused and went to bed early. It was then that I began to feel homesick, darling. It was all so strange and bewildering. But Lennie explained about the telephone and room service, 24 hours a day. It was tremendous fun. The chambermaid brought my early morning tea – a whole pot of tea at 6 a.m. and I ordered breakfast for 7.30 because Lennie had pushed a note under my door to tell me we should be leaving at 8 a.m.

Nigel had warned me we should only be enjoying the luxury of a hotel for one night, and in future we should be accommodated in lodgings. But I was still not prepared for the shattering change in our circumstances. The Bannisters hardly spoke a word in the taxi en route to the station. There were no porters at Paddington, and everyone carried their own luggage. Service personnel commandeered all the trucks and trolleys. Crowds of people and queues everywhere. You queued for tickets, for newspapers and cigarettes – the Bannisters are heavy smokers – and you queued on the platform. All the trains were late and we waited ages. Lennie managed to get us a compartment to ourselves because the young men and women in uniform were sitting on their baggage in the corridor. When the train pulled out of the station, darling, I wanted to cry very badly. The Big Adventure went as flat as a pancake. I had so wanted to stand on my own two feet, and to know the meaning of independence, but it was not what I had visualised. Don't worry, the feeling passed, and I had Lennie to remind me 'You'll be OK, kid'.

Our first lodgings are clean and our landlady most superior – 'too bloody superior' according to Lennie! It's such a cold house, and the meals are frugal, but of course we have to remember 'there's a war on'. Since we are constantly reminded of the fact, we are not likely to forget! Anyway, Nigel said not to worry, we could always have a meal in the NAAFI canteen.

Now, to tell you about the show. The first week of rehearsals was absolutely staggering to a novice who had to learn all the tricks of show business and discover all the moods of each individual performer. It didn't take long, Julian, to discover the Bannisters were second-rate and Lennie a real professional. No wonder they had to put up with his untidy appearance, and his rough language. The show would be a complete flop without Lennie. The Bannisters sing love duets and solos that were popular in the *last* war. They insist that audiences love to hear all the old favourites, but not these *young* audiences who shout themselves hoarse in the community singing at the end of the show. Very Lynn is *their* favourite. (We are giving several more shows in Salisbury for the different Army units that are stationed here. Then we move on to other camps, air force stations and factory canteens in the West Country.) I had only a small part in the comedy sketch because Nancy complained my voice did not carry to the back rows. She always seems to be complaining about something. Lennie calls her 'a green-eyed bitch!' Isn't he naughty? But they *did* like my Chopin, and I had to play an encore. We were invited to the Officers' Mess for a glass of sherry, before and after the show. I only took a few tentative sips of the sherry, and would have preferred a cup of tea. I suppose it's an acquired taste, like the wine we had with our lunch at the London hotel. Lennie likes to drink his beer in a pub. He only belongs to us on the stage. For the rest of the time he pleases himself. It leaves me feeling rather lonesome. Nigel will not allow any of the young officers to make a date with me. He is very conscious of his responsibility! Darling Julian, you are not to worry. *I am all right. Please, please* write soon.

Lots of love and kisses,

Wendy

He sighed, and glanced at his watch. Just time to reply. His poor little sweetheart had landed herself in a bit of a mess. Lennie – Lennie – Lennie. That name kept cropping up. He didn't trust that little twerp! With Nigel Bannister to keep an eye on her, she couldn't come to any harm – or could she? If only she had been content to put up with that Secretarial College for twelve months. If only she were not so strong-willed. If only Aunt Cynthia were not so domineering. This desperate urge for independence had been brewing for some time. The war had finally brought it into the open and paved the way to escape.

He rumpled his hair, reached for the notepad and pen, and began to write in a neat, flowing style, that quickly filled the normal two pages. He wrote lovingly and kindly. This was no time to condemn such an impulsive bid for freedom. It was too late, anyway. Reading between the lines, she was not only homesick, but struggling to keep her end up with that 'green-eyed bitch'. But she had guts, which was only another slang word for courage. Supreme courage was a quality that had constantly surprised him in the most unlikely chaps on the Station. You never could tell till the moment of combat what his reaction would be, even if you had known a chap as a friend and companion. One by one he had lost Pete, Dave, Mike and Johnny – and all had died courageously. He had been leading the squadron for more than a year, and surely that was a record. How much longer could his luck hold? They thought he had a charmed life, and that Spitfire Lucy held some magic formula for survival. The Luck of the Gods? More and more youngsters were being posted to the station, and some had not lived to see their 20th birthday. It made him feel old. He *was* old. Youth had passed him by in the relentless surge of manhood. Yet, if he had his time over again, he would make no major changes.

As far back as he could remember it had been aircraft, not trains or cars, that held such a fascination. He remembered his first Meccano set, and Uncle Bertie helping him to assemble the small models. Then it became an absorbing hobby, his only hobby, as a schoolboy. Gradually he had built up a fleet of model aircraft. If he closed his eyes, he could see them, for they were still there in his room at Russets, lined up on the mantelpiece, the chest of drawers, and the window sill, and pinned to the ceiling on long cords so that they moved with every current of air from the open window. They 'flew' in a most realistic fashion, and the ceiling was the sky. Aunt Lucy, bless her, had blue-washed the ceiling, but all the other bedrooms had white-washed ceilings. On cold Winter nights he would snuggle down under the blankets and watch his planes flying in the light of the candle till he fell asleep. He never heard Aunt Lucy come into the room to blow out the candle. On warm nights of Spring and Summer, with the window flung wide open and the curtains fluttering in the breeze, he would lie and watch them long after the sun went down. He could see himself as a boy, lying there, with his hands behind his head, and his eyes focused on every movement.

'You have your mother's eyes, Julian,' Aunt Cynthia had told him when he was very small, and he was puzzled. His mother had gone to Heaven when he was born, so had she left her eyes behind when she went to Heaven? Grown-ups often made puzzling remarks in those early years. His grandfather, Sir Neville Franklin, would scoop him up to ride on his big black stallion, then hold him firmly with one hand and the reins in the other hand. He was very proud to be the grandson of such an important person.

One day he had asked, 'Why haven't I got a Daddy like all the other boys?' The answer was puzzling. 'Your father went away, Julian, before you were born. When he comes back, I shall give him a good thrashing.'

'Why must he be punished? Was it wicked to go away if you were a father?' he had persisted, innocently.

'It was cowardly, and to be a coward is a disgrace,' Grandfather had explained.

He supposed his father had not come back to receive that good thrashing because it was never mentioned again. There were photographs of his mother and other members of the family in the parlour at Russets, including his handsome Uncle Charles who lived in America, and still sent money for his birthday and Christmas. But there was no photograph of that mysterious parent. Not that it mattered. He belonged to Russets, and Aunt Lucy adored him.

'Get up! Get up at once! We shall be leaving the house in twenty minutes!' Nancy Bannister's voice was sharp with irritation. She was never at her best in the early morning.

Six weeks had passed and they had reached Gloucester, where they expected to stay for ten days or so, putting on shows in factory canteens and hostels. The girl was playing up again. They had trouble with her last month at that RAF Station in Wiltshire. Whoever heard of a female putting herself to bed with the curse?

'Gran always allowed me to stay in bed the first day. I feel so awful.'

Silly little fool! Did she imagine her suffering was unique? Nigel would have kept her in bed. He was fond of the girl, and positively gloated over her performance as a pianist. Nancy had to admit, grudgingly, that Wendy had proved to be an asset, and not the liability she had expected. At every Forces show, in the Army camps and RAF stations, she had been obliged to play an encore, sometimes two. The young audiences loved her, but the factory workers, a mixed bunch of both sexes and all ages, clamoured for Lennie. Wendy would never have the true dedication to show business of the old troupers, Nancy had long since decided. She had no pity for the girl as she struggled into a sitting position, pushed off the bed-clothes, and swung her legs to the floor. Pale and listless, she was near to tears.

'Mrs Proctor is keeping your breakfast hot. She's a kind soul,' Nancy reminded her, as she turned to leave the room.

Wendy shuddered. 'I couldn't eat anything. It would make me sick.'

'Very well. I'll send Lennie up with a cup of tea.'

Wendy thanked her. She left the door open, and a few minutes later Lennie stood in the doorway.

'Feeling poorly, ducks?' he asked.

She nodded mutely, choked with tears.

He was sorry for the kid. He knew what the trouble was, and Nancy could be very scathing. But Nancy was no longer bothered with the curse. She was long past the age of menstruation.

'I – I'm not dressed.' Wendy pulled the sheet up to her chin.

He grinned. 'I don't mind, my ducks.'

She took the mug of tea and sipped it gratefully. She was shivering and wretched, and she wanted Gran. He could smell the warm blood and her stale sweat, but he was not revolted by such signals of femininity. It wouldn't be the first time he had counted himself lucky to be born a male. His lost love in Soho, all those years ago, had suffered in the same way. In her profession it had been a right nuisance – four days every month without customers!

'Jew know somethink, kid? I reckon you could eat a nice 'ot slice of buttered toast?'

'No thank you, Lennie. Just the tea. You spoil me. What should I do without you?'

'If it wasn't me it would be some other bloke playing nursemaid. I knew what I'd let meself in for soon as I set eyes on yer, that first dye in the 'otel. You was scared stiff, wasn't yer?'

She nodded. 'I was very nervous.'

'Lennie! Lennie!' Nancy was calling from below.

He pulled a face. ''ere we go agine!' and turned away.

'Is she getting up?' Nancy demanded.

'Dahn in a tick, Nance.'

Wendy sighed as he clattered down the stairs, then she pulled on her dressing gown and slippers and limped painfully to the bathroom.

The taxi was waiting and Lennie chatting to the driver. Nancy was fuming with impatience in the hall.

'Are you feeling better, dear?' Nigel asked kindly, draping an arm about her shoulders.

'Yes, thank you.'

'I told you so.' scoffed Nancy, and hurried down the steps.

They had a morning rehearsal and a lunchtime show that day in the canteen of an aircraft factory, spacious enough to serve a thousand workers at one sitting. The show would be accompanied by the clatter of plates and cutlery, and they all had to work hard to hold the wandering attention of an audience for the most part more interested in the food than the free entertainment provided by the management. Tomorrow they would be back to entertain those who had been allocated the second sitting. They were noisy and critical, these factory audiences, and had no use for Chopin and Schubert. They liked to choose what the pianist should play. The shouting match from a dozen or more dissenting voices had to be settled by Nigel, charmingly but authoritatively.

They had been served with coffee and spam sandwiches in the canteen before the workers' lunch hour, but Wendy passed her share of the sandwiches to Lennie, who was glad of them and never wasted a crumb.

'When I was a kid in Richmond Row, I went ter bed every night with an empty belly, and that's something yer don't ferget,' he had told her with that complete honesty that Wendy admired so much. Gran would have liked Lennie had she met him as an adult, but her memories of the O'Briens had a bitter taste. They were scroungers. They 'borrowed' but forgot to pay back. Their cottage was a disgrace, and their privy stank. Their children went barefoot to school in the Summer, and were kept at home in the Winter until boots had been provided by Parson's daughter, who distributed the Parish Relief.

Gran had written only one letter in the six weeks Wendy had been away, but she was a poor scholar, and avoided putting pen to paper as long as possible. Daddy wrote regularly. Mother not at all, which didn't surprise Wendy, but the estrangement saddened her. For the first time in her young life she was experiencing the misery of home-sickness, and the realisation that freedom was not something you automatically acquired when you abandoned the shelter and security of a good home. Freedom was an illusive quality she had not yet found in her new way of life. She was tied to her three companions by necessity and by a grudging sense of gratitude, yet she had little to thank them for. She contributed her share, made few demands on their company, off-stage – and had not yet received a penny for her services as an accompanist. She was too proud to ask, but she would soon have to draw on her modest savings bank account for small items such as stamps and toilet requisites. Somebody – she thought it was Lennie – was paying their lodgings and their train and taxi fares, but who was paying for the Bannisters' whisky and cigarettes?

It was a most unsatisfactory arrangement in so many ways, and it hadn't taken her long to discover the barrier that divided them in their private lives. There was no alternative in their dreary lodgings but to take a book to bed after supper, when Nigel and Nancy settled down to their drinking and smoking, and Lennie was on his way to the nearest pub till closing time.

It was even worse than last month, Wendy was thinking, desperately, nauseated by the overpowering smell of fish and chips in the factory canteen. It was Friday, and fish and chips took top priority on the menu.

Last month, at the RAF Station in Wiltshire, they had put on their show in the NAAFI, where only light refreshments were served. The audience of young airmen, WAAFs and maintenance crews had given their full attention to every item. When she had played 'The Moonlight Sonata' as an encore, the hushed atmosphere was so moving, she had been choked with tears. The misery and discomfort of that first day of her period had been overcome by the response of such an appreciative audience.

But not today. Tense with nervousness, her forced smile had no warmth when Nigel introduced her to the noisy audience, and she made her bow. He squeezed her clammy hand encouragingly. He had agreed with Nancy that the show could not be postponed because they had a tight schedule of engagements arranged with the various authorities before they left London. But he wished there could be a happier relationship between Nancy and Wendy. A kind word from his wife would help to lessen the strain. The poor girl had tried so hard to co-operate, but Nancy always found something to complain about. It had been a mistake to engage such a charming girl for she captured the hearts of all those young servicemen with her sensitive performance, and on one occasion, had a standing ovation, while Nancy's solo performance on that same occasion had received only polite clapping. She watched him all the time, suspicious of any little extra attention. A kiss on the cheek was frowned upon, but it was natural and spontaneous after a good performance. He often lost his temper at rehearsals, but there was no sign of friction on stage in front of an audience. Their false smiles and loving gestures were convincingly genuine.

Her mind was a blank as her fingers found the familiar chords of the opening duet, 'Tea for Two', then straight into the love duet from 'The Student Prince'. Then Nancy's solo from Ivor Novello's 'Dancing Years' followed by Nigel's evergreen 'Road to Mandalay'. She could have closed her eyes and not lost her way on the keyboard, but her eyes must reflect pleasure, not pain, and her own false smile would stiffen on her face before this critical audience.

She could sense the destructive element of a few dissatisfied groups of workers – the trouble-makers who delighted in spoiling the enjoyment of the rest. Nigel had already been warned. They complained about everything – the rates of pay – the food – the accommodation – the lack of facilities – and the free entertainment provided. So it was not too surprising when his 'Road to Mandalay' was rudely interrupted by a shop steward at a nearby table – 'Give us a break, Guv!' – and smothered laughter from his girl-friends. But Nigel, like a true trouper, carried on to the end, and Wendy was accompanied by the loud drumming of spoons on several tables. For the first time in six weeks, the urge to get up and walk out was so strong, she had to remind herself this was show business, and audiences were as variable as the weather.

Lennie was waiting in the wings, fully aware of the mood of the audience, and he bounded on to the stage with a couple of nimble hand-springs before the 'Road to Mandalay' had reached its destination. Nigel slipped away to join Nancy behind the scenes.

'Bastards!' he muttered, irritably.

'Poor darling. It was awful for you. But what can you expect from such an ignorant lot?' She kissed him affectionately and felt very protective towards him. At such times they shared an intimacy completely devoid of suspicion and jealousy.

They watched Lennie's antics and listened to the roar of applause that followed every vulgar story. He knew how to handle them, and if the majority of the decent, hard-working men and women felt embarrassed or disgusted, it was just too bad. Lennie was playing to the trouble-makers – 'an' I've got 'em by the balls!' he told himself, jubilantly.

A sudden crash in the background brought his head round sharply. Wendy was slumped over the keyboard. 'Blimey! The kid's fainted!' he announced, as though it were all part of the act. And when Nigel dashed across the stage, scooped her up in his arms, and carried her off, the audience cheered. Lennie stepped into the breech with his own particular talent for covering up a sudden emergency. A few extra jokes, a song and dance would hold their attention till Nigel and Nancy were free to lead the community singing so popular with these factory audiences.

The nursing sister who had come out of retirement, thankfully, at the outbreak of war, to take over the post of Matron at this big aircraft factory, had been sitting in the audience. She was on her feet and hurrying back stage in a matter of seconds.

'Bring her into my surgery,' she instructed Nigel, with the brisk manner she had retained since her hospital days.

'She's fainted, Matron,' he explained, breathlessly as he laid her on the couch and stood back, glad to be relieved of the responsibility. When she had taken her pulse, Matron confirmed it was only a faint, and nothing to worry about. Young girls often fainted in the factory, and more often than not it was menstruation trouble.

Nigel nodded. 'That's exactly the trouble with Wendy. I suppose we should have been more sympathetic after last month, when we had the same trouble, though she didn't faint. But it's quite impossible to put on a show of this kind without an accompanist.'

'Is she your daughter?'

'No, we only met up with her six weeks ago, in London.'

'She's young to be travelling around the country in wartime. Very young, and very attractive. Have any men tried to date her?'

'Yes, several, but I wouldn't allow it.'

'Very sensible. There, you see, she is coming round.' She smiled at the girl, a warm, motherly smile, and asked kindly, 'Feeling better?'

Wendy stared at her, then at Nigel. 'What happened?' she whispered.

'You fainted, pet.'

Pet? That was Daddy's name for her. Hot tears flooded her eyes.

'Don't cry,' he said, and kissed her cheek.

Nancy stood in the doorway with her false smile. 'Well, darling, if you wanted to steal the show, you

208

certainly succeeded!' she teased.

'I'm sorry.' Wendy knew it was not the end of the matter, and there would be another of those scenes she was beginning to dread, later in the day, back in their lodgings.

'Let her rest for an hour. She will be all right here,' Matron suggested, as she ushered them out.

When the door had closed, Wendy let the tears fall. She cried weakly and helplessly, and wished she were dead. Then she slept, exhausted, for nearly two hours, and it was Lennie who was waiting to take her back to their lodgings.

'Gimme a bloody fright you did, ducks. Thought you'd kicked the bucket,' he grumbled.

'Oh, *Lennie*! As if I would. I am much too fond of you.'

He grinned. ''ow abaht a nice cup of tea?'

She sat up, and discovered she was feeling better.

'Bless you, Lennie dear,' she said, gratefully.

PART III

PART III

Chapter Nine

As far as the family at Russets were concerned, the Battle of Britain was being fought by one heroic Spitfire pilot – their own Julian Franklin. Dick could hardly keep pace with the number of enemy aircraft shot down each day, and all the family had been recruited to make the tiny paper models to stick on the kitchen walls. The excitement was intense, and they listened, spellbound, to the 9 o'clock news. There was no question of the younger children being sent to bed. The school was closed for the long holiday, in which all the village children would be picking hops, but not the Russet children, who would be helping on the farm. Lucy always relaxed her strict ruling on 'early to bed and early to rise' in the holidays.

Katie was often to be seen on her hands and knees clearing up dollops of flour paste and scraps of paper. She grumbled about the clutter, but nobody took any notice.

During the second week of July, an incredible total of 441 enemy aircraft were shot down, and Dick was climbing on the step-ladder to reach the top of the wall. He was a very orderly boy, and liked the little models arranged in straight lines.

While the children were concerned only with the enemy aircraft that were shot down, Lucy, Tom and Carrie were constantly aware of the appalling number of our own aircraft reported missing. Maggie would bring in her friends from the Convent School at Marston Park to gaze in fascinated wonder at Dick's display. It was rumoured that the school would be permanently stationed at Marston Park, and when the war was over, the children would not return to London. There seemed to be some truth in the report, for several acres of parkland had been ploughed, and potatoes planted, the vegetable garden extended behind the stables, and sheep were actually grazing in the Park. It was sacrilege to Lucy, who had loved her lord dearly. Yet all these major developments had been sanctioned by Mr Maloney, according to his wife, Kitty, who was enjoying her new role as under-gardener.

Kitty and Sammy shared the self-contained flat in the Big House, and did all their own chores. The foreign servants previously employed in the house were working in factories and canteens. The war had changed all their lives. Sammy was supervising the various activities of the ladies of the WVS. The servants' bedrooms had been converted into a clothing depot, with rows of shelves lining the walls. They supplied their counterparts in London's East End with clothing for their bombed-out families. Sammy had acquired a second-hand van, and, with a small petrol allowance, travelled about the area, begging cast-off and outgrown clothes from reluctant upper-class housewives.

Diane Maloney had not been seen at Marston Park since the outbreak of war. She kept in touch by telephone. Her father was back in the States. His original plan to provide a worthy setting for his beautiful daughter was a failure; she did not want it. Harry B.

Maloney was a bitterly disappointed man, and he had long since decided to devote all his energy and enterprise to expanding the vast network of factories spilling out weapons of destruction. He hid his disappointment in his lovely daughter, increased her allowance, and wondered why his private world had been such a failure when his public world was so successful. It did not occur to him to blame himself. He was not a man to admit defeat readily. Yet those who knew him in those struggling early years remembered that he had idolised the child, spent money lavishly on her clothes, her dancing, music and riding lessons, while his poor little wife went without. So it had continued when he prospered.

Lucy was fond of Kitty, and always made her welcome at Russets. On warm Summer evenings, when her aching back and stiff muscles cried halt to the hard, manual work in the garden, she would take a bath, change her clothes, and walk across the Park, to relax in the old rocking-chair in Lucy's kitchen and listen to the chatter of the children as they ran in and out. With a cup of tea from the family teapot on the hob, and a slice of cake, she would enjoy the homely atmosphere that always surrounded Lucy.

Before the war, in the idle years at Marston Park, when Harry had reminded her that servants were paid to do all the work, she had envied Lucy Blunt, but now she had a useful job to do, and the shouts and laughter of the younger children playing on the swings in the courtyard kept her company. The aged gardener, bored with retirement, was back on duty. He was a great authority on vegetables and soft fruits, and glad to be employed again. Kitty was only a novice, but she was learning all the time, and a young lad, straight from school, helped with the digging and manuring.

Kitty Maloney was happy again, and she had not

known much happiness since Diane was a baby. She enjoyed her work, she enjoyed sharing the flat with Sammy, and she enjoyed visiting Russets on these warm, Summer evenings. It gave her a sense of belonging to the farming family. Each child had been made responsible for certain duties from an early age, and since the outbreak of war, when the arable work done by Tom and Dick had been greatly increased, the two younger children, John and Midge, had been put in charge of the poultry. They had often to be reminded, however, that the chores included keeping the hen houses clean as well as feeding and watering and egg collecting. Dick was responsible for the incubators. Maggie helped her mother in the dairy and on the market stall in the holidays. She spent all her free time at Marston Park. now her dearest wish was to become a Catholic, but she had to be content to watch all their religious practices. By watching and listening, Maggie would absorb the doctrine she was determined to embrace as soon as she had permission. But that permission would not be given till she left the village school, for neither her parents nor her grandmother trusted her change of heart. For a child who had once been obsessed by the desire to join Harriet and Philip at the Mission in the Congo, the change was too drastic, too unrealistic to be taken seriously, so they insisted. Tears were shed, and she begged Sister Theresa to intervene.

'Patience, child. Rome was not built in a day,' that pious soul reminded her. Poor Maggie. She had to be content, for the time being, with a picture of the Madonna and Child that she found on a stall in the market, and hung over the bed.

Dick was his father's deputy. There was a close affinity between father and son because they both loved the land. Of the four children, only John had a tendency to escape the tasks he had been allotted, but Lucy excused him for he hadn't the physical or mental stamina of the rest of the family.

With their children growing up and becoming independent, Tom and Carrie were still sweethearts. It was good to see Tom's quiet face light up with pleasure when Carrie walked into the kitchen; they had eyes only for each other.

'If only I had a daughter like Carrie,' Kitty would be thinking, 'and a grandchild like Midge,' for Midge was still her favourite. She had always been a friendly child, with a bright intelligence that emphasised the difference between her and her twin. There was little love between them now, only a kind of tolerance. Yet when he had developed bronchitis in that first Winter of the war, she could not bear to see him fighting for his breath, and actually allowed him to use her precious paintbox when he was convalescing.

Midge knew exactly what she would be doing when she left Grammar School. She would be enrolled as a student at the College of Art. The talent was there, and it was quite remarkable for her age. She recognised it and accepted it as natural. It was animals, not humans, she depicted with such life-like accuracy. And since she was surrounded by animals, she had no need to search for subjects beyond the scope of Russets. The Shire horses were her favourite subjects. She had outgrown the tendency to draw everything in miniature. She loved to perch on top of a gate, with a sketch book and pencil. Then her whole being was involved in tense concentration that nobody dare interrupt. It was the only time that Midge was seen to be still. Here was the third generation at Russets, plump and pretty, with golden curls and blue eyes. Lucy's curls were faded now, but her eyes were as blue and bright as her grand-daughter's. She had put on a lot of weight, but she was still an attractive woman.

By the Summer of 1940, the boys from The Firs Preparatory School were familiar to the local Cotswold shopkeepers. In their short grey knickers and blue blazers, they were a lively bunch of small boys, and all had settled down happily since the school had been evacuated from Tunbridge Wells the previous year. The two brothers, Mark and Matthew were not the only children to spend the holidays at school, for The Firs catered specially for children whose parents were working overseas and would not be on leave till the end of the war.

The cricket season was in full swing, and the boys were playing a team of village lads on the green on this Summer afternoon. It was just one of many minor events arranged by a sensible headmaster for those who were spending the holidays at school.

Matthew, the younger brother, sat huddled on the grass, feeling the pangs of defeat. To be bowled out by a freckled-faced urchin in a torn jersey before he had scored a single run, was the most humiliating experience of his short life. It was boring to sit and watch. He still had a penny left from his weekly allowance, and it was burning a hole in his pocket. On the other side of the road, Mrs King's little sweet-shop beckoned invitingly. A half-penny bag of sherbet and two sticks of liquorice would help to pass the time.

Nobody saw him slip away. They were all keen cricketers watching the match, clapping and cheering like mad when one of the school team added a couple of runs to the score.

A screech of brakes, a terrified scream, and silence. The small figures on the green seemed to freeze for a split second, then all started to run.

An elderly man was kneeling in the road, cradling a boy in his lap. 'It wasn't my fault,' he told the grey-haired master. 'He ran straight off the Green in front of my car.'

Both men were pale with shock. There was no blood, only a swelling bruise on the temple. The boys stood back, staring and whispering.

Mark pushed his way to the front. 'Is he dead, sir?' he asked, quietly.

'No – no. Just concussion. Will someone fetch Matron.'

Half a dozen boys shot off across the Green, each one eager to be the first to break the news of the accident. They remembered that Matron was also the grandmother of Mark and Matthew, though she did not favour them in front of the other boys, and they called her Grandma only in her private sitting-room.

She was enjoying a rest in a deck chair on the lawn. She loved these hot Summer afternoons when the school had broken up, and she had more leisure. Hetty would bring her a tray of tea at 4 o'clock. She had been dozing over her book. It was a habit that she found vexing, but she was no longer young. 'When the war is over, I shall be ready for retirement,' she had told herself, and she was not the only person on the staff thinking of retirement. The Professor who had been supervising the cricket match, had been at the school since the First World War. So had Cook and her handyman husband. The gardener was over seventy, and Hetty, the ex-housekeeper from Marston Park, would be in her mid-fifties. The younger members of the staff had left before the school was evacuated.

'Matron! Matron!'

It was young Jackson, sprinting across the grass with little Lowry close on his heels, and both shouting their heads off.

'I am not deaf,' she reprimanded them sternly, as they stood before her, panting for breath.

'There's been an accident, Matron,' Jackson gulped.

'It's Matthew. He's been run over. He looks sort of dead,' Lowry announced importantly.

'Matthew? – Oh, *no*!' she entreated, too stunned to move.

They took her hands, pulled her out of the chair, and hurried back across the garden. Four disappointed messengers of doom had got no farther than the gate. On the other side of the Green, a group of small boys stood aside to make way for the one person who would decide whether Matthew was alive or dead. If he was dead, the cricket match would be stopped, and the village team could claim to have won. It was not fair!

Matron was kneeling in the road. She had taken the limp little figure in her arms, and was sobbing wildly.

'My darling! My darling!'

The Professor had an arm about her shoulders. Mark stood there, not saying a word, not crying, white as a ghost till he suddenly turned away to be violently sick on the grass.

A group of Saturday shoppers was collecting, and the unfortunate driver kept repeating, 'It wasn't my fault. He ran straight across the road in front of the car. Didn't anyone see it happen? I must have a witness.'

'Yes, I saw the child dart across the road. 'e were making for my shop. Look, 'e's still clutching the penny,' the old woman was shaking her head, sadly.

'Will someone please telephone for the doctor?' the Professor was asking.

They were rather suspicious of the Professor in the village because of his foreign accent. But nobody could be less likely to be spying than this courteous, elderly schoolmaster with the Van Dyke beard.

'The police constable should also be informed. I'll phone them both,' the grocer reminded him, and hurried away importantly.

220

'Gosh! – the police!' gasped Penfold, the head boy, and dropped on the grass. The others followed suit, and they sat in a row, hugging their knees, the cricket match forgotten in this exciting event, important enough to bring the constable back on duty on a Saturday afternoon.

'Let me take him, my dear,' urged the Professor, kindly. 'Come, let us sit down on the grass. We may have to wait some time.'

So they sat down beside the row of small boys, and more people joined the group of interested onlookers, and hung about with their dogs and children, speculating on the fate of the driver, the headmaster's responsibility, and the terrible shock to the child's parents.

Matron was still crying quietly, holding the clenched little hand. 'A penny – only a penny. To be killed for the sake of spending a penny,' she sobbed.

'It is always a penny, not more, for the sweets. The shilling must last a whole week, and there is ice-cream to buy, and a stamp for the letter to the parents,' the Professor reminded her.

Nobody took any notice of Mark – a pale, silent boy, hugging his knees, too shocked to cry. It had happened so suddenly, he could not believe that Matthew was dead. People were killed in air-raids, but they had no air-raids here. It was a safe zone. That was why the school had been evacuated from Tunbridge Wells. How could Matthew be dead when he was standing at the wicket ready to slosh the ball only a short time ago? But he hadn't hit the ball. He was bowled out, and threw down the bat in a temper. Matthew was a poor loser, but then he was not keen on sport. He had to play. All the boys had to play cricket in the Summer and football in the Winter. Team spirit was important. The Head was terribly keen on the team spirit.

221

His mouth was dry. He could taste the sour vomit. Being sick was usually important enough to get you into sick bay, with Matron fussing over your temperature, but not today. Matron was Grandma, and she was crying.

'Can I have a drink of water, please?'

Grandma and the Professor stared at him in shocked surprise because he had called attention to himself, but the sweet shop lady, standing nearby, patted his head and invited kindly, 'Come with me, dear.' She took his hand. It was rather embarrassing, but of course she wouldn't know that a boy was manly enough to walk alone at the age of seven, when he was sent to preparatory school, and Mark was eleven. He was soothed by her kindness, and he went with her into her kitchen, and drank the water gratefully.

'Would you like a sweetie, dear?' she asked, as they came through the shop.

'No, thank you.'

'Your little brother was coming to spend a penny in my shop, and I knowed what it would be – sherbet and liquorice. Never 'ad no trouble with that one. Always knowed what 'e wanted. Some of 'em take 'alf the day making up their minds.'

'He's not dead, is he?' His eyes were wide with fear in his stricken face.

'Just concussion, I reckon, dear.'

'That's what I think,' he nodded. Then he pulled his hand away, thanked her politely for the water, and walked slowly back to sit quietly beside the Professor. As long as he lived he would remember that hot, Summer afternoon waiting for the doctor and the constable. He couldn't bear to look at Matthew, lying across the Professor's knees, and Grandma, her face wet with tears, holding that small, clenched hand. 'Take care of

222

Matthew, darling,' – his mother's last words, as his parents boarded the ship to take them back to the Congo.

'Keep an eye on Matthew, dear. He's only a little boy, and not very strong.' That was his dear Granny at Fairfields. If she were here, she would not blame him. But Grandma would blame him. She adored Matthew because he reminded her of his grandfather, who had died of a fever many years ago in the Congo. She had told them the story of the young Scottish missionary who had been invited to lunch at the Parsonage one Sunday, long ago. They had fallen in love, and she had left her post as governess to the two elder daughters of Sir Neville Franklin at Marston Park. Against her parents' wishes, she had married the young missionary, and sailed away for five long years. It had not been an easy life she had chosen. She was homesick, and often unwell in such an unhealthy climate. But she had her darling husband, and they were blessed with three children, Richard, Agnes and Harriet.

'I thought my heart had broken when we left Richard behind at The Parsonage on our first leave, to start school the following year,' she told them. 'But it finally did break when your grandfather died, quite suddenly, of a tropical fever. I came home to England with the two girls. Life has a strange way of repeating itself, my darlings,' she had reminded them. 'The girls grew up, Harriet married your father and went back to the Congo. Then you were born. Now you are here, at *your* preparatory school.'

Mark shivered on that hot, Summer afternoon, thousands of miles from their parents. 'Take care of Matthew, darling.' He was remembering his mother's last injunction. He wished he could run away and hide, but his legs wouldn't carry him far. Just crossing the road for a drink of water had taken all his strength.

When the constable arrived on his bicycle, the driver of the car repeated once again that it was not his fault, and he had a witness to prove it. The constable felt very important, and wrote busily in his notebook. In his serge uniform and helmet he was sweating profusely.

When the doctor arrived, the group of people on the Green closed in, but he waved them back, bent over the child, felt his pulse, and confirmed that Matthew was dead. The distraught driver felt obliged to repeat his story for the benefit of the doctor, but he was not listening. Glancing round the group of spectators, his eye fell on the burly figure of the butcher, in his striped apron and straw boater.

'Paterson, carry the boy to the school, there's a good fellow,' he commanded authoritatively.

It did not occur to the butcher to refuse. Leaving his young assistant in charge of the shop, he slipped off his apron, and stepped forward. The sad little procession followed him across the Green, through the garden gate, and across the lawn. The Head and his wife ran out in great consternation. Hetty and Cook stood back respectfully, waiting for instructions. Matron was leaning heavily on the Professor's arm, and his other arm was wrapped about Mark's shoulders. Then Hetty was asked to take charge of the boys, and to help Cook serve their tea at the trestle table on the lawn. Mark was pushed into a chair in the kitchen, to be out of the way, and he sat there, obediently, too dazed with shock to move. Appalled by the tragedy, the headmaster's wife was crying quietly as her husband led the way into his study.

When the dead child had been laid on the couch and covered with a rug, the Head immediately took charge of the situation, and poured a generous tot of whisky for the doctor, the constable, the butcher and the driver, the

Professor and himself. Matron was persuaded to drink a cup of tea laced with whisky, and to retire to her private apartment in a state of collapse.

It was a terrible shock, the Head was saying. In twenty years, they had never lost a child. They had had some bad scares with accidents and epidemics, but nothing fatal until today. Now it was his sad duty to notify the parents by cablegram, and the other grandparent by telephone.

When all had gone their separate ways, the Professor took up his duties again with the calm resignation of a man who knew the full meaning of tragedy. The First World War had robbed him of his home and his entire family. He had nothing more to lose. He was grateful for the kindness he had received from the headmaster and his wife, but he was still a very lonely man, still regarded as a 'foreigner' – that hateful word that segregated a man from his fellows.

Now he saw no reason why the cricket match should not be continued. The village boys were enjoying a strawberry tea with the rest. It had been promised, and was one of the highlights of this particular day. The long, light evenings had to be organised, and after what had happened this afternoon, the Head would be even more insistent on supervision. Yet who could have prevented that small boy from rushing off to spend his penny on the impulse of the moment?

So they went back to finish the game, leaving Mark with Hetty. The only sign of the accident was a skid mark in the road, and only the Professor was saddened by the tragedy as he took up his position to watch fair play. His thoughts wandered, however, to the grief-stricken woman who had leaned on his arm so heavily and trustingly in her hour of need. There was an affinity between them, and a common bond, since neither had a

225

home other than the school, and both were ready for retirement, but much too loyal to forsake the Head during the war. It would be quite impossible to find replacements for a preparatory school. If it was a long war – as long as the last – the Professor's hair and beard would be white, and Matron would have a double chin and no waist to speak of!

Martha was finding the school holidays much too long in her lonely cottage at Fairfields. No eyes but hers had admired the colourful flower borders, the smooth, green lawn and the neat rows of vegetables. She had picked gooseberries, currants, strawberries and raspberries in due season, made jam and bottled fruit, but it gave her no pleasure to see all the jars lined up on the pantry shelves. Most of her life had been spent in tending little children, and in caring for those who depended on her – her father, her two dead husbands, her son, and her two adored grandsons, when they were brought home from the Congo. Her father, the village wheelwright, was long since dead.

On this warm, Summer evening, she was staking a row of gladioli in the front garden. All the doors and windows were flung wide open. There was no sound but the distant rattle of the reaper across the fields. No child came to gather wild flowers in the lane. All the village children were out in the hop-gardens with their mothers. She was trying to make up her mind whether to offer her services at one of the farms. She had never picked hops, but there was always a first time. She had her bicycle, and the money she earned would buy coal and logs for the coming Winter.

The buzz of the telephone bell in the tiny hall sent her hurrying indoors, eager to talk to someone. She had not seen a soul all day. The milkman delivered at the crack of dawn in the Summer months.

'Hallo!' The eagerness was in her voice and in her bright eyes. It could be Carrie or Ruby, or the Vicar's wife reminding her it was her turn to provide the flowers for the altar next Sunday. A man's voice answered her, a cultured voice, speaking quietly. She listened in appalled silence, her bright eyes flooded with tears. When he had finished speaking, she answered him chokingly.

'Yes, of course I will come. I will catch an early train in the morning. I have no idea what time I shall arrive. How do I get to the school? Will there be a taxi at the station?'

'I doubt it. Just give me a ring and my wife will collect you. Will you take down the phone number, please.'

It was the first time she had spoken to the Headmaster of The Firs Preparatory School because there was no occasion for her to do so. The other grandmother, being the school matron, had naturally accepted the responsibility.

When she had hung up the receiver she stood there, trembling with shock, her face wet with tears. Matthew dead? It was inconceivable. Only this week she had posted another tuck-box – cakes, jam, home-made toffee and coconut-ice. Now she remembered the questions she should have asked. Had Mark seen the accident? How had he reacted? Would she be bringing Matthew back for burial in the family plot in the churchyard at Fairfields? Automatically, because it had always been done, as far back as she could remember, she put on the kettle and made a pot of tea. Sitting at the kitchen table in the window recess, she gazed out at the garden. The swing was still tied to the branch of the gnarled old apple tree. She had not taken it down, since it reminded her of the happy holidays before the war, when her grandsons stayed with her. They slept in the room she still called 'Philip's room' and rode his bicycle round the lanes. Even with the saddle lowered, Matthew could not reach it, so stood on the pedals.

In her mind's eye, she could see him showing off as she watched from the gate. Once he had got over the initial tears and tantrums of that first term at boarding school, he had developed into a manly little fellow, with a passion for sherbet and liquorice. Matthew dead?

She sipped the hot, sweet tea, and remembered the throttling hug at the garden gate when they said goodbye a year ago.

When she had finished the tea, she spent the next hour or so talking to Lucy, Carrie and Ruby, in a voice so choked with tears it was hardly audible. Their warm sympathy reminded her how fortunate she was to have these good friends. She had only to pick up the phone when she was feeling sad or lonely. She remembered how her dear Carrie had reacted when Andrew had died so suddenly. In less than an hour she was pedalling down the lane on her bicycle, and she stayed with her till after the funeral.

But now she had to face the long journey alone to that Cotswold village. She went to bed early, but could not sleep. At 5 o'clock, she was down in the kitchen making tea and eating a boiled egg with bread and butter. An hour later, she was on her way to the station with a small case strapped on the bicycle.

She would never forget that journey, or the return journey with Mark curled up beside her, and Matthew in the guard's van, surrounded by milk churns, sleeping peacefully in the small coffin.

Mark had clung to her like a limpet. 'Take me home with you, Granny. *Please! Please!* I don't want to stay here.' Dry-eyed and deathly pale, he had flung himself into her arms, and she held him protectively. Over the top of his head, she could see the questioning glance that passed between the headmaster and his wife. Perhaps they would be grateful to be relieved of further responsibility. She was concerned only for the child, and her first reaction was one of pleasure that he found comfort in her arms. Perhaps, in their determination to promote manliness and independence, these good people were sparing in affection. Perhaps it was asking too much to expect it.

Her own working-class background meant she deplored the necessity to send children away from home in their most formative years. Philip had attended the village school, then passed a scholarship to Grammar School where he was a day-pupil. But Philip had married into the upper class, and it was his young wife, Harriet, who had overruled the suggestion that Mark and Matthew should live with her at Fairfields and attend the village school. The other grandmother, already settled in the post of Matron at The Firs, had added her voice – an authoritative voice – to her daughter's. And Philip had acquiesced, as usual. If only they had listened to her, this dreadful tragedy would not have happened, she told herself, as she held the child in her arms.

Two days later they left for home. She had promised the Headmaster she would notify the parents by cablegram and a letter would follow, explaining that she would keep Mark with her till the end of the war, and when they came on leave, they could decide his future.

At the start of the new term, they would both be there, at the village school. For the remainder of the holiday, they would spend long days at Russets with Lucy's lively family. It would be like old times. There was no place like Russets for healing sad hearts. She should know.

Mark would be offered a puppy or a kitten. She wondered which he would choose. He would want to take the little creature to bed. Why not? Her grandson's happiness was all that mattered in the years ahead.

PART IV

Chapter Ten

He knew it must happen, eventually, because it had happened to all his friends. The Battle of Britain would go down in history as the most appalling sacrifice of the nation's youth since Kitchener's Army on the Western Front. If he lived to have a son, and if his friends had survived, their exploits would be told in the same way as fathers through the ages have recorded such tales.

These thoughts had occupied his mind on more than one occasion as they limped back to base. 'Old Jules' and Spitfire 'Lucy' had charmed lives, the youngsters maintained. He smiled and shrugged. Such foolish talk! The Squadron had lost so many planes and pilots in a few short weeks, it was sadly depleted. Crippling losses had been reported from all over the country. The German Luftwaffe, inflicting such deadly and devastating destruction, had seemed, in that crucial time of survival, to be indestructible, yet, according to young Dick at Russets, a total of 441 enemy planes had been shot down in a little over a week. It was certainly a fantastic figure.

Aunt Lucy's weekly letter always contained some encouraging episode to boost the morale, but made no mention of their own terrible losses. He could imagine the walls of the farm kitchen plastered with tiny paper planes, and the children busy with scissors and flour paste at the kitchen table. He remembered a time when he knelt on a chair at that same table, because he was too small to reach the bowl of flour paste. Carrie had rolled up his sleeves, and he and Uncle Bertie were making paper chains to decorate the kitchen and the parlour on Christmas Eve. He was a very privileged little boy, since he was the only child in the family, and hadn't to share anything. All his earliest memories were happy ones, and the farm kitchen the centre of happiness.

Limping back to base in the early dawn was a good time to remember his childhood at Russets. It was when he was physically exhausted that his mind was most receptive to the lovely pictures of those early years, before the village school dominated the scene. He seemed to spend a lot of time on somebody's lap, rocking back and forth in the old rocking chair. There were so many laps to choose from in those very early days, as far back as memory went, but Aunt Lucy's was the most comfortable. His senses had been lulled by pleasant smells – the smell of baking, of clothes airing on the fireguard, and geraniums on the window sills. Surrounded by love, he had responded with love. His every wish was gratified, and his small fears appeased. Because he was afraid of the dark, a night-light burned in his bedroom. He remembered the splendid figure of grandfather on the black horse, and the scarred face of Uncle Bertie. He remembered his first ride on a horse called Duke, with his short legs stretched across its broad back, and the two uncles walking on either side. It was much later when he discovered the two uncles disliked each other, and barely spoke.

But his first encounter with the antagonism between the two uncles had made no difference. He loved them both. The uncle with the scarred face and violent temper was never too busy to play games or read stories. It was much later that he discovered Uncle Bertie was not expected to work because he had been badly wounded in the war, so he accepted both uncles – the gentle Uncle Tom and the violent Uncle Bertie, with equal affection. They were part of his small world.

The servant, Katie, with her sniffing and her cackling laugh, was also accepted. She belonged to Russets. The horses, the sheep, the cows, the pigs, the dogs and cats, and the little brown hens he chased in the orchard, all belonged to Russets. His small world had seemed immense in those early years, when he went no farther than its boundaries, and before he discovered it was not the whole universe. Riding to market in the wagonette, wedged between Carrie and Uncle Tom, had been his first exciting encounter with the outside world. It was very surprising, and rather frightening. Too much traffic, too many people – too much of everything.

He tried to remember when Uncle Bertie helped him to assemble the first model aeroplane from his first Meccano set. It was before he started school, so it could have been the Christmas before his fifth birthday. He still had that little model, and all the others. Not one had been dismantled. When he had outgrown the Meccano sets, Grandfather sent to Hamleys, the famous London toyshop, for more complicated models to be fitted together like jigsaw puzzles, with a lot of patience. It was a fascinating occupation for a wet Sunday afternoon or for when he was kept in bed with a chesty cold. The smell of embrocation still reminded him of those happy hours. The stark reality of life was suddenly revealed in the school playground, when he found himself a tiny unit of no importance whatsoever. It was a bitter lesson to learn.

*　*　*

It happened suddenly, within sight of the coast. His last coherent thought, as he lost control and plunged into the sea, was of Russets.

All the family went to town on market days in the school holidays, leaving Lucy at home. She enjoyed the quiet day, and at 4 o'clock, she would drive the cows into the milking shed. It was like old times, and she had not lost that special touch the cows recognised. She had always been a good milker. Bert had taught her well. It was one of the most important tasks she had to learn when she arrived at Russets.

The prettiest girls in the village, with identical golden curls and blue eyes, plump and glowing with health and vitality, they were much sought after by the boys. But the twins had been clever enough to avoid the clumsy fumblings of every lusty village lad, and confined their courtship to these two steady young men with serious intentions. Both Tom and Bert were seduced quite happily in the sweet-smelling hay, and were only slightly surprised to find themselves prospective fathers three months later. Being decent, honourable young men, however, marriages were arranged.

From henceforth, the sisters' circumstances kept them apart for most of the year, though they lived within a couple of miles of each other. For Lucy, an only son to inherit the prosperous farm and a mellowed old farmhouse. For Ruby, a poorly-paid ganger and a rat-infested cottage, with a privy, in Richmond Row, the village slum. For Lucy it was a way of life strangely different and not altogether pleasant. The acrid smell of silage, the long, bleak winters, the mud and the mess, and no respite from the eternal drudgery, seven days a week. She carried her baby low, and she leaned over her bulging stomach to milk the cows with Bert, twice a day. On bitterly cold Winter mornings, Bert would pinch her bottom playfully, and remind her she was a farmer's wife. It was then that she actually envied her twin sister, who could lie abed till 6.30. Tom would bring her a cup of tea, pack his dinner box with bread and fat bacon, and kiss her goodbye. Bert expected Lucy to be downstairs by 5 o'clock, raking out the dead ashes, and lighting the fire to boil the kettle for the first pot of tea. They drank a lot of tea, and the pot stood on the hob all day. Bert's mother had waited on her husband and son hand and foot, like most country-bred women, so he naturally expected his wife to carry on the same way. Lucy resented it, and her strong personality soon changed his idea of the nature of a wife's role in the home. With only a 13-year-old servant girl from the orphanage for scrubbing and polishing, Lucy had never worked so hard in all her short life. The two years she had been employed as a house-maid at the doctor's house in the village had been easy in comparison, with one Sunday free in every month and two evenings after she had helped to serve the dinner.

Their babies were born the same week, both boys, and it didn't surprise them that both were blessed with three boys in five years – Lucy's boys as fair as lilies, and Ruby's as dark as gypsies. The only holiday the sisters enjoyed in their early married lives was a week's confinement, when the village midwife came in daily to attend to mother and baby. Ruby's status was definitely below Lucy's since she was employed as a charwoman at The Three Nuns public house. The wages were small, but supplemented with useful perks in the shape of soup, left over pies, and the remains of the cold joints of beef and mutton. This helped to feed the hungry family of boys, and they lived better than the other poor families in Richmond Row. Ruby had not lost her looks or her happy nature, and she was not envious of her twin in better circumstances. Lucy's family fed like fighting cocks at Russets. Bert was a tolerant, easy-going husband and father.

'Lucy Blunt do wear the trousers and old Bert the petticoats at Russets!' their farming neighbours declared.

There was a leisurely feeling about those quiet days with the family away to the market after an early breakfast. They enjoyed the hot supper she had waiting in the oven. The children brought her little gifts from the market stalls, and she kept them in the pretty chocolate boxes in the top drawer of her dressing table – brooches, handkerchiefs, scented soaps, lavender sachets and lace doilies. The chocolate boxes were a reminder of the birthday presents she had received from Squire Franklin, though she had no need to be reminded. Her lord was enshrined in her heart for ever.

When she had finished her morning work in the dairy, and sent the gardener from Marston Park on his way with the milk float, she made another pot of tea, and cut a thick crust from a freshly-baked loaf. With a piece of cream cheese and a pat of butter, she could make a satisfying mid-day snack. She carried the tray to the bench in the yard, and sat there in the sunshine with the two dogs stretched out at her feet, and the marmalade cat sunning itself at the wide-flung door of the Dutch barn. Her contentment was absolute in that quiet hour, and she had no premonition of the shock that would cast such a shadow over their lives.

When she had shared the last morsel of bread with the dogs, she strolled across the yard to lean on the gate, and stood there, in blissful idleness, reluctant to start on the next job. She hadn't expected any visitors today, and was surprised to see the boundary gate at the end of the cart-track swing open, and a small figure emerge, pushing a bicycle. When he had shut the gate, he climbed on the bike and pedalled furiously in her direction – a small figure in uniform. Her heart was racing, and she shivered in the warm sunshine, watching his approach with set lips.

'Good morning, Ma'am'. He greeted her with the solemn respect due to every recipient of an orange envelope, as he slid off the saddle. She answered him mechanically, and stared, in fascinated disbelief as he drew out the orange envelope from the leather pouch on his belt. She took it and slit it open. In that moment of agonising suspense, she was back in the First World War, waiting to read the brief announcement – 'We regret to inform you . . .' It was Harry, her first-born, then. Now it was Julian, the boy she had fostered, and the dearest of all her children, she realised with a cruel certainty when Death had divided them. When her clouded eyes had cleared, she looked up to see the boy had removed the pill-box hat, and was wiping his sweating head with a grubby handkerchief. It was a warm outfit to be wearing in the Summer, but he was very proud of his uniform, especially the pill-box hat. It was his first job when he left the village school on his fourteenth birthday, a year ago. A telegraph boy had a certain status. His friends were apprenticed to tradesmen, or working on the farms. In a sense, he was a messenger of doom, but his extreme youth, and the pride in his uniform, dispelled any morbidness that an older individual might have felt. To be singled out by the postmistress for this honourable calling was a big responsibility. As a trusted servant of His Majesty's Civil Service, he had been reminded that the penalty for disclosing the contents of an orange envelope to an outsider was instant dismissal. Even before the war, a telegram was regarded by the working class with some misgiving. It cost a shilling for twelve words, and nobody would waste a precious shilling for anything less than dire emergency. 'Bad news' would be the immediate reaction. The upper class normally communicated by telephone.

Since last September, the whole aspect of his job had changed dramatically. Every family in the village could expect to be the recipient of bad news at any hour of the day. The upper class were as deeply involved as the working class. Ladies and women were most unpredictable in their reaction. Some would burst into tears and slam the door, while others would thank him politely and ask him to wait for the small tip he always hoped to receive.

Mrs Blunt was tucking the telegram into her apron pocket. She was not going to cry.

'Would you like a glass of lemonade?' she asked, kindly, in a choked voice, and swung open the gate. He followed her across the yard and into the kitchen, with the dogs sniffing suspiciously at his trousers.

'Don't be afraid. They won't hurt you,' she said.

'I ain't afeared, Ma'am,' he told her. It wouldn't be the first time he felt the sharp nip of teeth. It was one of the hazards of wearing a uniform, he had soon discovered.

'Sit down,' she invited, still in that choked voice. She stood watching him while he drank the lemonade and ate a thick slice of cake, but she did not speak again.

So he thanked her politely, and pointed out, 'I'll be on my way now, Ma'am,' picked up his hat, and walked out.

'Listen to those cows. There's something wrong. They haven't been milked,' said Tom, anxiously, as they trundled slowly towards the farm in the loaded wagonette. Even Katie understood the importance of milking a cow twice daily, and she roused herself from the lethargy that followed her weekly rendezvous with the current swain to remark, 'The Mistress must 'ave fergot'.

The outcry from the family did nothing to dispel the pleasurable ache in her thighs. Sexual intercourse, for Katie, was as natural as eating and sleeping.

'Granny never forgets nothing!' Midge reminded her scornfully.

'Something's wrong,' Carrie echoed, and Dick stopped his shrill whistling as he climbed down to open the boundary gate. Midge slid off her perch on the tail-board, and ran on ahead to push open the yard gate. She always had to be first, and she raced across the yard to the kitchen, then stopped dead in the doorway.

Granny was slumped in the rocking chair. Her eyes were red and puffy. She must have been crying for hours.

'Granny, what's the matter? Why are you crying?'

The plump little figure bounded in her lap, and the old chair creaked under the double load. It was Dick who stayed behind to unharness the weary mare and see her settled comfortably in the stable, with water and oats. The others hurried across the yard and into the kitchen.

'Mum, what's happened? Are you ill?' Tom spoke for all the family. But his mother only shook her head, shifted Midge, took the telegram from her apron pocket, and held it out to him. He read it aloud, and they stared at him in stunned silence till Midge shrieked hysterically.

'It's not true! I don't believe it! Julian isn't dead!'

'Oh, *Mum*,' John whimpered, and Carrie drew him close, took Tom's hand, and gazed up at him with streaming eyes. Maggie murmured 'God rest his soul' and made the sign of the cross, but nobody noticed.

Katie was sniffing miserably.

When Dick walked in a few minutes later, he stood

241

transfixed, staring at the scene with a puzzled frown. Hundreds of paper planes hung motionless on the walls. He shivered, and understood. Then he turned away, and went outside. Julian dead? But Julian and his Spitfire 'Lucy' were indestructible. He could hear the cows bellowing in great discomfort, and he pushed Julian to the back of his mind, and called out, 'Dad! – the cows. You coming?'

Tom would have liked a cup of tea, but the tea-pot would be cold on the hob. The fire had burned too low to boil the kettle, and no hot supper awaited them in the oven. He had trained his son well. The animals came first.

'Coming, son,' he answered, dutifully. Then he dropped Carrie's hand, kissed her wet cheek, and followed Dick across the yard.

It was Maggie, not Katie, who went on her knees with a handful of kindling-wood, pulled out the damper, and soon had the fire blazing, and the kettle boiling. While Midge sobbed noisily in Lucy's arms, and John whimpered with his head on his mother's shoulder, Maggie brewed a pot of tea, collected mugs from the dresser, milk and sugar, then poured the tea. They watched her, but nobody offered to help. Katie sat slumped in a chair, waiting to be served.

'I'm Martha and Midge is Mary,' Maggie told her Granny as she handed her a mug of strong, sweet tea. Lucy looked at the child, surprised by this practical streak in her pious young grand-daughter.

'Thank you, dear. I always had a fellow feeling for Martha in my Sunday School days,' she said, and sipped the tea gratefully.

'Was he shot down, Dad?' Dick was asking, as they hurried towards the cows lined up at the fence.

'Yes.'

'I can't believe he won't ever come back to Russets.'

'Nor me.'

'Dad . . .'

'Yes, son?'

'Could I have his bike?'

Tom was so accustomed to his first-born speaking his mind frankly, he showed no surprise. 'You must ask your Gran,' he said.

Dick sighed. 'Gran won't let me have it. You know what she's like about Julian's things. She won't have anything touched in his room.'

'Then you must wait a bit, and we will look for a second-hand bike in the market.'

'I haven't any money, Dad.'

'What do you do with your pocket money?'

Dick looked guilty.

'Well?' Tom insisted, amiably.

'Buy smokes.'

'Since when have you been smoking?'

'Since I got into the Sixth. All the boys smoke in the sixth standard. We smoke in the lavatories.'

'I wonder the younger boys haven't reported it.'

'They daren't. They know what to expect if they split on us.'

Tom looked thoughtful as he pushed open the gate and the cows moved clumsily into the milking shed. 'I don't like it, Dick. You'll be leaving school at Christmas, and earning five shillings a week. If you want to smoke, you can do it openly. You don't have to hide in the lavatory. But your Gran won't like it.'

'I know she won't.'

Nothing more was said. They gave all their attention to the cows.

Wendy had never seen anything more beautiful than the lake, draped in a veil of mist, gradually lifting in the sun's warm rays. From her bedroom window the scene had a haunting loveliness that could only be described in music or poetry. Their lodgings at Windermere were comfortable, and their homely landlady a most obliging soul. Unfortunately, on the few occasions when they found comfortable lodgings, they had no leisure to enjoy them and hardly time to unpack before they were moving on again.

She found this new environment more disturbing to the senses than the bleak moors and bare hills they had left behind. Constantly reminded of her sad lack of knowledge about the landscape of her own country, on the long, tedious train journeys, she gathered impressions that would last a lifetime.

Already a seasoned traveller, she had learned to adapt herself to ever-changing circumstances, and to being left to her own devices. In the early days, she had found it depressing to be left alone to amuse herself in strange lodgings, but she no longer expected companionship. It was a working relationship, and they suited each other very well, provided they retained their individual contributions to the show, and kept up the pretence of a close partnership before an audience.

With the coming of Spring, however, the tension had lifted, and she was no longer obliged to stay indoors reading and writing letters. She could explore the nearest town or village, treat herself to a cup of tea or coffee and a slice of toast in a café, and watch the customers. The majority were in uniform, and she was often reminded of Julian. It was over a month since she had received his last letter. That was another hazard of being constantly on the move. She mustn't complain. They were keeping in touch – Daddy, Gran, Aunt Lucy and Aunt Martha all wrote regularly, but not Mother. She pretended she didn't care, but she would have welcomed a letter, if only to find it full of reproaches for her behaviour.

'Give my love to Mother' had received no direct response. 'We all send our love' was Daddy's way of avoiding the issue – her darling Daddy! He would love this view of the lake. She would try to describe it in her next letter. She always wrote home from each new address. It helped to minimise the strangeness and the loneliness.

Gran had enclosed another book of stamps in her last letter, bless her! She still had received no payment for her services as accompanist, and she would not ask, not until she had spent all her savings in the Post Office Savings Bank. Her expenses were paid, and she bought only the bare essentials, apart from the postcards she sent to the children at Russets, and the cups of tea and coffee.

Now it was mid-Summer, and the station at Windermere had been crowded with young service men and women returning from leave to their training camps, and a few elderly couples determined on a quiet holiday. They would find their favourite haunts swarming with evacuees, and their nights disturbed by the roar of bombers from the RAF Station, and the noisy columns of Army trucks en route to the coast.

Nancy had been complaining of toothache for several days, and Nigel had insisted that she see a dentist before they started rehearsing. He had telephoned for an appointment, and escorted her to the bus. The postman was delivering at the end of the road, so he waited in the doorway to collect any mail forwarded from their last billet. It was usually for Wendy. Poor darling. She was still homesick. It was doubtful whether she would ever make a good trouper in show business.

'Wendy! Letter for you!' he called up, and she ran

downstairs, flushed with eager anticipation, thanked him profusely, brushed his cheek with her cool lips, and scampered back to read it in private.

He sighed. 'Oh, to be young and in love!'

But it was not Julian's neat writing on the envelope. It was Aunt Lucy's large, sprawling hand. Her face clouded with disappointment.

Nigel had poured himself a generous tot of whisky, and was savouring the first sip when she screamed. He hurried upstairs, carrying the glass in a shaking hand, and found her sprawled across the bed. He put down the glass, sat on the bed, and pulled her into his arms talking soothingly.

'Hush, my little one. What has happened? Tell me.'

She beat on his chest with her clenched fists, sobbing hysterically. 'He's *dead*! Julian's *dead*!' she wailed, and lifted her tortured face to stare at him as though he were a stranger. He wrapped his arms about her so closely he could feel her fluttering heart and the tremors of her whole body in an agony of terrible weeping. He went on talking soothingly, stroking her soft, silky hair, and it seemed an eternity before she stopped crying. Her warm body, so young, so desirable, was limp and exhausted when he dried her tear-wet face and held the glass to her lips.

'Just a sip, my sweet, to please me,' he coaxed.

She took a sip and shuddered convulsively.

'One more, my sweet. It will do you good. Come, we will share it – one sip for you, one sip for me – one sip for you, one sip for me.'

When they had drained the glass, he laid her back on the bed and stretched out beside her. With her head in the crook of his arm, he began to unfasten the row of little pink buttons on the rose-patterned frock. Under the frock was a pink cotton petticoat, and under the petticoat a pair of matching knickers. All the garments had a childish simplicity, and were hand-sewn. Her eyes were closed, and she made no protest when he slipped the straps over her shoulders and began to make love to her with a practised hand. His caresses had an unaccustomed unhurried gentleness that surprised him, for his loins were throbbing and demanding. Limp as a rag doll, there was no response till his soft hand touched her thighs and her body quivered.

When he entered her, she gasped with pain and protest.

'No! No!'

But it was too late, and she was too weak and exhausted to push him away. The trickle of bright blood only served to prove what he had always suspected.

But Wendy was no longer a virgin.

Chapter Eleven

He opened his eyes and stared fixedly at the starched white cap perched precariously on the blonde head of the young nurse. Her hands were busy at the bedside-locker, and there was a strong smell of carbolic. He was stripped to the waist, and his chest felt uncomfortably damp.

'Nurse.' He spoke quietly, and she turned her head to look at him with startled grey eyes, and stammered, 'You're – you're awake?'

'Yes,' he said, surprised at the question.

'I must call the doctor immediately.' She dried his chest with a clammy towel, pulled up the bedclothes, and shook her head disbelievingly at the dark, probing eyes that followed her every movement. Then she folded the screen and hurried away with the tin bowl, and the towel slung over her arm.

He lay quite still, his eyes raking over the occupants of the other beds with only a vague curiosity. He lifted his hands from under the bedclothes, and regarded them with pleased satisfaction. He could feel his heart pulsing normally, and he could hear voices quite distinctly. All his senses were alerted now, but there was a strange numbness in the lower part of his body, as though nothing existed below the waist.

'Zo! You vake at last! Dat is goot!' The gutteral accent was unmistakably German, but the tone was kindly, and the massive grey head and bushy eyebrows bore a striking resemblance to the Grammar School headmaster. He had taken Julian's wrist, and had his thumb on the pulse. His patients were a mixed bunch of German and British, including civilians, but he treated them all with the same courtesy and consideration. He was a doctor, not a policeman, and he had no enemies.

'Doctor, where am I?' It was usually the first question, but this young man would be surprised at the answer.

'You are in de 'ospital on de island of Jersey, mein frient, an' you 'ave been lying dare for *sixty-seven* days!'

Julian smiled. It was a very disarming smile, and his nurses would spoil him, the doctor was thinking. His own two sons were serving the Fatherland, one in the air, the other in a submarine. He was proud of his sons, but secretly deplored the violence of the Nazi creed they had adopted.

'You are pulling my leg, Doctor,' the young pilot was saying.

'Vot you mean? I not touch your leg.'

'Sorry, I mean to say, you must be joking.'

'Nein. It vas no shoke. It vas concussion.'

'Concussion? – and I slept for sixty-seven days?'

'Dat is so.'

'Gosh!' The boyish exclamation was so typical of the British. They were so inarticulate!

'Ve 'ave ver' goot coast guart. Dey save many life. Dey save you. Dey tell me you are deat. I say no, dat boy is not deat. Zo!' He had drawn up a chair to the bedside. He had still to answer the most crucial question, and he never lied to a patient.

'Doctor – there is something wrong, isn't there? I can't

249

feel anything at all lower down? Tell me the truth. I can take it.'

'I speak alvays de truth, mein frient. It is de nervous system vot is damaged, you understant? So you feel nosing.'

'Paralysis?'

'Dat is so.'

'You mean, I can't walk? I shall never walk again?' The young voice was choked, the dark eyes anguished.

'Never is not for me to say. Meit Gott! I vish for you to walk. But this is not for me to promise, you understant?'

'But I can hope?'

'Dere is alvays de 'ope. No doctor in dis vorlt is – 'ow you say it?'

'Infallible?'

He nodded.

'One more question, please, Doctor. My family – have they been told?'

'Soon de Red Cross vil convey de goot news dat you are alive. Dat is all. It is for you to write a pose-cart ven you feel like it. Dat is all ve can permit. You understant?'

'I understand. Thank you, Doctor.'

'Now you vish a cup of tea – yes?'

'Yes, please.'

'Alvays de tea!' he chuckled – and pressed Julian's shoulder with a fatherly hand.

'Thank you, nurse.'

She had brought two more pillows, and she propped him up to drink the tea and smoothed the hair from his damp forehead. Poor Julian! What the doctor had just told him was enough to make anyone sweat, she thought.

'Say hello to the other patients. They have been very worried about you,' she rebuked him gently, like a

250

nanny whose charge was forgetting his manners. He raised a hand in greeting, and called 'Hello!'

'Hello Julian!' they chorused.

There was a screen round the bed at the far end of the ward, and another young nurse went behind the screen with a bowl of water, a soap dish, and a towel. Julian would soon discover they were very short staffed, and only very sick patients were washed and shaved. The others went to the bathrooms. The few nurses were either very young probationers or grey-haired women called back from retirement for the duration of the war.

'You'll be OK. Don't you worry,' the girl told him, with a pert self-assurance he found rather irritating.

'I'm not worried,' he lied. He was worried to death, and he desperately wanted Aunt Lucy. Surrounded by strangers, with this dreadful threat hanging over him that he might not walk again, how he would have welcomed that warm, motherly breast. It seemed an eternity since he was flying back to base, or thought he was. But he must have drifted several hundred miles off course. He must have been drunk – drunk with exhaustion.

'If you're a good boy, we shall get you up tomorrow and you can trundle yourself round the ward in a wheel chair.' Blast the girl! Why didn't she go away and leave him alone! 'It's scrambled egg and milk pudding for supper,' she added, as an afterthought.

'I'm not hungry.'

'Oh, but you must eat. It's a long time since you had a proper meal.'

A proper meal? He could visualise the family at Russets, sitting down to a supper of home-cured ham and home-baked bread, dairy butter and cheese, and a freshly brewed pot of tea on the hob.

'What's for afters?' Midge would demand.

251

How lucky they were to have their own produce. Even with the rationing they would not go short.

To shut out the grim bareness of the hospital ward, he closed his eyes and pictured that warm, cheerful kitchen with the family gathered round the table, and the marmalade cat stretched on the hearth-rug, or curled in the basket with a new litter of kittens. It was not the only picture he carried in his mind's eye, and both would be reflected again and again in the weeks and months that lay ahead. He could see himself perched on the gate in the lane, after his farewell visit to Aunt Martha. Wendy was wedged between his thighs, and her sweet-smelling hair tickled his chin. He had his arms about her, and his hands cupped her breasts. The picture was so real, so vivid, he could almost feel the pressure of her slight body against his chest, and her bare legs twitching. That was the moment when he knew for certain that he loved her dearly, and it was no longer the love of an elder brother for a little sister. Why had he waited so long to recognise in his young cousin his true love? He supposed he would not see her again till the war was over – his little sweetheart.

He touched the tiny silver trinket on a chain round his neck. She would insist that her faith in St Christopher had saved his life, and he must not disillusion her, though it seemed pretty obvious that it was the prompt action of the coast-guard.

Then he was struck by a sudden, disturbing thought. He was a prisoner of war! The Channel Islands were occupied by the enemy, and the presence of the German doctor should have reminded him of this obvious fact. He sighed. There was no hope of escape since he was also a prisoner of his own paralysed body. Tears pricked his eyes, but he kept them closed. Self-pity was not going to help. 'I can take it,' he had told the doctor, but that was bluffing. To spend the rest of his life a helpless cripple was a terrible prospect. It would demand a special kind of courage to face such a grim future, and he was afraid he hadn't got that kind of courage.

'Cheer up, me ole' cock-sparrer! you ain't the only one what's caught a packet!'

His eyes flew open. The badly scarred face reminded him of Uncle Bertie, but there was no bitterness in that chirpy Cockney voice. The stump of the right leg, amputated just above the knee, was covered with a pad, the left leg swathed in bandages.

'What happened?' Julian asked compassionately.

'Bloody torpedo!'

'I'm sorry.'

'That makes two of us, chum. I been watching yer. It ain't the end of the world, Julian. We still got two good 'ands. Pleased ter meet yer. The nime's 'arry – 'arry Sykes.'

'Pleased to meet you, Harry.' The grip of his huge hand nearly crippled Julian's.

'How long have you been here, Harry?'

'Six weeks. It ain't such a bad dump. Plenty worse, I reckon. 'Struth! I never knowed abaht these bloody Channel Islands. Jography wasn't my best subject, an' there was too many kids in that school ter be taught proper. We took pot luck as you might siy. If you was clever, you got full marks an' a certificit when you was fourteen, an' if you was as stoopid as yours truly, yer got chucked out wivaht a certificit, see? Blimey!' He chuckled at the memory. His hands on the wheelchair were the hands of a navvy, the fingers blunt, the nails broken.

'What's your job in peacetime?' Julian asked.

'Porter, Billingsgate Market. I was stinkin' o' fish when they called me up for the Merchant Navy. Didn't 'arf pong!'

Julian laughed, and heads turned to stare all down the length of the ward. Trust Harry to raise a laugh out of that poor lad. The pert young nurse, wheeling in the supper trolley, was pleased to see her advice had been taken seriously.

'I told him not to worry,' she said – and delivered a loaded tin tray to the nearest patient with the professional skill of a Lyons Nippy.

'Come and get your supper, *Mister* Sykes,' she called out authoritatively.

'I'll 'ave it 'ere wiv Julian, if yer don't mind, Nurse,' said Harry.

'Very well,' she conceded. 'But you will have to fetch your bed table. I'm not waiting on you. And you can bring one for Julian.'

'OK.' He swung the chair round and shot off down the ward at an alarming speed. Julian watched admiringly. He came back with the two tables balanced one on top of the other.

'Once a porter, always a porter, ah, chum?' He carefully arranged Julian's table over the bed clothes, then he collected the supper trays from the trolley, first Julian's, then his own.

'They got a lot ter do, these nurses. I like to give 'em a n'and,' he said, as they settled down to eat their supper. The egg was cold, the toast soggy, and the rice pudding draped in a covering of burnt skin. Julian shuddered and picked at the food distastefully. Harry crammed it into his mouth, belched comfortably, and leaned back to watch the young ex-pilot with amused grey eyes.

'You been spoilt in the RAF, I reckon, Julian. They 'ad ter give you fellers the best, an' I'm not siying yer didn't deserve it. Christ! You was bloody marvellous!' He wiped his mouth with the back of his hand, and wished the helpings were twice the size. He never seemed to get enough to satisfy his strong, heavy body.

Julian was scooping off the burnt skin. He sighed, and glanced at Harry's plate meaningly. Harry nodded and they exchanged plates with a deftness that would have surprised the nurse, but she was busy with the other patients and had no time to linger.

'Thanks, mate,' muttered Harry, chewing the burnt skin with relish.

'You're welcome. I have always disliked skin and have always been allowed to remove it. Ugh! Revolting!'

'Sahnds as if you ain't never been 'ungry?'

'No, never. I live on a farm, and we live like fighting cocks.'

'Didn't your Mum an' Dad mind jew joining' the RAF?'

'My parents are dead. I was brought up by an Aunt – a wonderful woman. She didn't object because she knew that nothing else would satisfy me.'

'What's she goin' ter siy when yer come 'ome in a wheelchair?'

'She won't say anything more than "Welcome home, dear" but I shall be hugged to her warm bosom – and it's quite a bosom, Harry boy!'

'Sahnds dandy,' Harry sighed enviously.

'Haven't you, I mean, isn't there someone waiting for you, old chap?' Julian probed gently.

'Nah. Lost the missus soon after I went ter sea. When I went back 'ome on me first leave, there wasn't nofink left of the 'ouse, only a n'eap of rubble. They caught a packet. All the 'ouses was flattened, an' a bloody great 'ole in the road. I stood there, gawping, crying like a baby, till a Bobby come along an' took 'old of me arm. "Come an' 'ave a cup of tea, mate," 'e says. "There's nofink like a cup o' tea".'

'But that's terrible, Harry. Nobody would ever guess, you're so darn cheerful.'

'It comes nat'ral. I got into the 'abit when I was a kid, an' I ain't never got aht of it. Mind jew, it comes over me nah an' then, an' I 'as a little weep. I won't never fergit it, Julian, not as long as I live.'

'What shall you do when the war is over?'

'Dunno. 'Tween you an' me, I ain't so keen for it all ter be over. This plice suits me fine an' dandy. Nah, why don't you 'ave a little kip while I collect up the trays on the trolley. You feeling OK?'

'Fine,' Julian lied. The scrambled egg lay heavy on his chest.

The weeks slipped away. It was a small, secluded world, and only the gutteral voice of Dr Muller to remind the patients they were actually living under German occupation.

Julian had been provided with a pulley, and quickly mastered the art of pulling himself up and swinging his lower half off the bed, and on to the wheelchair, with Harry there to steady it.

Harry was proud of his pupil. The lean young man had a suppleness that was lacking in his own heavy body, and the arms were finding an extra strength to compensate for the weakness of the legs. With so much interest and encouragement from the other patients, Julian found he was actually enjoying the exercise. He had always had an admiring audience at Russets; showing off his cleverness with the pulley would have reminded Aunt Lucy of his early riding lessons on his first pony.

The wonderful news that he was alive, conveyed on a Red Cross postcard, had been received with tears of joy and thankfulness. Maggie had been allowed to light a candle in the chapel at Marston Park, and Midge had given up sugar in her tea to make toffee for Julian's Christmas parcel.

For this second Christmas of the war, three of the

young generation would be missing. Aunt Martha would take Mark to Russets, for this would be the first Christmas without Matthew. Wendy was still travelling North. They would be spending Christmas Day in Oban, on the west coast of Scotland, and giving two shows, one for the RAF and one for the Army. A parcel of presents had already been posted from Tunbridge Wells, and there would be cards from the children at Russets. Also on the way was a Red Cross postcard inscribed – 'To my darling sweetheart. With love and best wishes for Christmas from Julian.' This would only add to the heartache of homesickness that nothing could dispel.

Why hadn't she taken her mother's advice and volunteered to serve as a VAD at the local hospital, or finished the course of training at the Secretarial College? Why had she persuaded herself that a musical career was so vitally important, and that independence meant more to her than a good home, loving parents, and the dearest old Gran in the world? She must have been mad, she told herself repeatedly in the weeks that followed that traumatic day at Windermere when she heard that Julian was dead – and Nigel had seduced her in their lodgings.

Nancy had returned from her visit to the dentist in a very good mood, having persuaded him that a 'filling' was more desirable than an extraction to a lady in show business! She listened to Nigel's explanation of the depleted whisky bottle, and agreed it was the best antidote to shock and ragged nerves. She sat on the bed and made a great fuss of Wendy, calling her 'my poor darling', and insisting that she spend the rest of the day in bed. They could manage without an accompanist since it was only a minor engagement at a factory canteen, and there would be the usual demand for community singing.

'Try to get some sleep this afternoon. I will leave you a

257

couple of aspirin. We are going out to lunch, but Mrs Goodwin will bring you up a sandwich and a cup of coffee. Now don't worry, darling. Just relax.' She pecked Wendy's flushed cheek and moved away. Nigel also pecked her cheek, but averted his eyes. What would Nancy say if she knew her husband was unfaithful? Perhaps it was not the first time. He was very attractive to women, but very conceited. She supposed it was show business that made them seem so artificial. They lived in a different world, a world she could never completely share, because she had no sense of belonging.

She heard them go out. Lennie had been out all morning. They had not seen him since breakfast. Nobody cared. She wished she was dead. She buried her face in the pillow, and wept.

London was still the Mecca for the young service men and women on leave, and the constant threat of raids added to the excitement. The only tangible enemy to be defeated was boredom, and the only situation to be avoided at all costs was loneliness. A single individual of the young generation was as rare as an empty pew in St Martins-in-the-Fields on Sunday night.

The herd instinct was not confined to the ranks. Youthful American officers could be seen escorting pretty girls and attractive women into hotels and restaurants. Generous with their money, and with presents of nylons and candies, no wonder they were so popular. But their popularity was a constant irritation to our less fortunate servicemen with their meagre allowances, often compelled to spend their leave in the company of men, watching the privileged young gods from overseas enjoying themselves with the opposite sex. They had the appearance of being made in the same mould, with their slender boyish figures and they all seemed desperately anxious not to offend the British public, and would refer to the little text books that were issued for guidance in conducting themselves in the approved manner.

Major Charles Franklin was no stranger to London. It was good to be back. The rank of Major had been conferred for the administrative post in which he found himself, due almost entirely to a chance meeting with a retired Colonel Brandon in a hotel bar. By such chance encounters Charles had escaped all the hardships of life, and enjoyed all the benefits. He had no intention of working for a living when he was obliged to leave England so suddenly, and when he had drained the last dregs of reluctant hospitality from his half-sister, Sylvia, and her husband, he moved into the apartment of Sylvia's friend – a wealthy widow, old enough to be his mother, and foolish enough to adore him. But money alone could not hold Charles Franklin, and his weakness for a pretty face of his own generation was no secret. Charles had no scruples; his motives were purely and simply self-indulgent. So he walked out on a mistress who had become too possessive, but not without his cheque book!

The house at Little Venice was a favourite rendezvous now for American officers spending their leave in London. The Canadians had been posted overseas, but Diane and her friends had no particular preference. They were enjoying the war, and they still had lots of fun. It was quite uncanny the way in which the reputation of Number 6 was passed on, over a drink in a Piccadilly bar, or a meal in a hotel restaurant.

Major Charles Franklin was intrigued, and anxious to make the acquaintance of the beautiful Diane Maloney. Not that he connected her with Marston Park – he had

259

lost touch with his mother at Russets for almost a decade, and the name meant nothing more than another attractive woman to add to his collection.

Charles had inherited his father's taste in women, and his father's good looks, but not his strong character. There was a weak streak in Sir Neville's only son that could not be traced to either parent. His mother – Lucy Blunt of Russets Farm – had discovered this flaw behind the charming façade whilst he was still at public school, but her influence was negligible since he no longer lived at Russets. More than one village girl had been seduced by the Squire's son, and his father had paid the parents of one girl generous compensation when she was found to be pregnant. They said in the village that young Charles Franklin was a chip off the old block, but that was not strictly true and his mother, who knew all his faults and loved him dearly, had been much troubled by his tendency to 'borrow' money and not return it. Lucy always excused Charles because of his mixed heritage. To have one foot in the upper class and the other in the working class was confusing, she contended. As a small boy of seven he had been removed from Russets Farm, and his three half-brothers, to Marston Park where he was expected to conform to the standards of the Gentry with its traditional pattern of boarding-school education. The boy had resented his father's arrogant treatment of his mother, and the relationship had been strained. To give Charles his due, he was neither ashamed nor embarrassed by his mother's environment, or the fact that he was born out of wedlock, and he rather enjoyed the notoriety of being the bastard son of Sir Neville Franklin.

'Hello, Mother darling.'

Lucy had been busy in the dairy and had not seen the

car. The handsome man leaning on the gate was so like his father she gasped with shock, and a hot flush swept over her neck and face. But his father had never worn a uniform or saluted her with such charming gallantry.

'Charles!' she cried, exultantly, flinging out her arms, her eyes bright with happy tears.

He caught her hands over the top of the gate and kissed her trembling mouth. 'How come you still look young enough to be my sister, and pretty enough to be my sweetheart?' he teased.

'You talk like an American?'

'I *am* an American.'

'You're not! You're British. You were born in this house, and you grew up at Marston Park.'

'I know, darling, but I changed my nationality some years ago.'

'But why?'

'I reckon it's a case of when you're in Rome you do as the Romans. Aren't you going to invite me in?'

'Of course. Forgive me. It was such a shock.'

'The prodigal's return!' he laughed gaily, pushed open the gate, and hugged her round the waist. 'You smell nice,' he said.

'Do I?' Choked with the memory of his father, she was torn between laughter and tears. But her son would not be here if his father were alive. He would not dare to show his face. They were so ridiculously alike, her son could make her blush with his flattery, but the flattery came too readily to his lips, and the smile was too disarming. There had been too many women in his life since he left England. Like father, like son they said, but she knew the difference, and had no illusions. Charles was only a poor copy of that man she had loved so dearly. A mother's love for her son was inborn. It was in her bones and her blood. That other love was a thing apart – enduring, eternal. She had not loved her dear, faithful Bert as she loved her lord, as she had called him. It couldn't be explained, for it brought her years of heartache and disappointment. He had taken her and used her, discarding and ignoring her. Finally, when it was almost too late, he came back to her, repentant, almost humble, and the long years between were forgotten, only the few short years they had left had any meaning.

'How long can you stay, dear?' she asked her son, and pushed away the memory of his father.

'Not long, darling. I have to be back in Town by early evening. Got a date with a pretty girl. Haven't met her yet, but I'm told she's a honey.'

'What's her name?'

'Diane Maloney.'

'*Diane Maloney?*'

'Sure. How come you sound so surprised?'

'You really don't know who she is?'

'Haven't a clue, darling.'

'Diane Maloney is the only daughter of the rich industrialist who bought Marston Park.'

'You don't say? And you've met her?'

'Only briefly. I haven't met the father, but I know her mother, and the ex-governess quite well.'

'What's she really like? Tell me more.'

'Come and sit down. Would you like a cup of tea?' He pulled a face. 'No cawfee?'

'Sorry, no coffee. We are great tea-drinkers, even in the summer. There's elderberry wine.'

'Thanks. Say, this is great! I mean, it can't be pure chance, can it, darling? There must be hundreds of guys making dates with pretty girls. Just the luck of the draw I reckon.'

'Diane Maloney is not just a pretty girl. She's beautiful, and she knows it. Don't imagine you have only to turn on the charm, Charles, to have her eating out of your hand. Diane calls the tune. She can pick and choose, and she's had her own way since her cradle days. She's spoilt, and she is utterly selfish.'

'That makes two of us, Mother darling!'

She shook her head reprovingly.

'Who did the spoiling?'

'Father. They say that Harry B. Maloney has only two absorbing passions in life – making money, and his adored daughter.'

'And the mother? What's she like?'

'A nice, homely little Irish woman. Rather pathetic, really. They practically ignore her. She once told me the happiest years of her married life were spent in a small apartment in a poor district of New York, before Harry made a lot of money. To this day she has no idea *how* he made his money. She asks no questions, and she is very loyal. Diane grew up admiring her father and despising her mother. I suppose her father saw Marston Park as a fitting setting for his beautiful daughter, and visualised her playing her part in the upper class. But they have no breeding, Charles, and money can't buy it. We call them the New Rich. You know Diane is married?'

He shook his head.

'She married the only son of a German industrialist. It was intended to be a merging of the two companies, but it didn't go according to plan. Diane's father gave them the London house as a wedding present. Carl seems to have spent more time in Germany than in England, according to the servants, and Diane was not invited to meet his family. Then Carl joined the Nazi Party, and that was the last straw as far as Diane was concerned. The war would have separated them, anyway.'

'She could be a widow.'

263

'Now, Charles!'

He laughed, drained the glass, and held it out to be refilled. His dark eyes were teasing. The years had dealt very kindly with her handsome son.

'Wish me luck, darling,' he coaxed.

'With Diane?'

'Sure.'

'You won't be the first Franklin to be attracted to that little Madam.'

'How come?'

'Julian.'

'*Julian*? But he's only a kid?'

'He *was*. He's a young man now, and a very good-looking young man. You forget how long you have been away.'

'He's not here? Am I likely to run into him? You haven't told him, Mother?'

'That he is your son? No. That skeleton is best left in the cupboard, Charles.'

'You had me worried, darling!'

'That could be a good thing. You seem to leave the worrying to other people. Somebody had to take the responsibility.'

'Is he farming?'

'A Franklin – farming? That will be the day!' she chuckled. 'He joined the RAF when he left Grammar School. By the time war was declared, he had his wings and was posted to a squadron. We are very proud of Julian. He was one of the fighter pilots in the Battle of Britain. We thought we had lost him. He was shot down and we were notified. Three months later we heard through the Red Cross that he was alive, in a hospital on the island of Jersey. With the Channel Islands under German occupation, we have to depend on the Red Cross for news of him, and he is only allowed to send an occasional postcard. So we still do not know if he was badly injured,' she sighed wistfully. 'It's not the first time I have known this terrible anxiety, Charles, and I hope and pray he will not be sent home a mental and physical wreck like my poor Albert, at the end of the last war. It's heart-breaking to watch your children suffer.'

He patted her hand, soothingly, and changed the subject. 'Tell me about Carrie and Tom. Why aren't they here?'

'It's market day, and Dick goes with them. Dick is the eldest of their four children. The others are at school. Why don't you wait and see them?'

'Sorry, Mother. I must get back to Town. Next time I sure would like to meet the family.'

But Lucy knew there would not be a next time.

He was taking out his wallet and peeling off the crisp banknotes.

'No, Charles. Put it away. A half-crown each, no more. They are not spoilt children.'

'OK.' He shrugged, slipped the bulging wallet back in his hip pocket, took out a handful of coins, and counted out the four half-crowns. 'I've got your present in the car, darling. You sit right there. I'll go fetch it.' He hurried back across the yard, wrinkling his nose at the acrid smell of silage. Such luxuries as a huge bouquet of roses and carnations, and a box of chocolates could still be purchased by a handsome American major.

'Charles! You shouldn't. Such extravagance!' Lucy exclaimed, as he thrust them into her arms and kissed her mouth. Her other sons kissed her cheek, but not Charles. He had to be different. They had called him 'a cuckoo in the nest'.

She laid his expensive gifts on the table and took his face between her work-worn hands, choked with tears. She pleaded, 'Keep in touch, dear. Life is so short, and I shan't always be here.'

'OK, Mother darling.'

He was smiling as he slipped out of her grasp. She had never been able to hold him. No woman could hold Charles when he wanted to get away – unless it was Diane Maloney? They were well matched.

Chapter Twelve

My Lady of the Lamplight,
My own Lily Marlene.

It was ironic, Wendy was thinking, that the favourite song for the community singing was invariably the one that belonged to the enemy. There was a poignancy even in the realisation that German youth were marching to war with this song on their lips, mothers, wives and sweethearts waiting for their safe return, only to be told their dear ones were not coming back. Goering was awarding medals to these women – posthumous medals for the gallantry and courage of his Luftwaffe pilots. He was especially fond of medals, and had them dangling in rows on his expansive chest, a figure of fun to our clever cartoonists.

Now that she knew Julian was alive, Wendy could sympathise with all women who had suffered the anguish of loss, and the aching loneliness of each new day. For her, it had lasted for a little over three months, but she had lived a lifetime and lost her youth in that brief period.

The burden she carried now would have been shared by Julian, though it was not his child that she carried. He would understand. Julian would not condemn as the rest of her small world would condemn – when they knew.

Nancy had remarked only recently to Nigel, 'You see, darling, I was right about Wendy. We have had no trouble with her monthly periods since we left Windermere. It took her a long time to accept the fact that menstruation is not an illness but a natural function. I blame the grandmother for encouraging the girl to spend the first day of the period in bed. It had a lasting effect on Wendy. She hasn't fainted again, has she?'

'That's true. But she doesn't look well. She has lost all her sparkle, and she's always tired these days.'

'Aren't we all? That's show business in wartime.'

'I expect you are right, darling. You usually are right,' Nigel conceded. It saved a lot of wear and tear on the nerves to agree with Nancy. It was the only sensible way to cope with such an emotional woman.

Lenny couldn't be bothered with their variable moods, and he had helped Wendy to cope with these difficult travelling companions. But now the doctor had confirmed what she had suspected, Wendy was frightened. How soon would it begin to show? If the morning sickness got any worse, Nancy would guess. Would it get any worse? If only she were not so appallingly ignorant – and too terribly ashamed to seek advice. Because most of the piano accompaniment was repetitious, and she had adapted herself to the routine, she managed quite a convincing performance. They supported each other, and she had accepted Nancy's stern reminder – 'The show goes on'. Self-discipline was an essential part of show business. She had seen Nancy, with a sick headache, swallowing aspirins, and Nigel, with a hangover, drinking strong black coffee. Only Lennie seemed immune from such obvious signs that the tour was a strain, and they were beginning to flag.

'You all right, kid?' Lennie would enquire anxiously if she faltered for a moment in the wings before making her entrance. He hadn't forgotten the time she fainted at the piano, and Nigel had dashed on stage to carry her off. But the audience had clapped and cheered, thinking it was all part of the act. He could usually manage to fool them.

It was Lennie who noticed Wendy was shivering in her print frock on a draughty makeshift stage, one evening, and insisted she bought a warmer garment.

'I can't afford it, Lennie,' she told him.

'You can 'ave it for yer Christmas present, ducks,' he said, airily.

'But it's not Christmas.' she protested, near to tears.

'Can't I buy me best girl a present when I feels like it then?'

It was embarrassing, but it wasn't the first time he had opened her handbag and pushed money inside. Gran would say it was important to receive a gift graciously, so she kissed his cheek, thanked him nicely, and took a bus into town. Nigel was offended because he had not been consulted, and he thought the dress – a saxe-blue velvet with a flared skirt – was unsuitable. It spoiled the image of the innocent young girl he had created. But it was nothing new to be the subject of an argument. It happened all the time, and Wendy had given up hoping it would ever be any different.

So another month passed and she hid her swelling stomach under the full skirt of the new dress. Every day was one day nearer discovery. There was no escape. She wished she had the courage to take an overdose of aspirin – but it took a special kind of courage to commit suicide.

It had been an hilarious evening at the Rose and Crown, and Lennie was still chuckling as he ran upstairs.

He was always allotted the attic bedroom in their lodgings, but it didn't bother him. One place was as good as another, and he hardly noticed his surroundings. The local pub – the working men's club – was the kind of environment to which he was accustomed.

On this particular night, however, he thought he heard Wendy crying as he passed her door, and he stopped to listen. Yes, he had not been mistaken. It was a muffled weeping as though she had her face buried in the pillow, and it had a despairing sound that could not be ignored. His gentle tap on the door brought no answer, so he opened the door and went in. The room was in darkness, and he whispered, 'It's me, Lennie. What's the trouble, ducks?'

'Nothing. Go away, *please* go away.'

He switched on the light, and the huddled little figure under the bedclothes turned over and sat up. 'Go away, *please*,' she pleaded, in a choked voice. Her face was flushed, her eyes swollen. She must have been crying for hours, poor kid, he thought, compassionately. It was the face of a child, crumpled in misery, and he had always thought of her as a child. It was part of the act.

He sat on the edge of the bed and wondered, not for the first time, why her parents had made no attempt to get her back. It was all wrong. She was not the type for show business.

'What's upset you, ducks? Is it that bitch, Nancy?'

She shook her head.

'What then? Tell ole Lennie. I won't say nofink to the others. Come on,' he coaxed, wiping her wet face with a grubby handkerchief smelling strongly of beer.

She shuddered involuntarily, which didn't surprise him. A fastidious little madam, young Wendy! Her hands were clutching at the bedclothes – those clever hands that could coax a tune out of any piano, and hold an audience spellbound with her 'chopping'. He took hold of her hands to quieten them. They were hot and feverish. The tears were still welling in her eyes, and her mouth trembling. He waited. She must take her time.

He remembered that night in the prostitute's flat in Soho, when she told him she was dying of cancer. They had lived together for several years, and their love was the best thing he had ever known. She was kind and generous, and when he had no money to pay his share of the housekeeping, she would laugh. 'Pay me next week, luv,' she would say. He had never forgotten her. She hadn't lived to share his success in show business. There would have been no need to sell her body on the streets of Piccadilly. Life was hard for such women. There was no physical resemblance between that dear woman and this child, yet, for a moment, looking into those tear-wet eyes, there *was* a likeness.

Then at last she told him. 'I am going to have a baby.'

He stared at her, shaking his head in disbelief. 'Christ! You must be kidding? Why you ain't been allowed to keep none of them dates with the fellers. Nigel 'as 'ardly let yer out of 'is sight. Nigel? NIGEL!'

She closed her eyes. She could not bear to look at his disgust.

'You let 'im do that? Bloody little fool! I could wring your neck!'

She opened her eyes. 'I couldn't stop him,' she said, quietly.

'You mean?'

She nodded.

'When? Where?'

'The morning I received the letter telling me that Julian had been shot down – in our lodgings at Windermere.'

'What abaht Nancy?'

271

'She had an appointment with the dentist that morning.'

His eyes were blazing now. He dropped her hands and rushed out of the room. She heard him clattering down the stairs. She heard the sitting-room door flung open. She heard him shout, 'You dirty bastard!' – and the thud of Nigel's heavy body as it hit the floor.

It was pandemonium. Nancy was on her knees, cradling Nigel's head in her lap, screaming abuse at Lennie, and the indignant landlady demanding to know what all the fuss was about.

'This is a decent, respectable house, and I won't allow such goings-on,' she insisted, when she could make herself heard. 'And look at the mess! I shall charge you for damages.'

'Shut up, for God's sake!' Nancy retorted, rudely. It would not be the first time they had been asked to leave their lodgings when she had used insulting language. Whisky was spilt on the floor, and a glass was smashed.

Lennie's eyes were still blazing in his ashen face. 'Get a brush and pan. I'll sweep it up,' he ordered.

Nigel was fondling his bruised chin and Nancy crooning 'My poor darling' when the landlady came back, swept up the glass and departed with the haughty ultimatum, 'I shall expect your rooms to be vacated by noon tomorrow. I have never been so insulted!'

'All right! All right! Now get out!'

Nancy was helping Nigel to stand up. His body sagged, and he had suddenly aged. But he was more frightened of Nancy's biting tongue than any physical blow.

When she had settled him comfortably in an armchair, she turned on Lennie. 'Now, *Mister O'Brien*, perhaps you will explain what you mean by your assault on my husband.'

'Come 'orf it, Nance. You know bloody well what 'e's done.'

'But I don't. I am waiting for an explanation.'

'Shall I tell her then?'

Nigel nodded, his shoulders hunched in readiness for the whiplash of her scalding condemnation.

''e's got young Wendy in the family wye.'

Her eyes bulged. He thought she would have a fit. Then she smacked Nigel's face a stinging blow, and his head rocked.

'You stupid fool! You blundering bloody· baby-snatcher!' she hissed. Picking up her own glass, she threw the dregs of whisky in his face and marched out of the room. Nigel wiped his face with a trembling hand. He was very frightened. If Nancy left him – as she had threatened a number of times – he was finished as an entertainer. With the double act and her driving energy, they had survived after a fashion. The war had saved them. Supported by Lennie and Wendy, they had enjoyed the tour, and expected it to continue to the end of the war. Now it was over.

Choked with tears of self-pity, he could only stare at the man who had carried them along by the sheer force of his own.talent as a comedian. Lennie would be welcomed by ENSA. He would team up with another comedian in a double act. After the war he would be back in London. There would always be a place for a clever comedian in show business.

'I was a fool,' he confessed, with rare humility.

Lennie made no answer. He had blown his top, and there was little more to say. Now he was no longer concerned with this man and his nagging wife, only with Wendy. He should never have got tied up with them in the first place, for it hadn't taken long to discover they were second-rate and their act out-dated. Old Time

273

Music Hall was their only hope of another engagement. They might be lucky in the provinces.

'What are you going to do?' Nigel was asking.

'Do? Clear aht.'

'We could finish the tour with another accompanist?'

'You've got a bloody nerve, Bannister!'

'It was only a suggestion.'

'Yer know what yer can do wiv it. Stick it up yer jumper!'

'What about Wendy?'

'I wondered when yer would get arahnd to 'er.'

'What do you suggest? I want to play fair with her.'

'It's abit light in the dye to talk abaht plying fair, ain't it?'

'I'm sorry.'

'*Sorry*? Blimey, you're a cool customer. Can't jew understand what you've done to that luvly girl? You've ruined 'er life.'

'Shall I go up and speak to her?'

'Nah, you keep awye from the kid an' tell your wife to keep awye. I'm phoning for a cab after I've packed 'er things, an' I'm tykin' 'er wiv me, back ter London, where I shall 'and 'er over to 'er Mum what's a Sister in an 'orspital, after I've been in touch with 'er Dad on the phone. Me an' 'im was neighbours at one time. A decent bloke, an' prahd as Punch of young Wendy. Goin' ter tyke it 'ard, both 'er parents, I can tell you.'

'Why should you do all this when I'm the guilty party? Let me take her back to London?'

'You keep 'aht of it. I don't want no interference, not from you or yer wife. I got it all organised! Jus' keep aht of it, Bannister.'

The door slammed, and he was gone.

In the little terrace house in Tunbridge Wells, Wendy's father was already in bed when the telephone rang. An extension in the bedroom had been Cynthia's idea. She always phoned if she was detained at the hospital, and when she was on night duty she phoned the following morning before breakfast. He was worried about her safety, but she was so dedicated to her nursing profession, she would not give it up. He was trembling as he reached for the receiver. In those few seconds he had visualised the horror and devastation of an air raid, and his beloved wife buried under the rubble with her patients. She had phoned earlier in the evening before she went on night duty.

'Hallo,' he croaked.

'That you, Fred?'

Fred? Nobody had called him Fred since those early days in Richmond Row.

'It's Len. Lennie O'Brien. Remember me?'

'Of course I remember you, Len. And Wendy always mentions you in her letters. What's happened? Why are you phoning?'

'I'm bringin' Wendy 'ome, Fred. Better 'ang on ter something, chum. This is goin' ter be a bit of a shock. She -- she's goin' ter 'ave a byby.'

'What did you say? Will you repeat it please. It's such a bad line.'

'Wendy is goin' ter 'ave a byby.'

'That's what I thought you said.'

The line crackled. 'You still there, Fred?' Lennie enquired anxiously.

'Yes, I'm here. Carry on, I'm listening.'

'It's an 'ell of a long wye from Scotland to London, an' it's goin' ter tyke all dye. What I 'ad in mind, Fred, was ter tyke 'er ter the 'orspital an' leave 'er wiv 'er Mum. What jew fink?'

'No, you can't do that. My wife is on night duty. I will come to London and fetch her. Where could we meet?

Do you know of an hotel? We might have to stay overnight if there's a raid.'

'I only knows one 'otel in London. Regent Palace in Piccadilly.'

'Right, I'll meet you there . . . I suppose you're the father, Len?'

'Christ! You've got a bloody nerve!'

'Who, then?'

'Bannister.'

'Bannister? But I thought his wife was with him on the tour?'

'She is, but that didn't stop the bastard from mykin' up ter Wendy when she was aht of the wye. It was the dye she 'eard young Julian was shot dahn. She broke 'er little 'eart, poor kid, an' Bannister gave 'er whisky an' made 'er tiddly. She ain't been drinkin' nofink only tea an' coffee an' lemonade. I been lookin' after 'er, Fred, like she was me own kid, only I wasn't in the 'ouse when it 'appened, see, or it wouldn't 'ave 'appened, that's fer sure.'

'Thanks, Len. I'm sorry I accused you. It just seemed the logical conclusion since Wendy always mentioned you in her letters and hardly mentioned Bannister.'

'That's OK.'

'What's happened to the Bannisters?'

'Left 'em in the lodgings. I give 'im a bashin', Fred. Nearly broke 'is bloody jaw – the bastard!'

'Thank you, Len, for taking care of her.'

'Okey-doke. I'll be seein' yer. So long.'

'So long.'

So long. A reminder of the village and his working class background. He hadn't said 'so long' since he married Cynthia.

The receiver clicked. He was wide awake now, and he knew he would not get any sleep. Lennie O'Brien must have thought he was a cool customer, but it was not his nature to rant and rave. His emotions had always been controlled. Even as a child he could hide his real feelings, and when he was hurt, he shed no tears. The last war had only strengthened his reserve; it had threatened his marriage for a time since Cynthia was an extrovert. Losing a leg had probably saved their marriage. She had always been the dominant partner, and now he did not mind. There was no more resistance. She ruled their lives. Sister Simmons was not a separate entity, though Cynthia tried very hard to leave her behind at the hospital when she came home.

The discipline had been strict for Wendy, but he hadn't interfered. When she ran away to join this touring company, he was utterly dismayed and ashamed, for he could have prevented it had he asserted his authority as a parent. He blamed himself, not Cynthia, for what had happened.

The tap on the door didn't surprise him. His mother was a light sleeper. 'Come in,' he called.

The dumpy little figure in the old-fashioned dressing-gown, smelled strongly of embrocation. Her legs had been bad for years, and getting worse, but she didn't complain.

'Was it the hospital?' she asked, anxiously.

'No, sit down, Mum.'

She sat on the edge of the bed looking at her son with faded blue eyes. She understood his reticence. He was not like her other children. Freddie was the clever one, and you had to make allowances for clever children. They were different, not so robust, more sensitive. His dark eyes were moist and his face quivered, but she knew he would not break down, no matter what had happened.

'Is it Wendy?' she prompted, gently.

'Yes. That was Lennie O'Brien phoning from Scotland. He is bringing Wendy home. She is pregnant.'

'*Pregnant*?' she gasped. 'Oh, Freddie, luv. I be proper flummoxed.'

His mouth twisted in a wry smile. The Richmond Row mother, hidden beneath a veneer of Tunbridge Wells refinement, always emerged in a crisis, bless her. It had taken her a long time to pick up those dropped 'aitches', but she had persevered for the child's sake. Wendy was her favourite grandchild. She loved his daughter dearly. They were very close, but Wendy had not confided in her, only in Julian. The young generation could be very secretive and disloyal.

She was crying quietly. He patted her hand.

'It's a shock, isn't it, Mum?'

She nodded mutely.

'Make a cup of tea, and I'll tell you all about it,' he said.

She slid off the bed and hobbled away. There was nothing like a cup of tea in a crisis. It helped to win the last war, and it was doing the same in this war.

The elderly porter had enquired about the trains and the approximate time of arrival, but nobody could guarantee punctuality. Freddie had been waiting patiently in the foyer for the best part of two hours, but there was plenty to interest him, with all the coming and going. Overnight guests were booking in, and casual visitors meeting for a drink or an evening meal. It was a popular rendezvous in the heart of London, and Freddie was fascinated by the motley crowd of people and the predominance of uniforms.

He had spoken to Cynthia on the telephone earlier in the day, but he had not mentioned Wendy, or the fact that he was coming to London. After a long night on duty, with an air-raid warning, and all the disturbance of moving the patients from the wards to the comparative safety of the underground shelters, she was tired, and ready for bed in the Sister's annexe. She would be home later in the week for her rest days, providing there were no more emergencies in the meantime. Doctors and nurses were often called back on duty, but so were ambulance drivers, firemen, and air-raid wardens. The Home Front was in line for devastating bombardments, and nobody could predict an end to the war. Freddie knew that Cynthia would have prevented him from making this trip to London, for she always spared him what she called 'unnecessary exertion'. His old wounds were often troublesome, and his artificial leg a permanent discomfort he had long since accepted as a permanent legacy of the last war. But he was determined to make amends for his lack of initiative and effort. It had been all too easy to sit back and watch Cynthia. She was so much his superior in every way, that he was inclined to wear a chip on his shoulder.

Of recent years, it was her regular salary that paid the bills. His own contribution would depend on whether or not his working-class clients paid for his services, and they were never pressed to pay. In his understanding and sympathy of the class to which he belonged Freddie Simmons was so like Dr Saunders, of his native village of Fairfields, who had also aggravated his lady wife by being so lax in sending bills to his patients. Cynthia held the sensible view that nobody should expect to receive services free, whether it was a solicitor, a doctor, or a plumber. She was right, of course. 'Your mother knows best, my pet,' he would remind his young daughter.

It was a mistake. It had made the child rebellious and a close relationship impossible between mother and daughter.

The revolving doors were constantly on the move,

spilling people out to the street and into the foyer. Strangers, all strangers. Then, all of a sudden, he saw her – the familiar little figure, yet different. She stood, hesitating, till the man joined her, carrying the two suitcases. He could sense her nervousness in the way she clutched the man's arm, her eyes searching the crowd. In that moment of recognition, he knew it was a woman who had come home, a woman who had left her youth behind. He pushed his way towards her, choked with sadness, and when their eyes met, she made no move to greet him. The girl who went away would have rushed into his arms and hugged him exuberantly. The girl who went away had glowing cheeks, bright eyes, and a cap of shining hair. There was nothing left of that girl, yet he had known her. She was still his beloved daughter. Why should she hesitate?

It was Lennie who spoke first, and he hadn't changed. ''ere she is, Fred. All safe and sahnd. Blimey, we thought we was stuck on that bloody train for the rest of our dyes, didn't we, ducks?'

Wendy made no answer. She was so pale, Freddie thought she was going to faint. He took her cold hands in a warm clasp, and kissed her gently.

'Welcome home, my pet. We have missed you. Come and sit down,' he said.

'Thank you, Daddy,' she whispered.

Then he shook hands with Lennie. There was no room for him on the seat, so he stood there, looking about the crowded foyer, obviously delighted to be back in London.

'This is where we met that dye. Remember, kid?' he asked.

Would she ever forget, she wondered. She was holding her father's hand, watching Lennie's ugly, familiar face.

'I'll be gettin' along nah I've delivered the goods,' he said, with that irresistible good humour that had saved so many tricky situations.

'Don't run away, Len. Stay and have a meal with us,' Freddie invited.

'Thanks all the syme, Fred, but me old landlady is expectin' me for supper. I phoned before we left, an' she said I could 'ave me old room back.'

'Just a cup of tea?'

He pulled a face. 'Gawd, we've 'ad enough tea on this lark ter sink a bloody battleship! I'll get a glass of beer in the bar.' There was really nothing more to say, only, 'Well, so long. I'll be seein' yer,' and to shake Freddie's hand. Then he kissed Wendy's cheek. 'Chin up, ducks,' he said.

'Thank you for bringing me back, Len.'

Freddie was still choked with sadness.

'Okey-doke,' Len grinned amiably, picked up his case, and walked away.

Wendy's eyes followed him wistfully. She was going to miss him. Lennie was the best friend she ever had, but she didn't expect to see him again.

'Are you hungry, dear? Did you get anything to eat on the train?' her father was asking.

'Lennie bought pies and buns at one of the stations when we had a long wait, but I just had a cup of tea. I was feeling rather sick.'

'Are you still feeling sick?'

She nodded.

'I thought you would enjoy a nice meal in the restaurant?'

She shuddered at the memory of that last meal.

'I'm not hungry, Daddy. Only tired. Do you think I could go to bed?'

'Of course. I have booked our rooms. They are not on

the same floor. I had to take what I could get. You don't mind?'

'No, I don't mind.'

He picked up the case, still holding her hand in a warm clasp. They stood pressed together in the lift that was packed as tightly as a tin of sardines. When they stepped out, Wendy swayed and clung to him.

'I'll be all right in a minute. Just a bit dizzy,' she told him, and he held her close till she had recovered. Then they walked slowly down the long carpeted corridor to the far end, where Freddie unlocked a door and stood back. The room was identical to the one she had occupied that night, but then she remembered it was a special feature of this hotel. An eternity had passed since that night. She sat on the edge of the bed and looked at her father with dull eyes.

'Does Mother know we are here?' she asked quietly.

'No.'

'Does she know about the baby?'

'No.'

'I'm sorry, Daddy.'

'You are not to worry, dear. I will cope with your Mother.'

'You will?'

He sat on the bed, a comforting arm about her shoulders. 'Gran will look after you. She sent her love.'

'She wasn't shocked?'

'No, only sorry that it had to happen to you, her favourite grandchild.'

'Mother will be horrified. She won't insist on having the baby adopted, will she?'

'Not if you want to keep it?'

'I do want to keep it.'

'Then you shall.'

'Can you afford to keep us both? I can get a job later.

Gran would look after the baby, wouldn't she?'

'Of course. Gran will love the baby. Now, stop worrying. We shall manage fine. Leave everything to me.'

She sighed, her eyes heavy with sleep.

'Now get undressed and into bed. I shall look in later. You know about room service? Just pick up the telephone when you are ready for something to eat and drink.'

'Yes, I know.'

He kissed her lovingly. 'Goodnight, my pet.'

'Goodnight, Daddy.'

He closed the door quietly, and limped back down the long corridor, his eyes smarting with unshed tears.

Back in the little house in Tunbridge Wells, wrapped in their love and understanding, Wendy wished it could stay that way with just the three of them, but the most important person of the family had still to be faced. Her father's repeated assurance that he would cope with her mother had yet to be proved, and dear Gran's tears of joy at her return, and her warm hugs had not dispelled the growing apprehension, or the certainty that her condition would be regarded as a shameful disgrace by a parent who had seemingly conducted herself with absolute decorum. Yet, in the back of her mind lurked a small doubt that the woman who ruled their little world at Tunbridge Wells, and the wider world in the big London hospital had not always been such a paragon of all the virtues. There had been tales of a young Cynthia Franklin who had rebelled against the traditional pattern of her own class of society, and escaped to London. And wasn't it Daddy who had jokingly remarked one day, 'Your Mother did the proposing, my pet. I should never have got round to it!'

Yet Wendy could not visualise that romantic young girl who had fallen in love with the solicitor's clerk her nervous horse had almost killed when he was thrown from his bicycle. All her young life had been directed and compelled by the strict supervision of a dominating person called 'Sister Simmons'. It was Gran who had explained to the child that her mother should not be blamed for her harshness. The last war had changed all their lives, and the young generation had suffered terribly. The boys who went away came back maimed, shell-shocked, or choking from the effects of poisonous gas. For a young wife to be faced with a crippled husband she hardly knew – for they had no time to get to know each other after a hasty marriage – it was a challenge to be met with courage and determination, or it was a tragedy.

'Your mother is a wonderful person, Wendy, and she saw it as a challenge. She took charge of everything. She had to. My Freddie was not capable. You see, love, a woman often has more endurance than a man, and she fights for those she loves with all her strength. You are too young to understand, but one day you may have to fight like your mother,' Gran had explained. Dear Gran. The sturdy little figure with her commonsense and cheerful philosophy had not changed her views. It was Gran who gave her the courage to face her mother and to fight for her unborn child.

Three days had passed, and Wendy was beginning to feel rested, and enjoying the appetising meals Gran prepared. Then, on the fourth day, that peaceful interlude was disturbed by an early morning phone call from London. It was Cynthia's rest day, and she would be home for a late breakfast. Almost immediately, a shadow seemed to darken the house, and their own breakfast in the warm, cheerful kitchen was a silent meal. Wendy had suddenly realised she must help with the chores, for she was not a guest in the house, and her mother would expect to find she was making herself useful. So she washed up the dishes, made the beds, tidied and dusted the bedrooms. The morning sickness had stopped, but she had little energy, and her nerves were ragged as she waited for the sound of that cultured, compelling voice.

She was sitting on the edge of her bed, holding the duster, when the car drew up at the curb, and her heart seemed to miss a beat then to race madly.

'Stay upstairs, pet, until I have spoken to your Mother,' Freddie had advised. Gran was on tenterhooks in the kitchen, with a hot breakfast waiting in the oven, and the kettle boiling. With her bedroom door open, Wendy could hear every word that was spoken in the tiny hall.

'Good morning, my darling!' Cynthia's exuberant greeting and Freddie's calm reply, 'Good morning, my dear.' His calmness was a pretence covering his own apprehension, and the fear that he might lose his nerve when the crucial moment arrived to defend Wendy. He had promised he would cope with her mother, but he was no match for her, and the natural tendency to accept her ruling could not be overcome by wishful thinking.

'It's good to be home, darling. It's absolute hell on earth in London these days,' she was saying.

He was hanging up her coat and hat, and he was pleased to see she had changed into civilian clothes, for when she came home in her uniform, its severity seemed to separate them. All her movements were brisk and decisive.

She hurried into the kitchen to greet her mother-in-law. 'Good morning, Mother darling. That smells good. I am going to enjoy it. I stopped only for a cup of tea before I left.'

Freddie joined them in the kitchen, and the door was closed. Now Wendy was cut off in complete isolation, waiting in fearful anxiety for more than half-an-hour, biting her nails, till her mother's voice reached her, raised in angry protest, and the kitchen door burst open. A firm step on the stairs and her mother was there in the doorway, her slight figure tense, her eyes blazing.

'You despicable little slut! How dare you!' she stormed.

And Wendy covered her face with her hands and sobbed.

Freddie's halting step on the stairs surprised them both, for he had never interfered between mother and daughter in these disturbing scenes. Cynthia was astounded when he spoke to her with a curtness that was alien to his gentle nature.

'Let her alone. I won't have her bullied. She has suffered enough.' He sat on the bed and clasped Wendy's shoulders with a comforting arm. Two pairs of dark eyes met and clashed.

'Well!' Cynthia was trembling with rage and indignation. Father and daughter had always been close, but for Freddie to condone such shameful conduct was too much for her overwrought nerves. She had to get away. She had lost control of the situation, and that in itself was humiliating. She spun round and walked out of the room. And they sat there, close together and let her go. The front door slammed, the car jerked forward and shot away.

'Don't worry, pet. She'll be back. It was a shock,' said Freddie, quietly.

'She hates me, Daddy. I wish I were dead!' Wendy sobbed.

He squeezed her shoulders protectively, and let her cry. Torn with compassion for both, he was more disturbed than at any time since Wendy ran away. He loved them both, and to choose between them had always been distressing. He had gained a minor victory over Cynthia's harsh judgement, but it gave him little satisfaction. That she was surprised and angry at his disloyalty was evident in her dark, expressive eyes. With this one redeeming feature, no face could be plain. Cynthia could not hide her feelings, and every emotion was revealed in those dark eyes. When she was angry – and she was very angry today – they were black as onyx, and in her rare moments of tenderness, they were soft as velvet.

Wendy's distraught sobbing would ease her tormented mind, but there was no such relief for his anguished Cynthia. She would not weep. She was too proud. This stiff, unyielding pride was a legacy from her own class of society. Cynthia was her father's daughter, and Sir Neville Franklin had a way of looking down his aristocratic nose on lesser mortals. His beloved wife had long since persuaded herself that the barriers between the classes had been broken down by her marriage into the working class. It was an illusion. Her voice alone betrayed her heritage, and the natural assumption that she must be obeyed.

He sighed, and kissed Wendy's tear-wet cheek. 'Come, my pet. Gran will be putting on the kettle for a nice cup of tea,' he coaxed gently.

The wailing sirens greeted her as she drove towards London. It was an eerie, nerve-racking sound that chilled the spine.

It had been a shattering discovery. Her gentle, biddable husband had spoken with the voice of authority, and she had not stayed to reason with him because of her hurt and humiliation. Freddie had leaned on her and depended on her judgement for so long that she thought her authority was absolute. When he came back from the last war physically disabled and broken in spirit, she had seen the future as a challenge, not a tragedy, and she had shouldered the burden of responsibility with faith and with courage. If, in the process of his slow recovery, she had become the dominant partner, it was unavoidable. Freddie had never questioned her authority until today.

'Let her alone. I won't have her bullied. She has suffered enough.'

His curt admonition echoed in her tired mind like a tolling bell. She had expected him to call her back, but he made no move to do so. In the wailing notes of the siren she heard the muted cry of suffering humanity, and her anger subsided. She would have turned back, and made her peace with Freddie, but her stubborn pride prevented her. So she drove on.

A short distance away, bombs were falling and the earth trembled. There would be more casualties, more terrible suffering, and more demands on her own strength and experience. Her personal troubles were forgotten, and her small world at Tunbridge Wells was lost in this vast city she had grown to love, fighting for survival with unsurpassed heroism.

She had no need to ask what had happened in her brief absence. It was all too evident. The Sister's Annexe had disappeared into a huge crater, and the East Wing had been sliced clean away, as though a giant's knife had cut through brick and mortar. Beds were hanging precariously in the wide open wards, and a solitary bedpan had lodged on a pile of rubble, an incongruous reminder of a probationer's last duty before Death had claimed her together with her patient.

Cynthia parked the car and stepped out. Rescue workers were digging in the craters. A strong smell of gas mingled with the dust. She groped her way to Out Patients, and tied a clean, starched apron about her slim waist. Sister Simmons was back on duty.

They waited all day, tense with anxiety, but she did not come back. The hours dragged by. Then it was 9 o'clock, and Freddie switched on the wireless to listen to the news bulletin. They learned of the heavy daylight raids on central London. Two hospitals had suffered extensive damage. Patients and staff had been killed and injured. The full extent of the casualties would not be known for some hours. A number of people were missing. The announcer's voice was calm, unemotional, unhurried. It was his simple duty to report, not to dwell on the horrors and havoc of this devastating war on the Home Front.

But for the three who listened in the little terrace house at Tunbridge Wells, it had a personal significance. In their separate ways they could visualise Sister Simmons back on duty, calming her nurses and comforting her terrified patients as the enemy planes roared overhead. Then the shattering explosion, and the few ghastly seconds as they were flung into space. Buried under the rubble, she could still be alive, but Freddie knew she was dead. All hope of her survival was lost in the compelling sense of tragedy. Without her, he was only half a man.

Stunned and shocked, he switched off the wireless, leaned back in the comfortable armchair and closed his eyes. Wendy came to sit on the arm of the chair. She was crying again, and his mother was crying. His own hot tears pressed on his closed lids. The tragedy was intensified by her angry departure and the bitterness of misunderstanding. The future was bleak. It had no meaning or purpose without her. They had depended on her for so long, it was impossible to imagine a time when she would no longer be there.

When the telephone rang in the office next door, Ruby

asked quietly, 'Shall I answer it, love?'

Freddie blinked his wet eyes. 'I'll take it. Thanks, Mum,' he said. Clients often phoned in the late evening to make appointments. They watched him limp away, and they heard the click as he lifted the receiver.

'Cynthia! My darling girl!' he shouted exuberantly, choked with tears. They heard him say, 'Thank God you are safe. We have been so worried.'

And Wendy got up to close the door. What they had to say to each other was too private to be shared. There would be no more jealousy, and Daddy must never again be compelled to choose between them. She had Gran, dear, understanding Gran.

Chapter Thirteen

The war had brought few major changes at Russets. It had been no surprise when Maggie was accepted into the Catholic faith and went to live at the Convent School at Marston Park, to help with the younger children. Several had been orphaned, and others had been sent from London to the care of the Sisters, as the bombing intensified. Older children had left to work on the farms, or in domestic service, thus replacing those who would never return. The young generation of servants would never know the contentment and continuity the older generation had enjoyed. A servant's hierarchy was a tale that was told, but hardly believed.

The Gentry had not survived a Second World War. It was sad to see the pathetic remnants of a lost society struggling to maintain a dignified existence in some obscure hotel. Bath and Bournemouth were often chosen because of the remedial waters and the milder climate. The harsh winters of the Weald had been made endurable by the comforts they enjoyed in their ancestral homes. All over the country, big estates had been converted into schools, convalescent homes and offices for the companies who had moved out of London.

For young Maggie Blunt and her sister Midge, Russets

was still home. Midge had won a scholarship to the College of Art, and came home at weekends. She had grown into a very attractive teenager, with a lively personality and a following of young admirers who seemed to compete for her favours, and for the privilege of spending a weekend at Russets.

For Wendy and three-year-old Peter, Russets was a second home. Lucy was glad of another pair of hands in the dairy and on the market stall, and Wendy grateful for the small wage and the free board and lodging they both enjoyed. Cynthia would collect them on Saturday afternoon to spend the weekend in Tunbridge Wells. She adored her grandson, and tried very hard not to interfere with her daughter's rather haphazard methods of training and obedience. Peter was a manly little fellow, with his mother's fair hair and blue eyes, and the inborn distinction of all the Franklins.

Lucy was delighted to have yet another small boy growing up at Russets – the third to be born on the wrong side of the blanket, as the villagers would say! There is nothing more certain in this life that a baby born out of wedlock will charm away all opposition with its first innocent smile. And Wendy's child was no exception. All was forgiven.

A new chapter had begun for the family in the little terrace house in Tunbridge Wells on that memorable day when Sister Simmons escaped death by a miracle. But the new chapter was truly blessed, three months later, when Cynthia opened her heart and her arms to her first and only grandchild. From the holocaust of a devastated city, to the blissful atmosphere of a maternity hospital in a Somerset village, was to be transported from Hell to Heaven, Cynthia had told her daughter with a wry smile, as she cuddled the tiny scrap of humanity and confessed, 'I don't feel in the least like a grandmother.'

'You don't look like a grandmother,' Wendy told her, quietly.

It was true. She had kept her youthful figure, there were no grey hairs, and her dark eyes had not lost their soul-revealing beauty. From the angry blackness of onyx, to the velvet softness of love and warm sympathy. It was all there. Cynthia would never be plain or non-descript with those expressive dark eyes.

As for Martha, when she stood at the gate of her cottage to wave to her grandson, Mark, on his way to the station, it seemed she had put back the clock to the days when her son, Philip, had raced away on his bicycle to catch the train to Tonbridge. Mark had also won a scholarship to the Grammar School, and they still joined the family at Russets most Sundays, after attending church and eating their dinner in companionable silence. Mark was a quiet, studious boy, competing for Midge's favours with the same dogged determination that his father had shown in courting Harriet, his future wife.

Martha had been teaching her Infants at the village school all through the war years, but now she was ready to retire for the second time, and devote herself to Mark. When she laid a posy of flowers on the small grave in the churchyard, she remembered the lively little grandson who had died so tragically that summer day. To be taken all the way to the West Country to escape the war, and to be killed by a car on his way to the sweet shop, seemed a sad waste of a young life, yet she did not question God's purpose. In her old age she was blessed with Mark when she had expected to be a lonely old woman. If his patience was rewarded, and he married Midge, it was too far ahead to cause her any anxiety. 'Sufficient unto the day' was a sensible maxim she had long since decided.

With the end of the war in Europe, Julian was expected home. Through the channels of the International Red Cross, Lucy had learned that he could not walk, and that he would be conveyed to Russets in an ambulance from the nearest port, one day in June. It was impossible to give an exact date or time of arrival.

For Lucy it was a time of sad reflection on the cruelty of war, but she knew she was only one of thousands of women who awaited the homecoming of their dear ones with anxious anticipation. The end of the last war had seen her third son, Albert, back from the prisoner-of-war camp in Turkey a pitiful wreck they hardly recognised as the same sturdy young farmer's son who had volunteered so readily in 1914. Of one thing she was certain, however. She would not make the same mistake twice. In persuading her niece, Carrie, to marry Albert, she had condemned the poor girl to years of fear and frustration. Albert had been physically incapable of a normal sexual relationship with his wife, and mentally disturbed by the abnormality. They all had endured his black moods and jealousy, for it was no secret that his brother, Tom, was in love with Carrie.

Now it was Wendy in love with Julian and determined to marry him. But what sort of future could she expect married to a cripple, even if he was willing to adopt another man's child? Remembering the suffering they had inflicted in the past by their interference, both Lucy and Cynthia resolved to let the young ones settle their own affairs.

So Julian came home to his small world, seemingly unchanged and incredibly lovely. When the ambulance drew up at the closed gate and the driver swung it open and pulled into the yard, the sweet scent of hay mingled with the scent of roses rioting over the mellowed walls of the old farmhouse. He opened the door of the ambulance and let down the ramp, exclaiming in wonder, 'My, but you're a lucky blighter, Julian, to come back to this. It's perfect!'

Julian shot down the ramp and on to the cobbles with the ease of over long familiarity with the wheelchair. A fitted cover was stretched across his legs. He was wearing an open-neck shirt, and his lean face was bronzed.

'Yes, I know I'm lucky, Jack. It hasn't changed. This is how I last saw it. I have carried this picture in my mind's eye.' Choked with tears, he waved a hand at the distant scene. The three figures in long print dresses and sunbonnets would be Aunt Lucy, Carrie and Katie. They were feeding hay to the figure on top of the piled wagon. That would be Tom. Several smaller figures darting about in the field with rakes could be Midge, Maggie and young John. And the stocky figure standing at the horses' heads could only be Dick, grown into a man since they last met. The dazzling sunlight reflected on the pitchforks as they were lifted high. His eyes scanned the scene. He was looking for Wendy and the child. Then he saw them, sitting together in a nest of hay, and his heart ached with love for her, and a great thankfulness that they both had been spared.

Somebody had seen him. They were waving and shouting. In a matter of seconds the scene had changed. Pitchforks were flung down. They were swarming over the field, leaving Tom on the wagon and Dick holding the horses. It was no surprise when Midge raced ahead. She always had to be first. He opened his arms and hugged her. Flushed and starry-eyed, with hay-seeds in her tumbled curls he thought he had never seen a lovelier girl. Then Maggie was there, smiling, undemanding, gentle. Julian reached out to kiss her cheek, and held her close for a moment. John was waiting to shake hands, a tall, gangling lad with nothing to say but a muttered.

'Hallo'. Midge had not stopped chattering, and his arm still encircled her waist.

It was some minutes later when the women joined them, and Aunt Lucy, with characteristic authority, pushed aside her clinging grand-daughter and wrapped Julian in her arms. Her hot cheeks were wet with tears of joy. She smelled of earth and sweat, and her warm bosom was the sweetest comfort he had known in a long, long time. A little plumper, a few more grey hairs, but otherwise unchanged. A wonderful woman, his Aunt Lucy.

Then it was Carrie's turn. How alike they were, these two dear women who had reared him. Katie stood there, giggling, waiting for a kiss, and last of all came Wendy, holding the small boy by the hand.

'Hello, sweetheart,' he said.

'Hello, darling,' she answered.

They were shy of each other and their lips touched briefly in their first kiss. It was Aunt Lucy who snatched up the child and sat him on the apron that covered Julian's legs. He stared at the stranger with wide solemn eyes, and Julian smiled.

'Say hello to Julian,' Aunt Lucy prompted.

''lo, Juyan.'

'Hello, Peter. Have you been hay-making?'

'Yes, I got a small little rake.'

'That's nice.'

'You can lend it if you like.'

'Thank you.'

'Have you got a Daddy?'

'No.'

'I haven't got a Daddy. I've got a Mummy.'

'Lucky boy.' Julian and Wendy exchanged an amused glance.

The driver had been standing aside, watching the

emotional scene. It was not the first time he had witnessed such a happy reunion, but it was certainly the loveliest setting. When he was introduced, he was immediately included and no longer an outsider.

'You will stay to tea, won't you?' Aunt Lucy invited.

'Thank you. I should like to,' Jack replied, promptly.

'Put the kettle on, Katie, and set the table,' her mistress instructed.

'Yes, Ma'am.' Katie always had to be reminded of her duties.

'I'll help you,' said Maggie, and they went away together.

'Would you like to see my baby chicks?' John was not often so friendly, but then it was not often they had a visitor, and he was proud of being in sole charge of the poultry.

'After tea,' Aunt Lucy prompted. She still had the last word it seemed.

Had anything changed? Julian wondered, apart from the small boy who sat so quietly on his wheelchair, surrounded by love. He could see himself at the same age. In his earliest memories, his short legs were stretched across the broad back of a very big horse, being led around the same cobbled yard by the two uncles. Now, on this memorable day, they both were sharing this love. It was so warm and tangible, he could feel its embrace.

'Come and see your room, dear.' Aunt Lucy was pushing him towards the house, with the small boy still perched on the apron.

'He won't recognise the parlour, will he, Gran?' Midge interrupted.

'The parlour? Have I been given the parlour? I feel very honoured,' said Julian.

'It was the obvious choice. Wendy and Peter have

your room upstairs,' Aunt Lucy explained.

Once more Julian and Wendy exchanged a glance, and now they were losing their shyness, and they were holding hands. They could hear the rattle of crockery as they passed the kitchen. The parlour door stood wide open. It would remain open always now, and Julian would not feel lonely or neglected. A little bell had been provided, and a night light. Nothing had been forgotten. He gasped when he saw the transformation. All his personal possessions had been brought down. The model aeroplanes decorated the mantelpiece and chest of drawers, and hung suspended from the ceiling, spinning slowly in the draught from the window.

'But this is marvellous, Aunt Lucy. Thanks a lot,' he said in a choked voice.

'Tom fixed the pulley. He's rather proud of it,' Carrie was saying.

'It's super. I'm really overwhelmed.' He rubbed a hand across his wet eyes.

'Can I have a n'airplane?' the small boy pleaded.

'You should have given him one,' Julian told Wendy.

She shook her head. 'Not without your permission. We all knew how you prized them.'

'I did, but that was a long time ago, before I encountered the real article. Let him choose one.'

Wendy lifted him up, and he reached out his hands to the smallest model, dangling from the ceiling.

'It's the Spitfire! Would you believe it!' Julian exclaimed, excitedly.

Midge climbed on a chair and cut it down. Peter's eyes were shining.

'Say thank you to Julian,' Aunt Lucy prompted, automatically.

'Thank you, Juyan. Can I keep it?' he asked, anxiously, knowing that John, and even Dick, who were grown men, had wanted one and been refused.

'Yes, it's yours to keep,' Julian told him.

Peter darted away. They watched him running around the yard, towing the tiny craft like a kite on the length of string.

Jack was seated on the bench with young John.

'I wanted one, but Gran wouldn't let me. He gets everything because he's the baby. It's not fair,' the boy grumbled sulkily.

'But it's for Julian to say who should have them, now he is home isn't it?'

'Yes, I reckon so.'

'Then why not ask?'

'I don't like to ask. He's not the same. He's different. Gran said we had to be very kind and we hadn't to bother him.'

'I think you will find he will not mind being bothered. Julian is still the same person, even if he can't walk.'

'Do you think so?'

'I'm sure of it. Anyway, you sit here and keep your fingers crossed. I'll ask.'

John crossed his fingers and waited. He heard a shout of laughter, then Jack's head appeared at the window.

'You're to come and choose one,' he called.

But John didn't hurry. He never hurried. Unlike Midge, his lively, intelligent twin, his mind moved slowly. So he took his time in getting to the room that had always been the parlour until a few weeks ago, when everything had been turned out. Dick had painted the walls bright yellow, his mother had stitched new curtains, and his father had laid a new green carpet. Only the piano was moved back, so that Wendy could play when she felt like it, after supper.

Julian grinned as he sauntered in, hands in pockets, humming tunelessly. 'Help yourself,' he invited.

And John went straight to the Gladiator on the mantelpiece. 'Thanks,' he said briefly. And that, too, was typical of John, who didn't believe in wasting words.

When Maggie came to the door to announce that tea was ready, both Midge and Carrie wanted to push the chair.

'But I don't have to be pushed. I still have two good hands and I can move myself along quicker than you could push me,' Julian protested, with a sigh of resignation as Midge won the tussle and went off down the passage. It was not going to be easy, adjusting to this home environment. They would smother him with kindness, wait on him hand and foot, and turn him into a helpless cripple. After today, he would make a firm stand. He must not lose the precious independence he had acquired in hospital, where every patient had been encouraged to help himself as well as to help those more badly handicapped. His hands had not been idle. Rug making and raffia work were two of the crafts he had been taught. Hand-made rugs and baskets would sell on the market stall. He had brought home enough material to keep him busy until he could get fresh supplies sent down from London. All this had been arranged through the channels of the Red Cross.

He had long since overcome the impatience he had known in those early months, when he thought he must go mad with frustration. He was no saint. In a way it was a good thing he had to spend that crucial period of adjustment in hospital, where self-pity was frowned upon.

Wendy was out in the yard, persuading Peter to come in to tea. Dick was leading the horses, and Tom sitting on the piled wagon as they lumbered into the yard. They would give the horses a rest and a nosebag, unload the hay into the barn, then finish clearing the field this evening. The fine weather could break at any time, and the hay harvest was valuable.

Gathered round the kitchen table, Lucy presiding, Julian was the focus of attention. It was embarrassing. He wondered if he would ever be regarded as a normal person again, for that is how he saw himself. Lucy was slicing home-cured ham, Carrie pouring tea, and Maggie cutting the freshly baked loaves. Midge had appointed herself his personal servant, and when she had collected the bed-table from his room and placed it carefully over the chair, she fussed about serving him, spreading his bread with butter, stirring sugar in his tea, as though he were a child. He reminded himself she would soon be gone back to London. He was really very fond of Midge. She had always been possessive, so it was nothing new.

When she seated herself beside him, in the chair that was intended for Wendy, nothing was said, and his darling sweetheart led Peter to the far end of the table. It was strange to see her as a mother, soothing him quietly, for he hadn't wanted to come in. The little aeroplane was placed beside his plate.

'It's mine,' he told them. 'Juyan gave it me for my own self. It's a Spitfire,' he announced importantly.

'I've got the Gladiator,' John reminded him. He hadn't brought it to the table. He was much too big for that sort of nonsense. After tea he would be taking his new friend to the orchard, to see all the hens and the newly hatched chicks. They said he had a chip on his shoulder, whatever that meant, because his twin was so clever, but it wasn't his fault he was slow and stupid. He was made that way. Looking at Julian, sitting so quietly in the wheelchair, he wished they could change places, for then he would feel important and everyone would make a fuss of him. Only in the orchard, surrounded by clucking hens who ran to welcome him with his buckets

301

of corn and mash, could he feel important. It was Gran who had put him in charge of the poultry. It was the only job he could manage successfully, for he was terrified of the huge Shire horses, and detested the smell of cows and pigs.

'Shall we go?' he whispered when Jack had refused a second slice of lardy cake.

'Will you excuse us, Mrs Blunt?' Jack asked politely.

'Certainly.' Lucy smiled at her grandson. 'Give Jack a dozen eggs to take home,' she instructed.

'OK, Gran.'

They went out together. The sweet scent of hay on the piled wagon started John sneezing. 'It's hay fever. I get it every year, but I still have to help with the hay-making,' he grumbled.

Back in the kitchen, Midge was holding forth about the American servicemen. 'They've got the most colossal conceit, those GIs,' she declared. 'They seem to think they have only to beckon and every pretty girl will be willing to hop into bed!'

'Midge!' Lucy was horrified, but Julian was grinning.

'You didn't oblige, I take it?' he teased.

'I did *not*!' She tossed her head indignantly. 'But I know someone who did.'

'Yes?'

'Diane Maloney. I saw her getting out of a taxi at the Regent Palace Hotel in Piccadilly with a handsome Major who was very attentive.'

'That would be your Uncle Charles. They are thick as thieves, so Diane's mother tells me, and her father is very upset because Diane is selling the London house and going to live in the States,' Lucy told them.

'With Uncle Charles?' Julian asked, guardedly.

'Yes, dear, with Uncle Charles.' Lucy had never divulged that Charles was Julian's father. That particu-

302

lar skeleton in the cupboard could stay there. Only one other person knew the truth. That was Hetty, one of the upper servants from Marston Park, much too loyal to the Franklins to confirm the rumour. In Hetty's opinion, the Gentry were privileged to enjoy certain standards of behaviour that would be condemned by the working class.

Wendy was spreading gooseberry jam on Peter's bread, and she did not lift her head, but mention of the Regent Palace Hotel sent a shiver down her spine. It evoked too many memories that were best forgotten.

When they had finished tea, and Peter had kissed everyone goodnight, they climbed the stairs together. She had not expected to feel so maternal, but every single day brought some fresh delight in her small son. Tucked up in bed, still clutching the toy plane, smelling sweetly of the Pear's soap Gran had hoarded from before the war, he looked angelic. But Peter was no angel.

'Goodnight, darling.'

'Goodnight, Mummy.'

She left the door open. He couldn't bear shut doors, and he was frightened of the dark, but she was always there to comfort him if he woke in the night.

By the time she had finished fussing over him and went downstairs, she found all the family had gone back to the hay-field, and Julian was alone in the kitchen. His smile had a tenderness she had not known for a very long time. He reached out his arms and she went into them, with a long-drawn sigh of relief. He was not going to blame her. She hadn't known what to expect.

When she lifted her head, he took her face in his hands and kissed her, with the same tenderness and the undisputed assurance that he still loved her.

'Don't cry, sweetheart. It's all over,' he said.

And she looked at him through her tears, and saw the marks of suffering on his lean face and in his dark eyes. He had lost his youth in the restrictive confines of a wheelchair – and she had lost hers in their lodgings at Windermere.

'Oh, Julian, will it always be like this?' she sobbed.

He answered her strangely. 'Not if you believe in miracles.'

'What – what kind of a miracle?'

'The German doctor in the hospital told me it was a miracle I had survived the crash, and the age of miracles is not dead. He also said Mother Nature is a wonderful healer, but she won't be hurried.'

'But it's already four years?'

'What's four years out of a lifetime, sweetheart?'

She choked on a sob. 'You shame me, my darling. I will have faith,' she promised.

In the peace of that Summer evening they found new strength and courage, for the love that was born so naturally as between an elder brother and little sister, had grown as naturally into this enduring love between a man and a woman. Separation and suffering had divided them, and the war deprived them of the years they might have been courting as lovers. But Julian was right. It was all over. They had all the time in the world to be together – well, almost. She mustn't disappoint Gran and her parents who expected her home, with Peter, at the weekend.

Yet Russets was her real home now, and her sense of belonging was intensified because Julian was here. And he was here to stay. That was the one certainty in their small world. His restless youth had been violently shattered, and in that long period of re-adjustment, he had found a new, surprising steadfastness and contentment. Unlike his Uncle Albert, who came home from the last war so terribly embittered, Julian had no bitterness, and no black moods. An occasional flash of temper was quickly over, and a sense of humour would save many a troubled situation.

Lucy had thought she knew every aspect of all her children, but she soon discovered in Julian a fundamental truth that could only be described as harmony. Sometimes she saw a likeness to his Franklin grandfather, and at other times to the young Penelope who had died so tragically in childbirth.

Instead of the disruption she had feared, Julian's homecoming had brought a wonderful sense of unity that now, at long last, the family was complete. With Midge back in London, and Maggie back at the Convent School, the normal routine of mid-Summer continued undisturbed. Lucy was a happy woman, as she packed a picnic basket after breakfast one morning, and strapped it to the base of the wheelchair. Tom had appointed himself the valet, and Julian was ready and waiting in the yard when Wendy and Peter ran out to join him.

The beechwood was their favourite haunt, not the river, which still had a reminder of that Easter Day and another family picnic, when seven-year-old Julian escaped drowning only by the prompt action of Martha's son, Philip.

With a little help from Dick, pulling on a rope, they climbed the rutted sloping path. Then Dick unfastened the rope, called 'So long!' and hurried back to work.

From the sunlit yard, Lucy could see the little group on the edge of the wood quite plainly. She saw Julian turn his head and Wendy's kiss. She heard Peter's happy shouts as he ran on ahead. Then they were gone.

She sighed with contentment, smoothed her clean, starched apron, and went back to the kitchen to put another batch of loaves in the oven.

THE END

THE VILLAGE
by Sarah Shears

Part one of the Fairfields Chronicles

Set in the heart of the Kent countryside and spanning the period from the turn of the century to the end of the Great War, *The Village* introduces us to the inhabitants of Fairfields Village, whose lives and loves become irrevocably entwined over the years. Richly evocative of Edwardian village life — from the brutal poverty of the slum dwellings of Richmond Row, to the grand splendour of Marston Park — this superb saga, with its wonderful cast of characters, depicts the changing pattern of English country life, portrayed by one of our best-loved novelists.

0 553 40161 7

FAMILY FORTUNES
by Sarah Shears

Part two of the Fairfields Chronicles

When Albert returned at the end of the First World War, his family welcomed him with open arms. So did Carrie, his young fiancée, who had waited patiently for him throughout the long and difficult years. But Albert has been a prisoner-of-war and had suffered terrible experiences. These were to affect his relationship with Carrie and with all those who came to the beautiful country farmhouse, Russets — a home that had always been a place of calm and comfort.

0 553 40262 5

RETURN TO RUSSETS
by Sarah Shears

Part four of the Fairfields Chronicles

'Russets' is the large comfortable farmhouse in the Kent village where Lucy, the matriarch, watches over her family. This new novel takes the family one generation further as Lucy's favourite grandchild, Midge, falls in love with the son of her oldest friend. The families are delighted and the young couple are very suited — but Sarah Shears shows how, in spite of all the love and good intentions, the first few years of a marriage are never easy ones.

Set against the background of the beautiful Kent countryside, and peopled with familiar characters including Tom and Carrie, Julian and Wendy, *Return to Russets* will take its place as one of Sarah Shears' most enthralling novels.

0 553 40264 1

IN SUNSHINE OR IN SHADOW
by Charlotte Bingham

Brougham is an imposing and beautiful house, the stateliest of stately homes, but to Lady Artemis Deverill it brings only sorrow and a lonely, crippled childhood. For Eleanor Milligan, born in downtown Boston of a poor Irish immigrant family, childhood means a continual battle against her bullying brothers and cruel father. When they meet on a liner sailing to Ireland, Artemis and Ellie couldn't have less in common or be more different in looks or temperament. But in spite of this they become friends, and when Ellie's cousin Rose asks Artemis to stay on at Strand House, County Cork for a few weeks of an idyllic pre-war summer, Artemis has little difficulty in accepting. It is there that Hugo Tanner meets both girls and is posed a question that will haunt him for the rest of his life.

0 553 40296 X

TO HEAR A NIGHTINGALE
by Charlotte Bingham

'A delightful novel . . . pulsating with vitality and deeply felt emotions, I found myself with tears in my eyes on one page and laughing out loud on another' *Sunday Express*

Brought up in smalltown America by a grandmother who despises her, Cassie McGann's childhood is one of misery and rejection. Fleeing to New York she falls in love with handsome Irish racehorse trainer, Tyrone Rosse, and when he marries her and takes her back to Claremore, his tumbledown mansion in Ireland, it looks as if she has found happiness at last.

Passionately in love as she is, Cassie finds the all-male world of horses and racing rather lonely. There is much for her to learn, not least about the man she has married. Tyrone's success depends heavily on the whims of the rich owners, men — and women — who can be very demanding. And Cassie must learn to endure the enmity of one in particular, who comes out of her buried past determined to destroy her.

When tragedy strikes, it seems that Cassie must once again face rejection and lose her hard-won security. But although the chances of success are slim and the cost in personal happiness considerable, she will not give in, and fights against all odds to survive in a world closed against her.

0 553 17635 8

A WORLD OF DIFFERENCE
by Leona Blair

Six-year-old Connor McKenzie is brought to Brandon Hall when his mother becomes nurse to the infant Georgia Brandon, whose own mother died in childbirth. Into this loveless household Connor brings his charm and fiery intelligence, sparking in Rhys Brandon more paternal warmth than he ever shows to his tiny daughter. Connor and Georgia grow up with a unique bond that suddenly, as she blossoms to womanhood, becomes a passionate love.

But Rhys Brandon cannot tolerate any man possessing his daughter, and turns on Connor as an ungrateful upstart. With Brandon now a dangerous enemy, Connor forges his own way in the world in an era when fortunes are made overnight. But the prize he has struggled for — Georgia — proves far more elusive.

0 553 40172 6

THE GREEN OF THE SPRING
by Jane Gurney

A heartwarming sage of love and separation during wartime.

The carefree days of lazy picnics and house parties end abruptly with the outbreak of war in 1914.

Separation and the testing of young promises form the trials of war as much as trench casualties and Zeppelin raids. Whether from the 'Upstairs' world of the Brownlowes or the 'Downstairs' domain of Mrs Driver's kitchen, each of the inhabitants of Maple Grange is affected by the conflict in Belgium and France, and in ways that they could never have foreseen . . .

0 553 40407 5

MAGGIE JORDAN
by Emma Blair

When most of Maggie Jordan's family are killed in a freak flood in the small coastal village of Heymouth, she is forced to find work in one of Glasgow's carpet mills. She becomes engaged to Nevil Sanderson, who suddenly decides he must go to Spain and join the Republicans in their fight against Franco.

Although she struggles on without him, Maggie eventually realizes her place is by his side and journeys to Spain to join him. But the newly promoted Nevil has become distant and ruthless, and is fiercely jealous of her new friendship with American journalist Howard Taft.

Years later, married and with an eight-year-old daughter, Maggie has returned to Glasgow. Astonished when Howard reappears, bringing light and laughter back into her life, she is forced to take decisions — decisions which threaten to destroy even the vibrant and courageous Maggie Jordan.

0 553 40072 X

SCARLET RIBBONS
by Emma Blair

Sadie Smith can't believe her luck when she is told that soon she will be like all other children *and* her mother buys her a pair of scarlet ribbons. For Sadie, born with a degenerative hip, is unable to walk. When she arrives at Babies Castle, a Dr Barnado's home, she is so excited that she fails to realize she will never see her beloved family again.

In 1927, once fully cured, Sadie is offered the opportunity of a lifetime: to start a new life in Canada. But when she arrives at the Trikhardts' farm in the heart of Ontario, her new life seems far from perfect. Worked from dawn to dusk, she treasures her scarlet ribbons and seeks solace in her friendship with fellow orphan, cheeky-faced Robbie. A freak hurricane finally provides Sadie with a lucky escape. From Canadian parlourmaid to pilot in Britain's Air Transport Auxiliary, from office clerk to managing director, Sadie has to draw on all her courage and strength in her determined struggle to find the lasting happiness that had always eluded her as a child.

0 553 40298 6

RICH MAN'S FLOWERS
by Madeleine Polland

From a miserable life of poverty in a small village in Ireland, Kathleen MacNally escapes to England and finds work as a maid. Fuelled by her burning obsession to make something of her life, she creates a new background for herself and marries Charles Delaney, who gives her the status that she had always craved. Years later, through her only daughter Sash, Kathleen pursues her social aspirations — determined that her 'golden girl' makes a good marriage. But it was to be the supreme irony of Kathleen's life that, through ruthless ambition, her own past is uncovered, and she flees to Ireland in shame. Unable to forgive her mother for the years of deception and abuse, Sash must face a disastrous marriage and an appalling tragedy before she can learn to love and trust again — and find the truth about who she really is.

0 553 40363 X

A SELECTION OF FINE TITLES
FROM BANTAM BOOKS

THE PRICES SHOWN BELOW WERE CORRECT AT THE TIME OF GOING TO PRESS.
HOWEVER TRANSWORLD PUBLISHERS RESERVE THE RIGHT TO SHOW NEW
RETAIL PRICES ON COVERS WHICH MAY DIFFER FROM THOSE PREVIOUSLY
ADVERTISED IN THE TEXT OR ELSEWHERE.

☐	40163 7	THE BUSINESS	*Charlotte Bingham*	£4.99
☐	40427 X	BELGRAVIA	*Charlotte Bingham*	£3.99
☐	17635 8	TO HEAR A NIGHTINGALE	*Charlotte Bingham*	£4.99
☐	40428 8	COUNTRY LIFE	*Charlotte Bingham*	£3.99
☐	40072 X	MAGGIE JORDAN	*Emma Blair*	£4.99
☐	40298 6	SCARLET RIBBONS	*Emma Blair*	£4.99
☐	40172 6	A WORLD OF DIFFERENCE	*Leona Blair*	£4.99
☐	40407 5	THE GREEN OF THE SPRING	*Jane Gurney*	£4.99
☐	40416 4	NO SAD SONGS	*Sarah Lyon*	£4.99
☐	40261 7	THE VILLAGE	*Sarah Shears*	£3.99
☐	40262 5	FAMILY FORTUNES	*Sarah Shears*	£3.99

*All Corgi/Bantam Books are available at your bookshop or newsagent, or can be ordered from the
following address:*

Corgi/Bantam Books,
Cash Sales Department
P.O. Box 11, Falmouth, Cornwall TR10 9EN

UK and B.F.P.O. customers please send a cheque or postal order (no currency) and allow £1.00
for postage and packing for the first book plus 50p for the second book and 30p for each additional
book to a maximum charge of £3.00 (7 books plus).

Overseas customers, including Eire, please allow £2.00 for postage and packing for the first book
plus £1.00 for the second book and 50p for each subsequent title ordered.

NAME (Block Letters) ....

ADDRESS ....

....